SILENCED

These are uncorrected advance proofs bound for review purposes. All cover
art, trim sizes, page counts, months of publication and prices should be
considered tentative and subject to change without notice. Please check
publication information and any quotations against the bound copy of the
book. We urge this for the sake of editorial accuracy as well as for your legal
protection and ours.

SILENCED

ANN CLAYCOMB

TITAN BOOKS

Silenced
Print edition ISBN: 9781803360584
E-book edition ISBN: 9781803360652

Published by Titan Books
A division of Titan Publishing Group Ltd
144 Southwark Street, London SE1 0UP
www.titanbooks.com

First edition: April 2023
10 9 8 7 6 5 4 3 2 1

A CIP catalogue record for this title is available from the British Library.

Printed and bound by 4edge Ltd.

For Paula (duh), a better friend than I could ever have invented or imagined. For Mirene, who would have rather liked this one, I think. And for Ryan, always, always, and with amethysts.

"'Why do men feel threatened by women?' I asked a male friend
of mine... 'Men are bigger, most of the time, they can run faster,
strangle better, and they have on the average a lot more money
and power.' 'They're afraid women will laugh at them,' he said...
I asked some women students in a quickie poetry seminar I was
giving, 'Why do women feel threatened by men?' 'They're afraid
of being killed.'"

Margaret Atwood *(Second Words: Selected Critical Prose,*
1960–1982)

"Having observed that the key to the closet was stained with
blood, she tried two or three times to wipe it off; but the blood
would not come out; in vain did she wash it, and even rub it
with soap and sand. The blood still remained, for the key was
magical and she could never make it quite clean; when the blood
was gone off from one side, it came again on the other."

Charles Perrault ("Bluebeard")

AUTHOR'S NOTE

Silenced deals with the theme of sexual assault and the silencing that many women experience when they try to report. The novel also includes brief descriptions of sexual assault. Although these descriptions are not graphic, they may still be upsetting for some readers.

So why write this book at all?

As a lifelong lover, scholar, and writer of fairy tales, I was brainstorming my second book in 2017. This was the year that revelations about the sexually predatory behavior of Harvey Weinstein, Matt Lauer, and numerous other powerful men emerged in the national media, propelling the #MeToo movement into the spotlight. I had rejected several Western fairy tales as the basis for my next novel, feeling frustrated by the constraints that each story would force me to place on my female protagonist. As more and more women added their voices to the #MeToo movement, I found myself looking at fairy tales differently. These stories don't just "constrain" women; they assault them. They trap women in comas, in towers with no way down, in the bodies of animals. They force women into slave labour, marry them to monsters, and punish them for daring to resist.

So I reconceived my book not as a retelling of a single fairy tale but as a #MeToo story incorporating several fairy tales. I also concentrated on not one but four protagonists, whose identities reflect the diversity both of my hometown of Washington, D.C. and of the women who have in the past few years come together to articulate a collective rage. *Silenced* does indeed deal with the theme of sexual assault and its aftermath. But my goal in writing it was to celebrate the survivors who, like my characters, refuse to be silenced or defined by what has been done to them. This is *their* story, and if it is your story too, I hope I have done justice to your courage.

JULY 27: ABONY

"Once upon a time," Abony said, "he'd have gotten away with what he did, but not today. We've got to make sure of that."

Ranjani, who was driving because she had to, pulled into a parking space near a sign that read *Police Station Visitors Lot Only* and turned off the engine. Then she sat desperately still, staring at the doors of the building.

"Breathe, Rani!"

Ranjani drew in a shaky breath.

"Is this it?" Abony asked. "Right station, right entrance?"

"Yes," Ranjani whispered, "this is where I came in May." She unclenched her hands from her lap to point down to the left. "I parked under that tree over there."

"Great. You feel okay to walk through the door?"

Ranjani put a hand up to the chain around her neck, pulled the pendant out from under her blouse, and closed her fingers around it.

"I feel okay," she said.

It was going to be a minute.

Rather than rush Ranjani even more—it was a small miracle she'd come this far—Abony focused on what *she* needed to do to get in there. She picked up her purse from between her feet and dropped her phone into it. She flipped the visor down and checked that her lipstick was still on and her hair was behaving as well as could be expected in peak-of-summer DC humidity. Satisfied, she flipped the visor back up, got out of the car, and shimmied as unobtrusively as possible to unstick her sky-blue sheath dress from the backs of her legs. She kept her face carefully blank of triumph or relief when she heard Ranjani get out and shut the driver's side door just as Abony shut hers.

As they neared the entrance, two women emerged, one Black and one White, laughing at some shared joke. They were both in street clothes, but as the White woman reached out to hold the door, the lift of her arm revealed a gun holster against her ribcage. Detectives then, or whatever rank police officers had to reach to wear plainclothes and carry weapons. Abony wondered if their guns made them feel powerful, made them feel safe.

"Hey, great shoes!" the door-holder said.

The other woman looked down at Abony's shoes and whistled.

"Damn. Pretty sure you're wearing my paycheck on your feet."

"And I'm pretty sure it's *my* paycheck," Abony snapped back. She swept inside the building, checking in the glass doors of the lobby that Ranjani was right behind her. As the doors closed behind the two police officers, she could hear one expressing indignation at Abony not being able to take a joke and the other teasing that anyone who could afford those shoes could afford to be a bitch.

Abony's high-heeled pumps were pearlescent patent leather, shimmering from pale blue to pink to rose gold as they caught the light. The soles were a perfect glossy red. The shoes had cost Abony $650, marked down from $800, which wasn't anything like her full paycheck. But that was just the one pair. Add $650 to the $775 for the pair the week before and the $1600 for the two pairs the week before that and...

"Abony, are you alright?"

Abony felt a prickle of sweat on the back of her neck. She drew in a deep breath and nodded without turning her head to meet Ranjani's worried eyes. She looked instead at their shared reflection, of a statuesque Black woman in a sleek fitted dress and fabulous shoes that added three inches to her already impressive height and a petite young Indian woman wearing coral silk and flat sandals, with gold beads wrapped around the end of her long black braid. They looked elegant, professional, each in her own way. They didn't look like rape victims too scared to come forward.

"Because we're not," Abony said fiercely to the in-the-glass version of herself. "We're doing this. We're not letting him get away with it."

She pushed open the inner doors and herded Ranjani into the building.

Things went wrong almost immediately. Confronted with a long curving "Information Desk" that looked like a check-in counter at a hotel, Abony waited her turn and then told the young man in a DCPD polo shirt that they were there to report a crime.

"What division, ma'am?"

"Division?"

"What happened, ma'am?"

The hollowed-out lurch that felt like hunger but wasn't hunger yawned in Abony's gut and the sweat bloomed again on the back of her neck, under her arms, on her palms and the soles of her feet, making her feel like she might trip and fall if she had to walk too far now in her goddamn $650 shoes. She pushed through it to get the words out.

"We need to talk to someone in Sex Crimes."

The young man's face fell. He put down the clipboard he'd been about to offer and instead lifted the phone on the desk and made a call, speaking softly and rapidly to whoever picked up. Then he gestured them over to the right of the desk.

"Wait there and someone will be right down."

Right down. Abony stepped far enough in the direction the young man had pointed to see the building directory on the wall and the bank of elevators beyond that. According to the directory, Sex Crimes was on the fourth floor, which meant that to get up to that office via elevator Ranjani would have to go through a door she'd never gone through before. They could take the stairs instead—but no, duh, there was a door to the stairwell too.

Abony wheeled on Ranjani as she heard the younger woman's sharp intake of breath.

"We don't have to go up," Abony said. "When someone comes down, we'll just ask to take a walk, okay? We'll go sit on a bench outside. We've talked about this."

"I know," Ranjani said, but her eyes were huge and her knuckles white around her necklace. Meanwhile, Abony's own resolve was buckling under the sweaty, shaky, nauseous wave of need that she wasn't going to be able to resist much longer. If she kept trying she'd black out, the nice young man at the desk would call for EMS, and Ranjani would probably bolt, leaving Abony to blame her faint on heat stroke, convince the paramedics *not* to take her to the hospital, and then have to call an Uber to get home.

One of the elevators opened and a woman strode toward them. She had olive skin, curly graying dark hair, and a frown that might have been intended to convey the seriousness with which she was ready to treat their report, but which Abony could only see, through her own increasing dizziness, as irritation. She hadn't thrown up from the need before, but it felt like a possibility now and she couldn't let that happen, couldn't vomit on the scuffed marble of the police station, all over her iridescent So Kate 120 pumps, or God forbid all over a Sex Crimes detective's sensible black loafers.

Abony turned on her heel and headed back outside. She managed not to run because she couldn't run in these shoes, not with her feet sweating inside them, not on this expanse of polished floor. She heard the woman's raised voice behind her—*Ma'am! Ma'am? Can I help you?* —and Ranjani's sobbing breath over her shoulder because of course Ranjani hadn't needed much incentive to give up on this stupid doomed attempt to report what he'd done to them.

Because he hadn't stopped at raping them. He'd done something to each of them afterwards—drugs? some kind of hypnosis?—then planted these intense, implausible blocks in their subconscious so they couldn't report him no matter how hard they tried or how many times. He'd made Abony feel helpless, and Abony didn't *do* helpless, goddamn it. She did *not*.

Out on the sidewalk Abony fumbled for her phone, found the eBay app, and bought the shoes that she'd made sure to put in her virtual cart this morning. They were a bargain at $665 and as soon as the *Order Received* notification text popped on her screen she swallowed the flood of saliva in her mouth. She wasn't going to throw up or faint. She was still sweating, but now it was from standing outside in the July heat. Dropping onto the nearest bench, Abony pulled a package of scented wipes out of her purse, patted her face, and held the wet cloth to the back of her neck until the damp cold made her shiver. Then she was able to look over at Ranjani, on the bench beside her.

"You okay?" Abony asked.

Ranjani was sitting very straight as she always did, with her hands clasped in her lap now and the pendant tucked away again.

"I'm okay. Are you alright?"

"I'm fine," Abony said.

"Did you buy some shoes?"

"Yep. I told you I'd do it if I needed to."

"I'm sorry you had to."

"I know." Abony also knew she should apologize on her end for dragging Ranjani down here. Ranjani hadn't wanted to come, terrified as always of encountering a situation that would force her to walk through a new door, but as soon as she'd told Abony that she'd already been to the police station near her house once, Abony had convinced her that they had to try.

"Excuse me?"

They both turned to see the woman from the elevator squinting at them in the blazing afternoon light.

"The folks at Information said you wanted to report a sex crime," she said. "It can be scary but we're here to help. You sure you don't want to come back inside and just talk? Get out of this heat for a minute?"

This woman, this police detective who specialized in sexual assault, was so close. She wanted to help. It was her job to believe them. She *would* believe them when they told her what had happened. But would she believe the rest?

Abony couldn't even explain the rest. The shuddering was already starting again, and if she talked to this woman any more she'd end up having to buy another pair of shoes, which would make two pairs in one day, which would negate the bargain price she'd gotten on the first pair, not to mention that she didn't have a second pair saved at Gilt or on eBay or Saks or Neiman's so she'd have to hunt one down and probably pay more, which would bring her monthly total up over $5000 and—

Abony heard a choking sound, realized it was her own voice trapped in her throat, and then felt Ranjani's small, cool hand on her arm.

"Thank you," Ranjani said to the woman. "We appreciate your help but we're fine."

"Your friend doesn't look fine."

"I am though," Abony said, and felt her symptoms ease like a wave receding.

"We're sorry to have bothered you," she added firmly. She tucked the wet wipe inside her fist and stood up, swinging her bag over her shoulder and letting the shoes tell lies for her, about her confidence, her power, her sense of control.

The detective looked from one of them to the other and Abony could almost see her confusion in a thought bubble over her head. Ranjani was young, beautiful, and soft-spoken, but Abony had fled the building and let Ranjani speak for her a moment ago. So which of them had been the victim of a sexual assault and which of them was trying to talk the victim out of reporting—and why?

"I'm going to leave you my card," the woman said finally, and made a point of handing one to each of them even though she had to step around Abony to put a card in Ranjani's hand. As she walked away, Abony imagined calling her back, asking her to sit on the bench with them, telling her why they'd come. But she pictured the scenario almost idly, like playing out a possible car crash while sitting at an intersection: *What if that Corvette ran the red light? What if that blue truck failed to yield?* And she was done courting disaster for today.

She stalked to the nearest trash can to throw away the cleansing wipe and the detective's card, then fished her sunglasses out of her purse and put them on, welcoming both the relief from the glare and the fact that the glasses hid her eyes.

"You ready to go?" Ranjani asked behind her.

Abony nodded without turning around. She thought about the things she should say to Ranjani right now: *I'm sorry. I shouldn't have asked you to do this. We knew it wouldn't work.* She thought about the other things she might say, ways to brazen this out: *Well, it was worth a try. We'll find another way, Rani. We'll figure something out.*

She didn't say anything. They drove in silence to the nearest Metro station, where Ranjani let her out.

Waiting on the platform for the next train, Abony got a text notification from her company's emergency alert system: *Urgent: Please read.* The link took her to a screenshot of a Discord channel, of all things. She was poised to delete it and send the IT team a warning that they'd been hacked when a phrase caught her eye. She read the whole thread, then found the channel it had come from and scrolled through the recent content, baffled. Had the CEO sent this to her himself, or did someone else at the company know what he'd done to her? Abony wasn't sure which was worse, or whether the conversation she read on her phone was meant as a taunt, a warning, or a riddle that—should she solve it—might point to how she could be free.

Fairy Tales Forever Discord Channel

*We are an inclusive community; we celebrate all voices and identities. Expressions of hate, bias, or general assholery (yes, we know it's not a word) will not be tolerated. For full channel rules and guidelines click **here**.*

Discussion Boards

• **Fairy Tale of the Day**—*submit a summary of a fairy tale you love, hate, or just think more people should know about and invite people to share their thoughts.*

• **Question of the Day**—*submit a question about fairy tales, or about a specific fairy tale, for discussion. We welcome questions you actually want answered, questions that keep you up at night, and rhetorical questions designed just to spark conversation.*

• **Fairy Tales for Our Time**—*seriously, these tropes are everywhere! Submit a real-life story that reminds you of a traditional fairy tale and invite our community to be amazed along with you at the way life really does imitate fairy tales. All the fucking time.*

Question of the Day: What is it about women's feet in fairy tales?
submitted by bellerules (member since 2015)

Jess: it's a good question. There are So. Many. Fairy tales that seem like they're about messing with women's feet. "Little Mermaid," anyone? And no not the Disney version the real one.

Eden: yes that one totally! And while we're on Andersen has anyone read "The Red Shoes." Go read it now but also don't because it's AWFUL. About this girl who is poor her whole life, has no shoes at all and just really wants a pretty pair of shoes, but then when she falls in love with these red shoes in a store, everyone tells her that good Christian girls don't wear red shoes (!) and tries to guilt her into boring black ones. She gets the red ones anyway and wears them to church and everyone is *gasp* and someone (pretty sure it's a man, duh) curses her so that she can't get the shoes off and has to keep dancing in them forever!

badassvp: Agree, I hate that story. I hate Andersen in general for attitudes towards women, but that story is bad! WOMEN SHOULD BE ABLE TO WEAR WHAT THEY WANT. One note is that she doesn't wear them forever. She finds a man with an axe and begs him to cut her feet off, which he DOES!! and then the shoes go dancing off down the road with her feet still in them and she gets crutches and wooden feet and becomes a beggar. It's fucked up.

steph: I didn't know that story but went and read it just now. Wow! That's horrible. Thanks for sharing it though. Are there others?

Jess: Well, speaking of gross cut-off feet, remember notdisneyCinderella. When the stepsisters try on the glass slipper and it doesn't fit, the first one cuts off her toes to make it fit and the second one cuts off her heel. So when that shoe gets to Cinderella, it would have been literally sloshing with other people's blood.

steph: Ewwwwwwww.

Jess: Also, GLASS slippers? How are those a style ideal? They just sound so painful to wear.

Eden: Agree! How about Grimm's "Snow White," where the wicked stepmother (thanks to fairy tales for giving all of us stepmothers a bad rap, by the way) is forced at the end to put on red-hot shoes made of iron and dance in them until she dies?

Jess: These stories are so fucked up.

badassvp: Ummm, hello, the way women's feet are fetishized is fucked up generally which is WHY the stories are fucked up. I mean, how many of us own high-heeled shoes that give us mad blisters or just tear up our feet but we wear them anyway because we're told they look "sexy" by men (and by women too by the way)? Right?????

<click to see more comments>

JULY 27–29: JO

Before she understood the full extent of what he'd done to her, Jo simply fled. She got out of the building by keeping her head down in the hall, on the elevator, and through the revolving door that led to the street. No one stopped her to comment on the fact that her ponytail had slipped halfway down the back of her neck and she was collapsed in on herself like someone huddled over a wound.

She claimed an empty row on the Metro and put her bag squarely in the middle of the seat beside her. It was 2:45 p.m. She had a 3 p.m. meeting with Ranjani from Creative Services about the promo campaign they were launching next month. She emailed Ranjani that she needed to reschedule, then turned her phone off and dropped it into her purse.

Jo's apartment complex backed onto a state park. She ran the trails nearly every day, as much to avoid the silence that had settled over the apartment these past few months as anything else. The whole place was quiet and cold and clean now, had been since May, when Eileen had left.

So Jo had already run five miles this morning before work. But the moment she got in the door, she stripped and pulled on shorts, a sports bra, a red t-shirt. Her hair spilled out of its ponytail when she pulled the shirt over her head. She rewrapped it ruthlessly, tight enough that her scalp stung, then laced up her shoes. She kicked the heap of clothes on the floor aside as she left. It had been her best skirt suit, but she wouldn't ever wear it again. Jo thought fleetingly of what she would be doing differently right now if she'd come home to find Eileen here, curled on the sofa reading, looking up with a smile when she heard the door . . .

Jo didn't know what she'd have done then. She only knew what to do now.

In the woods, she didn't set a pace. She just ran. She wanted to run right off the trail and into the trees, because you stayed on the trail to stay safe and if you weren't safe anymore anyway, what difference did it make? But even as she ran, Jo knew there were worse things than what the CEO of her company had just done to her. A young woman's naked body had been found in this park just a few months ago. Her ex-boyfriend had carved his name into her stomach before he'd killed her.

Jo stayed on the trail. She made it to the dog park that was the turn-around of her usual route before her breathing broke and she had to stop. In two hours, when all the dog owners got home from work, the park would be the scene of joyful chaos. Now it was deserted. Jo paced the perimeter, hands on her waist as she caught her breath. Her legs burned.

You must be a runner, Jo. I can tell from those long legs. Do they go all the way up under that skirt?

When she'd gotten a calendar request from the CEO that morning with the event title *BOD PR Issue*, Jo assumed it was something urgent to do with the company Board of Directors— the *BOD* of the event title. They were meeting the next week and it was almost a given that at least one director would have ruffled feathers about something. But before she'd even had the chance to sit down, the CEO had been talking about her legs.

Shit, Jo thought—and tried to say. *Dammit.* There was a wriggling, writhing feeling in her mouth, like the words were struggling to get out.

That fucking bastard. He fucking planned it—

There were things coming from her mouth instead of words. She put a hand up automatically and caught them: two tiny black spiders and then, horribly, a centipede, the too many legs tickling her lower lip. She screamed and flung the things away, shook her hand to get them off.

Nothing but sound had come out of her mouth when she screamed. Jo gagged and tried again.

"Hello," she said to no one. "Anyone hear this or am I talking to myself here?"

Nothing but her own wavering voice.

"Great. I'm literally talking to myself in the woods."

She tried again.

The CEO of my company just raped me—

But these words turned into *things* as they left her throat: a trickle of red ants and something covered in bumps that she could feel against the roof of her mouth—a fat little toad. She felt them swell into being the moment she would have spoken, then drop onto the back of her palate. Ant, ant, toad: not an exact ratio of creatures to words, but that was hardly a consolation. It was either get them out or choke on them. Jo spat the creatures onto the ground, wiped her chin. And finally understood what he'd meant when he'd smiled at her as she left his office. She'd been unsteady on her feet, shaking, but already angry. She'd been ready to go straight to the cops.

You won't want to talk about this, Jo, he'd said. *You think you do now but trust me. You won't.*

Jo walked home, feeling chilled and clammy in her sweaty clothes despite the heat. She told herself to be rational—ha!—and assess the situation one problem at a time.

What about what he'd done to her in his office? She was sore, between her legs and deep inside. Her back hurt from her futile twisting beneath him and her palms stung, imprinted with deep crescent marks from her fingernails digging into them. He had forcibly restrained her effectively enough, with his bodyweight on hers and his hands as manacles around her wrists, that she had barely been able to breathe, much less fight him off. But she wasn't bleeding or even noticeably bruised, at least externally.

As for other problems, Jo was on the Pill for her menstrual cramps, so no risk of pregnancy. She tried to find this bleakly funny, that as a lesbian on the Pill she was now unexpectedly relying on it to perform its primary function. But she could only feel relief.

But she'd need to go get tested to see if he'd given her an STD. Fuck.

And what about what he'd done—what seemed to be happening to her—in the aftermath of the attack? Start with whether it was really happening, which seemed at once like the obvious question and the most ridiculous, because *of course* it was really happening. She wouldn't suddenly hallucinate spitting out toads and bugs. Still… alone on the trail, Jo said again—tried to say—*he raped me.* Instead, she gagged and spat out a half-dozen iridescent green and gold beetles that looked like they wanted to fly away when they got over the shock of being spit out.

They were also really there, or at least her phone camera saw them, and so did the Insect Identifier app she found, which told her they were Japanese beetles that could wreak havoc on rose bushes but were not harmful to humans. Jo begged to differ but supposed the app wasn't accounting for people having the damn things materialize in their throats. She picked one up, feeling the prickle of its legs as it tried to escape her cupped palm. Back at her apartment building, she stopped and stretched near the door until one of her neighbors came out to walk a pop-eyed Chihuahua. Jo recognized the woman from the mail room and encounters like this one but didn't know her name. She waited until the woman was near and then let the beetle fall from her hand onto the sidewalk.

"Hey, be careful," Jo said, pointing. "I don't want your dog to eat that bee or whatever it is."

The woman stopped and looked down, while the Chihuahua, utterly uninterested, strained at its leash.

"It's just a little beetle," the woman said, "but thanks." She bent closer. "He's kind of cute, actually."

So the things Jo was spitting out were real.

That night, she tried over and over to say out loud what the CEO had done, but every time the words emerged as bugs and toads and snakes. The snakes were awful; they swelled into existence in her throat and then kept coming, slithering out over her tongue while she gagged convulsively. But the centipedes were still the worst. Jo tested to see if there was any relationship to the words she wanted to say and the things she spit up by standing at the kitchen sink and trying to say the same sentence—*my CEO raped me today in his office*—over and over, running the water to drown the hapless creatures that spilled out. If she could figure out how to avoid the damn centipedes... but it was a confusion of things with too many legs or no legs at all.

She found that she could write down whatever she wanted, so she documented the whole encounter in a clinical third-person narrative—*the employee attempted to leave the office but the CEO forcibly restrained her from doing so*—the way detectives did in serial killer novels. She even saved the document in a password-protected file. But what was she going to do with it? She could email it to the police and to the company's anonymous HR reporting portal, called "Tell Someone," but that was precisely the problem. Eventually *someone* would want her to say, face-to-face and in real time, what had happened. And what would they do with a woman who says she wants to report a sexual assault and then proceeds to spit insects out instead of words?

The safest thing to do would be to just run away: quit her job, pack up and move, and never talk about what had happened. Safest—but Jo couldn't get past the tightness she felt in her chest at the thought of leaving DC, of leaving Eileen and the chance that she might come back.

Jo put in for sick leave for the entire next week. The rest of the weekend, she slept heavily and long, then ran every morning, pushing herself so hard she ended up walking the last mile of her route. Mid-morning, she showered and tackled breakfast.

Eating was a minefield. She was starving from running so much, but the physical sensation of certain foods between her teeth—particularly anything juicy or bursting or with seeds—reminded her of the things that were coming unbidden up into her mouth. Jo dug the protein powder out of the back of the pantry, where Eileen had stashed it because it tasted like shit, and made smoothies. They still tasted like shit. Bread was good, but chips shattered under her teeth like beetle shells. Meat was right out, as were noodles. Ice cream was fine but not with any add-ins, and what was the point of plain ice cream? Jo drank coffee by the pot and then paced her apartment, too jittery to sit.

Monday evening, she rebelliously got dressed in jeans and a nice top. A group of friends was meeting for drinks and she might as well try being out in public by starting with a dimly lit bar and a bunch of people who were unlikely to suddenly turn and ask her probing questions.

As soon as she got to the restaurant, though, Jo knew this was a mistake, and would have been even if she didn't have this literally unspeakable secret. These were—had been—*their* friends, hers and Eileen's. Jo wondered if they'd only invited her after they remembered that Eileen, who taught history at a private high school, was chaperoning a summer trip to Asia. The other five women in their group all gave Jo hard hugs and told her they loved her and no one mentioned Eileen at all, though Jo knew Eileen had been posting Facebook updates from China for the last two weeks and that everyone at the table followed her. They ordered tapas that Jo didn't touch and a pitcher of sangria that she did, putting her finger in the pour spout to keep any fruit out of her glass.

Two glasses in, she realized she'd better eat some bread. She was reaching for the basket when someone asked if they'd all heard the latest: another politician had been accused of sexual misconduct, in this case of having a camera installed under his desk so he could look up women's skirts when they sat across from him, and of storing extensive video footage from that camera on his work computer.

There was a collective shudder.

"Do you know what gets me the most?" one woman asked. "His assistant said that when she found the camera and confronted him with it, he just kept saying it wasn't what she thought—"

"Oh, yeah, I read that!" someone else burst out. "He said it wasn't a big deal because he hadn't touched her. He has a camera looking up between her legs for almost a year before she finds it, and video footage—and you know exactly why he has *that*, eww— but he never touched anyone so no big deal."

Jo looked down into her glass. Despite her efforts to keep the fruit out, there were bits of orange floating in the wine. They looked like translucent legs.

"I've got to go," she said. There were murmurs of dismay and another round of hugs, but she imagined that they all breathed a sigh of relief when they sat back down after she'd gone.

Back home, she tore into a croissant, heated a mug of tomato soup in the microwave, and tried to calculate what time it was in whatever part of China Eileen was in now. Jo texted before she could stop herself: *I miss you. Hope you're having a good trip.*

She watched her soup circling on the glass tray and thought about the politician and his camera and about her CEO. She wondered if there was a hidden camera—or cameras—in his office too.

Probably not, she muttered—or meant to. *In the sexual predator hierarchy, I bet rapists think voyeurs are pathetic.*

She had a brief suffocating sensation of something like a bundle of wool fiber materializing in her throat, then gagged up a tarantula, its hairy legs all tangled together.

So she couldn't even refer to him as a rapist in the abstract. Good to know.

Her phone pinged just as the microwave finished. Jo got the mug out and read the text from Eileen: *I miss you too. How are you?*

Yeah, no way to answer *that* question. Jo watched the tarantula sort itself out on the kitchen counter and wave a tentative feeler while it tested the best direction to go.

The soup was too hot but she gulped it anyway, scalding the inside of her mouth and throat. Then she lowered the mug and poured the rest over the tarantula, sluicing the thing across the counter and into the sink on a scalding red tide. It seized up and rolled over on its back, twitching. Jo contemplated her options— the disposal or the garbage can—and imagined shreds of spider flying into her face from the bottom of the sink. She scooped the thing into the can with her mug, then tied the bag tight and took it out to the trash room.

Another text came in a few minutes later, while she was brushing her teeth.

Dammit, Jo. Can you just please TALK to me?

Jo typed, *I can't. I know that's the problem,* and then stared at the words, her finger hovering over the Send arrow. Another text came in as she hesitated, this one from the company's emergency alert system—*Urgent: Please read*—and she clicked the link automatically, half-relieved to have to think about something besides whether or how to reply to Eileen. The link took her not to a company message but to some kind of crowd-sourced fairy-tale encyclopedia, which was weird, plus the story tagged in the link was definitely not one she recognized. Jo read it in growing horror, because this had to be from the CEO—who else could have sent it?—and it suggested that whatever it was he'd done to her, it was somehow her fault.

Fairy Tales Forever Discord Channel

*We are an inclusive community; we celebrate all voices and identities. Expressions of hate, bias, or general assholery (yes, we know it's not a word) will not be tolerated. For full channel rules and guidelines click **here**.*

Discussion Boards: **Fairy Tale of the Day** | Question of the Day | Fairy Tales for Our Time

Fairy Tale of the Day: "Toads and Diamonds"
submitted by happilyneverafter (member since 2018)

Once upon a time, there was a beautiful girl whose mother died and whose father remarried a woman who had a daughter already. These two were lazy and arrogant, and when the father died suddenly, they made their poor stepdaughter/stepsister into their servant. One day, the stepmother sent the girl to the well for water. There the girl found a frail old woman who begged for a cup of water because she was too weak to pull the bucket up herself. "Of course, Mother," the kind girl said, and drew a bucket of sweet water for her. "Bless you, child," the old woman said. "From now on all shall know how precious you are whenever you speak." The girl came home late and her stepmother threatened to beat her. "Oh, please don't!" the girl cried, and a diamond fell from her lips. Astonished, the stepmother asked how this had happened and the girl told her, dropping jewels, nuggets of gold, and flowers with every word. The stepmother then called her own daughter and urged her to go at once to the well to draw water and be sure to give some to an old crone she would find there. The lazy girl slouched off, but when she got to the well she saw a fine lady clad in silk and jewels, who languidly asked for a drink. "No!" cried the arrogant girl. "You're rich enough, get it yourself." But of course, this was the same fairy who had appeared as a crone. "I see your character is as ill-favored as your face," she told the rude girl. "And so shall everyone know who hears you speak."

The stepsister stormed home to tell her mother what had happened, at which the mother screamed, for foul toads, spiders, snakes, and insects tumbled from her lips. The stepmother most unfairly blamed her stepdaughter for her own daughter's misfortune and threw the poor girl out of the house. She fled to the forest and wandered there for days, living on berries and nuts. One day, the king passed by with a hunting party and seeing the beautiful girl under a tree, asked for her name. When the girl told him, a ruby fell from her lips. Astonished, the king asked for her story. She told him, while flowers and other gems tumbled out, whereupon he put her on his horse in front of him, took her to his palace, and married her.

The stepmother and her daughter, for their part, lived on in their cottage and no one dared come near for fear of the dreadful things that the daughter spit out whenever she spoke.

JULY 27–31: RANJANI

Ranjani was trapped in summer weekend traffic on the DC Beltway when she saw the email from Jo canceling their design meeting that Friday afternoon. She was simultaneously horrified and relieved, because she'd been so anxious about the planned trip to the police station with Abony that she'd forgotten to clear her calendar.

She didn't bother to reply to Jo, who was probably headed to the beach or something fun anyway. The traffic started moving and Ranjani focused on driving. It took her another hour to get home and her silk dress was sticking to her back by the time she pulled into her driveway. Her car's air conditioning worked just fine, but there was only so much it could do to counter the heat and humidity in stop-and-go traffic.

Amit's car wasn't in the garage, which wasn't surprising. He almost never left work early, even on holidays, and given the constraints Ranjani had put on their schedule over the past few months, he probably hadn't felt any incentive to slip out today. Ranjani let herself into the house quietly, praying that her mother would be napping or watching television as she sometimes did in the afternoon. That would give Ranjani a few minutes to change out of her sweaty dress, splash cold water on her face, and remind herself that despite Abony's best efforts, nothing bad had happened this afternoon. She hadn't had to face those elevator doors.

Shreshthi was indeed watching television, an Indian interview show, and while she offered her cheek for her daughter to kiss, she also waved an imperious hand.

"Ssh, Rani! Let me finish my program in peace, please. It's been a busy day."

Going into the kitchen, Ranjani saw evidence of that busyness. A pot of dal simmered on the back of the stove and puri dough rested in a covered bowl beside the front burner, where a pan of oil was ready for frying. Ranjani checked to make sure that only the one flame was on under the dal. Then she slipped into her bedroom and shut the door, allowing herself a sigh of relief at being alone in the quiet. She unzipped her dress and tossed it onto the dry-cleaning pile, then climbed into bed wearing just her underwear and necklace, which she didn't dare take off even now. She waited until the air conditioning raised goose bumps on her bare skin before she pulled the covers up.

Her mother's dementia had been mild and stable for a long time after the diagnosis last year, but it was nonetheless progressing. Some days, like today, Shreshthi was mistress of all she surveyed, cooking a feast for dinner and cleaning the entire house, then settling in front of the television to offer sharp commentary on whatever show she chose. Other days, she started cooking only to wander away leaving things bubbling on the stove or plugged in the vacuum and left it leaning up against the couch with the motor on. Then she tried to watch television with her hands over her ears to block out the noise, which meant she couldn't hear the show and ended up rocking back and forth in a paroxysm of frustration. Ranjani and Amit paid their neighbor Deb, who was a retired nurse, to check in on Shreshthi several times a day and to stay with her when she was really distressed, but soon it wasn't going to be enough.

Ranjani couldn't think about "soon" right now. She thought she might cry; she felt the pressure behind her eyes almost constantly these days. But though a few tears leaked out, she was too tired for a storm of weeping. She exhaled and imagined herself sinking into the mattress, where it was white and soft and clean. When Amit got home two hours later, he had to shake her awake. Ranjani pulled him down beside her and pressed her ear to his chest to hear his heartbeat. Amit was home and Shreshthi was at the stove frying up puri; Ranjani could smell from here that the oil was at the perfect temperature. Everything would be okay. They didn't need to go anywhere new.

Ranjani had taken Monday off to be home for the plumber who promised to show up sometime between ten and four. She savored her unexpected long weekend, running errands to familiar stores, cooking, doing laundry, working beside her mother in the garden, watching movies with Amit on the couch after they'd gotten Shreshthi to bed. When she sat down at her desk on Tuesday morning, she felt more settled than she had in weeks. She worked on the edits for a single-image multimedia campaign, finally getting the color bleed where she wanted it. Then she turned to the project she was supposed to be working on with Jo and remembered the canceled meeting. She started to reply to Jo's email with times when she was available, but then noticed an out-of-office message; apparently Jo was on sick leave all week.

Ranjani was debating replying anyway, just to say she hoped Jo felt better, when her cell phone buzzed. She snatched it up.

"Hi, Mami."

"Rani—you're still at work?" Shreshthi had a beautiful voice, deep for a woman, with the lilting accent of British-educated Indian women from her generation. Ranjani had learned only recently to hear tremors of uncertainty in that voice.

"I'm at work until five, Mami. Then I'm coming straight home. We can make dinner together."

A pause. Ranjani's hand went unconsciously to grip the pendant tucked inside her blouse.

"It's—what time is it, Rani?"

A few weeks ago, Shreshthi had forgotten how to tell time. She could look at a clock and read the numbers on the face, but they didn't translate into a signifier by which she could measure her day: time to get up, time to eat, time for Ranjani to come home. Some days this didn't seem to faze her at all, but other days, Shreshthi knew there was something off about her sense of the world, and the awareness alternately enraged or terrified her. More and more, Ranjani didn't like leaving her mother home alone. She and Amit had been asking more of Deb recently, but Deb understandably was reluctant to give up her retirement and had urged them to hire a full-time home health aide.

And of course, they could do that. But as Shreshthi's symptoms worsened, they'd also have to go back to the doctor, who would send them to new specialists, to new labs for more bloodwork, to new clinical centers for MRIs and CT scans.

Infinite, necessary new places. Infinite, unpassable new doors.

Ranjani calmed her mother down as best she could, then called Deb and confirmed that today she was free not only to check in on Shreshthi but to stay for an hour or two. When Ranjani hung up, she had a headache. She knew she needed some food, but the thought of microwaving leftover dal and eating it at her desk made her feel trapped and depressed. Instead, she went outside to grab something from one of the food carts that always ringed Franklin Park at this hour. No new doors to go through to get there and she'd welcome the sun and the heat. She felt chilled from the inside whenever she thought about her mother's illness or about what had happened in the CEO's office and its impossible, dreadful aftermath, as though she'd swallowed a ball of ice that had lodged in her stomach and refused to thaw.

She got a gyros and a diet soda, then found a perfect spot to sit near the fountain, so that an occasional breeze blew a fine mist at her. She unwrapped the sandwich and ate a loose piece of cucumber before it could fall on the ground. Her cell phone buzzed with a text message: *Hey how's in-person work life?*

Ranjani smiled. Maia English was the company's chief information security officer. She had been one of Ranjani's first colleagues to become a friend but had started working from home six months ago because of a mysterious health issue.

I was just thinking about you, Ranjani wrote back. *Eating alone in Franklin Sq. Wish you were here.*

Me too. Pizza or gyros?

Gyros! Ranjani typed. *Will try not to drip on phone screen. How are you? How is working from home?*

Not all it's cracked up to be.

Ranjani took a bite of her gyros, did indeed narrowly miss dropping a blob of tzatziki on the phone screen, and wondered how to get Maia to *really* talk to her. Texting wasn't a medium for intimacy, and when she'd gone remote this past winter Maia had deflected Ranjani's offers to drop off food at the house or set up a Zoom call. Whatever health issue she was dealing with, it seemed to make her so tired that anything more energetic than texting was too much.

But even as Ranjani was trying to think what to say next, another text popped up from Maia.

Okay weird question. You ever read fairy tales?

Ranjani wiped her mouth and wished she'd gotten a few more napkins, though it was a rule of gyros that however many napkins you got wouldn't be enough.

Snow White, Cinderella, Rapunzel? she wrote. *I know them but not super well. My mother wasn't a fan of fairy-tale princesses. Too helpless.*

She's not wrong. Have you ever read Bluebeard?

Ranjani sent back a confused emoji, then watched as three dots popped up from Maia, went away, then came back again. Finally, her reply appeared: *I think you need to read it.*

And she sent a link.

Fairy Tales Forever Discord Channel

*We are an inclusive community; we celebrate all voices and identities. Expressions of hate, bias, or general assholery (yes, we know it's not a word) will not be tolerated. For full channel rules and guidelines click **here**.*

Discussion Boards: **Fairy Tale of the Day** | Question of the Day | Fairy Tales for Our Time

Fairy Tale of the Day: "Bluebeard"
submitted by JennyK (member since 2017)

Once upon a time there was an incredibly wealthy man known as Bluebeard who was looking for a wife. He'd had several wives already, who had all disappeared, but he was so rich that a woman agreed to marry him. After their wedding, Bluebeard took his new wife to his castle and told her he had to go away on a business trip so she'd be there alone. He left her with a key that would open any door in the castle but warned her sternly not to open a certain locked door.

Bluebeard's wife explored the castle while her husband was away, opening every door but the one he had told her not to open, but he was gone so long that at last her curiosity got the better of her. She opened the door and found to her horror the hacked-up bodies of all her husband's previous wives. She tried to close and lock the door again, but her hands were shaking so much that she dropped the key in a puddle of blood on the floor. The wife picked the key up, locked the door, and ran to wash the key, but no matter how hard she scrubbed or what cleaner she used, the blood would not come off.

When Bluebeard returned, he asked for the key back and his wife tried to say she had lost it, but he became so angry that she was frightened and handed him the bloody key with trembling fingers. As soon as he saw the blood, Bluebeard knew that she had disobeyed him and announced his intention to kill her. He gave her an hour to say her prayers while he sharpened his sword, and the wife went to the tallest tower in the castle to pray desperately for help. Just as her husband rushed up the stairs to murder her, her brothers burst through the castle doors and struck him down. Bluebeard's wife returned to her family and eventually married a good kind man who helped her forget all about her terrible ordeal.

JULY 31: RANJANI

Ranjani read the story Maia sent her with confusion that coalesced into terror while the ball of ice refroze in her stomach, congealing her lunch until she felt ill. She didn't "click to see more comments." Instead, she went back to her text screen and reread her exchange with Maia. In retrospect, it was clear that Maia had reached out specifically to send her this link. Ranjani typed *Why*, then accidentally hit send without knowing exactly what question she'd wanted to ask.

Why did I send you that? Maia replied.

Ranjani took a gulp of her soda. Sure, that question would do. Had the CEO put Maia up to this? Because he'd figured out that Ranjani and Abony were trying to help each other?

Maia's next text seemed to confirm this: *I know what he did to you.*

Ranjani fumbled her reply: *How? Did he tell you?*

Jesus no. No!

Ranjani set the can down and wiped her damp fingers on her skirt. She asked, *Then how could you possibly know anything?* just as another text from Maia came through.

I know about Abony too.

Ranjani went from chilled to sweating and back again in an instant. Maybe it wasn't even Maia texting her, maybe it was the

CEO himself. And even if it was Maia, he had to have told her. But what did the fairy tale mean? She stared at the three dots promising another text as though they were the countdown on a bomb, then realized she didn't have to wait for it to come through. She flung her phone into her purse and gathered up her trash. Her phone pinged with texts as she walked across the park, clammy with flash-sweat. Another horrible thought occurred to her: if this *was* the CEO, had it been some kind of trap?

She veered off onto a bench and pulled on the chain around her neck so hard she nearly broke it when it caught on her hair. The pendant hanging from it could have come directly from the fairy tale she'd just read: a key nearly the length of her palm, exquisitely carved out of some gleaming, translucent white material. It emerged blindingly white in the noon sun and Ranjani slumped in relief. Still, she couldn't bring herself to keep ignoring her texts. What if someone besides Maia was trying to reach her, especially her mother or Deb? She pulled out her phone again—all Maia. Ranjani read them through.

I can see why you think that he told me, why you'd be afraid it's that, but it's not I swear.
I've been trying to figure out how he's doing it to stop him.
Ask me something only I'd know if you need to know I'm me.
Rani?
I didn't reach out because he made me. Think about it, Rani. He didn't tell me a damn thing. So how else could I know?

Ranjani thought about it. She reread their text thread to reassure herself that indeed, she hadn't actually *told* Maia anything. There was no reason for the key to trigger. But Maia had found out anyway.

Maia was brilliant, everyone who worked with her knew that. She was also a badass. Her Casual Friday t-shirts said things like *My Dragon Ate Your Patriarchy* and *The Bridges I've Burned Light My Way*. Ranjani wanted to believe that Maia wouldn't ever sell out another woman. She did believe it, as much as she could believe anything right now. But how else could she have known about both Ranjani and Abony?

Oh.

Why did you start working from home? she asked.

Exactly, Maia typed back.

Have you tried to report him?

Of course. I can't, any more than you or Abony can.

Three dots again, and Ranjani braced herself to hear what the CEO had done to her friend, but Maia's next text avoided the unspoken question:

I knew I couldn't be the only one because, hello, Matt Lauer, Harvey Weinstein? I didn't know how to find anyone else. But men are nothing if not predictable so I started looking for a pattern.

And Abony and I fit the pattern? Ranjani asked.

Yes, I can explain how. More important—I know what he's doing and why he's doing it.

I don't care why. How do we stop it?

Don't know that yet and not for lack of trying. But he just did it to someone else.

Ranjani moaned in distress. *From the office?*

Then even as Maia replied—*yes, not sure if you know her*—Ranjani thought of last Friday. She tried to ask: *Jo Miller*, but hit send too soon and left off the question mark.

So you do know her.

We were supposed to meet Friday but she canceled, Ranjani typed. *She's out sick all this week.*

Again—exactly.

So what…

Ranjani paused to figure out what she actually wanted to say or ask next. She'd been swept along by Abony's determination less than a week ago and Maia was just as much of a force of nature. It would be easy to just finish the question: *So what do you want to do?* but then Maia would say what she wanted to do and if it was something bold or dangerous—something involving a new door—Ranjani would have to say no to it.

She deleted the phrasing that created a question and typed instead.

She must be so scared. I can reach out to her.

Good, Maia replied. *Just be aware that I think her curse is like mine, not yours—it's constant, not on a trigger.*

Curse??? Ranjani added extra question marks for good measure this time, because now she felt lost. What was Maia talking about?

Like I said, I know what he's doing and now I know why. Jo was the key to figuring out the pattern.

But you said you don't know how to stop it.

Hoping we can work together to figure that out.

Ranjani choked on a humorless laugh.

Seriously? I can't go anywhere new and you can't leave the house.

You can come to my house, Maia said. *You've been here before, remember? I hosted Wendy's baby shower.*

Yes, Ranjani remembered, which was a relief and a new problem, because now she had basically committed to reaching out to a colleague she didn't know well to ask her if she'd recently been sexually assaulted—and by the way, had anything *else* awful happened as a result? Anything really, really weird? Ranjani thought of that ugly Bluebeard story and wondered wildly if the

CEO could have turned Jo into a frog or a beast—weren't those things that happened in fairy tales? But they happened to men, not women.

Okay, Ranjani said. *Thanks for remembering that. Just give me a few days to get Jo and Abony to come with me.*

Of course. Text me when you've picked a time to come. Simon can let you in.

Ranjani had met Maia's husband Simon several times. He was shy and awkward and seemed relieved to be Maia's sidekick in social situations.

Simon knows?

No way he couldn't.

Did you tell him right away? I . . .

Again, Ranjani hesitated and didn't send, this time because she had too many questions herself and didn't know which to ask, if any. Had Maia told Simon right away or only later, when she couldn't hide some strange new behavior from him? Had it broken him, to know that she'd been hurt like that? Had he tried to report the assault himself? Was that even feasible, or did it make things worse?

Her alarm went off, reminding her to go back to her desk. Ranjani refastened her necklace, tucking the key away again.

You there? Maia asked.

Ranjani finished her last text with what amounted to an open question and a buried one.

Did you tell him right away? I haven't told Amit. I wasn't sure I could.

Maia's reply took a moment to come in and was a longer block of text: *Like I said, there's no way Simon could NOT know what happened to me. I don't think this guy cares if you tell someone so long as it's not officially reporting him. He's counting on us not telling anyone because we're afraid they won't believe us.*

Three dots, then she added: *But you could tell Amit! He loves you so much. He'll believe you.*

He would. Ranjani knew that. She stood at the corner waiting for a walk sign and craned her neck to take in the façade of her office building, all the way up to the top floor where the CEO's office was. Was he in there now? The floor-to-ceiling windows flashed like mirrors and gave nothing away.

I'm sorry if the Bluebeard story freaked you out, Maia said, *but you can see why you had to read it. When you get a chance later, read this too.*

Ranjani saw that she'd sent a link to a different post on the same channel, but didn't click on it until that evening, as she was getting ready for bed. Then she read with the prickling sense that Maia had sent this particular story hoping it would make Ranjani angry, and she didn't feel angry so much as scared. She turned off her phone and focused on brushing out and rebraiding her hair, then clicked off the light and slipped into bed. Amit was already half asleep, but he rolled toward her instinctively and slung one long arm over her waist, anchoring her to him.

Ranjani recalled the drive home from the doctor's office when her mother had gotten her diagnosis, the silence in the car rising and pressing against them like a mass of yeasted dough. Finally, Shreshthi had said crisply, "I'm not afraid, Rani. I choose not to be afraid. As a surgeon, you learn to do this, because if you are afraid, you put your patient at risk. You become angry instead. You choose anger, not at your patient, but at the injury. It is a better way."

Mami, Ranjani had thought, *it's okay to be afraid.* But she had known better than to say so out loud.

Fairy Tales Forever Discord Channel

*We are an inclusive community; we celebrate all voices and identities. Expressions of hate, bias, or general assholery (yes, we know it's not a word) will not be tolerated. For full channel rules and guidelines click **here**.*

Discussion Boards: Fairy Tale of the Day |
Question of the Day | **Fairy Tales for Our Time**

Fairy Tales for Our Time: "The Women Who Told the Truth"
submitted by legalprincess (member since 2015)

Once upon a time, a scholar (yes, children, a woman) learned that a certain man had been offered the scales of justice in the kingdom and would have authority over the laws of the land. This same man had once tormented this scholar such that she did not believe he could be trusted to always be just and wise. She left the tower where she studied, went to the king and court, and told them all that she knew of the man's wickedness. Some of the courtiers were impressed by the scholar, but most refused to believe her. They said that women, even great scholars, were often mistaken about men's intentions. So the scholar went back to her tower and the man was given the scales of justice, which he wielded for ill as she had warned.

Years went by, during which time other women of the kingdom sought out the scholar to tell her that they too had suffered at the hands of the same man, or other men like him. Many in the kingdom vowed that the next time a woman told the court what she knew of a man's wickedness, they would be sure to believe her.

In time, another man was offered the scales of justice, and another woman—a healer—went to the king and the court and told them that when she had been a young girl and this man not much more than a boy himself, he had held her down and tried to kiss and touch her.

Women across the kingdom waited to see what the king and court would do, sure that this time the woman would be believed. Some at court were shaken by the healer's story, but others were unmoved. This man too was given the scales of justice, and he too wielded them for ill.

The women of that land wondered if there was an enchantment laid upon their kingdom that kept those in power from believing the truth when it was told to them. They wondered too what it would take to break such an enchantment. They saw that it couldn't be broken by a prince with a magical sword, a clever tailor, or a handsome youngest son—yet these were the only heroes permitted. The women vowed to continue to tell the truth about wicked men. They declared the scholar, the healer, and other women who had come forward to be heroes of a new kind. And they tried not to give up hope that someday they would all be believed.

AUGUST 1: ABONY

In line at Starbucks on Wednesday, Abony reminded herself that she could still afford to buy a damn coffee in the morning and handed over her credit card without blinking. It was $4.73, for God's sake.

"Nope." The barista shook her head. "He took care of it." The girl jerked her head toward the high-top table in the bay window, where a man was busy dumping an appalling amount of sweetener into his cup and studiously not watching Abony's reaction to his generosity. Abony had to wade through the pile-up of people at the sugar and cream station to get to the table and was at the man's elbow before she registered that he was both young and extremely good-looking.

Okay, maybe not *too* young. The lines that crinkled around his eyes when he turned to smile at her looked like they might leave their mark when the smile faded, and there was a thread, just a thread, of silver in the hair at his temples and over his ears. He was dressed like all of DC, in a navy-blue suit and white shirt, but he wore the suit like he was used to it, not half-strangled to have a tie on, and his briefcase appeared to have been through a warzone and only barely survived.

"Thank you," Abony said. "You didn't have to do that."

He stirred his coffee, still smiling at her.

"I do plenty of things every day because I *have* to," he said. "I try to balance them out with things I *want* to do, like buying a beautiful woman a cup of coffee."

He had nice hands, clean and square and long-fingered. No rings.

"Exactly how many sweeteners did you put in there?" Abony asked.

The smile became a grin. "Just enough to make it too damn sweet, which is the only way I can drink coffee. I hate the stuff."

That startled a laugh out of her. "Then don't drink it."

He rolled his eyes. "And lose all my cred as a serious professional? Please." Finished stirring, he wiped his hand on a napkin and held it out. "Jonathan Martin—Jon to my friends."

"Abony, with an 'a'."

"Beautiful," he said, then let go of her hand to smack himself theatrically on the forehead. "I've only been talking to you for five minutes and already I'm repeating myself!"

Abony pressed her lips together to keep from laughing again, only because he so clearly wanted her to, then saw his eyes drop to her mouth and felt herself flush.

"I have to get to work, Mr. Martin—"

"Jon."

"Jon, I really do have to get to work."

The barista called out her order and Abony hesitated. She knew prolonging this conversation was a bad idea, but just now it was hard to remember why.

"I have to get to work too," Jon said. He took a sip of his coffee and made such a horrible face that Abony had to stifle a giggle. "I'm a forensic accountant, which I'm only telling you because I want you to trust me and really, how can you not trust a forensic accountant? So I have to get to work and you have to get to work, but eventually we both leave work, and sometimes, almost every night in fact, I eat dinner. You?"

God, she was tempted. She must have looked torn because he pressed on and said the worst thing he could possibly have said, though of course he couldn't have known.

"I promise to take you someplace worthy of those shoes."

And Abony went cold and still inside, must have gone cold and still on the outside too from the look on his face. She turned her back on him, grabbed the coffee he'd bought her, and walked away. He'd almost had her, Mr. Jon Martin with his dazzling smile and his wit and his excellent hands. She might have agreed to have dinner with him. Thank God he'd reminded her why she couldn't.

Abony's shoes today were leopard-print pony hair with a red cap toe studded with spikes and a three-inch heel. They weren't even beautiful; they were ferocious. They made her calves pop and her butt sway when she walked and their heels didn't give a rat's ass about sore feet or twisted ankles. All they cared about was keeping Abony literally on her toes. Those heels were so sharp-edged and slender that they'd make excellent weapons in a pinch. As she pushed open the door of the Starbucks, Abony imagined stabbing one of those heels right into the CEO's neck. It might ruin the shoe, but it would be worth it.

Out on the sidewalk she slipped her sunglasses on and started mentally going through her day: meetings all morning starting at nine, but only two in the afternoon, which wasn't the worst line-up she'd ever had. She'd be able to grab lunch and would also have space at the end of the day to actually *do* some of the work those meetings would generate.

"Abony."

She almost walked right past, but then heard her name again, more urgently— "Abony!"— and turned to see Ranjani rising from a nearby bench. Ranjani's glossy black hair was braided to the side today, wrapped in red silk cord that matched her top.

Abony stepped out of the flow of pedestrian traffic. "What's wrong? Did something happen?"

Ranjani's pretty mouth twisted. "Is it that obvious?"

"I figured you'd had enough of me for a while after last Friday," Abony said, biting her tongue to keep from adding *and I don't blame you*, because dammit, she wasn't going to apologize for trying to get them both free. "But here you are on a bench right between Starbucks and our building," she went on, "and you're not just taking time with your own drink. You don't even have one."

"I wasn't stalking you or anything!" Ranjani cried. She sat down abruptly and started pleating her skirt in her hands. "And I don't like coffee. I just figured most people from the office start their day here so it was a good bet you did too. I didn't . . ." she faltered. "I could have texted you but—"

"It's fine," Abony said. "Scoot over."

Ranjani slid down to one side of the bench and Abony sat down next to her, took the lid off her cup, and took a healthy swallow.

"You think he's watching us right now?" she asked idly, which made Ranjani jump and clutch her braid.

"No! I mean—is he? Do *you* think he is?"

Abony shrugged. Since Friday's debacle at the police station and the creepy text message suggesting—what? that what the CEO had done to her had something to do with *fairy tales*?—

she'd been sleeping badly. Several times she'd jerked awake and lain still with her heart racing, half-convinced that her feet had been chopped off while she slept and that when she turned on the light she'd see red stains on the sheets.

Now she looked over and saw that Ranjani was pressing her whole body back into the bench, her eyes huge.

"I don't actually think he's watching us, Rani," Abony said. "I just feel paranoid, probably the same sort of thing that made you try to meet me here rather than texting or calling. Wait—is that why you wanted to talk to me? Did you get that weird text on Friday?"

"What text?"

"It looked like it was from our IT alert system, one of those mass alerts that goes to everybody, but it was clearly just for me. Whoever sent it knew what happened—at least the part about the damn shoes."

Ranjani peeled herself off the bench.

"What did it say?"

"It linked to a website," Abony said. "Some discussion board about fairy tales of all things. Creeped me out."

"I didn't get the text," Ranjani said. "But I know who sent it."

"Him?"

"No." Ranjani shook her head. "But it's related to why I need to talk to you. Can I see the message?"

She held out her hand with such unexpected assurance that Abony scrolled to find the message and handed the phone over. Ranjani clicked and actually smiled when she first saw the Discord site header. Her face fell as she read the discussion thread, though, and she bit her lip.

"Wow," she said as she handed the phone back. "I didn't know any of that stuff, did you?"

Abony shook her head. "So who sent it to me and why shouldn't I be freaked out?"

"Maia English, from IT. You know her, right?"

Ah yes, the ever-present assumption that HR knew everyone at the company. Abony rolled her eyes behind her sunglasses even as she registered that she *did* know Maia, had worked with her on several company policies and protocols around personal content on company computers. She'd also processed Maia's work-from-home request at the end of January, though that wasn't something she was at liberty to share.

"We're friends," Ranjani went on, "I mean, not best friends or anything, but we used to go to lunch and stuff and we've texted since she] started to work remote. I should have been more worried about that at the time," she added, half to herself. "I mean, I thought it was super weird that she suddenly had to work from home, couldn't even call into meetings, nothing, and wouldn't let me come by to visit. But it didn't occur to me—"

"Oh shit, are you kidding? Her too? *Six months ago?*"

Ranjani nodded miserably.

"Yes. I mean—I think so. I'm pretty sure."

"You *think* so? What did he do to stop *her* from reporting him?"

"I don't know. But, Abony, listen. Maia says he assaulted someone else from the office last Friday, a woman named Jo Miller; she works in PR."

Abony's hand twitched hard enough to slosh hot coffee over her wrist.

"Dammit!" She held the cup at arm's length in front of her and glared at Ranjani. "How the hell does Maia know this?"

Ranjani looked like she wanted to retreat into the bench again, but she returned Abony's look steadily.

"I was suspicious too," she said. "I flat-out accused her of being his puppet. But I don't think she is. And she could be right about Jo. We were supposed to meet last week but Jo canceled at the last minute and now her out-of-office is on for this entire week saying she's sick. Look—here." Ranjani pulled out her own phone, tapped, and then handed it to Abony.

"Read my whole thread with Maia. You'll see. Start with the link she sent me."

Abony had to take her sunglasses off to read, drawing in her breath sharply when she recognized the website Maia had sent Ranjani. And that story…

"'Bluebeard.' I've never even heard of this story. Have you?"

"No."

"I can't imagine why Disney hasn't remade it yet," Abony murmured.

Ranjani let out a startled, breathless laugh. Abony kept reading.

"So Maia wants us to track down Jo and get her to tell us if the CEO attacked her—let's ignore the fact that I'm not a fan of the head of HR asking *anyone* why they took sick leave—and *then* she wants the three of us to go to her house to hear some theory she has about all this shit?"

"Well…" Ranjani was pleating her skirt in her fingers again, "I did tell her I had to talk to you and Jo first."

"I saw that." Abony passed Ranjani back her phone. "What's Maia's secret here, do you think? Has she written an algorithm that reveals his motives?"

"She says she knows why he's doing it," Ranjani said.

"Sure, why and what, just not how. But stop looking like I'm about to scold you, Rani. I'm inclined to have confidence in Maia too, and probably for the same reasons you do."

"Because she's terrifyingly self-confident and unfiltered?"

Abony laughed. "Exactly. And if something did happen to her all those months ago, *of course* she's been determined to find a way out. So yeah, I'll go with you to talk to Maia. The bigger problem right now is Jo. Miller, you said?"

Ranjani nodded.

"Did you reply to her email canceling your meeting yet?"

"No, I was going to but then I saw that she was out all week."

"Good," Abony said. "That gives you an excuse to reach out, to reschedule. And I'll tell my assistant to work with you so I can be there once you find a time. But could you set something up outside the office?"

Ranjani went still again, in that disconcerting way Abony had gotten used to already—disconcerting because it wasn't the abrupt, jerky movement you would expect from someone under stress. It was an encompassing held-breath stillness that was all the more alarming because it wasn't clear Ranjani knew she was doing it.

"You think he'd know if we met inside the building?"

"I don't want to chance it," Abony said.

"But then—" Ranjani faltered. "Won't he know I've emailed her? And then know when she responds? If we set up a meeting somewhere else, he'll know that too!" Her voice rose perilously close to hysteria and her pleating fingers lost their rhythm in her skirts.

"He doesn't know everything, Rani," Abony said, trying to invest her own voice with sureness. "He's a man, not a magician."

"I'm not so sure," Ranjani said. "Maia used the word 'curse,' remember? And she also said…"

She trailed off, then drew a steadying breath to try again.

"She was surprised I hadn't told anyone, besides you I mean."

"How did she know you'd even told me?" Abony asked.

Ranjani hunched her shoulders. "I don't know. I didn't ask. Maybe just because she knew he'd assaulted us both already and then she saw on our calendars that we met, what, was it two weeks ago? When I asked to talk to you about my mom?"

Ranjani had asked for an appointment with HR to discuss all the permutations of caring for her mother as her illness progressed, from the health insurance options to medical leave for Ranjani as a caregiver and work-from-home options. Having helped care for several of her grandparents through long-term and eventually terminal illnesses, Abony was an expert in the resources available that many employees didn't even know to ask for, and she also liked meeting with people in this situation herself, since she'd been there. She hadn't even blinked at Ranjani's abashed request to meet in the conference room on her floor rather than in Abony's office. Then halfway through the meeting, Abony had gotten a text from her assistant about a complaint against their chief financial officer for retaliation. The idea was ludicrous—the company CFO was one of the kindest, most ethical people Abony had ever worked with—and Abony had set her phone down with an apology to Ranjani. *Sorry. Some people think it's always open season on leadership, apparently.*

Ranjani had gone absolutely still in that disconcerting way that Abony was now used to and asked, in an almost inaudible voice, whether someone had complained about the CEO. Then she'd scrabbled at her throat to pull out the necklace she was wearing and peered urgently at whatever was at the end. And Abony, staring at the young woman in front of her, played her own offhand remark back in her head and somehow *knew*.

"I'll buy that," she said. "Especially if, as you say, Maia already knew about both of us herself. She'd have been on the lookout for any time any of our paths crossed."

"I thought I wouldn't even be *able* to tell you," Ranjani said. "Even though we were in a room I'd been in before so the key wasn't triggered, I didn't think I could tell you."

"Well," Abony smiled wryly, "as I recall, I mostly just told you to be quiet and let me tell you a story, see if it sounded at all familiar."

"Yeah," Ranjani said quietly. "So is that what you'll do with Jo?"

"I suppose so."

"But what if—what if Maia's wrong? What if he didn't assault Jo? Would you still tell her what happened to you?"

Abony checked her watch as discreetly as she could on the pretext of placing her coffee cup on the ground beside her. She still had a few minutes.

"Rani, what are you getting at?"

"I don't know!" Ranjani burst out miserably. "I just hadn't thought about it the way Maia clearly does. I mean, her husband *knows*. He's going to be at their house when we go over there."

"It sounds like whatever the CEO did to Maia might be—" Abony tried to say something besides *awful* or *completely debilitating*, but Ranjani cut her off.

"I know. I mean, it sounds like she needs Simon and I've been trying not to think about what he could have done to her for that to be true. I guess we'll find out. But," she went on, "what I realized when Maia was so surprised is that I can't imagine telling anyone besides you. I know you had to drag it out of me because I was so scared—"

"For good reason," Abony said, "as we both discovered last

Friday, by the way, when I dragged you on that fool's errand." There, she'd admitted it.

"But that's not why I don't want to tell anyone else," Ranjani said. "I'm *glad* you know. It helps. But when it comes to anyone else—Amit, my mother, my friends…"

She trailed off for good this time and resumed plucking at her skirt, but half-heartedly now.

They sat in silence long enough for Abony to realize that it was officially unbearably hot in the sun, not just about to be unbearably hot. And it was nearly time for her first meeting, which she was leading. Fuck it.

"Let me say this and let me finish it, okay, because what I have to say up front sounds—I can't believe I'm even saying this phrase. But if all he'd done was assault us, Rani—and I know, as if that's "all"—but if he'd done that and then we'd walked out of his office, each of us, you, me, Maia, maybe Jo, we would have had choices to make. To report the asshole. To get a rape kit done. Quit our jobs. Sue the bastard. See a counselor. Tell our families."

Her sunglasses were sliding as sweat beaded on the bridge of her nose. She pushed them up.

"But he didn't—and here's another phrase to make you cringe—he didn't 'just' assault us. He did it and then took away our choices. Even Maia. It sounds like she didn't have a choice to tell her husband or not, so don't let her judge you for not telling your husband. She's not in your shoes." Abony grimaced. "Or mine. I always assumed that if a man raped me, I'd see him in jail, fired, facing a civil suit—you name it—all within a week. *Then* I'd be able to tell people what he'd done. But only then."

"So you haven't told anyone either?" Ranjani asked.

Abony shook her head. "Does that make you feel any better?"

"No," Ranjani said.

Abony smiled mirthlessly. "Honest at least."

"I'm sorry," Ranjani said. "It does make me think we're doing the right thing in talking to Jo, though."

"To let her know she's not alone?"

"To remember that none of us is, even though it sometimes feels that way."

Fairy Tales Forever Discord Channel

*We are an inclusive community; we celebrate all voices and identities. Expressions of hate, bias, or general assholery (yes, we know it's not a word) will not be tolerated. For full channel rules and guidelines click **here**.*

Discussion Boards: Fairy Tale of the Day | Question of the Day | **Fairy Tales for Our Time**

Fairy Tales for Our Time: "The Princess and the Conservatorship"
submitted by amyc (member since 2016)

Once upon a time, there was a princess who loved to sing and dance, and her performances captivated not just her own kingdom but kingdoms around the world. People traveled from far and wide to hear her sing and watch her dance, and the princess grew both wealthy and famous. The more her fame spread, however, the more the people wanted of her, so that they were not content to hear her sing or watch her dance. They wanted to know more: what foods she ate, what clothes she chose, how she wore her hair, where she slept and with whom. Many people cared so much about what the princess did—or didn't do—that when she made a choice they didn't like, they lashed out at her in rage. And when she tripped and fell, or cut her hair too short, they laughed at her.

These same people never would have been so cruel to an ordinary person. It was because she was a princess, you see.

The princess seemed to grow richer each year, for people flocked to see her sing and dance—many of them the same people who laughed at her, mocked her, or scorned her for choices she made when she was not on the stage, when she was not being their beloved "Princess of Pop." But in truth she was trapped, not in a tower but by a piece of paper. This piece of paper decreed that she could not control her own wealth and gave that control instead to her father and a lawyer.

This piece of paper which decreed that the princess could not be trusted with her own wealth was called a conservatorship, and for many years the princess struggled to be free of it. She also longed to be free of her father, who saw her still as a little girl and not as a grown woman. At long last, she was granted that freedom, but there is no "happily ever after" here, children, just more legal battles and depositions and revelations that over the decade and more of the conservatorship, the princess made millions and millions of dollars that went to the men controlling her money, her career, her day-to-day actions, her very life . . .

AUGUST 8: JO

Jo had been annoyed when Ranjani suggested rescheduling for someplace outside the office, but by that afternoon, she was grateful for the excuse to slip out. They were going to the coffee shop just a block from Metro Center, so she could get on a train afterwards without having to come back to her desk. And they weren't meeting until 3:30, but Jo was always starving these days, so she left her desk at three to walk over and get an iced latte and a cheddar cheese scone—she looked longingly at the sandwich menu, but it was a textural minefield—then stake out a table in the shade on the patio.

Jo slurped the coffee gratefully. She hadn't been sleeping well even before the assault because she missed Eileen in the bed, but in the past two weeks it had been even worse. She woke to frequent charley horses, which were her own fault for running so much, and to the conviction that she was bruised and abraded inside, which was decidedly *not* her fault. She had also discovered—painfully, mid-leg-cramp—that cursing even generically in those first waking moments was enough to make her cough up a pair of crickets. She was carefully quiet after that, gritting her teeth and pounding on her thigh.

She wasn't sure what alarmed her more: the fact that whatever the CEO had done to her meant that even her half-asleep invective produced bugs rather than words, or her response to the fact, which was to stop talking even alone in her own bed. What the fuck should she care if the whole thing filled with beetles and snakes? They never seemed inclined to bite or sting her and she wasn't squeamish about killing them. But still Jo knew herself silenced. She was reluctant to speak the few times she went out in public or picked up the phone and had to control an instinctive flinch when she heard her own voice; how brittle it was, and sharp.

She took advantage of waking before dawn to run before it got too hot and ran again in the evenings even when it still was, trying to tire herself out enough to sleep at night. She abandoned the wooded path in the park behind her building in favor of Connecticut Avenue, which was always seething with people on their way somewhere. Jo weaved through commuters, nodded to other runners, waved to dogs and solemn babies in strollers, and felt pathetically grateful when people *saw* her, even if only to step out of her way.

Eileen would have said that there was no reason to describe her gratitude as "pathetic," of course. Eileen believed in expressing emotion, all the time and even when it was pointless. She thought that Jo was stifled by her parents' divorce and her mother's admittedly arm's-length approach to parenting while she made a ruthless climb up the corporate ladder of an international law firm. It had been a joke at first, what Eileen called their radically different "love languages," but it wasn't funny two years later when the two of them sat at opposite ends of the couch, Eileen sobbing listlessly and Jo clutching a pillow to her chest like a shield. Eileen said that telling people how you felt didn't make you weak, it made you *vulnerable*, and Jo hunched her shoulders and said she wasn't sure what the difference was.

And so Eileen moved out.

But now at least they were texting again. During her cool-down at the end of each run, Jo took pictures she knew Eileen would like.

She snapped an ancient Italian man eating antipasti on a restaurant patio, wearing a thin white sweater, white pants, and no shoes on his gnarled brown feet, and captioned it *I want to be this guy.*

She sent a photo of an ice-cream store menu featuring a flavor called "Girl Scouts Gone Wild." *Hey, weren't you a Girl Scout?*

She sent a picture of a dog waiting for her owner outside a coffee shop. The dog was nothing but a mop of coarse white and gray fur with liquid black eyes and a comically pronounced underbite.

That poor thing, Eileen texted back. *How does she even chew her food?*

Underbite or no, the dog looked prepared to enjoy whatever she slurped up. Jo envied her.

Because Eileen was still in China, sometimes they'd communicate in real time, while Jo was finishing an evening run and Eileen was getting ready in the morning. Texts Jo sent in the morning, though, would go unanswered all day. Then Eileen would send her own pictures, of shrines and street vendors, the plate-glass front of a McDonald's entirely obscured by a technicolor painting of a Big Mac. She fretted that they should stop texting each other: *You know this is just making me miss you more and it doesn't change anything.* She worried that Jo was not taking care of herself.

Are you okay, really? I just want you to be okay, she said. Then the next evening: *I want you to be happy. Even if you met someone else I would be okay with that if you were happy.*

Jo was debating getting up from the table to snap a photo to send to Eileen of a food truck across the street advertising footlong hot dogs with the scrawled slogan, *Come on, ladies, you know nothing less will satisfy,* when Ranjani materialized beside her.

"Sorry I'm late!"

"It's like 3:33, Rani. You're fine."

"Thanks. Sorry." Ranjani was gorgeous as always, in a pink silk top and vividly patterned full skirt. She'd sweated just enough walking over from the office that her skin was dewy and Jo could smell the delicate perfume she wore. "Do you mind if I run in and grab something really quick? I could just skip it if we need to start…"

"I don't have anything after this," Jo said. "Seriously. Go get something. I'll work on my scone." She popped a bite in her mouth to prove it.

"Okay. I'm gonna leave my bag if that's okay." Ranjani settled her tote bag in the chair across from Jo, fished out cash and her phone, and then stood another moment beside the table, biting her lip.

"I forgot to say, umm, Abony's joining us. Abony LePrince from HR? She's getting her coffee now so she might get here before I get back."

"I'm here," said another voice over Jo's shoulder, and Abony set her cup down on the table, swung out the chair to Jo's right, and sank gracefully into it.

"Hi, Jo." She held out her hand. "I don't think we've met."

"Okay then," Ranjani practically squeaked. "Be right back."

Jo shook Abony's hand. "I suppose me seeing you in the company orientation video doesn't count as meeting," she said.

Abony grinned. "I do make an excellent HR video."

She took the lid off her cup, which held what appeared to be iced tea, added a packet of sugar, and stirred thoroughly.

Jo sipped her own drink and waited. Abony'd crashed this meeting, after all.

Abony tasted her iced tea and made a face.

"It's a problem," she said, waving at the cup with the wooden stirrer. "I'm not a sweet tea person, but I can't get to liking it totally black either. And I *hate* artificial sweetener. So it's a question of using just enough sugar to cut the bitterness." She took another sip. "I envy you your latte, to be honest, but I had one this morning and I don't have your metabolism."

"What do you know about my metabolism?" Jo asked. "Maybe this is the first thing I've had to eat or drink all day."

Abony considered her.

"Looks like it might be, at that. I apologize."

Jo deliberately chewed another bite of scone, though it was pretty stale, and sat back to assess the other woman. Abony was wearing a draped-neck white silk blouse, a red pencil skirt, and red-soled peep-toe pumps in white linen printed all over with clusters of cherries.

"Whoa, are those Louboutins?"

Ranjani, arriving at the table at that moment, gasped, and looked from one of them to the other with something like panic on her face.

"Something I said?" Jo asked.

She knew she was being a bitch but also knew that there was something off about this whole thing. What was the head of HR doing here? And why was Jo noticing her damn designer shoes a big deal? They were pretty fabulous shoes and Abony's whole outfit was clearly designed around them. Then Jo thought of something.

"Are you here about that text?"

Abony cocked her head. "What text?"

"The one I got from IT like a week ago or something. I was going to report it because there's no way that was an authorized company email—"

Jo broke off, pressing her lips together as if to seal any future words inside. She wasn't feeling the telltale swelling sensation in her throat but she wasn't going to take a chance on saying anything else, not in a public place, for God's sake, or to two women who were basically strangers.

"Actually," Abony said, "I am here about that text. Sort of. I asked Ranjani to invite me. This isn't at all how I like to approach an employee, believe me, but can you just give me one minute?"

Jo glanced at Ranjani, whose return gaze was an eloquent plea—though for what, exactly, Jo didn't know.

"One minute," she said.

Abony nodded.

"I'm going to tell you a story," she said. "And depending on how this story—let's say depending on how it lands with you— then I want you to know that I'm here, we're both here, to listen to yours. Now," Abony swung one long leg in Jo's direction. "You asked about my shoes. They are Louboutins. This pair was a bargain on eBay—only $670—"

"Christ," Jo muttered. "*That's* a bargain?"

Abony acknowledged the interruption with a raised eyebrow but kept talking.

"I used to love Louboutins," she said. "I told myself that when I got promoted to VP for HR, I would buy myself a pair, which I did. Not these." She twitched her foot again. "These are ridiculous. I bought the shoes that you buy when you're splurging on one pair of designer shoes—black patent leather, mid-height heel. And I was wearing them when the CEO of our company raped me in his office four months ago."

Jo clapped her hands over her own mouth.

Nope. Nothing wanted to come out. Though why should it? *She* wasn't talking.

Abony, meanwhile, had *stopped* talking. She and Ranjani were both gazing at Jo. Ranjani's eyes were full of tears, while Abony's face was inscrutable.

Jo brought her hands down and folded them carefully in her lap.

"I think you've used up your minute," she said. "But that wasn't the whole story."

Abony wiped the condensation off the side of her cup with a long, elegant finger.

"The whole story'll take longer," she said, "and you might not believe it."

"Try me," Jo said.

Four months earlier, on a Friday in March, Abony had been in a consultation with the company's General Counsel about an employee grievance. Abony was pushing for a harder line with this employee, whose grievance was pretty thin, and she was frustrated that Suzanne, the lawyer, was recommending that they go ahead and allow the guy to report to a different supervisor. When Abony's cell phone chimed to let her know that a meeting had just been added to her calendar, she initially picked it up just to silence the alert, then cursed inwardly when she saw that the meeting was for that very afternoon. *Somebody has some nerve,* she thought as she tapped to see the details, *scheduling a Friday afternoon meeting on a Friday morning.*

Then she saw that it was a one-on-one with the CEO, with the bland event title *Personnel Question from BOD.* Abony cut the conversation with Suzanne short, explaining that something had come up she needed to prep for and promising to send over HR's proposed response to the employee by Monday. The lawyer left with her lips compressed in a disapproving line, which was hardly surprising since she hadn't gotten her way on the grievance. As she sat down at her desk and began to review all the open HR cases, Abony briefly wondered whether it would be worth raising her concern about Suzanne's general risk aversion with the CEO.

He had stepped into the role at the beginning of July eight months earlier, following a closed-door search by the company's Board of Directors. He was a fascinating enigma in the industry: at less than fifty, he'd already led several large companies through massive growth and change and he was known for making bold, unconventional moves that always paid off. As a member of the leadership team, Abony was supposed to meet with him in a group setting weekly, but he rarely joined those meetings in person, choosing instead to call or Zoom in. Sometimes he didn't show up at all and the VPs took turns running the meeting.

Abony was also supposed to have a monthly one-on-one with him, but so far they'd only managed to connect once face-to-face. That had been right after he started and Abony had treated the encounter like a job interview that she had to knock out of the park, even though she'd been head of HR for two years by then and was widely respected in the industry. She was a Black woman in a leadership role at one of the largest corporate employers in DC; she knew perfectly well that she could prove herself every single day of her professional life and still be labeled "a diversity hire." The CEO had impressed her in that initial meeting with his focused attention and his understanding that HR decision-making was both an art and a science. He also seemed to be interviewing *for her*, which she decided afterwards had been a performance, but a good one.

Since then, their mutually crazy schedules had prevented another one-on-one. Abony assumed that this particular Friday, in addition to the question from the Board that he needed to discuss with her, the CEO would want a briefing on her whole portfolio.

But that wasn't what he wanted. He opened the door to his office and ushered her in with a gallant flourish, joking about how long it had been since they'd seen each other, did Abony even remember what he looked like? And just as she stepped far enough in for him to close the door, he shoved her hard from behind to send her stumbling toward his enormous desk, shoved her again before she could catch herself, and then the weight and length of his body was over hers, and for all that she was a tall, strong woman, he was taller and stronger.

She'd come prepared to brief him on her *work*. As the rape was happening, she felt a thread of incredulity that he would do this to the head of HR at his own company. How could he not imagine that she would report him, see him prosecuted, make sure he went to jail?

When he was finished, he stepped back and zipped his pants and Abony flung herself up and around—then found that she couldn't move any further. She wasn't paralyzed by fear or indecision or shock. On the contrary, she would have physically attacked him in that moment if she could have. But she was frozen facing him, drawn up to her full height and with her dress falling back down over her thighs at least, but otherwise unable to move. Had he somehow given her an actual paralytic drug, injected her and she hadn't felt it?

He assessed her from head to foot, his eyes lingering, then sweeping back up again. And he smiled.

I love your shoes, Abony, he said. *They're absolutely erotic on you. You'll want to buy them every time you think of sharing this moment, more and more beautiful, red-soled shoes. You'll find you can never have enough of them.*

Then he walked away from her into his private bathroom, and with the snick of the door lock Abony could move again. She got the hell out of his office, into the elevator, down the hall into her own office, and safely behind the locked door. She cleaned herself up, shaking, and then called 911. It wasn't until the operator answered and Abony broke out in a full-body sweat and had to hang up that she began to understand why the CEO hadn't been worried about her reporting the rape.

"Had to hang up—but why?" Jo demanded. "Because you were *sweating*? It sounds like a panic attack, which I get, but you could have pushed through it—"

"Did *you*?" Abony asked.

"Did I what?"

"Did you push through whatever it was he did to you?"

Jo pushed her chair back; the metal screamed against the patio.

"Why do you think he did anything to me?" *Careful, careful*: apparently that was close enough to a denial that nothing threatened to emerge.

"Why?" Abony retorted, her level voice a mockery of Jo's raw one. "Let's start with the fact that a coworker tells you she's been raped by your mutual boss and you—well, you felt some kind of way, but I don't think it was surprised."

Abony looked as relaxed as ever in her seat; only her foot in its insanely expensive shoe twirling idly suggested any inner agitation.

Ranjani cut into the charged silence.

"Jo," she said, "that text you got, the one that looked like it was from IT? The person who sent it is a friend. She told me that she thought he'd hurt you too."

She faltered when Jo turned to look at her, but then kept going. "It happened to—I mean, he did something to me too, two months ago. We weren't sure he'd done anything to you, but we thought we'd better—"

"What? Test me?" Jo threw the questions at Ranjani because now in addition to feeling horribly exposed, she also knew that Abony must be furious with her. Panic attack indeed. *You could have pushed through it.* Shit.

"No!" Ranjani protested. "We just thought that if it had happened to you, you'd want to know you weren't alone."

"But what made you even think of me? Because I took leave last week?" Jo glared back at Abony, because screw it, she was pissed too. "Is HR monitoring every woman at the company? Too bad you couldn't figure out how to warn people instead of just coming at them afterwards."

"Don't be an idiot," Abony said. "He texts, right, day-of, urgent meeting with just the two of you? How the hell is anyone going to monitor for those appointments?"

"I have no idea, but clearly you should have tried," Jo snarled. "I thought protecting employees was your *job.*"

"Jo—" Ranjani tried, just as Abony said, "You're right."

There was a moment of silence at the table.

"You're right," Abony said again. "I don't know how I might have tracked who he was attacking, or stalking, or whatever, but I should have thought of a way. The thing is…" She hesitated for the first time since she'd started talking. "Until I met Rani and realized that he'd assaulted her too, I wasn't thinking about other women he might have raped. I was too busy dealing with my own shit, with the aftermath of what he'd done to me, the part that doesn't make any sense. And I can beat myself up about that for the rest of my damn life but it's not going to change anything now."

She was looking not at Ranjani but at Jo, and Jo knew with certainty that this was because Ranjani didn't blame Abony for not protecting her but Abony blamed herself and was inviting Jo to pile on.

Christ, Abony was as bad as she was.

Jo picked up her chair enough to bring it back to the table without scraping this time.

"My girlfr—my friend—is a teacher and she loves to do this thing where when a kid is acting out in class, she offers them a 'reset,'" she said. "She has them go out into the hall with their books and their backpack, even their coat, and come back in like they're literally starting the school day over. It honestly sounded incredibly stupid to me when she first told me about it but apparently it works like magic for a lot of the kids." She shrugged. "So I still have a lot of questions, including how you knew to talk to me, but we can come back to that." She turned fully towards Abony. "Like you said, I was being an idiot. And I'm not interested in helping you beat yourself up. But could we do a reset on the story you were telling me? You were explaining what happened when you tried to call the cops."

"A reset," Abony repeated. Then she grinned. "When we were little and came downstairs in a mood, my mom used to send us up to our rooms and make us get all the way back into bed, lie there remembering what side we'd gotten out on, then get out the other side."

Jo unclenched her hands on the arms of her chair.

"You had to hang up," she said. "but I'm guessing you called back."

Abony nodded.

"The second time I forced myself to stay on the line even as the symptoms got worse. Flash sweat, chills, nausea, full body shakes so bad that I was sore the next day. Then I passed out. When I came to, I tried calling again. Same thing. Those are all symptoms of a panic attack. They're also symptoms of withdrawal."

Her voice remained even, but as she reached for her iced tea, there was an almost imperceptible tremor in her fingers. Jo watched it run up Abony's arm like a current when she closed her hand around the cup.

"He made you addicted to something," Jo said, "and you go into withdrawal whenever you try to report him... Jesus." She dropped her gaze to Abony's feet. "To the shoes?"

"To the shoes."

"Those things are—I mean—are you bankrupt? You said this was more than *four months ago*?"

"That first day," Abony said, "when I came to the second time, I was about to call again when a Neiman's ad for Louboutins popped up on my phone. I bought three pairs without even checking the sizes. Spent $2500 in two minutes. And over the next month, I tried every avenue I could think of to report the assault—my own HR channels, the police, the Board, investigative reporters with the *Post*, sexual assault survivor hotlines. Every time I got to the moment of trying to write or say what had happened, the withdrawal symptoms hit and I had to stop and buy shoes."

Abony's iced tea was gone. She took the lid off, popped an ice cube in her mouth, and crunched on it.

"In that month," she said, "I spent more than $30,000 on Louboutins."

Jo heard Ranjani draw in a horrified breath. Apparently she hadn't heard this little detail. $30,000. Obviously, Abony made more than either Jo or Ranjani did, but still. That had to be several months of salary.

"I can see why you stopped trying," Jo said.

"I didn't stop!" Abony snapped. "I just forced myself to confront reality. I was distracted at work, and I couldn't afford to lose my job. If I did, I'd need to find another position making at least what I'm making now, and *fast*."

"I'd also be worried," Ranjani said, "that if you quit you could make things worse. I mean—*he* might make things worse."

"What would that even look like?" Jo asked, but then waved her hand. "Never mind, I can imagine it and it's mind-bogglingly expensive. What does 'confronting reality' mean, Abony?"

"It means finding ways to minimize how much I pay for the damn shoes. Now I buy on consignment, on eBay, at flash sale sites, and I put available pairs in my cart for the times when I try another way to report him." She slanted a glance at Ranjani. "Like a couple weeks ago. I put a pair on hold and just have to click 'buy.' As soon as I do, the symptoms stop."

"Still," Jo said, "you've got to be spending thousands of dollars a month."

"Yep." Abony cracked another ice cube. "I also vowed only to buy Louboutins that fit me, in styles I like." She pointed her red-lacquered toe, peeking out from white linen printed with cherry clusters, at Jo.

"You know what's funny? In interviews, the designer's always talking about how he designs his shoes for strong women, because walking around in stilettos—note the pun—

with that bright red almost as an afterthought makes the wearer powerful."

"Huh," Jo said. "I wonder what the people who write into that fairy-tale channel would think of that argument. As I recall, women's feet come up in a lot of those stories."

"How did you know that?"

Jo shrugged. "I took a class in college. But I'm with you on only buying shoes that fit. It's bad enough you have to buy them to begin with, you might as well be able to wear them." She tried a smile. "And you *look* powerful."

"I haven't felt powerful since March 23," Abony said, "but I'll keep wearing them. Because fuck him."

Fairy Tales Forever Discord Channel

*We are an inclusive community; we celebrate all voices and identities. Expressions of hate, bias, or general assholery (yes, we know it's not a word) will not be tolerated. For full channel rules and guidelines click **here**.*

Discussion Boards: Fairy Tale of the Day |
Question of the Day | **Fairy Tales for Our Time**

Fairy Tales for Our Time: "Belling the Cat"*

submitted by Jess (member since 2018)

*author's note: This is an update of an old story about some mice and a cat, which you can read here. In the original, the mice are the heroes. In my version, they're the villains. Also, men are mice. Just saying.

Once upon a time, a colony of mice grew dissatisfied with the cats in their midst, who didn't want to eat them or kill them, but who were better than they were at a lot of things and also sometimes wanted them to do things differently, which the mice didn't want to do. So they went to a wizard, who happened to be a very old White man, and asked for help.

"Well," the wizard said, "you could hobble the cats' feet so they can't move as quickly."

"We tried that," said the mice. "We did that for hundreds of years and then the cats started fighting back so we had to stop."

"Pity," the wizard said. "Have you tried forcing them into tight collars that cut off their circulation? Might make it hard for them to think."

"Tried that too," the mice said. "They're refusing to wear the collars."

The wizard suggested making sure the cats had to have litters of kittens regularly, whether they wanted to or not. The mice were interested in this idea, though they suspected that forcing the cats to have kittens and not letting them choose to have them might prompt a ferocious response. Nevertheless, they formed a committee to discuss the matter.

Meanwhile, they pressed the wizard for an easier, more immediate solution, "something that the cats might not even realize we've done."

The wizard thought and thought and then created some strange, beautiful, but uncomfortable ornaments for the cats to wear.

"Give them these," he said, "and tell them that all the best cats wear them."

"But how will these help us stay ahead of the cats?" the mice wanted to know.

"Because these make noise. You see?" The wizard demonstrated the brisk tap-tapping noise the ornaments made as the cats walked.

"These won't make you smarter than the cats, or faster, or better in any way," he explained, somewhat apologetically. "But at least you'll always hear them coming."

AUGUST 8: RANJANI

"Jo," Ranjani said, "do you know Maia English, in IT?"

She heard her voice rise and turn the statement into a question but couldn't help it. This would be so much easier to explain if Jo knew Maia.

But Jo clearly didn't recognize the name.

"Is she the one who sent me that text? Why? And how did *she* know?"

Abony stood up. "I need to use the restroom," she said. "Rani, keep talking. I've heard this part."

She strode away before either of them could protest, not that Ranjani would have done so. If *she'd* just told the whole horrible story of what the CEO had done to her, she'd have needed to lock herself in a bathroom stall and make sure the key was still white, then splash cold water on her face and let it run over her wrists as her mother had taught her to do whenever she got anxious as a child. Two weeks ago, before they went to the police station together, Ranjani would have sworn that Abony not only never revealed that kind of weakness, she didn't even feel it. But having seen Abony in withdrawal, Ranjani knew better now.

"Abony gave a lot more detail when she told the story this time," she said to Jo. "I knew the basics but not how bad the withdrawal symptoms were or…"

"Or how much money she's actually spending? Yeah, those numbers are terrifying. There's no way she can keep fighting without completely wrecking her finances."

That was exactly what Ranjani was thinking, and yet she wondered if they had the same attitude toward Abony's situation. Ranjani wanted to beg her to stop trying to report the CEO, to take care of herself instead. It sounded like Jo, on the other hand, admired Abony's the-hell-with-it determination.

Jo reached for her latte. "So tell me about Maia English from IT and the text messages. Is she the one who told you to talk to me? Because I got that text from her more than a week ago."

"Yes," Ranjani said, "and she wants to explain some stuff to us, but we'll have to meet at her house."

"Why?"

"I don't think she can leave. She started working from home at the end of January, really suddenly. Like, she went home on a Friday and she hasn't been back to the office since."

"Ah." Jo set her coffee cup down. "Her too?"

Ranjani nodded.

"So more than six months ago," Jo said thoughtfully. "Then two months later Abony was assaulted and two months after *that*, you were. If I didn't know better, I'd say there was a pattern."

Ranjani noticed that Jo didn't mention her own assault—she still hadn't even acknowledged that it had happened—or the fact that the timing of it made the pattern even more obvious. Ranjani pressed on, trying to explain as much as she could before Abony got back so that hopefully they could call Maia then. They'd been sitting at this table for nearly an hour and she was starting to worry about time. Her mother's

confusion and anxiety got much pronounced later in the day—
the doctor called it "sunsetting"—and Ranjani not being there
made things even worse.

She was letting Jo read their text thread when Abony slipped
back into her seat. Jo handed Ranjani back her phone.

"So Maia knows *what* and *why* but not *how*," Jo said. "And
she's talking about curses. Magic, is that what she's suggesting?
Like, witchcraft and sorcery? Is she into that sort of thing?"

"Not really," Ranjani said. "I mean, she's a Comic-Con nerd—
that's what it's called, right? She's obsessed with the Joker's
girlfriend from Batman."

Jo laughed. "Harley Quinn? So is she a lesbian?"

"No," Ranjani said, confused. "I've met her husband."

Abony cut in. "Listen, Jo," she said, "I want to hear what Maia
has to say. If she's discovered a pattern, then maybe we *can* prevent
other women from getting hurt."

Jo looked thoughtful. "I guess I want to hear what she has to
say too," she said, "including what exactly he did to her and why
she couldn't tell Ranjani even over text."

She turned to Ranjani.

"You haven't told me what happened to you either."

Ranjani's hand went instinctively to the chain around her
throat.

"Don't be a bitch, Jo," Abony said.

"Did *you* try to report him?"

"I tried once," Ranjani said. "Once was enough."

"But nothing bad happened when you told Abony?"

Ranjani's fingers twitched around her necklace.

"I didn't exactly tell Abony. She got it out of me. But when
she—" she shot a glance at Abony— "when we tried to report him
together, we couldn't."

"And when you talked to Maia over text, you told her too?"

"You saw the texts," Ranjani said. "She already knew."

"I don't think I'm saying this right," Jo said. "My point is, you *can tell* people what happened to you, right? The way Abony just told us? You can say the words out loud to anyone you like, so long as you're not talking to—what, a cop? A doctor? Any mandatory reporter?"

"Actually," Abony said drily, "I *am* a mandatory reporter. Ironic, isn't it? I could get fired for not reporting what he's done to us."

"You think *that's* ironic?" Jo sneered—or tried to. Her face betrayed her, crumpling with self-loathing and fear. Jo had beautiful bone structure and a deliberately austere attractiveness, but in that moment, her cheeks hollowed out and she reminded Ranjani of a comic-book character, all shadows and exaggerated lines conveying extreme emotion.

"You know something more ironic, Jo?" Abony asked, but gently, not pushing this time.

"Yes," Jo said. "The fact that even if I wanted to tell you what happened to me, I wouldn't. I *couldn't*. This is what happens when I try."

She drew in a shaky breath and then blurted out what Ranjani had braced herself to hear: *The CEO raped me twelve days ago, in his office—*

Except that she didn't. When Jo opened her mouth, instead of speaking she vomited out a black substance that heaved and hung in the air before settling on the table and starting to spread.

Ranjani flung herself backwards and pressed her hands to her mouth, so nauseated she was afraid she might throw up herself. Abony leapt off her chair, cursing. A woman at another table screamed. An employee passing with a laden tub of dirty dishes said, "Jesus, what the actual fuck?" dropped the tub with a crash and backed inside.

Jo wiped her mouth.

"Fuck," she said. "Sorry."

Her face crumpled into what Ranjani first thought was another spasm of vomiting but turned out to be tears instead, which Jo immediately hid behind her hands.

In the shocked, silent aftermath, Ranjani tried to avoid even glancing at the table. She turned instead towards Abony, but Abony *was* looking at the table, her eyes wide in horror. And Ranjani could hear the tabletop buzzing.

She made herself look. The glistening black stuff that had spilled from Jo's mouth was resolving itself into a seething mass of tiny black flies. They stumbled over and around each other, then seemed to all remember at once that they could fly. They swirled up in a cloud that pitched itself first at Abony, who stumbled into the chair behind her as she beat them off, then at Ranjani, who threw her arms up to protect her head. When she dared peek, she saw the cloud dispersing as it gained altitude and moved away, until the flies were just individual insects, specks in the air... and then they were gone.

The woman who'd screamed had been sitting alone. She bolted from the patio, her tote bag banging against her hip as she ran. Those at other tables who'd heard the commotion but hadn't seen anything looked at their group for a minute and then, with nearly the same synchronicity as the flies had displayed, went back their drinks, their conversations, their laptops.

Abony took a step back towards her chair, though she didn't sit down.

"Jo—"

"Shut up!" Jo said from behind her hands. Then she lifted her wet face and glared at Abony. "I tried to tell you! Why is that you and Rani can get the words out but I can't? What the hell does that *mean*?"

Abony shook her head and said nothing. Over her shoulder, Ranjani saw the employee who'd dropped his tray returning, accompanied by a man who she guessed was the manager.

"Everything alright here, ladies?" he asked.

Jo tensed like a runner in the starting blocks. Ranjani put her hand lightly against Jo's back.

"A bug flew into our friend's mouth," she said. "She's fine, but could we get a glass of water, please?"

"Of course," the manager said, "but I thought…" He scanned their table, the ground around it, then turned back to the server.

"Sir, I swear, there was this whole—and she—" He gestured at the table and then at Jo, who was looking at a fixed point straight ahead of her.

Abony stepped directly into the manager's line of sight. In her heels she was taller than he was.

"She nearly swallowed a bug," she said crisply, "and she's allergic to bees, so we were all understandably extremely upset. She coughed it out and it was just a fly, but…" she turned to address the young server, whose forehead was crinkling as he tried to make this recital of events match his own memory of what he'd seen, "it was pretty scary for a minute there."

"We appreciate you coming out to check on us," Ranjani said. "A glass of cold water really would be helpful."

"Of course."

"And no ice, please."

"Absolutely. And we'll get this whole area picked up shortly." The manager motioned for the server to pick up the trash he'd dropped, then hurried inside and brought Jo back a glass of water himself.

"I'm surprised you don't have measures in place to keep bugs off the patio area," Abony said as she sat down again. "This incident was just a nuisance, but it would have been terrible if our friend had been stung."

The manager assured them all that he would personally look into that sort of thing, though of course it was difficult to keep insects away from open-air spaces and they didn't want to spray because they served food here... finally he trailed off and left them.

Jo picked up the glass of water and gulped half of it.

"You two just gaslit those poor men," she said without inflection.

"Yep," Abony said. "You want me to go in and apologize?"

"No," Jo said. Some color was coming back into her cheeks. She slanted a look at Ranjani.

"*No ice?*"

Ranjani bit back a sudden mad urge to giggle. "I just—it just came out."

"Good thing, too," Jo said. "After I've spit out a swarm of bugs, the last thing I want is ice."

Once they all started laughing, they couldn't stop. Ranjani gave in to her giggles, clutching her stomach. Jo kept trying to drink more water and spluttering before she could get it down. Abony would get herself under control, look at Jo, and double over again.

Ranjani couldn't remember the last time she'd laughed like this. It wasn't just laughing in general, it was *this* laughter, irresistible because you knew it was inappropriate, and intoxicating because you knew if you stopped laughing you might cry.

Finally, Abony wiped her eyes and sat up straight in her chair.

"So that's what happens whenever you try to talk about what he did to you?"

Jo drank the rest of her water. "Also when I try to curse out—" she paused to swallow and then continued carefully— "people who might hypothetically have done certain things I don't like."

"So you can't talk back to your television."

Jo half-smiled. "Exactly."

"And it happened even with us," Ranjani said. "Does it happen when you're alone?"

"Yeah."

Ranjani checked her phone—she had maybe fifteen more minutes before she'd need to call Amit and tell him she was going to be late—and saw the text thread with Maia still up on the screen.

"Wait," she said, "that's got to be true for Maia too. That must have been what she meant. I didn't understand it but here—" she scrolled to find the text and read it aloud. "*Just be aware that I think her curse is like mine, not yours—it's constant, not on a trigger.*"

"So let's go see her," Jo said. "Text her now, tell her we're willing to come hear what she has to say—when? This weekend?"

"Hell, I'd rather get it over with," Abony said. "I could do tomorrow night after work."

"Me too." Ranjani knew that if she told Amit she had a late design meeting he'd take care of everything at home without question. She'd bring him his favorite takeout to make up for it, and deal with the sick plunge in her stomach at telling him the lie later.

"Tomorrow, then," Jo said. "It doesn't sound like Maia's got a busy social calendar."

Ranjani texted Maia and got a thumbs-up reply almost immediately.

"I've got to go," she told the other women. "I'm sorry, but I really do."

"Go," Abony said. "Let's meet in the parking garage tomorrow at five. That way you can drive."

"Can't we just take the Metro?" Jo asked.

"No," Ranjani and Abony said at the same time.

Right. Ranjani still had to tell Jo about the key and all the doors she couldn't pass through.

"I can't," she said miserably. "I just—not now. I *can't*."

Ranjani didn't wait for a reply or look back as she left the patio. Once in her car, she turned music on as loud as she could stand it for the whole ride home. She needed to *not* think about everything she'd learned this afternoon, or about what she had committed herself to for the next day. She needed to see her mother's face light up when she walked in the house, with a relief so pure it might have been joy. She needed to put her arms around Amit and feel his tighten around her, so that her head rested on his chest and his breath stirred her hair as he breathed her in.

Fairy Tales Forever Discord Channel

*We are an inclusive community; we celebrate all voices and identities. Expressions of hate, bias, or general assholery (yes, we know it's not a word) will not be tolerated. For full channel rules and guidelines click **here**.*

Discussion Boards: Fairy Tale of the Day | **Question of the Day** | Fairy Tales for Our Time

Question of the Day: What's going on with "Bluebeard"? Just read it for the first time and I'm so confused!
submitted by tiffwithane (member since 2017)

tiffwithane: Hey, FTF community, thanks for helping me with this one. I'm writing a paper on fairy-tale tropes, including rules in fairy tales and what happens when you break them. The "Bluebeard" story is making my head hurt. (If you haven't read it, @JennyK submitted it as a FTOTD here.) My question is: are we actually supposed to think the wife deserves what happens to her? Because I definitely do NOT but I feel like the story says she does.

Natalie: Oh you are not wrong! There are so many fairy tales where people get in trouble for doing the one thing they weren't supposed to do: go off the path in the forest, talk to strangers, stay out past curfew... and this reads just like those. You have to stop and really just go—wait, a guy whose wives have all disappeared and never been found tells someone not to go into a certain room and when they do it and find the dead bodies THEY deserve to get in trouble?? Umm, hello, serial killers get off on power! We shouldn't be taking orders from them!

TaqwaT: The sick thing about the story is to think about his whole signature as a killer, and yeah I know I watch way too much *Criminal Minds!* ☺, but play it out: he kills his first wife, panics and hides her body in the house but he got off on it and now he wants to kill again. So he gets another wife, tricks her into discovering the first wife's body, and then kills her "because he has to because she disobeyed." And then he just hits repeat on this pattern and gets away with it.

Jess: The magical key that gets covered in blood that then won't wash off is a nice touch I guess but you don't even need it for the story to basically be a serial killer horror story with some blame-the-victim shit added.

Angelofthehouse: Yeah, the bloody key is super-creepy, but what I hate is that the wife is sort of set up to be at fault because she married him for money, which women HAD TO DO back then just to survive, and also because she "disobeys" him by opening the door he told her not to open. There's a reading on this @tiffwithane about how scared the patriarchy was—and is!—about women not doing exactly what they're told and that's why so much bad shit happens to women in fairy tales when they break a rule.

JennyK: Absolutely! I want to point out that the whole thing about the husband's "blue beard" is almost certainly coded racist language suggesting that the character is non-white. A lot of the male villains in fairy tales are coded as non-white, either in the text or the illustrations, and that's clearly not okay. But talking about sexism not racism here, my thing with "Bluebeard" is that the limits on women are really right in your face because of the door. In the story it's a literal door hiding the dead wives, but think about the metaphor: unlocking a door means opening up new possibilities, new potential, new choices...

tiffwithane: This is amazing (not the icky stuff in "Bluebeard" but what you all are saying). Thanks for helping me think through this story. It really felt to me like she was a prisoner in the castle as soon as he left her alone there, even though she had this key. Because it doesn't seem like she has any way to leave and there's no one else there. It feels so creepy, and like OF COURSE you'd want to open the door you couldn't open, because you just felt so trapped.

Jess: And then the key getting permanently stained with blood is so obviously an indictment of her, like, "if you want to escape the confines set out for you, we're going to make sure you're marked forever."

Natalie: *shiver*

<click to see more comments>

AUGUST 9: ABONY

Abony was reviewing a new position description that the Sales Team wanted to create when her assistant knocked on her door.

"Sorry to interrupt, but the General Counsel's here."

Abony managed not to roll her eyes. She did *not* need this today. "Suzanne?"

"Yes. She says it's urgent but it'll only take a minute."

That was probably true. Suzanne talked fast, got right to the point, and was always laser-focused on getting what she needed or wanted out of a conversation. Today promised to be no different. She came into Abony's office already talking— "thanks for the time, Abony, this'll really only take a minute, I promise"—as she pulled out a chair, sat down, and touched her fingertip to her tablet screen.

"Hi, Suzanne," Abony said drily. "Nice to see you."

Suzanne spared only a glance from her scrolling screen.

"Bullshit," she said. "Nobody likes to see the GC's office, not even when they've asked to see us, and you don't even like me. Now, here's the deal."

Abony blinked. Well.

Suzanne launched into the reason for her pop-in—a Board member had stumbled onto a company employee's activist presence on social media and was deeply offended by it—while

Abony noted that the other woman was wearing a pantsuit that was both shapeless and insanely unseasonable. She must just melt whenever she went outside. She was also growing her hair out of the sharp, angled bob that she'd worn for years. Now it was clipped back at the nape of her neck and visibly gray at the roots. Abony recalled that when they'd first met, Suzanne had favored pencil skirts, silk blouses, and high-heeled boots. She was nearly as tall as Abony, full-figured, and she had always worn tailored, elegant clothes that suggested that she knew how to dress the part of "female high-powered corporate lawyer" and derived satisfaction from doing it flawlessly.

When had she stopped dressing like that? When had she let her chic haircut go?

"So anyway," Suzanne said, "the Board member called the CEO at home to complain and of course was assured that we'd look into the matter. What the member wants—and you're going to love this—is for us to force the employee to A. to take everything down, B. apologize to the Board for their stance, and C. accept a censure in their personnel file."

She ticked off the stipulations on her fingers.

"Please tell me you explained that we're not going to do any of those things," Abony said.

"Not yet," Suzanne said. "I'm prepared to, obviously, but I'd rather not get into a back-and-forth with this guy. What I need from you is an example of the kind of thing we *would* take action on in an employee's social media presence."

"Threats of imminent violence to oneself or others, to start with," Abony said. "It's in our policy."

"I know, but this guy is being really literal-minded. He keeps saying that if we've never done anything per our policy then how can he trust that we ever will. Do you have an example you can send me—we'll redact it, obviously—of a time when we did take action?"

"Probably," Abony said, "but it'll take some digging."

"I need it by end of day tomorrow," Suzanne said. She flipped the cover over her tablet.

Sure, no problem, Suzanne, Abony thought. *It's not like I have anything else to do between now and then.*

She also thought about her own enduring dislike of the GC, which wasn't anything virulent; Suzanne just made her bristle. And having registered just now the changes in the other woman's self-presentation, along with her brusque opening salvo, Abony knew that she couldn't let her feelings stop her from asking.

"I'll get you something," she said. "But before you go, Suzanne—are you okay?"

Suzanne froze halfway out of the chair, then sat back down.

"I'm fine," she said. "Busy. Why?"

Abony resisted the urge to fidget with her pen. "I don't know," she said. "I just thought I'd ask. It's part of my job."

"Got it," Suzanne said. She stood up. "Thanks for asking."

"What do you think of the CEO?" Abony blurted out.

Again Suzanne seemed to freeze for just a second and then deliberately move, this time towards the door.

"I think he's used to getting results," she said, "and getting what he wants. Good qualities in a CEO, don't you agree?"

"I haven't had the chance to work with him closely at all," Abony said. She paused to check—her heart rate was still steady. "I was just interested in your opinion because I assume that as General Counsel you've worked with him a good bit more."

"I have," Suzanne said, "of course I have. But we're certainly not out getting drinks and having laughs after work."

"That wasn't—" Abony began, but Suzanne was gone. She left the door open behind her and Abony watched her stride down the hallway to the elevators, head up, arms swinging.

Abony's assistant stuck her head in.

"So, what did Ms. Humorless want?"

"Don't call her that," Abony said absently.

She waved her assistant into the room and tasked her with finding an employee case file that would meet the GC's needs. Then she went back to her comps review, feeling slightly buoyed by the fact that she had asked Suzanne those questions: *Was she okay? What did she think of the CEO?* It didn't matter that the questions had been rebuffed. Knowing now that the CEO had assaulted four women in the company, Abony also knew she had to be actively on the lookout for others. She wasn't going to let any woman feel like she was alone and losing her mind, even if that woman was a humorless pain in the ass.

Abony took the elevator straight down to the garage at five and headed towards where Ranjani said she'd parked her car. Ranjani was standing by the trunk, reading something on her phone, but as the staccato sound of Abony's heels reached her, she snapped her head up. *Overly sensitive startle reflex,* Abony thought, *common in victims of personal violence.* There was nothing she could do about her shoes—hot-pink tie-dye pumps today—but she made sure to wave to Ranjani as she approached and saw the other woman's shoulders drop.

"Hey," Ranjani said, as Abony drew near, "Jo just texted to say she's trying to wrap up a call, but it's with a vendor in California so they're not quite getting that it's the end of the business day here."

"No problem," Abony said. "You let Maia know?"

"Yes. She's fine with it."

"What about you? You okay?" Abony asked. "Was everything okay at home last night?"

Ranjani nodded, but distractedly. "My mother's got a doctor's appointment tomorrow—just at the usual office, but they're moving the practice at the end of the summer."

"Shit."

"Yeah."

Abony resisted the urge to say something stupid, like that maybe by then they'd have found a way to get Ranjani through new doors.

"Anyway," Ranjani said, dropping her phone into her bag and making a visible effort to change the subject, "I was thinking that I should tell Jo when she gets here."

"I don't think she's going to demand that you do," Abony said.

"I know."

They both turned at the sound of more heels on the concrete and saw Jo headed towards them.

"Well," Abony said, "if you want to talk in the car, I'm happy to drive."

Ranjani frowned as she thought the offer through. "Oh—you could, couldn't you? So long as I'm in my own car—and I've used the passenger doors before too, because Amit sometimes drives."

Abony felt her stomach clench at the reminder of just how many obstacles Ranjani encountered every day. No wonder she jumped and started at every noise.

"It's up to you, Rani," she said. "If you want to drive, you should. And if you want to wait to tell Jo later—"

"No," Ranjani said. She thrust her car keys at Abony and opened the back door of the car. "This way no one else has to sit in the backseat, which is a mess."

She climbed in, shut the door behind her, and leaned over to, presumably, deal with the clutter in the back of her car.

Jo reached Abony's side. "Hi. What's up? We still going?"

"Yes," Abony said. "I'm going to drive, though. Ranjani wants to finish our conversation from yesterday."

Jo looked briefly puzzled, then her face cleared. "Jesus," she said. She marched around the car to open the front passenger door and lean in.

"Rani," she said, "you don't have to tell me. I mean—you can but you don't have to, and for sure not on some kind of timeline. It's not like we're not going to go to Maia's unless you tell me."

"Hi, Jo," Ranjani said. "Can you just get in? We're already late."

Jo got in, but turned around immediately, clearly intent on still engaging Ranjani.

Abony opened the driver's side door and assessed the seat, which was pulled so far forward to accommodate Ranjani's smaller frame that she'd be lucky to squeeze in. She leaned over to put her bag on the floor on Jo's side, pulled on the lever to move the seat back, then climbed in and adjusted the steering wheel and the mirrors.

"You're going to have to move everything back next time you drive, Rani," she said. "Sorry."

"It's okay," Ranjani said. "Amit's six foot one. When I get in after he drives, I feel like I'm practically sitting in the backseat."

"Rani," Jo cut in. "I'm serious."

"So am I," Ranjani said. "I dropped a hundred hints yesterday but I didn't tell you what he did to me and I *have* to tell you so you understand a lot of things, like why we're in my car, why it matters that I've been to Maia's house before today, and why I'm so scared all the time instead of being angry like you two are. Probably Maia too," she added. "Knowing Maia, she's pretty pissed off."

Jo opened her mouth—presumably to argue with some part of this—caught Abony's eye, and turned back to put her seatbelt on.

"The thing is," Ranjani said as Abony started the car, "I wish I *was* angry. I'm just mostly scared, like I said, and ashamed."

"Ashamed!" Jo burst out. "For being raped?"

"He didn't rape me," Ranjani said. "Just—just let me tell you, okay?"

At the end of May, the CEO had put a meeting on Ranjani's calendar on a Friday afternoon with the topic *Urgent: BOD Design Need*. She'd been so thrown by the invite that she hadn't questioned it. She'd debated bringing her hard-copy portfolio and decided that looked presumptuous; she would just give him the link to her online portfolio if he asked.

But the CEO didn't ask. He forced Rani to her knees with his hand wrapped around her braid, and while she did what he was making her do, he unraveled her braid so her thick hair tumbled loose around her face and he could grip hanks of it in both hands and yank on it. He did this whenever she gagged or tried to pull back, right up until he finished, when he slid his hands under her hair to clasp her scalp. With her eyes squeezed shut, Ranjani felt how easy it would be for him to turn her head sharply to the side and break her neck.

Afterwards, he pulled her to her feet, smiled at her, and said warmly, as if he was reassuring her: *You can't tell anyone about this. I'll send you something to explain why not—a present. It will look lovely on you.*

Ranjani took the elevator straight down to the garage, got in her car, and drove home. Her hair kept slipping over her bare arms and distracting her. She never wore it loose outside of the house. Later she had no recollection of the drive at all, only came to herself when she pulled into the driveway and felt a pang of mingled relief and despair that Amit's car wasn't there yet. She should go to the police station right now. And she would. She just needed a minute first. She huddled down in the seat, wishing she were in her bed where she could pull the covers up over her head to cry. She imagined telling Amit, pictured his soft face crumpling. His gangly scarecrow's frame—wide, bony shoulders and long arms over a narrow chest and no hips at all—would sag under the weight of it. He would hold her and she would know it was not her fault. But once she told him, something would be spoiled between them forever.

Their marriage five years ago, when they were both twenty-five, hadn't been *arranged*, exactly, except in the way that marriages in many American-based Hindu families evolved. Ranjani had heard a great deal about her mother's friend's son over the years—he worked with computers, did well at the University of Maryland, then landed a good job right away, a government job, and such a nice boy too, never in trouble—while Amit had heard the same sales pitch about her. When they'd see each other at family parties, they would spend a few minutes in awkward conversation, asking questions they already knew the answers to and trying to convey tacit agreement that their mothers' matchmaking was heavy-handed and unwelcome.

They'd forgotten to stop talking one night and Amit had made Ranjani laugh so hard she snorted lemonade out her nose and couldn't stop coughing. Mopping her eyes and blowing her nose, she'd smacked him on the arm and told him to stop looking at her.

"But you look beautiful, same as always," Amit said. He sounded puzzled, as if he really couldn't see her as anything *but* beautiful. Ranjani wondered how long he'd been pretending not to want to marry her and whether she'd been pretending too, each of them waiting for a sign from the other all this time.

They were both virgins and they learned together. Making love with Ranjani on top, her hair veiling them as if in a private tent, felt deliciously intimate. And when she slithered down Amit's body, letting her hair catch on his nipples and under his arms, until she lowered her mouth onto him, she thrilled to the way he surged up into her, groaning.

Of course neither of them had ever done any of the things they did together with anyone else. But her taking him into her mouth—that had been the erotic thrill that Ranjani savored when she heard her mother say proudly that *her* daughter had married exactly the man her family hoped for, like a good girl. Because she wasn't a good girl with Amit, and only the two of them would ever know.

So she couldn't tell him what had happened.

And she couldn't tell her mother either. A year ago, Ranjani wouldn't have told her mother for fear that Shreshthi would have blamed her for not fighting harder, no matter that it was the company CEO and he'd been gripping the roots of her hair. Shreshthi, who had been the top surgical resident in her class at Georgetown, never thought her daughter strong enough. Then she began to forget and misplace things and went from a woman like a steel blade to a reed, still slender and elegant, but brittle and even occasionally pliant. Ranjani couldn't possibly tell this new version of her mother what had happened, because Shreshthi herself was no longer strong enough to bear it.

Ranjani's miserably circling thoughts were interrupted by someone rapping on her car window. She jerked upright and braced herself to see Amit, or even her mother come out of the house to see why Ranjani was just sitting in the driveway. But it was a FedEx delivery man. Ranjani swiped at her cheeks and fumbled the button to roll the window down. The guy thrust his electronic signature pad at her, then traded it for a FedEx packet. As he drove off, Ranjani tore the envelope open and spilled the contents into her lap: a length of chain with a curious pendant on the end, a long white key that shone faintly as it caught the light, as though it had been carved from mother of pearl.

There was also a folded note, handwritten on heavy cream-colored paper in slashing, forward-leaning black letters. *The rules are simple*, it read. *As you love your mother, any familiar door will be fine. Any new door might not be. The key will tell you whether you've made a mistake or not, but unfortunately, it can only tell you too late. Best to just avoid new doors.*

"As you love your mother?" Jo repeated. "Who the fuck—?" She started gagging, hit the button to roll her window down, and heaved convulsively into the sudden rush of hot air.

"Dammit," she said weakly as she rolled the window back up. "Sorry."

"I didn't understand at all at first," Ranjani said. "Familiar doors, new doors—it didn't make any sense. And I definitely didn't know what the key meant."

"So you tried to report him?" Jo asked. "You said that yesterday, that you tried once before you and Abony went together."

"I stuffed the note and the key back in the envelope and drove to the police station," Ranjani said. "I thought I could use them to prove that he was threatening me after the fact."

"It was a good idea," Abony said. "Those things also proved that there *was* an assault to begin with. You don't warn someone not to talk about something that never happened."

"First rule of Fight Club," Jo murmured. "So what happened?"

"They asked me what kind of crime I needed to report, and before I could even try to answer, my phone rang. I knew it was my mother because it was her ringtone." Ranjani drew in a breath. "I always take her calls these days. Always. This time I needed not to. Except that when I went to silence the phone, I dropped the FedEx envelope and the key fell out. Oh, wait," she said. "Here."

Abony glanced in the rearview to see Ranjani lifting the chain from around her neck and threading it out from under her braid. She turned her eyes back to the road as Ranjani passed the pendant up to Jo, then at the next red light looked over. Jo held the key puddled in its chain in her palm and was examining it with the same mixture of incredulity and disgust that Abony imagined she otherwise reserved for the things she spit out when she tried to talk about her assault.

Abony had seen the key before but still found her eyes drawn to it. Amidst the myriad sources of harsh, glaring light provided by DC rush hour, the key looked both fragile and precious, like a gift rather than an instrument of punishment.

"Hold on," Jo said suddenly. "'Bluebeard.' The fairy tale Maia sent you. Let me guess—when the key fell out at the police station, it wasn't white anymore."

"It turned bright red at first," Ranjani said. "It could have just been paint. But then it started darkening—there isn't anything that color red but blood. And it turned almost black at the edges, like it was—oxidizing, that's the word, right?"

"Jesus," Jo murmured. "Or scabbing over." She closed her fingers around the key. "But whose blood—I mean, it's not literal blood like in the damn fairy tale, right?"

"No," Ranjani said, "and sort of. If the key turns red it means my mother has been hurt. That day at the police station, I ran back to my car as soon as I saw the key, even before I had any idea what it meant. And my mother called again. She'd cut her hand so badly she could see a tendon—"

"Christ," Jo breathed. "I'm surprised she didn't pass out."

"Oh, no chance of that—former surgeon, remember? But she needed eleven stitches in her palm." Ranjani half-laughed. "She predicted ten to twelve and she was very pleased that it was eleven. Our neighbor drove her to the emergency room and when I got there someone had called Social Services."

"What? Why?"

"Because they were worried that we'd left her alone at all, which I'm worried about too! We're *trying* to make sure she's safe all the time, and sometimes she's fine, so fine that she gets annoyed, but… but in this case, the hospital was concerned because my mother's narrative of what happened didn't make sense."

"What did happen?" Jo asked.

Ranjani leaned forward to pantomime the incident.

"She was cutting up chicken, like this—she's right-handed. And she was using a cutting board and a good knife, with her left hand just stabilizing the meat to cut it. And all of a sudden, the knife turned nearly a hundred and eighty degrees while she was holding it—she said she could feel it turn but she couldn't stop it—and it sliced across her left palm from underneath."

Abony had heard this part and seen Ranjani re-enact it. She didn't consider herself particularly squeamish but visualizing what had happened to Shreshthi made her feel cold all over, not just because of the visceral nature of the injury but because of the viciousness of it, and the terror that Shreshthi must have felt when her own hand—her surgeon's hand—turned against her.

"Was she okay?" Jo asked. "I mean—did she sever the tendon or…"

"No, it missed the tendon by millimeters. The doctor said she got lucky," Ranjani said.

"But you knew better," Abony put in. "Tell Jo about the key."

"Right. Even after I left the police station and went to the hospital, the key stayed red. It wasn't until we pulled into the garage of our own house that it turned back to white."

"Because you'd been going through new doors?" Jo hazarded. "Not just the police station but then the hospital too… but that means you can't go *anywhere*, Rani! I mean—have you tried since then? Didn't the note say that *some* new doors might be okay?"

"Doesn't matter." Ranjani held out her hand and Jo dumped the necklace into it. "I can't take the risk. And I wear this thing all the time now, even in the shower and when I sleep. I probably don't need to but…"

"But you can't take the chance," Abony said. "I'd wear it too, Rani. What did you tell Amit about where it came from? He must have wondered."

Ranjani refastened the chain around her neck.

"I told him it used to be my grandmother's, that my mother found it in her jewelry box and insisted I wear it for luck. It's the sort of thing she *would* do now, get really fixated on something like a necklace. And I told my mother it was a present from Amit."

She tucked the key under her dress.

"I don't call attention to it as much at home. I mean, I worry about it a lot when I'm out, but when I'm at home I *know* my mother's safe. Neither of them questioned my explanation." She tried and failed to laugh. "My mother thinks it's beautiful, actually. She was delighted that Amit had given it to me."

Jo was still sitting half-angled toward the back seat.

"Have you ever lied to them before?" she asked. "To either of them?"

Ranjani shook her head.

"And now you've had to—you *had to*, Rani. Worse, you're practically a prisoner in—not your home, exactly, but in whatever version of your regular routine you were in when he…" Jo broke off, swallowed hard, then started over on a different tack. "And your mom is sick."

"Yeah," Ranjani said softly. "I was just telling Abony—her doctor's office is moving their practice at the end of the summer."

"Shit."

That about covered it. Ranjani looked out the window and registered where they were.

"We're almost there," she said. "Abony, you should probably grab any spot you see."

"I'm on it," Abony said.

"What I still don't understand is what all these fairy tales that Maia's been pointing us to have to do with anything," Jo said. "I mean, there's a key in 'Bluebeard' that gets stained with blood, but otherwise the story has no relation to what's happened to you. The one she sent me is pretty on point—assuming of course that I'm a wicked stepsister. But Abony's feels more metaphorical in terms of the shoes…"

"Which I suppose I should be grateful for," Abony said, "given the things that happen to women's feet in various fairy tales. As I recall, most of them involve searing pain."

"That doesn't make what you're dealing with any less awful!" Ranjani cried.

Abony found a miraculous parking spot at the end of the block, which meant she could just pull in and didn't have to parallel park. She turned off the engine.

"You're right," she said. "We start being 'grateful for small favors' or relieved that he *only* did what he did to us—we can't go there."

"That includes you, Rani," Jo said, "saying you weren't—damn it—talking about certain physical acts as if one is more or less than another one—" She broke off, coughed, and opened her door to hack something into the gutter. "Abony, can you…?"

"He raped you, Rani," Abony said. "Pretty sure that's what Jo means. What he did to you was sexual assault, pure and simple, just like what he did to both of us."

Jo nodded. "Yes. That. What you said. And what I was getting at before—whatever it is Maia has to tell us, I hope she can explain the fairy tale teasers. Are they supposed to be literal, metaphorical, symbolic? Because I swear to God, if she's going to suggest bringing a handsome prince into the mix, I'm *out*."

The front door to Maia's Capitol Hill brownstone was at the bottom of a half-flight of stairs, which left all three of them crowded onto the small landing while Abony rang the bell. The man who answered looked like a college student they'd caught cramming for exams. He was slight and pale, wearing a too-big hoodie and jeans, his brown hair sticking up in a way that suggested he'd slept on it funny and then spent the day running his fingers through it.

"Hi, Simon," Ranjani said, sidling up beside Abony to make sure he saw her.

"Oh, hey, Rani." He stayed in the doorway, for all the world like he was not just barring them from entering but keeping them from even peeking inside. He held out his hand as Ranjani introduced him to the two other women, then seemed to realize that he was actually supposed to let them into the house.

"Right," he said. "Right, you're coming in. Sorry. Umm, it's… uh. Come on in."

It was, or had been, a beautiful house, decorated with the kind of flair that made the most of old bones and oddities, from the exposed brick along one wall to the slightly scuffed and water-stained parquet floors. The bold-patterned rug, blue and taupe linen furniture, and blond-wood tables and bookcases made for a stylish Scandinavian-inspired space—or would have if everything hadn't been rearranged and even upended to a bizarre mazelike effect. The seating was all pushed together, forming a lazy arc around the room. At the end nearest the front door, where they all stood, a bookcase lay on its side, flush to the arm of the sofa, and apparently serving as a side table; there was a fabric coaster on it along with the TV remote. The actual end tables and coffee table had been pushed out of the way into a corner of the room. Another bookcase lay on its side at the other end of the chain of seating surfaces, this one also pushed right up to the arm of a chair and extending out of sight into the next room.

Abony's initial impression was of kids building a fort, the ones she and her brother used to make, throwing cushions onto the floor and shrieking to each other that the carpet was lava and anyone who touched it was dead. But it also reminded her of the living room in her grandparents' house when her grandmother had come home from the hospital to die, all the furniture pushed aside to make room for the metal-barred bed, the beautiful rugs rolled up out of sight and the tools and detritus of illness piling up on ordinary surfaces: pill containers in the basket that had once held her grandmother's needlework, plastic sick buckets and bedpans stacked on the coffee table, piles of blankets and clean laundry that never got folded taking up the sofa.

Abony could tell that Ranjani and Jo were having the same shocked reaction. Simon, when he turned back from shutting and locking the door, took in their confusion and shook his head.

"Yeah, we moved some things around. Come on in. Maia's in the dining room."

He led the way around the wall of furniture, following the line from bookcase to sofa to chair to chair to bookcase again, into the dining room, where the bookcase ran right up against the dining-room table. It was too short to come out even, flat surface to flat surface, but someone had laid a series of slim hardback books on top of the bookcase to make a shallow staircase of sorts from the top of it to the tabletop. Abony's eyes followed this curious set-up irresistibly, from the bookcase up those little stairs to the table and across to the bank of computer equipment that took up most of the table, a veritable fortress of keyboards and monitors, wires and hard drives and speakers. Maia stood in the middle of it all with her arms folded, looking exactly the way Abony remembered her, from her unruly mass of caramel-colored hair to the expression of ill-concealed impatience on her face, as though she knew not only where any conversation was headed but where it would end up—and she wished they could just get on with it.

There was one difference, though. She was no more than four inches tall.

Fairy Tales Forever Discord Channel

*We are an inclusive community; we celebrate all voices and identities. Expressions of hate, bias, or general assholery (yes, we know it's not a word) will not be tolerated. For full channel rules and guidelines click **here**.*

Discussion Boards: Fairy Tale of the Day |
Question of the Day | Fairy Tales for Our Time

Question of the Day: Is Hans Christian Andersen's "Thumbelina" meant to be metaphorical?
submitted by TaqwaT (member since 2018)

Natalie: Wow, I never thought about it, which is embarrassing I guess, but I always loved "Thumbelina" when I was little. I had a picture book of it and everyone was just so cute, even the creatures that are supposed to be the villains, like the toads that steal Thumbelina away from her house, the beetle, the mole. But what do other people think?

steph: I haven't read this one in a long time but I remember being really scared by all the things that happened to her and really wanting her to find someplace safe. I mean, first she's kidnapped by some toads, right? She gets away from them when her lily pad floats away, but then she's kidnapped by a beetle who wants to marry her until the other beetles tell him she's ugly (because she's not a beetle). Then she nearly starves in the fields—I remember this illustration of her trying to pull a single grain of corn out of an ear—until a fieldmouse takes her in. I don't know if it's meant to be metaphorical but it's a wild ride.

Angelofthehouse: It's interesting that this is one everyone had a picture book version of; I did too. "Thumbelina" is often illustrated like "Wind in the Willows," with chubby pastel animals, but it's a story of serial kidnapping and, honestly, trafficking. And the female characters are just as bad as the male ones. First a mother toad steals Thumbelina for her son to marry, then a bunch of female beetles shame her for not conforming to their beauty standards, then the field mouse who takes her in basically tries to pimp her out to her next-door neighbor, who's a literal mole. I'm telling you—DARK.

badassvp: @Natalie, don't feel bad. I still have my copy of this book from when I was little and I've read it to my daughters. We do talk a lot about how Thumbelina is too passive and just sort of lets things happen to her. My girls like to say they'd have punched the toads and gotten away right from the start. ☺

DrHarleyQ: Has anyone even READ the original story? Go do it and then talk to me about whether it's metaphorical. First off, the actual title is "Little Tiny or Thumbelina" and throughout the story she's called Tiny. Everyone who encounters her also calls her "little"— little wife, little maiden, little creature—and they're attracted to her BECAUSE OF her smallness and helplessness. This whole story fetishizes the ideal woman as one who is literally so small that she would fit in the palm of a man's hand. It makes me sick. It should make all of us sick.

Angelofthehouse: Mike drop!

<click to see more comments>

AUGUST 9: MAIA

Ranjani's legs buckled. She sank to the floor, pulled her knees up, and pressed her face into her skirt. "No, no, no, no, no, no."

Abony let her bag fall and dropped into the nearest chair, never taking her eyes off Maia.

The other woman—Jo—stayed on her feet. "A curse," she said rather hoarsely. "A literal fairy-tale curse. I thought it was a figure of speech."

All in all, Maia thought they were taking it rather well.

"Nice to meet you, Jo," she said. "I'd shake your hand, but..." She held hers out to illustrate the sheer impossibility of it.

Jo didn't move or smile.

"'Thumbelina?'"

Maia shrugged. "*Obviously.* He seems to know the whole Western fairy-tale canon pretty well, but he has a definite preference for Andersen."

She had turned the dining-room table into her work surface and kept the lavalier microphone that amplified her voice nearby. It was far too heavy for her to wear around her neck, so she dragged it like a sled behind her as she went to the side of the table to look down.

"Rani?"

Rani's voice was muffled by her skirt but her distress was clear enough.

"I didn't understand why you wouldn't let me come over," she wailed, "and I was really hurt about it. But if I had come over, I would have shown up with—with soup or something and you were—you were..." she trailed off and shook her head against her knees.

Maia couldn't go right up to the edge or she'd get dizzy from the sight of the drop. She got to her knees and scooted as close as she dared.

"Rani," she said, "you couldn't possibly have known why I wouldn't let you come over. I don't blame you for being pissed; I wish I'd kept in better touch with you. But for the first couple weeks we were just trying to keep me alive."

"Keep you *alive*?" Jo asked. "Why? Was there something else going on besides—"

"Besides the fact that I'm the size of a *Star Wars* figure?" Maia asked, while Simon, who had been hovering in the doorway, stepped forward with a shaking finger aimed at Jo.

"Are you kidding right now? Seriously?" he shouted—Simon, who never shouted. "Look at her!"

Jo turned white and backed away.

"Do you know how dangerous, say, a sofa with separate cushions is when you're that small? Or a blast of air from a vent?"

"I'm an idiot," Jo said. "I'm sorry."

"I hope you keep that in mind when you start talking," Simon said. "Maia insisted that we let you in the house, but if you put her in danger..." He trailed off, realized he was still pointing at Jo and visibly backed down, shoving his hands in his pockets and dropping his gaze to the floor.

Jo pulled out the chair beside Abony.

"So you know what he did to me?" she asked.

Simon nodded.

"And you're worried that I'll try to say something and that whatever comes out instead could hurt Maia." She scrubbed her hands over her face. "That's fair. I'll be careful, I promise. I don't always know when I'm crossing the line in terms of what I can say and what comes out with legs and feelers and shit, but I'll be careful."

"It's good enough for me," Maia said, shooting her own warning glance at her husband. They'd *talked* about this, about how they had to let Jo into the house.

"I remember *Star Wars* figures," Abony said. It was the first time she'd spoken since she arrived. "My brother used to play with them. They were always getting lost in the sofa and under furniture, or you'd step on the damn things in your bare feet…"

She flung out her hands, palms up, a disconcertingly helpless gesture coming from her.

"I don't know what I expected. Like Jo said, when you talked about curses, I thought you meant something about how it felt, what he'd done to us, that it *felt* like being cursed. But that these things are literally curses—I don't *believe* in curses. I don't believe in magic or sorcery or whatever you're going to tell us he's using. And you're going to say he's—what—a wizard? I don't believe in wizards either. There's no such thing, for God's sake. They're not real."

Ranjani picked herself up off the floor and came around to sit at the table. Simon scooted the box of tissues toward her.

Ranjani was upright and Abony was talking. Progress!

But also, Abony had to believe that this shit was real or they weren't going to be able to fight it. And so what Maia herself said next was important. If she said the wrong thing, Abony might bolt. They all might.

Maia crossed an acre of table to stand in front of Abony.

"So you weren't a *Harry Potter* reader then."

Jo drew in a sharp breath. Ranjani froze with a tissue halfway to her face. Abony stared down at Maia, her face stony, and then slowly, reluctantly cracked a smile.

"Goddamnit," she said, "you're as bad as my father and my brother. Both of them know how to come right into the most serious, tense situation and just—bam—drop some idiotic line and suddenly everyone's laughing."

"It's a gift," Maia said.

Abony snorted. "Mm-hmm. And no, I never longed for some owl to come and take me to Hogwarts—"

"Actually," Jo said, "the owls just tell you that you got in. You have to take the train to Hogwarts."

Ranjani wiped her eyes and blew her nose. "I'm sorry," she said. "I know you guys are trying to get around how horrible this is by making jokes and stuff but I'm just—Maia, what exactly happened to you?"

"You mean after the CEO of our company sexually assaulted me?" Maia asked. "Isn't it obvious? Or you want the gory details?"

"I didn't mean it like that!" Ranjani protested.

"It's okay if you want them," Maia said. "I would if I were you. And it might make you all believe in magic because there's really no other explanation."

The thing he made her do—sucking him off—Maia had never liked doing under any circumstances. She actually thought for a moment, with his hand in her hair and her skirt bunched uncomfortably under her knees, that he was an idiot. Because there was no way she wasn't sinking her teeth into him. But then he muttered something and suddenly he had her wrists pinned over her head with one hand and her jaw locked open with his other. It was impossible: that he'd moved that fast, that his hand was that big, that strong, but it was happening, it happened, he was done.

He backed off to let her spit and cough, then wipe her mouth and clamber clumsily to her feet.

"You son of a bitch," she said. "There is no way you're getting away with this. No fucking way."

Maia, Maia, he said. *So little and yet so fierce, isn't that how you think of yourself? I wonder just how fierce you'll be by the time you get home.*

She made it to the elevator before the first wave of dizziness hit, to her office before she had any sense at all of what was happening. She was going to the police, but first she sat down at her desk to lock her computer down so the bastard couldn't get into it. She wouldn't put it past him to try to plant something that made it look like she had an axe to grind against the company, but he wouldn't get past the safeguards she had on her system. Fuck him. He might be a financial genius, but she knew IT.

Another dizzy spell as she reached for her cell phone and then it was too far away; the phone itself, right on her desktop, was out of reach. She had to stretch for it, when a moment ago it had been right below her hand. Now the desktop itself was too high, as if her chair had dropped, but the chair hadn't dropped. It had expanded somehow, was too big for her, her feet barely touching the floor when a moment ago they'd been comfortably planted.

Maia looked at her left hand and actually saw it shrink, felt the twitching, tightening sensation as it happened. Then there it was again, still her hand but smaller, enough so that her wedding ring was in danger of slipping off. She closed her fingers around the ring and slid off the chair. She pushed outward with her whole being, pressed against the sense of herself contracting, tried to prevent it from happening with the sheer force of her considerable will. No. Just—no. Then she bolted from the office, both hands under the straps of her backpack to help bear the sudden weight of it. What the hell had she put in the thing this morning, anyway, bricks?

She shouldn't have driven. By the time she got home she could barely see over the steering wheel and her feet were slipping so much in her boots that she'd kicked them off to press the pedals in her too-big socks. She threw herself against the car door, leaving her backpack and boots behind as she climbed down, and didn't even bother trying to close the door behind her. Her skirt was falling off, but that hardly mattered because her blouse was as long as a dress, the sleeves trailing over her hands so that she had to push them back to get the key into the front door. She was forced to stand on tiptoe to do it, fumbling blindly over her head to insert the key, and she only managed to open the door by hanging from the knob— feet off the ground by now—and letting her weight turn it. And still she kept shrinking, growing smaller and smaller as she shrieked for Simon, who worked from home. Even as he came tearing into the foyer to stare at her in horror, she kept shrinking and screaming "No! Stop it! Stop it!" until she was lost under her own clothes and couldn't find her way out. When Simon finally got to her she fit in his cupped hands, naked and exhausted. She tried to tell Simon what had happened, but he talked over her in his now booming voice, told her he had her, he wasn't going to drop her, she was okay now.

And Maia realized that he couldn't hear her. Her voice wasn't loud enough, not unless he held her right up to his ear. From farther away she was just squeaking unintelligibly, like a mouse or a baby bird.

The lavalier mike crackled as Maia finished talking, an ironic touch she might have appreciated if she hadn't felt abruptly exhausted and exposed, as though the tabletop was a stage with no wings she could retreat into. She turned in a circle to escape her audience and saw that Simon had taken a seat at the far end. When he saw her looking at him, he laid his cupped hands on the surface in invitation.

Maia shook her head, but she badly wanted to run down there, clamber onto his palm, and hide. Having these women here was harder than she'd imagined it would be. They were all staring at her, their faces so enormous and mobile, shiny lips moving over shiny teeth, big liquid eyes staring down at her through thickets of black lashes, each one as long as her hand. She hadn't seen anyone except Simon in six months and she'd grown used to him as her very own giant, to the overwhelming animal smell of him and to the many textures she'd never noticed before on his body, from fingernails to callouses to the hairs on his jawline, which made her bleed if she pressed on them too hard.

Now she had to get used to new giants if she wanted them to help her, which she did. She turned back to face them, though she did allow herself to sit down cross-legged, feigning relaxation and hoping she was too small for them to notice her legs trembling.

Jo had clearly been waiting for Maia's attention to return.

"I really would have preferred an owl," she said, "or a magical wardrobe that opened up near a lamppost."

Abony and Ranjani both looked blank.

Maia laughed despite herself. "And thus we recall that most of our fantasy lit is *extremely* White."

"Fair," Jo said. "But what I mean is that when characters in books are confronted with evidence that magic is real, it's usually something cool, not awful."

"They're kids' books," Maia said. "Reality is a lot darker, or at least more complicated, and the good guys don't always win."

"*That* I won't argue with," Abony said, "any more than I want to argue with you about whether magic is real or not. I believe you about what happened, Maia," she went on, "I mean—I'm looking at you and I *see* what happened to you, but I don't see how labeling it a curse and the CEO as a wizard gets us anywhere at all."

"It makes it worse," Ranjani said. She was tearing a tissue into shreds. "I mean, if what he did involved magic then there's no way we can stop him or undo anything. *We're* not magicians."

Maia blew out a breath. "There's the rub."

"So we're just trapped like this forever?" Ranjani cried.

"Maybe not." Maia turned to address Abony. "You all want to hear my whole spiel? I get that you don't entirely believe in how he did what he did to us, but everything else hangs together. Logically, I mean."

"The what and the why," Jo said.

"Yeah."

Abony sat back and folded her arms. "That's why we're here. Is there a PowerPoint?"

Maia grinned.

"Actually," she said, "there is a *killer* PowerPoint. Why don't you ladies all slide around to one side of the table so you can watch it. Oh, and wow, we suck at hosting. Simon, we didn't offer anybody snacks or drinks or anything!"

"I'm good," Ranjani said quickly.

Jo looked up. "I'd love a glass of water if you don't mind. Want me to get it?"

"I got it," Simon said. "The kitchen's kind of a mess these days."

He left while Maia pulled up her slides and the other women moved their chairs so they could see her screen. She thought briefly about pointing out the upside to her new size: she could be right in front of her PowerPoint and everyone could still see, but suspected that at least some of her audience had had enough dark humor for the evening. Jo was probably game—Maia liked her already—but Ranjani looked like one more shock to her system was going to push her into hysteria.

Simon came back in with a plate of cookies, a bag of pretzels, and water glasses, then made a second trip for the Brita filter and a bottle of Pinot Noir.

"I found this in the cabinet. I think it's a pretty good bottle," he said. "I figured I'd ask."

"Simon, you are my new best friend," Jo said, which made him start in alarm.

Abony uncrossed her arms. "What the hell," she said. "Pour me one too."

Simon tilted the bottle at Maia, who shook her head.

"Okay," she said when everyone else had a drink, or two in Jo's case—she gulped a glass of water without pause, refilled it, then sipped at her wine at a more measured pace. "The caveats here are that first, like Simon said, we didn't start trying to dig up dirt on this asshole for a couple of weeks. We had to figure out how to live day-to-day. Second, I did try to figure out the *how*—as in, I did look for ridiculous obvious shit that might have pointed to magic, like whether he played a lot of D&D as a kid or was in a LARPing group—"

"I'm sorry," Abony said, "a *what*?"

"Right, sorry. Live Action Role Play."

"People who dress up in costumes and whack each other with foam swords for fun," Jo said helpfully.

Abony stared at them both. "You're kidding." She shook her head and took a large-ish drink of her wine. "Go on."

"No on those things," Maia said, "or on credit card purchases at Wiccan stores or online sites that might have suggested an interest in magic."

"You hacked his credit cards?" Ranjani squeaked. "What if he noticed?"

Maia exchanged a small smile with Simon. "We were careful, Rani. And also…"

"Also," Simon said, "we're really good."

"Anyway, my next thought was whether he'd done anything like this to another woman, and I don't mean the curse business, I mean just plain old sexual assault. He's only been CEO here a little while—only six months when he assaulted me—and so I checked out his last company."

So far her slides had been just text headers to guide her narrative: *Evidence of interest in magic? Past history of assaulting women?* Before she clicked to the next one, Maia paused with her hand over the button on the mouse. She had to lean on it with both hands to force a slide change and she wanted her audience ready for what was coming next.

"Turns out," she said, "there was something at his last company. Nothing was proven, but he left abruptly, and I think it's because of what happened to one of his employees."

She clicked to a slide featuring two side-by-side photos of a young Asian-American woman. One was a professional headshot, in which she was all glossy elegance with her hair pinned up in a twist and her smile just wide enough to look genuine. In the other, she was straddling a dirt bike, spattered in mud and grinning broadly.

"Whoa," Jo said. "Are those the same girl?"

"Emily Sato," Maia said. "She was twenty-eight."

"*Was?*" Abony asked.

Maia advanced the slide and let them absorb the contents themselves: newspaper clippings along with court docs that she'd hacked into, all telling the story of the tragic accidental death during cosmetic surgery of young marketing professional Emily Sato. Her grieving parents had filed two different suits: a malpractice suit against several plastic surgeons for irresponsibly performing procedures on their daughter and a civil suit against the CEO himself for "brainwashing" her into believing she needed them.

Both suits had been dismissed. The malpractice suit was determined to be groundless: Emily had lied to her doctors, gone across state lines, falsified psych signoffs, and generally done whatever she could to conceal how many procedures she'd had in a short span of time. And the suit against the CEO was dismissed because it was just unbelievable. As the judge put it, *If not for the Court's deep sympathy for the family in this matter, the obligation would be to dismiss this suit with prejudice and describe it as frivolous, which it clearly is on its face. Given the gravity of the family's situation, however, the*

Court expresses hope that they can be content with knowing that their tragedy is understood to be just that—a tragedy—but not in any way attributable to any action on the part of the respondent.

Ranjani sucked in an unsteady breath as she read. Abony cursed softly. Jo put her wine glass down on the table so hard that the glass made a flat, unmusical sound.

"I hope someone else gets it," she said. "Because I don't think I'm going to be able to talk about this one without, you know, freaking everyone out."

She drank her second glass of water nearly as fast as she'd downed the first and then sat rigid in her chair until Ranjani asked, "You're thinking he assaulted her and then did something to her so she'd constantly think she needed surgery?"

Maia waited. Jo nodded somewhat frantically but kept her mouth shut tight.

Abony slapped her hand on the table.

"'The Ugly Duckling'! That's a fairy tale, right?"

"Yep," Maia said. "It's another Hans Christian Andersen one, actually."

"Jesus." Abony looked nearly as sick as Jo did. "So he did whatever he does—cursed her, whatever—to believe she was so ugly that she couldn't stop getting cosmetic surgery?"

"That would be even more expensive than your shoes, Abony," Ranjani ventured.

"No shit," Abony said. "And unbelievably dangerous. I mean, Jesus, look what happened."

Jo tapped out a text that made Abony and Ranjani's phones ping, then held out her own phone so Maia could see the screen.

Do you think he meant to kill her? Or that he knew it was a possibility?

"There's no way to know," Abony said.

"Maybe not," Maia said. "But I think the fact that he jumped companies after the suit was filed—even after he was found not responsible and the Board stood by him—suggests that he didn't intend for Emily to die. I think he was careless with the curse he gave her, didn't think it through, and then wanted to get away from the fallout."

Ranjani was reading the PowerPoint again. "In the suit they filed against him, Emily's parents claimed he raped her," she said. "So she told them what happened and they tried to report it on her behalf."

"But it didn't matter," Maia said. "By the time they came forward their daughter was dead and it was just assumed they were grasping at straws."

"Jesus," Jo said. She used a slender finger to click back to the photos of Emily Sato. "That poor family. That poor girl."

"But do we know what would have happened if they'd tried sooner?" Abony asked. "Simon, did you try reporting what he did to Maia?"

"I wanted to," he said, "but—"

"But I talked you out of it," Maia interrupted. She swung around to address the other women.

"What could he say? That the CEO had assaulted me, I wanted to press charges, and by the way I was now pocket-sized? And then what? Was he going to carry me to the police station in a Tupperware container with airholes poked in the lid?"

"I think it was probably good you didn't try," Ranjani said before anyone could counter that. "Emily's parents did try to report him when she was alive. See?"

She had advanced the slides again and now drew her finger across the screen from one document to the next.

124 | ANN CLAYCOMB

"Emily's mom confronted her after her fifth surgery because she was so freaked out and worried. That's when she says Emily told her she'd been assaulted and when she—the mom, that is—tried to report the assault to the police."

Simon came around the table to see the dots Ranjani was connecting.

"And then Emily went and got a procedure *the next day*," he said, "one that should have been minor. But because she'd had so many surgeries, she got a blood clot and died. Shit."

He looked down at Maia, alarm and relief warring in his expression.

"Looks like it's a good thing you convinced me not to try." He sucked in a shaky breath. "It might have made things worse."

"It would have," Maia said firmly. She reached for her mouse again.

In the reflection of the screen, she caught Jo flick a measuring glance at Simon. Maia knew what she saw: a slacker who lived his life indoors and online, who'd been powerless to protect his wife from the worst possible violation and its aftermath, who'd let her convince him that he couldn't report her assault for her because it wouldn't work anyway, and who was now feeling justified in his own cowardice.

When he'd leaned forward to read the screen, Simon had set one hand down on the table in what had become an instinctive placement, bracketing Maia between his thumb and index finger. If she wanted to, she could sit on the back of his hand, to get a little height and relief from sitting on the tabletop. She could also sit comfortably in the notch between his fingers, which made a backrest. She did that now, sliding the mouse with her and tucking herself against him. There was no way to convey to

Jo how Simon had grown to fill the space Maia had literally left empty in their marriage. But she could make sure these women didn't discount or dismiss him.

"Okay," she said, trying to pick up her thread, "let's say that the CEO himself is freaked out by Emily Sato dying, not because he cares about her but because her death prompted all these lawsuits and media coverage. He jumps to our company, which is where we went looking next. With Emily in mind, plus what he'd done to me, we figured we might as well look for other things that screamed 'curse.' That's how we found Rani."

"Me? How?"

Maia wished they could skip this next part.

"I hacked his emails," she said.

"The CEO's emails?" Abony said. "How did that lead you to Rani? He didn't say or do anything over email."

"True," Maia said, then quietly—"You want me to explain it, Rani?"

"It's okay,' Ranjani said. "I emailed him. After that night in the ER, after I realized what he'd done to my mother."

"You emailed him," Jo repeated. "To say what?"

"To ask him to undo it! Or change it even a little, just so we could go to the doctor's offices we needed to go to…"

"To beg," Abony said flatly.

Ranjani was silent. She put her hand to her throat in a gesture that Maia at first thought might signal that she felt choked by the other women's scorn. Then Maia saw the glint of the gold chain in Ranjani's fingers and realized what must be at the end of it. She got up from her niche in the curve of Simon's hand. She felt like making a noise in her throat as she crossed the table, as if she were approaching a frightened animal, which was ridiculous given the difference in their sizes.

"I knew we'd find someone else," she said when she stood directly below Ranjani. "The way he acted—it was so clearly about power. Why would he stop with just me? Who's to say that at our company he'd *started* with me—which by the way I don't think he did? But when we figured out he'd done it to *you*…"

She put out her hand—slowly, carefully—but then dropped it because what was she doing? Offering comfort? How? Ranjani was looking down at her with enormous, frightened eyes, but her cheeks were enormous too, and her teeth, and her dimpled brown hands. And Maia hadn't touched another human being other than Simon in six months.

"She wanted to kill him," Simon said into the silence. "Like, actually kill him. She made plans. I think she was angrier when she found out about you than after what he did to her."

He risked a glance at Ranjani's face, then flushed and turned away from what he saw there.

"You wanted to kill him, Maia," Ranjani whispered. "You wanted to kill him and I—I begged. You would never have done that, not in a million years. None of you would."

"Maybe, maybe not," Maia said. "I showed your emails to Simon, and you know what he said? *I know you'd never beg him for yourself, but isn't there anyone you* would *beg for?*"

Simon straightened up and ran his hands through his hair, making it stick up even further.

Jo and Abony looked at him, but appraisingly this time.

"He's right," Jo said, then directly to Simon, "you're right. If it had been Eileen—my girlfriend—ex-girlfriend now, but still. If it had been her…"

"We've all got people we would beg for," Abony said. "I can't say how I would have reacted if he'd targeted someone I love."

She jerked her chin at the PowerPoint, currently showing just a transition slide titled *Finding the Pattern*.

"So you found Ranjani's emails. Had he replied to any of them?"

Ranjani shook her head.

"Right," Abony said. "I figured he'd be too smart to do that. Then what?"

"I figured out where her curse came from. When you look up fairy tales with keys as prominent elements, 'Bluebeard' comes right to the top."

"But," Ranjani said, "when you texted me you said that I wasn't the one who unlocked the pattern, nor was Abony. Jo was. So even after you found my emails you weren't sure?"

Simon grabbed the rolling stool from his own workstation, dropped onto it, and scooted to sit across the table from the women.

"The thing about patterns is that you need a minimum number of data points to identify one," he said. "You were the third point on one pattern. What he'd done to you told us that he was definitely putting curses on the women he assaulted, curses he pulled from fairy tales."

"And the fact that he used 'Bluebeard' meant he wasn't limiting himself to Andersen stories," Maia said. "But we didn't know anything beyond that, anything *useful*."

She tipped her head back to look up at Ranjani.

"Rani, as soon as I knew he'd hurt you, I wanted to reach out to see if you were okay."

Ranjani's gaze was steady. "Why didn't you?"

"Because," Maia said, "like I said, I didn't have anything to offer you. We didn't understand anything yet, couldn't *do* anything."

"I couldn't have done anything for you either," Ranjani began, "and I'd still—"

But Maia cut her off.

"You don't get it! We—damn it. Once we realized he'd assaulted you, Rani—I know I said we expected it, but still, I'd convinced myself that finding a second woman at the company would be enough for us to not just track him but actually get ahead of him. But it wasn't! It was just puzzle pieces still."

"Which left you still steps behind him," Abony interjected, "looking for assaults that had already happened instead of being able to prevent new ones."

Maia twitched a shoulder in acknowledgement.

Abony laid one long-fingered hand on the table near where Maia stood.

"If it makes any difference, I know how that feels. Like you've failed before you've even begun."

"You know what else feels like failing?" Maia burst out. "Being fucking four inches tall. Without a microphone, I can't speak loudly enough for anyone to hear me. Without Simon building a whole crazy maze so I can get from one place to another, I'm trapped right here on this table. I can't get my own food or get water to wash myself with or… or even go to the bathroom by myself. I'm just too *small*!"

Maia stared at her reflection in the computer monitor to avoid the people looming behind her. She was too small, and they were too big. She heard her own ragged breath emerge as amplified static from the mike.

Apparently, they all needed a break. Ranjani murmured something about calling home to check in. Jo asked Simon if she could use their bathroom. Abony announced that she needed to stretch her legs. The front door opened and shut, then a moment later Ranjani's voice drifted in from the living room.

Maia sat down and rested her chin on her knees. She'd found that if she deliberately narrowed her field of vision to only her own body and the very small space around her—in this case a wooden surface that looked like a floor—she could briefly escape the constant oppressive awareness of her size. She did it now and got a few minutes of relief before Simon broke the illusion by crouching in front of her. She didn't have to look at him, but she could tell he was there; his breath ruffled her hair and his shadow changed the light on the surface of the table.

"Hey," he said. "You're doing amazing."

"Oh yeah, I'm killing it here. Half my audience doesn't even believe my basic premise and all of them are pissed—or about to be—about my information-gathering methods."

"They'll get over it," Simon said. "Also, I thought you might be getting hangry. Here."

He used one finger to slide a scrap of paper towel toward her, on which rested a single mini chocolate chip, and then lifted his finger to stroke her hair. They both knew from experience that if he wasn't careful, he'd knock her over, but Simon had perfected what must have felt to him like a whisper-light caress.

Maia turned her head slightly so that Simon's finger brushed her cheek, making sure not to look at him. Simon's face filled with wonder whenever he touched her now, and Maia knew that she was infinitely precious to him. But he'd never looked at her like that before, when she was 5'4", 135 pounds, and often referred to, even by her closest friends, as *a lot*.

"Thank you," she said. "Chocolate makes everything better."

Simon withdrew his hand, got up, and made room for Jo to sit back down. She took a drink of her wine and took in Maia's chocolate fix.

"Don't take this the wrong way," she said, "but it's kind of a relief to know that someone else's curse has really fucked up their eating habits."

Maia spun around on her butt to face the other woman.

"I can see that," she said. "What do you miss the most?"

"Dishes," Jo said at once, "like—things made out of lots of ingredients and with lots of textures. I can't do a lot of textures now and I *definitely* can't combine things. I have to eat everything alone." She laughed, though her mouth twisted with it. "Which is exactly as sad an experience as it sounds like."

"Me too," Maia said. "I mean, there's just no way to make the food small enough for me to eat things mixed together. And I miss having control over my food."

She picked up the chocolate chip, which filled her palm. "I used to eat these things by the handful when I was working late. They were my favorite all-night coding snack, not because they tasted better than other chocolate, but because I could literally eat one tiny chip at a time, you know, spacing them out to motivate myself, or shove a whole handful in my mouth—whatever."

She put the chip down without taking a bite.

"I hadn't thought about it that way," Jo said. "But yeah, it would be nice to be in control again, even if that did just mean picking all the broccoli out of my Pad Thai."

"Goddamn broccoli," Maia said, and they grinned at each other.

Ranjani slipped back into her seat, and a moment later, Abony opened the door and strode back into the room to take her seat as well. "All of your neighbors are walking their dogs," she reported. "Like, *all* the neighbors, all the dogs."

"Yeah," Simon said. "It's a big dog neighborhood."

"Well," Abony said, "where were we?"

"Wait!" Ranjani said, then flushed. "Okay, maybe not 'wait,' because what I have to say is exactly where we were. I just want to say that I don't blame you, Maia, for not reaching out to me earlier than you did. You were dealing with something awful, something I can't even imagine. I think we just need to not blame each other for not being able to deal when we couldn't—or can't, because there might be another time now, going forward, when you all want to do something and I just can't. Or I don't want to, whatever way you want to put it. But it will be because I'm struggling with the specific curse he put on *me*, just like all of us are."

"Bravo, Rani," Abony said. "And I'll add that I think we're pretty clear here, Maia, that you dug into all of our business to find us and figure out what he did to us, so just tell us what you know, okay? I mean, I assume you figured out what he did to me by looking at my credit card bills?"

Maia could practically hear the sound of the conversation booting back up. She got to her feet and went back to her monitor.

"Yes," she said. "Credit cards, phone records—" she jerked her head at Jo— "camera footage from outside your apartment building where you're showing your neighbor a bug?"

They'd tried all kinds of searches and cross-references, pulling employee cell phone records and looking at 911 calls—especially hang-ups, which is how they'd flagged Abony. Then her financials had revealed the shoes as the trigger. They had a pattern emerging by then and were watching for someone else to be assaulted the very day he raped Jo.

"Just *watching*?" Jo asked. She looked from Maia to Simon and back again over the rim of her wine glass.

"No," Maia said. "No—God. We're just explaining it that way—"

"Just the facts, ma'am," Jo said. "I get it."

"But you don't!" Maia said. She cast an anguished glance at Simon, wishing either of them was up to the task of explaining how frantic they'd been that Friday when they'd picked up the trail—or thought they had—in time to stop him.

"Another woman from the company canceled all her afternoon meetings for that Friday and the following Monday," she said. "We had alerts set to go off when women at the company did things like that with their schedule. It made sense that this woman had gotten summoned to the CEO's office and had cleared her afternoon and the next Monday to work on the big project she assumed he was going to give her."

Jo put down her wine glass.

"But that wasn't it."

"No," Maia said miserably. "Her sister in Virginia had gone into labor."

Ranjani made a small sound, quickly choked off. Abony, arms folded, was watching Jo.

"Your alerts wouldn't have picked me up anyway," Jo said after a moment. "Not until after. I assume that's what happened?"

It was. When she put in for sick leave for the following week, Simon pulled the footage of the cameras around her apartment complex and caught her spitting things out several times on her way back from her run. Maia, meanwhile, hacked Jo's Dropbox and found the account she'd saved there of the rape itself.

"Did you read it?" Jo asked.

Maia nodded.

"Good," Jo said, "since obviously I can't tell you any of it."

"Jo—" Ranjani tried.

Jo waved her hand. "So I confirmed the pattern. Does that mean you finally got something out of all this? Like, something that explains—anything?"

Maia advanced the slide and let them all absorb the timeline.

"You've got to be fucking kidding. He's doing it to—" Jo clapped her hand over her mouth, darted to the kitchen, and turned the faucet on almost enough to drown out the sound of her retching.

"Simon," she called. "Is this switch here for the disposal?"

Simon half rose from his seat. "Yeah," he said. "You need help?"

The disposal ran briefly, then Jo reappeared, wiping her face with a paper towel.

"You okay?" Abony asked.

"Yup." Jo took a gulp of her wine. "The caterpillars taste like rotten strawberries."

"So I'm going to spell this out," Abony said, "what I see here and what I assume Jo saw. He's assaulting someone right before every Board of Directors meeting, and then shortly after each assault, the company stock price shoots up, or some other revenue indicator goes crazy—after he raped me it looks like a big real estate deal went through for way over asking—"

"Right in time for the Board to see," Maia finished. "Yep. That's the pattern. That's his why."

"And that means that we have, what, another six weeks before—" Jo broke off and tried again— "the next Board meeting, assuming one just happened. Or does their schedule change in the summer? I know some Boards take a summer meeting hiatus."

Abony shook her head. "Ours doesn't. They have a retreat out of town at the beginning of August—which means they meet at a member's estate on some private island near Annapolis and go sailing in between sessions—but they still meet on schedule. So we've got until late September before he'll presumably do this again."

"But I don't get it," Ranjani said. "I mean, I see the numbers but… do you mean that attacking us *gave* him power? I thought your whole point was that he *used* power—magic power—to do this to us."

"But that's it exactly, Rani!" Maia said. "Only what you're forgetting to account for is that he has some power to start with, power he can use to get him what he wants."

"And what he wants," Simon said, "is so straightforward it's almost boring. He wants to be rich and powerful and have his name in some bullshit list of 'America's Top CEOs'."

"Right," Maia said. "Let's say you believe that we *are* talking about magic, okay? He's a wizard and he wants to send company stock or valuation skyrocketing. But that's got to be really hard to do, right? I mean, if we assume that what he needs to do is work a really big magic spell to force the financials to behave improbably, then he needs a lot of power to work that spell."

"But the idea is that he *gets* power every time he successfully assaults a woman and then curses her to keep her quiet?" Abony asked. "Enough power to work his big money spell?"

Maia nodded.

"Batteries," Jo blurted, then pressed her lips together. Nothing came out.

"Batteries," Abony repeated. "That's what we are to him." She crossed her arms over her chest as though she were cold. "Jo, honest to God, if you want to spit something out right now, I'm right there with you. Jesus Christ."

They all fell silent. Maia knelt and took a bite of chocolate. She reminded herself that this shared realization of just how deeply they'd all been violated, and why, was preferrable to the other women still not believing her. At least now they could work together to *do* something. It still felt like shit, though.

"What's the deal with those first six months?" Jo asked after a moment.

She pointed to the left-hand side of the slide.

"Yeah," Simon said as Maia got back to her feet, "this is a little weird."

They'd marked an initial disproportionate jump in company performance nearly three months into the CEO's tenure, before his first Board meeting, and another one two months later. But there was also a sharp dip in performance in the intervening month.

"That's the only time financials have faltered since he's been CEO," Abony said, pointing to the bottom of the "V" on the timeline. "I remember that. It was the end of October, which is when the Executive Team starts gearing up for the December Board meeting and that plummet just came out of nowhere. We were having meetings where we thought we'd be talking about the menu for the holiday party after the Board sessions and instead everyone was just waiting for the CEO to tell us what to do, how to pivot in our presentations. I mean, I thought I might have to draw up layoff projections."

"What did he tell you to do?" Maia asked.

"Nothing!" Abony said. "He never addressed it directly. Then right before Thanksgiving he wished us all a good holiday and told us to stop worrying."

She shuddered. "I think his exact words were, *I've been doing this a long time, folks. It'll turn around. Wait and see.* And then, bam, the Monday after, our stock soared and everything was rosy again."

She looked from Maia to Simon. "You haven't found any women he assaulted connected to these dates?"

"No," Maia said. "There's no woman at the company whose behavior fits the pattern of being assaulted and then cursed during that whole initial six-month period, and we also can't figure out what caused the dip."

"Maybe that's what happens when someone he curses escapes?" Ranjani wondered.

"Or dies," Abony said grimly.

"We looked at both those possibilities," Maia said. "We looked for women who left the company at that time and for employees who died. No one."

"Damn," Abony said. "I mean, I'm glad you didn't find any more deaths but—feels like we've got the *why*, like you said, but we're nowhere near the *how*. All we've got are questions."

Finally.

"Maybe not," Maia said, and thought she might actually be able to smile now as they got into this part of the presentation. If the problem they were trying to solve hadn't been one of literal life and death, she would have called this the fun part.

"So," she said, "you can track the company's financial success on all kinds of public-facing sites, it's not a secret. I mean, the whole point is for the Board to see how well we're doing under this asshole's leadership, blah blah blah. So it occurred to us to check for other companies that had the same weird, inexplicable success—jumps in stock prices at just the right moment or against market trends, higher profits than should be feasible for their business model, that sort of thing. We started with companies in DC and got a hit."

Abony sat up straight. "Wait, so there's another evil wizard in town?"

"Not necessarily," Simon said. "I mean—yes, we think there's another magic-user, but not necessarily an evil one."

"And if they're not," Maia said, "then maybe they can help us."

"Where there's an evil wizard there's always a good one to counter him—or her," Jo said, nodding sagely. "Dumbledore, Aslan, Gandalf... I mean, I think it's a rule in fantasy novels."

"Aslan's not a wizard," Maia said absently, "he's Jesus. But never mind. We didn't find a wizard but we might have found a witch."

She clicked to the next slide, which captured a screenshot of a website.

"I give you," she said, "The Gingerbread House."

The name was clearly a doubled joke, partly a nod to its proximity to the White House—the store windows were painted with trompe l'oeil white pillars and portico—and partly another reference entirely. The store logo featured a smiling little woman in a checked apron stirring a brimming round pot.

"Oh for God's sake, is that a cauldron?" Jo asked.

"Might be," Maia said. She *knew* she was right about this. "But you see the shape of the thing, right, the stirring stick and the bowl of the pot? Turn it upside down and you also see what The Gingerbread House is apparently known for."

"Candy apples," Ranjani said, leaning in to run a finger down the screen. "A dozen flavors of candy apples, plus award-winning gingerbread tiles. What on earth is a gingerbread tile?"

"Some kind of cookie, I think," Maia said. "Now look at this."

She showed them the store's financials. The rent for the space, right in the heart of the business district, was astronomical and should have been utterly out of reach for an independent business. Moreover, the street was a retail dead zone, but the profit-per-square-foot number that The Gingerbread House owner reported to the IRS made Abony's eyebrows fly up.

"Damn."

"But, Maia," Ranjani ventured, "witches in fairy tales are *bad*."

"She runs a fancy candy store," Maia said, "not an evil empire. If she's an evil magic-user, she's not a very ambitious one. She hasn't franchised the place, doesn't have a mail-order business—and, I don't know, the fact that she calls the place The Gingerbread House makes me think she's got a sense of humor."

"The CEO has a sense of humor," Abony said. "I just don't much care for it."

"I agree with Abony," Ranjani said. "I'm not sure we want any more magic on top of what we're already dealing with. Maybe she's good, maybe she's not—how could we even find out?"

Abony looked thoughtful. "One of us could go check out the store."

"No!" Ranjani cried. "Isn't it also a thing in fairy tales that witches and wizards enchant people with food? What if she makes money by getting people addicted to her candy?"

"That's a good point," Abony said. "But we've got to keep the stakes in mind here. Ideally, we want to find a way to get these damn curses lifted—broken—what's the terminology there?"

"I think either works," Jo said. "And I agree that it's worth taking some risk to see if this woman would be willing to help. It's got to be better than doing nothing."

Maia felt a zing of triumph and disbelief. They'd actually gotten here—and with the help of a PowerPoint no less. She shot a glance at Simon, who winked at her.

"*Anything* is better than doing nothing," she said. "And don't forget that in addition to getting our own curses taken off, we've also got less than two months before he assaults another one of our colleagues."

"None of us are likely to forget that," Abony said. "But to Rani's point, whoever goes—and I'm willing to do it—would have to be careful not to eat anything at the store, not until we've got a better sense of this woman anyway."

"If you're willing to go, Abony, I think you're our best bet," Jo said. "Maia can't, obviously, and I'm probably also not a great bet, just because if she does turn out to be a baddie and she pisses me off in front of other people…" she tried for a casual shrug, "I mean, you saw what happened at the coffee shop."

"And I can't because I've never been there," Ranjani said. "I'm sorry, Abony. That's really not fair to you."

"I'll be fine," Abony said. "I've got a new pair of shoes to break in and no place to wear them. I'll pay our potential witch a visit tomorrow after work."

Maia let out a breath she hadn't realized she was holding. "Thank you."

"And we'll convene again here after you've checked the place out, right?" Jo confirmed, looking around at all of them. "Only, Abony, if she invites you to look in her oven, don't do it."

"And if she offers you an apple, don't take it," Simon said.

Abony rolled her eyes.

"You guys," said Ranjani darkly, "are *not* making me feel any better about this."

Fairy Tales Forever Discord Channel

*We are an inclusive community; we celebrate all voices and identities. Expressions of hate, bias, or general assholery (yes, we know it's not a word) will not be tolerated. For full channel rules and guidelines click **here**.*

Discussion Boards: Fairy Tale of the Day | Question of the Day | **Fairy Tales for Our Time**

Fairy Tales for Our Time: "The Man Who Kissed Women"
submitted by imwiththedragon (member since 2016)

Once upon a time, and not so long ago, there was a man who bragged to other men that he often kissed women without their consent. "I better use some Tic Tacs just in case I start kissing her. You know I'm automatically attracted to beautiful... I just start kissing them. It's like a magnet. Just kiss. I don't even wait. And when you're a star they let you do it. You can do anything."

When he said this, the man was famous in a curious way, not so much for anything extraordinary he had done, though he had erected buildings of pink marble and gold in a number of cities—buildings that aspired to be palaces. Nevertheless, his fame came from the widespread belief in the world he lived in that because he was rich and owned faux palaces, he *ought* to be famous, he *deserved* to be. But he sought more than fame. He sought power. And he bragged that he could do more than just kiss women without their consent. "Grab them by the pussy," he said. "You can do anything."

Fortunately, the people of his country, when they heard these boasts, were disgusted by the man and rejected his bid for power, telling him to return to his pink marble and solid gold palaces and to give up his delusions that because he was rich and famous, he could do whatever he wanted.

Oh, who are we kidding? No, they didn't.

AUGUST 10: ABONY

The next morning, knowing she had to do her reconnaissance mission at The Gingerbread House after work, then go back to Maia's to report her findings, Abony made sure to get to the gym in the morning. She was doing her cool-down on the elliptical, eyes shut as she got her breath back, when someone said, "Abony," close enough that she startled, opening her eyes and grabbing the handrails.

In front of her, looking chagrined, stood the gorgeous man from the Starbucks, the one she'd walked out on. Jonathan? Jon.

"I'm sorry," he said, "I didn't mean to scare you. I saw you when I came in but you were pushing hard enough I didn't want to interrupt."

Abony was dripping sweat, her hair sticking to her cheeks and her scoop-neck top clinging to her sports bra. Aware of Jon's admiring eyes on her, she kept pedaling, but swiped her towel over her face and neck.

"You work hard," he said. "It looks good on you."

"It looks like I stink," Abony said, but when he just grinned at her she smiled back. "I've never seen you here before," she said. "You just hide out on the weight floor?"

"I usually come in after work," Jon said, "but I've got a late meeting today, so here I am. As for the weight floor…" He shook his head sadly. "I do my reps, sure, but have you seen some of the lifting going on? That's way out of my league."

"Out of your league," she asked, "or just not your style?"

There was that grin again, taking up his whole face like a little kid's grin did.

"Maybe," he said, "I'm too old for that kind of peacocking."

"I doubt it," Abony said, and was immediately torn between delight at his appreciative chuckle and an arrowing pang of alarm, like a sudden side stitch. Her elliptical program finished and started scrolling through the stats of her workout, but she didn't get off the machine. It would put her closer to Jon and open up new uncertainties, like how bad she smelled up close, how good she suspected he smelled, and whether he'd want to walk with her over to the locker room to continue their conversation. Balanced up on the pedals, she could still hold him off.

As if he knew her thought process—and maybe he did—Jon put a hand on the railing of the elliptical, near where hers rested but not touching.

"About that dinner invitation the other day," he began. "I didn't mean to—"

Abony cut him off. "You didn't say a thing wrong. I wanted to say yes, want to say yes. But I can't. I'm sorry."

He looked up at her a long moment. Abony tried to smooth the blankness onto her face that had carried her out of the coffee shop the last time they'd talked, but she could feel the corners of her mouth tremble. She broke his gaze and wiped her face again.

"Okay," Jon said. "You can't. That's okay. Well, you have a great day, Abony. Have a great weekend."

He patted the bar several times, looking as miserable as Abony felt, then walked away.

––––––––––

The Gingerbread House was several blocks from the nearest Metro station and the street parking all along the block was reserved by the valet service of a restaurant around the corner. It was hard to understand how this place made any money with those obstacles to walk-in traffic; Abony could see why Maia and Simon had flagged the financials as unusual. She called an Uber to get her there, and then was even more curious when the driver seemed not only to know the store but was unsurprised that Abony wanted to visit it at five on a Friday afternoon. He dropped her off across the street and warned her playfully not to buy too much—*but of course you will. No one ever comes out of there without a bag. Good weekend!*

The storefront itself was half-elegance, half-kitsch, with white scrollwork all around the enormous windows and a white awning extended out over the sidewalk, supported by poles festooned with white ribbons that seemed impervious to the weather. The design was obviously mimicking the front of the White House itself, but with enough whimsy in the size and fullness of the bows on the poles and the intricacy of the scrollwork to suggest an elaborately frosted cake version of the building rather than the real thing.

Abony crossed the street to join the line waiting to get into the shop. Inside, the place was packed with people, tourists from the looks of them, laden with Smithsonian gift shop bags and cameras and wearing sensible walking shoes.

"They'll be gone in a minute," the woman in front of Abony assured her. "That's why locals know to come just before closing. They're sold out of some things, of course, but at least you don't have to elbow your way to the register."

"I've never been here before," Abony said. "A friend recommended it and I thought I'd check it out. I had no idea it was so popular."

"Girl!" the other woman gaped at her. "You've *never* been here? How long you lived in DC?"

"I'm local," Abony said, "from Maryland, but I've lived downtown for five years now."

"And you've *never* been to The Gingerbread House." This wasn't a question so much as an incredulous acknowledgment. The woman was in her fifties, with close-cropped natural hair and bejeweled eyeglass frames. Her skirt suit and shoes were both off-brand, but the Coach bag was real. Government job, Abony guessed, and a lifer.

"Well, I'm here now. What should I try?"

Her new friend's face lit up, her eyes shining behind her glasses. "Oh, honey, everything is good. But you get yourself a cinnamon apple if you get anything, alright? I get one every Friday just to reward myself for making it through another week." She winked at Abony. "I could tell you where I worked but then I'd have to kill you, see?"

Uh-huh, Abony thought, *pegged it*. Federal government alright.

"A cinnamon apple—is that like a candy apple?"

The other woman laughed. "Sure it is, yes. And you're thinking, 'What the hell is this woman selling me on a candy apple for? They're sticky and sweet and bad for your teeth.' But you just wait, honey. This candy apple is as much like other candy apples as ..." She flicked her eyes over Abony's own skirt suit (not off-brand) and down to her shoes. "As those shoes of yours are like the pair my daughter got at Ross last weekend. You'll see."

Abony managed a smile at the implied compliment. She remembered Simon telling her the night before not to eat an apple if the store owner offered it to her. But what about an apple that a customer tried to talk her into trying? Would that be dangerous too? She eyed the woman as a charter bus pulled up to the curb and the crowd inside the shop surged out. The woman didn't look like she was under a spell, but then neither did Abony. What was it Ranjani was afraid of—that this place made money by selling treats that you just had to have once you'd tried them? The tourists pushing past were red-faced and excited, talking too loudly about the things they'd just bought.

Those gingerbread tiles, did you try those?

I got two boxes, one for the cat sitter and one for us, I couldn't resist.

I know, I think I spent more in there than I did at the outlets on the way down, isn't that crazy?

Not when everything is so good! I swear, I didn't know candy apples could even taste like that.

I wonder if they ship?

Then the bus swallowed them all up. The people who had been waiting outside moved forward eagerly, but Abony stood rooted where she was. What if the door to the shop *was* the oven door, and all it took for the witch to get you was to step into her lair?

But the woman Abony had just met was holding the door open.

"Come on. They'll take good care of you in here, you'll see. You'll wonder how you went so long without finding this place."

"I'm already wondering that," Abony said. "If it's as famous as you say. Seems like I should have heard of it before."

The woman cocked her head. "Maybe," she said, "you just didn't need it before."

And that phrasing was at once so odd and so alarmingly potentially true that Abony walked into The Gingerbread House before she could reconsider.

Inside, she was instantly beguiled. The white-frosting excess of the exterior was not continued here. Instead, the shop was paneled in warm wood, with boxes and cellophane bags of candy displayed in floor-to-ceiling bookcases and on red-and-gold-skirted occasional tables. The arrangement of the tables encouraged lingering over the treats heaped on each surface but never impeded a customer's movement to the register or the glass display case beside it. And inside the case—!

It made Abony think of Tiffany's or Cartier, of a jewelry case from within which beautiful things glinted and sparkled enticingly. This was a bakery case, of course, upright and angled, and the items inside were much larger than gemstones, but they gleamed all the same: glossy candy apples in shades from amber to a crimson so deep it was almost purple, with green and dark gold and mahogany interspersed in between. The woman from the sidewalk was already at the register, pointing to the apple she wanted, shellacked in a vivid red.

"Here's my Friday treat," she said, turning to smile at Abony over her shoulder, "a cinnamon candy apple. And I just realized what color it is, you see?"

She nodded at Abony's feet and Abony felt her belly clench. It was true. The apple was exactly the color of the soles of her shoes, the red that Christian Louboutin had decreed to be "the perfect red." Her discomfort returned with the reminder of why she was here, only to dissipate again as she watched the chosen apple being delicately removed from the case and wrapped.

One of the girls behind the counter had already laid out a double layer of square cellophane sheets, one gold, one red. Now she placed the apple exactly in the center of them, holding it by the gold-dusted stick that had been inserted into the top, right near the stem. She gathered the cellophane in one swift sweeping motion of both her hands, pulled the sheets up, and twisted them around the apple so it was both protected and showcased, shining through the tinted film like an enormous jewel. An elasticized gold ribbon seemed to materialize in the girl's fingers—though really, Abony saw, she'd just been storing it on her wrist—to secure the bunched packaging tight to the stick. Then she affixed a label bearing the store logo to one side and lifted the apple delicately into a red gift bag just large enough to hold it without letting it tip over or bang around.

The woman took it with glee and then said to the girl, "Now you be extra nice to this lady here. This is her first time in the shop, can you believe it? And she's a local!"

Abony turned to watch the woman leave, wishing she could stop her and ask: *Can you afford this weekly apple of yours? Do you get panicky on the weeks when you don't get one? Could you share it with someone, or do you have to eat every bite yourself?*

When she turned back, the girl was practically prone on the counter, leaning over to see Abony's shoes.

"Oh my God, are those Louboutins? They are, aren't they? They're amazing! Are they comfortable, or do they hurt your feet? My mom says heels are stupid, that women just wear them so their butts look good to men, but I think they're beautiful. Still, Louboutins! How much did those cost you? Five hundred dollars, I bet, am I right?"

The shoes in question were mustard-colored patent leather slingbacks—the very shoes, in fact, that Abony had bought the afternoon at the police station two weeks before, $665 on sale.

"You can get them cheaper if you shop on the internet," Abony said mildly, and the girl tipped her head up, then righted herself completely.

"Well, I'm saving up," she said. "I want a pair for prom next spring."

She couldn't have been more than sixteen and she was adorable, plump and curvy, packed into a denim button-down shirt that she'd knotted at her waist and painted-on red jeans. Her hair was set and curled and her dark brown eyes were round with mischief, a child's eyes in a young woman's face.

"You haven't tried our apples, then," she said, "or the gingerbread tiles. It's your first time here. First-time customers get a taste. Hold on, I'll come around."

"But—" Abony tried to forestall her— "aren't you closing soon?"

"It's fine. There's two of us to close." The girl ran a quick appraising eye over the few other customers remaining in the store. Then she ducked through a door in the back wall and emerged a moment later holding a gold tray covered with an assortment of small square cookies and apple slices arranged in semi-circles across a red linen napkin. None of the apple slices was touched by the browning that usually happened to apples exposed to air, even though there was no way the girl had just cut them. Magic, Abony wondered, or just some special preservative?

"Now," the girl was saying, "we've got all kinds of candy here, chocolates and caramels and licorice whips, hard candies too. But these are our specialties, my mom's secret recipes. These here—" She gestured with an amateurishly hand-painted fingertip, turquoise with silver polka dots— "are our gingerbread tiles. There's three kinds, which you can tell from the glaze color. This one's honey, this one's golden syrup, this one's blackstrap."

Abony had promised not to eat anything, and fortunately this wasn't even a temptation. She didn't particularly like gingerbread. Still, the round brown eyes were fastened expectantly on her, so she selected a square. It was about the size of one of those tiny post-it notes that she always had too many of in her desk drawer, and the glossy dark brown of a leather executive chair. Blackstrap, whatever that meant.

"Thank you," she said. "I'll just nibble this while I look around. And I was actually hoping to talk to the owner. Is she here?"

The girl nodded, but her eyes were on the square that Abony was holding between thumb and forefinger.

"You're not going to eat it," she said. "I can tell." She pursed her lips, staring hard at Abony, and then gasped. "You're scared to eat it! You think it's dangerous."

"Is it?"

The girl shivered and her whole face crinkled with disgust. "We don't *make* things like that. Bleagh!"

Abony burst out laughing, reminded of the look on her nephew's face the time he snuck a bite of what turned out to be not regular honey but honey with black truffles in it. It was hard to imagine faking that look.

She lifted the gingerbread square to her mouth and took a bite.

It was somehow both a cookie and a candy, melting and crumbling in her mouth in a slow surfeit of flavor—spice, sugar, butter. But she got no further than that before she was suffused with the most glorious sensation, tingling from her scalp to the back of her neck and down to her fingertips and toes. Without volition, she felt herself smiling—no, grinning, her mouth stretching and her belly filling with the urge to laugh from sheer excitement.

Christmas! Christmas was in her mouth and in the back of her throat and all through her. Christmas morning when she'd wake up and look over to the other bed to see Darnell still asleep, his thumb in his mouth and his cheeks all puffed out around it, and she'd whisper, "Darnell, wake up, wake up, it's Christmas!" and his eyes would pop open and he'd be grinning at her from around his thumb before he was even awake. They'd be out of bed, then, running light as they could on bare feet, Abony holding up her nightgown, to peek over the banister and see the tree in the living room below, the lights already on, even though Daddy always turned the tree off before he went to bed. Santa had turned them back on, no other explanation. And sure enough there were packages there that hadn't been there the night before, piles of packages, some in *Star Wars* paper—"Those are yours, Darnell," Abony whispered to him, pointing through the railings, and he wriggled delightedly beside her—and some in a beautiful shiny red paper with gold flowers all over it that had to be Abony's because red was her favorite color in the whole world. Darnell would want to creep downstairs to look at the presents—"I just want to feel them, Abby, I just want to see if there's a landspeeder set in there, come on, please!"—but Abony knew they shouldn't do that, even though she was eyeing those red boxes herself, could see that at least one looked like it could be a Barbie doll, maybe the Barbie she'd asked for, who was Black and had straightened hair down past her waist like a White girl but still was beautiful. No, they had to creep back down the hall and push Mommy and Daddy's door open just a crack, very quietly, so as not to wake them up, but still just open the door and look in because what if maybe they *were* awake already and then they could all go downstairs? And at first when she'd look in—making Darnell stay behind her because he couldn't be quiet enough—she'd think they were still asleep, but then Daddy would shift and turn over and yawn and say something like, "Hmmm, I thought I heard something out there, like little elf feet on the stairs, think I might need to go check it out." And then she and Darnell would start giggling and not be able to stop and they'd rush into the room and jump on the bed and shriek to Mommy and Daddy to wake up and come downstairs and see because Santa came and it was Christmas!

Abony swallowed. The flavors receded and Christmas slipped away, but gently, like a tide going out. She remembered standing by the tree ripping back the paper from a tiny package, the very last package, and glancing over at her mother in disbelief. Could it be, really? Mommy had said she wasn't old enough yet. But inside the box were three pairs of starter earrings—gold studs, gold hoops, and a pair glinting with little diamond chips—and Mommy was smiling over the rim of her coffee cup.

Her mother had been dead for five years now, but when Abony put the remainder of the gingerbread tile in her mouth she could smell her mother's perfume and feel the nubbly softness of her mother's bathrobe against her cheek. Then she swallowed again and her mom was gone.

"So," the salesgirl asked, "what do you think?"

"It was delicious," Abony said. "You really make these yourself?"

"I do a little bit of everything," the girl said, "although I'm only just getting into the kitchen. My mother owns this place."

She stuck out her hand. "I'm Ebonie, by the way—that's with an 'i' and an 'e' at the end, my mom's idea of a fancy spelling."

Abony burst out laughing and slipped her hand into the girl's. "Your mom and my mom had the same idea, sweetie," she said. "I'm Abony—with an 'A' at the beginning."

Ebonie's eyes lit up with delight, but then she dropped them to where she held Abony's hand and her smile faded. "It's nice to meet you, Abony," she said carefully. "But, umm, you said you wanted to see my mom, didn't you? I'll go get her for you."

Before Abony could say anything, Ebonie had released her hand, set the tray down on the nearest table, and ducked back through the door in the back of the store.

"Don't leave," she said over her shoulder. "Please? She'll be right out."

Abony looked around and realized that she was the last person in the store. She wondered fleetingly whether she'd lost time when she'd eaten that gingerbread square, but a glance at her watch reassured her that it was just 6 p.m. Outside, the street was deserted; this really was a block that turned into a ghost town once the business day was over. Abony looked down at the tray of cookie tiles and apple slices. She didn't feel a compulsive urge to eat another. She just felt happier than she'd felt in months, as though the memories the gingerbread had triggered had lifted the tangle of the curse off her for a moment and it was only now settling back into place. Whatever magic was at work in The Gingerbread House, it felt *good*. Abony could practically hear Maia scoffing at her: *So, you taste something yummy that makes you remember being a little girl and that makes it automatically 'good magic'?*

The door to the back opened again and a woman stepped out, with Ebonie on her heels. Abony couldn't tell if Ebonie was herding her mother into the store or hiding behind her; it might have been both. The other woman was close to Abony's own age, in her mid-forties, lean in that way that suggested she'd never worried for a moment of her life about what she put in her mouth, that as a girl she'd bemoaned her flat chest and her spindly arms and legs. She wore jeans and sneakers with a berry-colored tank top, straightened hair, and a suspicious frown. As soon as she saw Abony, she stopped in the doorway and folded her arms over her chest, leaving Ebonie to peer over her shoulder.

"Mom?"

"Ssh. You were right, Ebonie. Stop pressing on me." The woman stepped all the way into the shop. "Go lock the front door, change the sign. Then I need you to go on in back and get the dishwasher going."

"But—"

The woman swung round to give her daughter what Abony could only assume was a ferocious look. "Nuh-uh, girl. Do *not* press on this. You were right and you did good. But this isn't something you can practice on, you understand me? This is way beyond that. You do as I say."

Ebonie's shoulders slumped as she slipped around her mother to lock the front door. When she passed Abony on the way back, she didn't look up, merely darted out of the room again, shutting the door behind her.

"Your daughter had just about talked me into buying some of your gingerbread tiles," Abony said. "She's a very good saleswoman."

"She's a child," the other woman said, "and she's still in training. She could sense your fear right off—says you were worried we tainted our food, which I'll let pass because I can understand now why you'd be scared. Ebonie felt the curse on you when she shook your hand."

Abony had her feet planted so she didn't sway, though she felt the ground shift under her feet. *The curse.* As if it was just a fact, not a wild speculation by a couple of comic-book nerds.

She held her hand out again, her eyebrows lifted in challenge. "I'm Abony," she said. "Ebonie and I bonded over our names."

The woman uncrossed her arms and took Abony's hand.

"Chantal," she said. "I'll shake your hand, though I don't need to touch you to see the curse. And I'll sell you some gingerbread, but that's all I can do, you understand? I can't help you."

"Did I ask you to help me?"

"With that thing wrapped around you?" Chantal snorted. "Why the hell else would you be here?"

"What does the curse look like?" Abony asked.

Chantal rolled her eyes. "It looks like a hedge of thorns, baby, like patent leather chains, like a spiderweb you walked into and got stuck all over. You can describe it however you like; it looks to me like a hell of a curse, a sorcerer's curse, and nothing I'm going to mess with."

"But can you tell what it's done to me?"

"Sure, I can tell what it's done to you—more or less. I can see the intent, anyway. It's twisted your power and your sexuality into hobbling chains is what it's done." She shook her head, crossing her arms again and drawing in on herself. "Nasty work. And yes, I know whose work it is. He didn't exactly hide his light under a bushel when he moved in here a year ago. Whole goddamn building's afire with the magic he's been burning to make things go his way."

Abony named her company and the CEO.

Chantal nodded. "That's right."

"So he's, what, an evil wizard?"

"Sorcerer."

"Sorcerer. And you're not surprised to see what he's done to me. Would you be surprised to hear that he's cursed at least five women that I know of, four besides me?"

"No."

Abony took a step forward. "Would you be surprised that one of those women is dead because of what he did to her?"

Chantal's shoulders twitched. "No."

"What are you, exactly? What are you training your daughter to be? Another sorcerer?"

"I wouldn't let Ebonie near sorcery," Chantal said. "She's learning witchcraft, same as I learned from my mother and my mother learned from hers."

"And of course you're a *good* witch," Abony said.

Chantal laughed shortly. "You tasted my food. What do you think?"

"I think you can help us," Abony said. "I don't know what you can do, exactly, but I refuse to believe that you can't do *something* because—what?—you're just a witch and he's a sorcerer? Or is it because you're a Black woman and he's a White man?"

"The only reason I'm not telling you to get out of my store right now," Chantal said, "is that I know you're in pain and I'm sorry for you."

"The hell you are," Abony said. "You don't even know what to be sorry for."

"Fine. Tell me what he did."

Chantal swung away to pace the shop while Abony talked, but she didn't interrupt. Abony told their stories in order, starting with Emily Sato. When she was done, Chantal glowered a minute at a display of prettily packaged chocolates that she'd been rearranging.

"Your friend Maia. How little did he make her?"

"Little enough," Abony said. "What difference does that make?"

Chantal snorted. "I was wondering how little she had to be to make him feel like a big man, that's all. Some of what he's done to all of you sounds like he's having fun, playing the evil wizard and making fairy tales into private jokes. But there's that viciousness at the core..." She trailed off and adjusted another tier of candy boxes. Abony waited.

"You taste my gingerbread?" Chantal asked.

"Ebonie gave me a piece."

"Where did it take you?"

"Where did it—oh. Christmas morning when I was little." She smiled despite herself. "I could feel my little brother's hand— how'd that boy's hands get sticky before he even got out of bed in the morning? And I could smell the tree."

"It took me years to perfect that spell," Chantal said. "Something small like that, and so personal? It's like..." She shaped a sphere with her hands. "Like blowing glass. It kept bursting on me before I could get it stabilized. It had to be pure nostalgia, you see what I'm saying? Not 'Christmas,' because Lord knows there are plenty of people who walk through this door who've got nothing but bad memories of Christmas, and plenty more for whom the day doesn't mean a thing. I had to create something that didn't have me or my idea of perfection at the center of it. That spell goes out and latches onto *you* when you eat my gingerbread, finds the memory *you* need."

"It's a gift."

Chantal smiled, the first real smile she'd offered. "It's a gift."

"And I'm not addicted to it now," Abony said, aware that there was still a thread of question in her voice.

Chantal turned to face Abony fully. "I'd no more do that with my magic than I would use it to rape or kill someone. I *wouldn't* work magic like that. But you don't know me. Maybe it will help you to know that I also *couldn't* work curses like the ones your CEO's put on you."

"Why not?"

"You said it yourself. He's a sorcerer and I'm "just" a witch."

Chantal wove her way across the room to where Abony stood. "I'll explain it to you as best I can. We've all got talents, right? And passions, things we love? For me, it's always been baking and feeding people. Only since I was born a witch, I've also got some power, personal power, that my mother taught me to use from the time I was little to fuel those talents and passions. First I used it to be a better baker, then to be a better magical baker— to successfully imbue magic into recipes—then finally when I was ready, to make my own magical recipes."

"Like the gingerbread."

Chantal nodded. "Like my gingerbread. Now, I inherited my power, all witches do. So think of it like a literal inheritance—a certain sum of money that was essentially willed to every witch in my family before we were even born, and which each of us can nurture or squander to feed the spells we want to do. The core power never gets any bigger from generation to generation, but it never gets any less either, not so long as the witch believes in it."

"Never gets bigger or smaller," Abony said thoughtfully. "So the magic you use for your spells is like the dividends you're able to generate—and then spend—from this fixed amount of power?"

"Yep. And that means it's limited. Sure, there are witches who've got very little talent for getting the most from their power and others with more—I'm fairly talented, more than my mother was to hear her tell it—but regardless, we're limited to the scope of what one single person can accomplish with the magical equivalent of at most, say, a couple of million dollars. And that would be a *really* gifted witch."

Abony refrained from asking Chantal just how much money was in her magical bank account, partly so Chantal didn't think she was being snarky and partly because she was getting worried about the fact that she had to not only understand all this but also explain it to the others later.

"And even a million-dollar witch couldn't accomplish curses like the ones the CEO has put on all of us?" she asked instead.

"No way," Chantal shook her head. "*No way.* That's *billion*-dollar magic, if we're sticking with the money metaphor."

"So how the hell is he doing it? How is sorcery so different?"

Chantal sighed and reached out to absently untie and retie the ribbon on a bag of licorice.

"I should probably be careful here," she said. "I don't like sorcery. My grandmother used to warn me not to be prejudiced against the whole lot of them just on account of a few that do stuff to turn your stomach but..." she turned back from the shelf... "in my experience it's more than a few operating like that."

"And are witches always women and sorcerers always men?" Abony asked.

Chantal made a face. "Not necessarily to the first. As for the second, I wish I could tell you different but, yes, they're almost always men. Which makes sense when you understand where they get their power. See, instead of being passed down from parent to child, sorcery is a mentorship. One sorcerer can teach or train a half-dozen young sorcerers, with varying success of course, but still. I suppose we should all be grateful that they're a suspicious, power-hungry bunch and so they don't tend to be all that interested in sharing power or spreading the wealth, as it were. But still, they do pass it down."

"Okay," Abony said. "So far you're describing our CEO. But how does his power *work*?"

"Sorcerers don't have personal power," Chantal said. "What they have instead is an awareness and understanding of how to tap into much broader power. Infinite power, in many cases."

"Enough to do billion-dollar magic," Abony said.

"Oh, enough to do magic like those curses he's crafting every day of his life without feeling a pinch," Chantal said, and nodded at the look on Abony's face.

"Yep, you *should* be terrified. See, the thing a sorcerer does have in common with a witch is that he has a talent or passion he wants to fuel with magic. The difference is that without any power of his own, he taps into Belief."

She said this last word as if capitalizing it. Abony lifted an eyebrow.

"Let's say you're a sorcerer who's also a football coach," Chantal said. "You want to become, I don't know, the winningest coach in NFL history. You need power to work the spells to make that happen—to make your quarterbacks unsackable, to curse opposing teams with sudden clumsiness, to beguile the fans to think your temper tantrums on the sidelines are charming. Where do you get the power for those spells, really big spells that need to affect hundreds of—thousands of—people at once?"

"I have no idea," Abony said. At least she was following the football metaphor.

"You tap into the belief in this country around football," Chantal said. "If my power is a tidy inheritance, a sorcerer's power is a Swiss bank, assuming he picks the right belief to use to fund it. In the case of football, there's an unimaginable amount of power to draw on. There's millions of people who *believe* football is the greatest professional sport in the world, because it's uniquely American. Who *believe* the men who play it are superhuman, and sometimes above the law. Who *believe* that their team is good and the rival team is evil. Who *believe* that games between rival teams mean something about the future of our world. Who *believe* that NFL players deserve to make millions of dollars a year, more money than most people make all their lives. Who *believe* that tickets to the Super Bowl are worth $5000. Each."

"Jesus," Abony said. They were both silent a moment. Chantal walked around behind the counter, got two bottles of water out of a cooler, and brought one back to Abony.

"So our CEO. The belief system he's tapping into is what, sexism?"

Chantal took a long drink of water.

"Go further."

"Right." Abony took her own drink. "It's not just the belief that women are inferior to men," she said slowly. "Not garden-variety sexism, if you will. I mean, yesterday we talked about how he's just using us as batteries for his bigger spells to get rich. If there's a belief there, it goes way beyond 'listen to your husband, ladies.'"

"Damn right," Chantal said. "It's everything men have believed over the centuries and have convinced plenty of women to buy into—that we're property, ornaments, pets, slaves, vessels to carry their sons, plus whatever you want to add to that list. You think about those fairy tales he's messing with. He didn't make them up. He just opened a book and there they were, and what, hundreds more where they came from? Stories of girls getting their feet chopped off, being raped by their own fathers, locked in towers or put to sleep forever, tongues cut out, eaten by wolves—"

She broke off, took another drink of water, then started again.

"He's tapped into so much power that it's unquantifiable," she said. "The things that people have believed about men's power over women—that they still believe—"

She compressed her mouth like she was tasting something foul.

"But *we* don't believe these things," Abony said. "And we're helping each other. Isn't there something we can do with that?"

"Maybe. I don't know."

"And you don't care, or not enough, to help us figure it out? Even though you yourself *believe*—" Abony stretched the word out— "that what he's doing is the worst kind of magic."

They faced off, silent. Abony started counting in her head, a trick she'd learned in a professional development class to distract yourself from how long a silence was stretching, make you less uncomfortable so you wouldn't feel like you had to break it. Chantal worried her lower lip with her teeth.

"Dammit," she burst out finally. "I can't take the risk."

Just then there was a knock on the back door, which turned out to be Ebonie's way of warning her mother that she was about to open it and pop her head into the shop.

"Abony, you want to buy a package of those gingerbread tiles you tried?" she asked, all dimples and eyes. Honest to God, Abony thought, that girl could sell a fur coat to a mink. "What about an apple? I'm just about to close out the register, so if you want anything I can ring you up now."

"I'll take a package of gingerbread," Abony said, "and an apple. Whichever kind is your favorite."

"Don't ring up the apple, Ebonie," Chantal said. "Give her one of the smoked honey ones on the house and just ring her up for her tiles. Give us two more minutes then she'll be leaving."

Chantal had stepped back just enough to prevent Ebonie from coming fully out into the shop without having to ask her mother to move. Ebonie shut the door and Chantal relaxed fractionally.

Abony felt like a fool. "You're scared of what he'll do to her if you help us and he finds out—"

Chantal rounded on her. "You *know* he'd go after her! Don't pretend he wouldn't."

"No," Abony said, "I won't."

"And then what? You want to get a book of fairy tales and find one for Ebonie? She loved 'Cinderella' when she was little, so what's she going to get, tiny little feet she can hardly walk on? Shards of glass embedded in the soles?"

"She's not—no one's asking you to risk that."

Abony stopped short of saying she was sorry she'd come.

"I'll go," she said instead, reaching into her bag for her wallet. "I'll get my cookies and let you close up. I'm not asking you to work some spell that he could trace to you. I swear I'm not asking you to do that. But if you can't help, there's no one else." She heard the crack in her voice and steadied it, holding out a twenty-dollar bill and trying to make Chantal meet her eyes. "Is there *anything* you can do, anything that won't put Ebonie in danger? Is there someone else I can ask? Someone else you can send me to?"

Chantal laughed. "Girl, you've been watching too many movies. Let me just go call my coven, that what you're looking for? There's no one else. Not only because there's no good-witch book club in this neighborhood, but because anyone else I would send you to is going to be just like me, and that means they won't touch the stuff this man is working."

Ebonie emerged again, carrying two gift bags stuffed with tissue and smiling tentatively. "Here you go, Abony. It's fourteen ninety-five for the gingerbread. You don't need to refrigerate the apple until you cut into it, then you should just keep it in the fridge with some plastic wrap on the open part."

Abony exchanged her money for the bags. "Keep the change, Ebonie, unless your mom doesn't let you accept tips."

Chantal gave a one-shouldered shrug. "That's alright. Something tells me this girl is going to be saving up for a pair of fancy shoes like yours, so she'll need every penny she can get."

She looked back at Abony. "You want to keep fighting this man."

"I hope that's not a question," Abony said.

"No, I know you do. But I do have a question," Chantal said. "Are you going to meet with these other women when you leave here? I assume they're waiting for your report on me."

Abony smiled slightly. "You assume right."

"Fine. Good." Chantal nodded at the bags dangling in Abony's fingers. "Cut into that apple when you're all together."

"Why?"

"You want to explain it, Ebonie?"

Ebonie was clearly bursting to do just that. "It'll make you more yourself," she said. "That's what our apples do. You know how you can start to feel scattered and sort of stretched thin, not sure how you even feel about things because your friends are telling you one thing and your parents another and—" She broke off and giggled— "well, maybe not exactly like that for you, but still. It will settle you into yourself."

She glanced at her mother, who nodded.

"And if you eat it with other people," Ebonie finished, "not only will each of you feel better, you'll feel more like you belong together, to each other. So you should only eat it with people you really trust, because it will strengthen the bonds between you."

"How long did the spell take you to perfect?" Abony asked Chantal.

"I can't claim this one," Chantal said. "I've worked on it, sure, but it was handed down on my mother's side some six generations back."

Six generations back: the woman who made this spell would have been a slave, and she used her power to remind the people around her who they were, as individuals, as families, and as a people.

"Sounds like it's good witches all the way back in your family," Abony said. What else could she say? "I can't wait to try that apple."

She turned to go. Ebonie darted around her to unlock the door.

Behind them, Chantal sighed.

"Wait," she said.

Abony spun around.

"The only way to undermine a magic—spell, curse, whatever—is to shake the belief of the person who cast it," Chantal said. "You'd have to destroy a witch's belief in herself to undo her power. With a sorcerer, you have to find cracks in his belief in whatever it is that fuels him."

"You want us to shake his belief in White patriarchy?" Abony asked incredulously. "Seriously?"

"Listen," Chantal said. "He believes that men have silenced, shrunk, and caged women for centuries. That's a fact. He also believes they should be able to keep on doing it. That's not. Try showing him you've still got power in those stories he's trapped you in, take them back. Confront him that way and you might shake those curses loose."

"How?"

"Don't move!" Chantal snapped, dropping her arms to her sides.

She was glaring, not at Abony, but at something over Abony's shoulder. Abony stood still as ordered while Chantal shook her hands as if working pins and needles out of them.

"Ebonie," she said, "get back to the kitchen."

"But—"

"*Now*, Ebonie." Chantal's eyes had gone completely black, even the whites, and a glittering lattice of gold was flickering in them. Ebonie squeaked.

"It's just her power," she assured Abony. "She's not going to hurt you, she's just gathering it." She ran back across the store.

Abony heard a faint whispering noise behind her. She turned her head just enough to see a pattern etching itself across the windows in the front door, moving from pane to pane like fast-growing vines. No, it *was* vines, vines that climbed over one another and wove themselves together, sprouting thorns and leaves but no flowers.

"Oh no you don't," Chantal murmured. "Not my own windows, you don't, not my own shop."

She stepped around Abony, put a fingertip on the nearest pane, and then leaned in and blew on it. Abony smelled spices: ginger and clove and something rich and burnt. The whole etched pattern shook, little flakes of glass raining down onto the sidewalk outside like shaved ice, and the vines grew the flowers they'd been missing, roses in every stage of bloom. Then they went still.

"What did you do?" Abony gasped. "What *was* that?"

"That was a warning," Chantal said. "Now get out of here. Go on," she said, when Abony hesitated, still staring at the windows. "Get out of here and don't come back. Or don't you remember what happens to the people in the castle inside the hedge of thorns?"

Fairy Tales Forever Discord Channel

*We are an inclusive community; we celebrate all voices and identities. Expressions of hate, bias, or general assholery (yes, we know it's not a word) will not be tolerated. For full channel rules and guidelines click **here**.*

Discussion Boards: Fairy Tale of the Day |
Question of the Day | Fairy Tales for Our Time

Question of the Day: Why are witches in fairy tales always evil?
submitted by blackcatlover (member since 2016)

Jess: Short answer to this one: because men find powerful women scary and need other women to also find them scary. How to do this? Make sure that the women exercising power in these stories are always doing it for evil purposes.

Rebekah: Seriously evil purposes too, not subtle. Like, "please cut out my stepdaughter's heart and bring it to me so I can EAT it." Or "please cook my grandchildren in a special sauce so I can EAT them."

Eden: Okay now I have to come in and point out that there's also a stepmother/evil witch overlap that really pisses me off. It's not 100% for sure, but it's a lot, and even when the stepmother isn't also a witch, she's still evil. I know that's not the question you asked but as a step-mom myself (and it is no picnic let me tell you) this just makes me so mad.

Angelofhehouse: @Eden you should post that question sometime so we CAN talk about it. Because there's some historical context around second wives wanting their biological children to get food before their stepchildren, which is horrible but also was a reality.

DrHarleyQ: Agree that in fairy tales, women who demonstrate power are so scary that they have to be shut down immediately. But they're not even supposed to WANT power. If you take @Rebekah's examples where they want to eat their stepkids or grandkids as metaphorical, it's about not wanting to give up actual power over a kingdom, which women back then could only have had as regents for their sons or as "the power behind the throne."

Cleotheprettyrat: The term "witch" in fairy tales is pretty much synonymous with evil, isn't it? I mean, there are Good Fairies but no good witches until *The Wizard of Oz*. Right?

Rebekah: Ooo—me, me, me! (Yes, I am Hermione, who is also a witch.) In the book of *The Wizard of Oz*, the witch of the west isn't even green (!) and the good witch of the north is a little old woman. But then when Hollywood gets ahold of the story, the wicked witch turns green and shrieky and Glinda is basically Fairy Princess Barbie.

Jess: Right. The ugly factor is intense. The hunchbacks, hooked noses, warts, long crooked fingers… the whole trope of the "ugly old witch" works two ways. It undermines the trope in a lot of cultures of the wise old woman and it makes all women scared to try to BE powerful because in these stories, being powerful pretty much means you're hideous.

Cleotheprettyrat: "I'm not a witch, I'm your wife!" #princessbrideforever

<click to see more comments>

AUGUST 10: MAIA

Since Abony had planned to go to The Gingerbread House after work and the shop closed at six, they had all agreed to convene at Maia's again right around that time. Maia had plenty of work to keep her busy, but at 5 p.m., when she imagined Abony was heading over to the store, she gave up and just scrolled The Gingerbread House website.

"I don't think it's been updated since you last looked at it, you know, two hours ago," Simon said.

"Shut up," Maia said. "I'm checking the reviews. I mean— there's literally no bad ones. Not even on Yelp! Don't you think that's weird?"

Simon rolled his chair over from his workstation.

"Why are you freaking out about this now? Abony can clearly handle herself."

"Not if this woman, Chantal, is another bad actor." Maia clicked back to the store's menu. "By which I mean a literal evil witch. When we found this place online, it seemed so obvious that someone should go check it out, but now I feel like, easy for me to say…"

"You didn't ask Abony to do anything you wouldn't have done yourself," Simon said. "You would have marched in there without even telling anyone where you were going if you could have. My question is, what if Abony comes back with a plan that means you *do* have to leave the house? Are we really going to do it?"

Maia grinned at him over her shoulder. "I think last night I proposed going out in a Tupperware container like a firefly."

He didn't smile back. "No, you pointed out that doing that would be a *terrible idea*."

"We have a whole protocol, Si," Maia said. "Why shouldn't we use it?"

Her cell phone buzzed. Saved! She ran across the table to check the message.

She's a witch alright, and he knows I went to see her. Will explain when I get there.

"Shit," Maia said, even Jo and Ranjani replied that they were both on their way. "That doesn't sound good at all."

Simon pushed back the hood of his sweatshirt. He was on a deadline for a work project and hadn't showered since the day before. His hair currently stuck up in a curving sweep forward from his crown like the plumy tail on a dog.

"Should I clean up?" he asked. "Order some food? We didn't eat dinner yet, did we?"

Maia winced. She ate so little now that Simon essentially cooked for himself. He lacked both the talent and inclination to do it and often ate only when she asked him to make food for her. She worried that he never really got enough to eat.

"Why don't we order Thai?" she suggested. "Everybody likes spring rolls, isn't that, like, a universal truth or something? And you know I love those adorable ears of corn."

This was an old joke, no longer funny, except that she willed it to be. Maia *had* always loved those weird little ears of corn. Now that each ear was half as long as she was tall, they'd lost their allure. Besides, cut into pieces small enough for her to eat, they didn't taste like much of anything.

"You're not funny, you know," Simon said, but he smiled down at her and put his hand out palm up. Maia clambered on, feeling his supporting fingers close around her.

There were so many things that they'd had to figure out in the first weeks after she'd been assaulted and then shrunk that it had taken Maia a while to notice that they had stopped laughing. So many things that might have been funny in the abstract were terrifying in reality. Once Simon had sneezed in her direction and knocked her off the arm of the sofa; she'd saved herself by catching hold of the fringe on a throw blanket. Another time she'd gotten stuck in the folds of their comforter, trying to pull herself up slick brocaded hills only to slide down again, gasping, and unable to make a noise loud enough that Simon could hear, as he searched the house screaming her name.

Then too there were the more mundane struggles, like finding her things to wear and eat, a way to get cleaned up, brush her teeth, and (mortifyingly) use the toilet. They'd solved some dilemmas more easily than others; who knew there were dozens of people on Etsy who *lived* to make tiny custom-made clothes. Maia had never spent so much time or money on her clothes when she was 5'4", but, as Simon pointed out, there was no such thing as T. J. Maxx for people the size of dollhouse miniatures.

"Well, there should be!" Maia had snapped. "I'd shop there."

"I know you would, honey," Simon had said, "but you'd be the only one, and you'd shop the clearance rack and so they still wouldn't make any money off you."

That had been one of the first times they had laughed, each catching the other's lips twitching, and Simon visibly waiting for Maia to laugh first so he knew it was safe.

But the thing that had saved them had been Simon's idea. Maia had been against it, horrified by the cost and by the competing emotions it aroused in her: hope at the possibilities it might open up and a nauseous fear that if those hopes were realized, she might allow herself to settle, grow accustomed to being four inches tall, call this size— God forbid—her new normal.

So she hadn't wanted the 3-D printer. But Simon had bought it anyway, using his own credit card. The thing took up a whole counter in the kitchen and reminded Maia of the machines that comic-book villains were always building and then testing on themselves: a cube with an open core. She could easily have stood on the tray where the products took shape and waited to be zapped with some super-charged beam of energy or cocktail of chemicals, emerging horribly modified and primed for revenge.

Instead, the first thing Simon produced was a cup, stark white and so thin that he was afraid to touch it. Maia darted into the middle of the printer and touched the thing with one finger, found it cool, then picked it up.

"Well?" Simon asked.

She turned the cup in her hands, lifted it to her lips. The smell of hot plastic was already fading and the rim was exactly the right thickness. She'd been trying to drink from dollhouse tea sets they'd ordered online, so heavy she could barely lift them, the cheap porcelain so thick that she had to slurp without tipping her mug until it was at least half empty, for fear of pouring the contents all over her front. But this felt like, well, just a cup. Holding it, Maia was not, for the first time in months, too small.

"Make me another," she said. "And a plate and a bowl and some utensils and a bed…"

Simon had laughed, reaching for the rolls of filament that came with the machine. "As you wish, m'lady. Do you want to choose your colors?"

The doorbell rang much earlier than Maia had been expecting anyone. Simon tried to leave her in the dining room while he checked the peephole, but she made a face at him and clung to his finger.

"It's Jo," he said. "Damn, she looks like she ran here from the Metro."

Jo hadn't run from the Metro; she'd run from her apartment.

"I was more than halfway here, according to my damn watch," she said when Simon let her in. "I figured I could either run three miles home, shower and drive over, or I could just run the rest of the way here and apologize for being sweaty. But then…" she glared at her wrist as she swiped at her dripping face with the bottom of her tank top, "when it was too late to turn back, the three-mile estimate turned into five." Jo dropped the tank top, which had revealed a flat belly and the bottom of a sleek black sports bra, and shrugged. "So here I am, even more disgusting than I thought I'd be. Sorry."

Her ponytail was coming out and strands of her dark hair stuck to her cheeks and neck. She gave off the sharp, salty sweat of pure exertion. Maia knew that smell; she used to go to spin class three times a week and feel that same sweat rising on her arms, streaming down her legs. Then she'd come home and fight with Simon about how good she felt and how good *he'd* feel if he'd exercise, ever, just once a week even, go for a walk for God's sake, get out of the house...

"Do you want to take a shower?" Maia asked. "None of my clothes will fit you properly, but you could tie a scarf as a belt, something like that?"

"That would be amazing, thanks," Jo said. "I don't know what I was thinking." She pushed her hair back and a drop of sweat splashed into Simon's palm, a single bead nearly enough to fill Maia's 3-D printed water bottle.

Simon took Maia back to the dining-room table, then walked Jo upstairs. Maia watched them go, registering that Jo was as tall as he was even with her shoes off and reminding herself that Simon, as Maia knew well after twelve years of marriage, didn't exactly have an insatiable sex drive. It had been a longstanding source of tension between them before she'd been cursed: that Simon never wanted to have sex and she always did. Now, of course, it was a non-issue.

Despite the assault, Maia missed sex. She'd probably never give another blowjob again in her life, but she was okay with that. What she missed was the sex she'd craved when she'd been her own size—her *real* size—and in charge of what she did with her body. She missed the gasps of pleasure she could wring from her husband when she finally cornered him, the cool dry friction of his hands on her body, his fingers initially reluctant but eventually marvelously dexterous.

Now Simon's penis was taller than she was, and Maia couldn't move past the reality of it to any kind of longing. She shrank from Simon's physicality in a way she'd never have thought possible, shutting her eyes so she wouldn't see him naked, shrinking from his hot damp breath when he spoke too close to her. His body, which had always been hard-to-get, was now overwhelming.

But the CEO hadn't destroyed their marriage. There was that. Their marriage had not merely survived her assault and this damn curse, it had thrived in the aftermath. Simon had risen to every challenge, solved every new problem, from the need for a lavalier mike to the purchase of the 3-D printer. So he didn't miss having sex with her; Maia could live with that. Another man following Jo up the stairs might not have been able to resist watching her perfect butt flex in her black shorts, might have tracked the rivulets of sweat that ran down her shoulder blades under her tank top, might even have lingered outside the bathroom door to sneak a peek as she stepped into the shower. Simon was back downstairs before the water had even begun to run. And a good thing, too, because the doorbell rang again announcing the arrival of their delivery order.

Ranjani and Abony both arrived while Simon was setting out containers of food, Abony still in her work clothes and Ranjani in clothes she would never wear for work: a vivid pink tunic that reached to her knees, with loose white cotton pants underneath. They were just loading up their plates when Jo came downstairs wearing one of Maia's favorite dresses, a blue smocked cotton with red and white flowers. Of course, on Jo it was a different dress entirely, hitting well above the knee and blousing out above and below the fabric Jo had knotted around her waist. She looked younger and more relaxed than the night before, with her hair loose on her shoulders and her cheeks still flushed from her run.

"I assume that was your bathrobe belt I stole," Jo said to Simon as she picked up a plate. "I'll give it back, I promise."

Maia had been trying to see differences in the other two

women, whom she'd known before and now after they'd been assaulted and cursed, but it was hard to get past the added strangeness of their size. Ranjani did seem more tentative, and even more fidgety, which was saying something. But Maia was also distracted by the astonishing porelessness of the younger woman's skin now that it was magnified for her. And Abony seemed to move with a new leashed aggression, but that could be an extrapolation of Maia's own terror at the thought of being in the path of those four-inch heels. With Jo, Maia had no "before" to contemplate, but she'd bet Jo had always been pretty tightly wound and only very rarely willing to show this barefoot and beautiful version of herself.

Simon dished up a piece of a noodle, a shred of carrot, and a sliver of a shrimp for Maia, then used a knife to cut all of it into the finest dice he could manage. Maia settled cross-legged on the table and picked up her plate.

"So she's a witch," she said to Abony. "Let's hear it."

When Abony had told them the whole story, they all burst out at once.

"She said it was a warning?" Maia demanded. "To who? To her or you? And she was sure it was him?"

"And she *stopped* him?" Jo asked. "She actually did something that countered the curse he was trying to put on the shop?"

Abony nodded around a bite of spring roll.

"It doesn't matter," Ranjani said. "We can't ask her to get involved, not if her daughter could get hurt."

"Well, I *did* ask her to get involved and she won't," Abony said, "for exactly that reason. "The only thing she'd give me was that we try to show him we have power over the stories he's cursed us with. Maybe we need to find ways to take the stories back, like— I don't know—if I could find actual glass slippers."

"And then what?" Jo asked. "You—" She swallowed hard, set her plate down, and took a drink of water. "Dammit. I can't even ask fucking hypothetical *questions*."

"Let me try," Maia said. "You get some glass slippers or—Christ, I don't know—I bet Louboutin makes clear plastic heels—"

"I have a pair," Abony said.

"Right. So what do you do with them? Wear them into his office and show him that you're in on the joke?"

"I wish I knew," Abony said. "He started his little attack on Chantal's store windows before I could get anything else out of her. But this woman has *power*. I saw her use it."

"And you think she's—I don't know—*good*?" Ranjani asked. "Because you ate the cookie she offered and it turned out okay?"

Abony put down her plate, stood up, and went out to the foyer. She returned with an elegant gift bag from which she extracted a box of dark brown cookies and an enormous candy apple wrapped in red cellophane.

"I didn't intend to try anything they gave me," she said. "But when I didn't take the gingerbread from the girl, she *knew* that I thought it might be tainted in some way, and she was absolutely horrified. That's what changed my mind, that reaction."

She ran her nail under the tape sealing the box of cookies and lifted the lid. "Everything I learned after that, from both Ebonie and her mother, confirmed my instinct. But none of you were there. I don't blame you for not believing in someone only I've met—" she nodded at Maia— "and who we only learned about from Maia and Simon's reconnaissance. Now, personally, I'd like to figure out how to show the CEO we still have power in these damn stories. But, I'd like you all to try one of these first."

Ranjani's eyes widened and she pressed her hand to her chest, where the key lay under her tunic.

Maia crept over to the box, which came up to her chest, and looked at the neat stacks of square cookies inside, as big as paving stones. She doubted she could even lift one. "They're beautiful," she said. "And they smell amazing."

"They're gifts," Abony said, "or rather, the spell baked into them is a gift. That's how Chantal explained it, and how I experienced it."

"I think we could all use a gift right now," Maia said. "I'll try one, but can someone get it for me?"

Simon lifted out one of the gingerbread tiles and broke off a corner for her. Maia cupped it in both hands. It smelled so strongly of molasses that it reminded her of dark rum and she had a flash of a college party, a drink sweating in her hands—cupped just like this—while a dark-haired boy laughed down at her and splashed Captain Morgan into her cup.

She took a bite and sank into the memory.

"Christ," Maia said when she swallowed. She was pretty sure several minutes had passed. "A gift, she called that?"

"The gift of a specific positive memory," Abony said.

"Well, it worked for me."

Abony's grin was tinged with relief. "I told you. And yet, you don't *need* another bite, right? You don't suddenly crave it."

Maia shook her head. She felt flushed and shaky, the way she had that night, the way you do when you've been making out with someone who turns you on so much you want to practically crawl inside of them.

She didn't look at Simon as she deposited the crumbs on her plate and wiped her hands on her skirt. What had *he* remembered with a rush of overwhelming sensory pleasure? Or had he even eaten his cookie? Knowing Simon, it was entirely possible he'd only pretended to try it.

Ranjani, who had initially taken the barest nibble of her gingerbread square, ate the rest in quick eager bites. Her eyes filled and overflowed.

"You okay, Rani?" Abony asked.

Ranjani smiled through her tears. "Baskin-Robbins."

"The ice-cream chain?" Jo asked. "Are they even still around?"

"I have no idea," Ranjani said. "It was a memory, like Abony said it would be."

She leaned in, clearly eager to tell them the story.

"I was six when we moved here from India. My mother had a surgical fellowship and my father had a job lined up, but there were issues with his visa and while he waited for it to come through he drove a cab. He'd pick me up from school and we'd go get ice cream, which my mother disapproved of—she disapproved of all American junk food. My father never went against her on anything else, but almost every weekday for months he'd take me to Baskin-Robbins and get me a single scoop, a different flavor each time so I could try them all. Just now… it wasn't even that I could taste the ice cream. I could smell the cab, hear my father laughing. I could feel his arm—he'd fling it across my chest if he had to brake suddenly. And he'd put his hand on my head afterwards, ask if all my thoughts were still safe inside my brain."

She dabbed at her eyes, dried her fingers on the hem of her tunic. "He died of a heart attack when I was in high school."

"I'm sorry," Abony murmured.

Ranjani shook her head vehemently. "Don't be!"

Jo set the remainder of her gingerbread on the edge of her plate.

"Sounds like Chantal's gift works for everyone," she said. "Not sure I needed that particular memory right now, but..." she twitched her shoulders, "it didn't feel evil. I don't have the impulse to spit up a toad now or anything."

"For which I am personally grateful," Maia said. She wondered what Jo's memory had been, and whether she too had remembered something—or someone—she'd since lost.

"What about that thing?" Jo asked, nodding at the candy apple that Abony had placed in the middle of the table.

Maia crossed to it and set her hands on the cellophane, pressing a section flat across the rounded curve of the fruit. The poured candy coating gleamed like chrome and the smell—of apple juice, honey, and something almost savory, like woodsmoke— was overpowering from up close.

"You want me to get a knife and a cutting board?" Simon asked.

He was eyeing the apple dubiously. Maia didn't blame him. She wasn't sure even their big carving knife was up for tackling that apple.

"I didn't try a piece of apple at the store," Abony said. "I can't tell you how it works. Ebonie said—and I quote—*It'll make you more yourself.* And also apparently bring us all together somehow."

"Well that's not cryptic or anything," Maia said.

She reached above her head to tug at the ribbon around the apple, then stopped at the sudden discordant beeping of twin alarms from both her computer and Simon's.

"What the hell?" Jo asked.

Maia rushed over to her computer.

"I've only got the first alarm set, remember?" Simon said, swinging onto his stool and sliding in to see Maia's screen over her shoulder. "You've got them sequenced on yours."

Maia heaved her mouse over to him. "Here, you drive. I'm too slow."

Simon clicked rapidly through the results of the alerts they'd set, while Maia stared at the screen in mounting unease. It could be nothing but...

"Did we get the timing wrong?" Simon asked. He clearly saw the same thing she did. "I thought there wasn't another Board meeting until the first week in October."

"There's not," Abony said from behind them. "Can you tell us what's going on, please? Does this have to do with the CEO?"

Maia turned around.

"So remember I told you we set up a bunch of alerts attached to employees at the company? Well, two different ones just went off for the same person, which is why our system alarms went off."

Jo had gone white but clearly didn't dare say anything.

Ranjani pressed her fist to her mouth as if stuffing back a scream.

"He's assaulted someone else?" Abony asked. "Do you have a name?"

"Yes," Simon said, still focused on Maia's screen. "At four p.m. and again at four-thirty, we have two 911 hang-ups from the same cell phone, belonging to a woman named Renee Peterson. Then at six-thirty we have an ER admit for the same woman." He clicked to one more screen. "Looks like she checked in with the ER front desk but then walked out."

Ranjani dropped her hand. "So she could be okay?"

"She could be okay," Maia said. "And, guys—seriously—this could be unconnected. We're flagging patterns, is all. Remember the sister in labor. For all we know, Renee Peterson got a migraine, and when her phone kept dropping her calls, she hailed a cab and went over to the ER herself."

"And then she saw there was a really long wait, so she left," Simon added. "It's possible."

"Renee is in webinar development," Abony said. "I remember the name because a pipe burst in her apartment a few months ago and we got her corporate housing while they fixed it."

"Okay, and I know you're saying it could be nothing," Ranjani said, "but it could also be that he did something to her."

"And if there's no Board meeting until October, then why?" Jo asked. "The obvious answer is because Abony went to see Chantal, which we know he's aware of. It means that if he assaulted this woman—"

It's our fault.

No one finished the sentence aloud.

"It's not how he works, though!" Maia burst out. "I mean, between what we'd already figured out and what Chantal told us about how a sorcerer works, doing this to—what? Punish us for daring to find each other?—isn't getting him anything."

"Isn't it?" Ranjani asked, her voice shaking. "If he's doing it to scare us, it's working."

"He did try to scare Chantal," Abony acknowledged, "but he knew she was a witch. I can see him being angry that I went to see her, but beyond that—I don't know. And assuming he *has* done something to Renee Peterson, how could he even be sure we'd find out and understand that it was a message to us? The threat to Chantal was immediate and blatant."

"That's what I'm getting at," Maia said impatiently. "We should stick to what we know about him and the way he works. If he gets power from assaulting a woman and then cursing her, what did he need it for *now, today*?"

"Shit," Simon said quietly. He'd gone back to his own computer to run a different search so they could do nothing but wait, staring at his hunched back, until he swiveled to look at them.

"*Forbes* magazine just tweeted out this morning that they're adding a 'Five Under Fifty' category to their annual list of the top CEOs in America," he said. "It could be unrelated but—"

"It's absolutely related," Abony said bitterly. "He's forty-eight. And the timing is perfect. I mean, to make the very first iteration of a new *Forbes* list—"

"It's exactly the kind of thing he would want power for, to make absolutely sure his name was on that list," Maia said. "We did not do this! *He* did this."

"If in fact he did anything," Abony said. "We're still not sure. But we can find out. Simon, what's Renee's number?"

She typed it into her phone as he read it off, then stood up. "Let me make this call from the other room," she said, "just so you all can keep talking."

"What are you going to say?" Maia demanded. "I mean, if she even picks up, what's your story for why the head of HR is calling her at—" she glanced at her computer screen— "eight on a Friday night?"

"We've asked the insurance company to let us know when an employee makes an ER visit," Abony said without hesitation. "It's complete bullshit, you understand, and would be a HIPAA violation if we actually did that, but if she's in crisis, she's not going to realize that or care."

"Maybe not," Jo said. "I agree that we have to find out if Renee's okay. And if—" a pause to make sure the words would come— "if we can help her. But—" she hesitated again, but this time her throat didn't clench like she was swallowing things back— "Abony, you could get in trouble for this call. If nothing happened to her, or even if she's so scared that she pushes back—"

"Oh, I could get fired," Abony said. "No way around it."

"Oh no!" Ranjani cried. "But, Abony—"

Abony put up a long-fingered hand and hit the call button on her phone. "I got this."

She stalked out of the room and Maia drew in a steadying breath.

"There's probably still ways we can find out what happened if she doesn't get anywhere," Simon ventured.

It was Ranjani who said, softly but firmly, "She needs to do this though. For herself."

Maia and Jo both nodded, then Jo leaned across the table towards Ranjani's plate.

"Can I take this?"

"Oh, right!" Ranjani jumped to her feet and, seeing that Jo was already stacking dirty plates, started closing the takeout containers.

"I can do that," Simon protested.

"We need to *do* something," Jo said. "This is easy." She slanted him a glance. "But we won't take stuff into the kitchen if you'd rather we not."

"No, it's fine," Simon said. "I did dishes this morning. Here—" he got up and held out his hands for some of Ranjani's boxes— "I'll show you where to put stuff."

But of course it was a matter of only a few minutes to remove the detritus of their meal from the table and then they were all back again, hearing the murmur of Abony's voice from the living room. Jo refilled everyone's water glass and gulped down her own. She eyed Maia's cup.

"Do you want more?"

"I'm good," Maia said. "Unless we're switching to tequila?"

Jo grinned. "Why am I not surprised that you're a tequila drinker?"

"When this is over," Maia said, "I've got a bottle of *extremely* good añejo we can break into to celebrate."

Ranjani made a choked sound of protest. "When this is over?" she asked. "You really believe it *will* be over? That we'll find a way to get free of this—of him?"

Abony appeared in the doorway.

"We have to find a way," she said grimly.

She didn't take her seat again, just picked up her own water glass and drained it, then set it down again. No one else spoke.

"I didn't talk to Renee," Abony said. "Her sister answered her cell phone. She's a college student at Georgetown and she and Renee apparently share the apartment. I'm heading over there now to talk to her. She's just a kid and she's practically hysterical. Their parents are flying in tomorrow, but this is a situation where I can absolutely legitimately step in and activate emergency medical leave, smooth the path with insurance, that sort of thing."

She leaned down for her tote bag and slung it over her shoulder.

"And in case you're wondering," she said, "he didn't bother searching for an obscure fairy tale this time. Renee Peterson just can't stay awake."

Jo made a sound that might have been the start to a word, then clapped her hand over her mouth and visibly tried to keep from retching, her eyes watering and her face flushed.

"Si, pick me up," Maia gasped. She clambered up onto his proffered palm, her mike dangling.

"Jo," Abony said, "you're going to choke to death. Let it out."

"I've got Maia," Simon said, while Ranjani jumped up from her seat and backed across the room.

They were just in time. Simon had closed the one hand around Maia and cupped the other on top, but the microphone wire threaded between his forefinger and thumb had forced a gap. Maia crouched down to peer through and saw first a slender forked tongue and then the entire golden-brown head of a snake thrust insistently between Jo's fingers. Jo dropped her hand and coughed violently around the length of the thing as it slithered out of her mouth and onto the table, where it lifted its head and flicked its tongue out again, tasting the air.

"Jesus," Simon said. "Is that thing poisonous?"

"It might be," Jo croaked, "but it won't hurt me."

She picked up the snake in one hand and took it into the kitchen. A moment later they all heard the thunk that Maia recognized as a carving knife hitting their cutting board, then Jo reappeared, swaying slightly.

"It's in the garbage can and I tied up the bag," she said.

"You couldn't have just not said anything?" Simon half-shouted.

His hands were shaking, making it hard for Maia to stand up. She pounded on the fleshy part of his palm with both hands— "Si, I can't breathe in here, come on"—until he reluctantly lowered her back to the table.

"I'm sorry," Jo managed. "You'd think I'd be able to keep it in by now."

"That's exactly what he wants," Maia said. "Not just that you can't say anything about what he's done or how horrible he is, but that you don't even *want* to anymore."

"And you have to want to call him out, tell people what he's done to you," Abony said. "We can all acknowledge that it's not smart to do it right now, but if we actually stop wanting

188 | ANN CLAYCOMB

to?" She shook her head in a single violent gesture of negation. "He just assaulted and cursed another woman," she said, "just so that he can get his name in a goddamn magazine. Now, I'm going to go over there and see what I can do to help her and her family."

"Wait, what about the apple?" Maia asked. "Should we cut into it first?"

"And what about what Chantal said?" Jo put in. "We were going to try to brainstorm things we could all do."

"So we do that on our own this weekend," Abony said.

"And you'll tell us what you find out about Renee?" Ranjani asked. "So we know how we can help her?"

"I will. As for the apple…" Abony eyed it speculatively. "The way Chantal and Ebonie talked about it, it sounded like something we shouldn't rush."

"I can't stomach anything right now," Jo said. "Sorry. I don't mind if the rest of you try it, but—" she made a face— "I'd really rather not."

"Are you headed to the Metro?" Abony asked her.

Jo nodded. "I've run enough for one night."

"I'll walk with you."

Maia cast one more look at the apple. She had to admit that it looked serene and impervious to the crisis swirling around it, as though it was prepared to wait for them until they were ready to taste it. She started to say as much out loud, but by the time she turned back, Abony and Jo were halfway out the door, Simon had disappeared into the kitchen—probably to make sure the snake was really dead, and Ranjani was shouldering her purse.

"I have to go too," she said. "I told Amit I was coming back to the office for a work emergency and that I'd be home before my mother went to bed."

"Rani," Maia said, "you have to tell him."

She knew even as she said the words that though she meant them, she was also feeling so helpless that she wanted to scream.

Ranjani's braid had slipped forward when she reached for her purse. She pushed it back over her shoulder.

"I don't know how," she said. "It will hurt him so much. And it's been so long since it happened… I don't know how to even start."

"Find a way," Maia said. "You know I don't know how to tiptoe around things. And do you really think he hasn't noticed that something is wrong, really, horribly wrong?"

"There was already something wrong before this happened, though," Ranjani said miserably. "Nothing's been right since my mother got her diagnosis."

"Oh, Rani." Maia sat down on the table. She really did suck at anything but the bluntest advice.

"You're in that together, aren't you? Can you imagine trying to take care of your mom and having Amit not helping, just ignoring what was going on?"

"He would never—"

"And what if something horrible had happened to him? Would you want him shielding you from it and trying to bear it alone?"

"Of course not!"

"So let him help you with this, Rani," Maia said, gently as she could. "Tell him."

"You're really bossy, you know that, right?"

"Yep."

"It's been really good to see you again, though," Ranjani added, her eyes filling. "I missed you."

Then she turned and darted out the door, leaving Maia blinking back tears herself—and aware that Ranjani hadn't promised to even think about telling her husband what the CEO had done to her.

"You're being really hard on her, you know," Simon said, coming back into the dining room.

"She needs to tell him."

Simon sat down at his workstation, his back to her, and began shutting things down for the night.

"If what he'd done to you hadn't been so obvious, I don't think you would have told me," he said. "I think you would have been so angry that you would have wanted me to figure it out on my own and then when I didn't, you would have just left."

Maia stiffened in surprise. "You think I would have *left* you?"

"It's okay," he said. "Because you did tell me. And that makes me feel like shit because it sounds like I'm glad you *had* to tell me, that what that asshole did to you was so obvious."

"I know that's not what you mean," Maia said. "Si, can you turn around, please?"

Simon turned around. His eyes were full of so much tenderness when he looked at her that Maia felt like a bitch for noticing that he looked awful, pale and greasy.

"The thing you're not considering with Rani is that she's probably also scared Amit won't believe her," Simon said. "You've got to remember that for us, there wasn't any question of me not believing you or walking out on you."

"Any more than I would have walked out on you," Maia said. "I love you, Si."

He smiled. "I love you too. And I really, really need a shower. You okay here?"

"I'm fine," Maia said. "Take your time."

She stayed where she was for a long time after Simon left the room, pulling in her focus to try to stop feeling small for a few minutes. When she lifted her eyes from her feet, she saw a crumb of gingerbread tile that hadn't been picked up when the others had cleared the table.

It hadn't been addictive. She hadn't felt, when she finished eating it, that she *needed* another taste. But it had been a gift, and one she hadn't savored earlier because she'd been in the room with all the others.

Maia picked up the crumb, which was the size of a jumbo muffin in her hand. She breathed in the scent of molasses that reminded her of dark rum and it happened again before she'd even put the cookie in her mouth: the flash of a college party, a drink sweating in her hands, while a dark-haired boy laughed down at her and splashed Captain Morgan into her cup.

She took a bite.

The dark-haired boy's name was Owen and he had crashed the party by literally scaling the building with his rock-climbing gear and flinging himself over the windowsill. He was all angles and limbs, sweaty and smelling of dirt and metal, and he carried his own drink supplies: Captain Morgan and Dr. Pepper. It was disgusting in the cup but delicious straight from his mouth, tempered by heat and the friction of his tongue against hers.

"You taste amazing," he whispered when they came up for air. "What the hell do you taste like?"

"You're just drunk," she whispered back, kissing from his mouth to his chin and then down his neck to the warm hollow of his throat.

"I'm not though," he said. "I'm not drunk. It's you."

Maia swallowed and drank the last of the water in her cup. When Simon came downstairs, smelling of soap and toothpaste, she climbed gratefully into his proffered hands. He carried her to the bathroom and helped her get cleaned up before bed. They hadn't figured out a toothbrush solution, so Maia just swished with mouthwash several times a day and hoped for the best.

As she rinsed away the taste of gingerbread, she decided that it had been a gift, that memory. For most of their relationship, Simon hadn't looked at her with the kind of wonder that boy had, as though he couldn't believe his luck. Now he did, every day.

Fairy Tales Forever Discord Channel

*We are an inclusive community; we celebrate all voices and identities. Expressions of hate, bias, or general assholery (yes, we know it's not a word) will not be tolerated. For full channel rules and guidelines click **here**.*

Discussion Boards: Fairy Tale of the Day |
Question of the Day | Fairy Tales for Our Time

Question of the Day: Where can I find a fairy to help me sleep for a hundred years—or even just a week?
submitted by renfestmom (member since 2017)

AngelaC: I'm guessing this is kind of a joke question?

renfestmom: No, I really want to know what people think about this. I'm a mom of four who hasn't slept more than six hours a night in I DO NOT REMEMBER HOW LONG. But seriously, reading "Sleeping Beauty" right now feels like wish fulfillment for me.

Natalie: There are those spas in Sweden? Switzerland? where they'll just give you meds so you sleep for like days and then you wake up feeling refreshed. Those might be a myth, but I can see the fantasy. I don't even have kids and I crave more sleep all the time. It's because we have no work-life boundaries anymore.

Eden: And the fairy who casts the sleep-for-a-hundred years spell is a GOOD fairy, remember? Because the original spell was a curse that the princess would prick her finger and die instantly. So sleeping is clearly the better alternative.

AngelaC: But for a hundred years?

Eden: That's why I like the versions where everyone else in the castle falls asleep too, so that when the princess wakes up she's not alone trying to adjust. Everyone she knows is there too.

bellerules: I think we do have a different attitude towards sleep now that we are all so sleep-deprived? I mean—and @renfestmom, you probably know this—I read a study recently that when you have a baby, by the time the baby is six months old, the average mom is two months behind on sleep. That's insane.

renfestmom: It makes you feel insane, that's for sure.

badassvp: Chiming in late because I agree about the fantasy of sleeping as much as you want, but that's not what happens in "Sleeping Beauty." She doesn't WANT to go to sleep, the fairy PUTS her to sleep.

DrHarleyQ: Which is what we say we're doing to our pets when we euthanize them.

<click to see more comments>

AUGUST 10: ABONY

Renee lived in a garden apartment complex just across the river. When Abony knocked, a dog began barking immediately. A woman's voice followed, shushing the dog without rancor, and the door opened on a blonde girl in a t-shirt and shorts, her hair in a messy ponytail and one hand tucked into the collar of a golden retriever who really, really wanted to say hello.

"Penny?" Abony held out her hand. "I'm Abony LePrince, from Renee's office. We spoke on the phone a little while ago."

"Oh my gosh, you actually came over." The girl opened the door wider. "I hope you're okay with dogs. I can lock her up but then she just cries."

"I'm fine with dogs," Abony said, which was the girl's cue to let go of this one's collar. The dog ushered Abony into the apartment with joyful thumps of her plumed tail, then sat down and gazed worshipfully at her.

Penny, for her part, seemed not to know what to do once Abony was actually inside. They stood together awkwardly on the square of wood floor that delineated the foyer, beyond which stretched a carpeted open-concept space. There was a TV on the far wall playing HGTV on mute to a sectional sofa with its back to the door.

"You okay?" Abony asked.

"I'm okay, yeah. My mom and dad will be here tomorrow."

"And how's your sister?"

"She's still asleep." The girl scrubbed both hands over her face. "Sorry, I really don't know why I'm so freaked out. It's just—here, sorry, come on in."

She led the way into the living room and clicked off the TV. The dog trotted along beside Abony, then jumped up and wriggled into a non-existent space between the back of the sofa and the back of the young woman who lay on her side, so deeply asleep it was impossible to imagine her eyes opening. She was breathing in little sips, her lips parted, strawberry-blonde hair fanning out behind her head and her cheek pillowed on her hand.

"Stupid dog," Penny said, her voice catching. "She keeps trying to wake Renee up, but she doesn't even stir."

"She won't wake up at *all*?" Abony asked. "I thought she just fell asleep abruptly a couple of times this afternoon, then woke up pretty soon after."

"Yeah," Penny said. "But it was scary. She came home from work early—I don't have any classes on Friday so I was here studying—and I heard her slamming around in the kitchen. She sounded really, really mad. I thought something bad had happened at work so I came out of my room and she was making a phone call. She held up her hand for me to be quiet, but then as soon as the other person picked up, Renee's eyes rolled back and she just pitched over on the floor. Then I could hear that it was a 911 operator on the other end."

The girl drew in a shaky breath. "I thought she'd had a heart attack or something, I don't even know. She woke up after a few minutes and I tried to ask her what was wrong, but she shushed me and called 911 again—and the same thing happened. This time she didn't wake up for a while, which freaked me out. I was about to call my mom and tell her what was going on when Renee opened her eyes. I convinced her we should go to the ER. But after we checked in and she started filling out the forms, she suddenly went 'fuck' under her breath, kind of slammed the clipboard down, and told me we had to leave."

So had Renee guessed by then that she couldn't indicate on the form that she'd been assaulted without falling asleep with the pen in her hand? That made sense, but it was just a theory. Abony looked down at the sleeping woman, who seemed not the least disturbed by their conversation right above her head.

"So we left," Penny said. "She wouldn't really talk to me in the car on the way home, just said she was 'perfectly fine'—" she winced, remembering— "and to please stop bugging her and focus on my driving. But then right as we walked in she got a call-back from 911. They wanted to know if everything was okay, I guess, because she'd called twice and hung up. Renee opened her mouth to say something and—just like that—she was asleep again. She was in the kitchen and she almost hit her head on the counter that time. I managed to get her onto the sofa and I put a blanket on her." She looked down at her sleeping sister. "I'm sure she'll wake up soon."

Abony felt sick with rage. "I'm sure she will," she said. "Meanwhile, I'll go ahead and put Renee on medical leave effective immediately. That way she doesn't have to worry about coming back to work until she feels better and you all have figured out what's going on."

"It could be narcolepsy, right?" Penny asked. "I mean, I've obviously heard of that. I don't know what else would make her just fall asleep like this, like out of nowhere."

"Why don't you wait to see how Renee feels when she wakes up?" Abony said. She looked closely at the girl, who was weaving on her feet. "And why don't you go make yourself something to eat, take a minute? I can sit here. I want to leave Renee my contact info anyway."

Penny stared at her. "Eat?"

"Or just go to the bathroom and splash water on your face," Abony suggested. "You've had a long evening."

"I—sure." The girl blinked. "Thanks. I'll—I'll be right back."

Penny disappeared down the hall and a moment later Abony heard water running. She sat down in the chair beside the sofa and watched Renee sleep, feeling at once like she was intruding on the other woman's privacy and bearing witness to what the CEO had done to her. Renee was wearing a pale green linen shift dress and a thin gold chain spilled sideways across her neck, whatever pendant was at the end of it trapped under her hair. She looked like a princess in a tower, like she could sleep for a hundred years, easily. The golden retriever had dropped its head to rest in the hollow between Renee's rib cage and hip, but its enormous brown eyes were fixed mournfully on Abony.

"We're trying," she told the dog. "We're trying to stop him."

Renee was going to wake up, surely. This must be a curse that worked the way Abony's did: you try to report, you're Sleeping Beauty. You stop trying to report, you're fine. He wouldn't just leave a woman like this indefinitely—but then again why not, if it got him the power he needed? Unlike Emily Sato, Renee hadn't even had time to tell anyone she'd been assaulted before she'd started falling asleep without warning.

Abony dug in her bag for a business card and a pen, turned the card over, and wrote a note on the back: *You're not alone— and it wasn't your fault. Call me whenever you need to.* That sounded generic enough that if Renee's family read it, they wouldn't read too much into it, not unless she was awake to tell them what had happened to her. Abony put the card on the coffee table, then stood as Penny burst breathlessly back into the room.

"She's still asleep, she's fine, nothing's happened."

"Thanks! Jeez—thank you." The girl had washed her face and brushed her hair. She looked just as agitated but a bit more alert. "I really did have to go to the bathroom, get a drink. It helped. I didn't even realize."

"Do you have someone else who can come stay with you until your parents get here?" Abony asked.

"Maybe, I mean, I could call a friend to come over. But we'll be fine."

"I left my card," Abony said, "and a note for Renee to call me any time."

"Thank you," Penny said. She bit her lip. "Do you know why she was trying to call 911? I mean, you said you're from HR so I just wondered—did anything happen to her at work? Is there something we should know about?"

Good girl, Abony thought. Aloud she said, "I don't know of anything that happened to Renee at work, no. But you should ask her when she wakes up. And tell her to call me, okay, any time? Maybe even instead of 911."

Penny had been about to open the door for Abony. Now she stopped with her hand on the knob.

"What do you mean, 'instead of 911?' Renee's not—she wouldn't do that unless she needed to, unless something had happened to her. You want me to tell her not to try to report something that happened to her? Because—" Penny set her chin— "it kind of sounds like that was what you said."

Even before she opened her mouth, Abony felt her heart speed up and sweat prickle on the back of her neck. Apparently, even encouraging *another* woman to try to report the CEO was going to trigger her damn curse.

"If Renee believes that she needs to report a crime, then she should do that," she said. "Tell her I'll help her do whatever she needs to."

Once out of the apartment, Abony stopped on the sidewalk and ran a quick search on her phone. There weren't any Louboutins in her size on any of the online sites she had bookmarked, but the Neiman Marcus store at Tysons Corner had two pairs in stock. If she hurried, she could get there before they closed and quell the panicky craving that was just beginning to gibber in her brain.

The good news was that Neiman's was running a sale for cardholders. The bad news was that sale was ridiculous: $100 off every $1000 you spent. Abony tuned out the shoe salesman who wanted her to buy *both* the pairs they had in her size and focused on the shoes on her feet.

They were amazing: gray suede booties that came to her ankles, with four-inch heels, gray patent-leather toes, and decorative silver buttons up the side like old-fashioned Victorian boots. She hated that her appreciation of them was muted by the queasy insistence in her gut that she *had* to buy them, and *right now*. Abony stood up and took a turn, then checked the foot mirror, noting how the matte texture of the suede set off the warm tone of her skin.

"I'll take them," she said.

"Fantastic!" the salesman exclaimed. "That'll get you the $100 off. You sure you don't want to try the other pair too? Remember, when you hit $2000 you'll get that extra $100 off."

"Just run the card, please," Abony said. She slipped the shoes off and nestled them back in their tissue-lined box.

She felt the moment the transaction went through in the easing of the tremors in her hands and the pressure behind her eyes. She handed the shoebox to the salesman to put into a shopping bag, then signed the card slip, letting her eyes skip over the total. A hundred dollars off meant the shoes cost less; it didn't make them affordable.

The store closed at ten on Fridays, and Abony was one of the last customers there. Maybe that was why she noticed the woman in Career Separates, a slight frown of concentration on her face as she held up an unconstructed gray blazer.

At the sight of the woman, Abony felt a rush of dizziness so intense that she worried her withdrawal symptoms were returning. She gripped the bag containing her shoes and rode out the feeling, until on the back end of it she recognized it as not withdrawal but rage. A young woman had just been assaulted and cursed in a way she didn't yet understand, Abony herself had just had to buy a fucking pair of shoes for $950 dollars *on sale*, and this woman was just browsing Neiman Marcus at nearly 10 p.m. on a Friday night like she didn't have a care in the world.

Abony pivoted to push her way through the racks of clothes, feeling reckless and wild in a way she'd never felt in her life. She didn't even care if she triggered her curse again. Hell, what better time to do it? She was just a few yards away from the shoe department and she already knew they had a pair in her size.

"Hello, Suzanne," she said. "Looks like we're both doing some late-night retail therapy."

The General Counsel looked up, startled.

"Hello, Abony," she said. "It looks that way, yes."

"Tell me, do you *have* to buy that blazer? You know, the way I *had* to buy these shoes—" Abony brandished her bag— "because earlier tonight I tried to help someone report a sexual assault? That happen to you too?"

"You tried to help—" Suzanne broke off, wet her lips, and tried again. "I'm so sorry. What's happened? Can I help?"

Abony did a quick inner check for withdrawal symptoms— nope—and then focused on the other woman, noting as she had earlier that week Suzanne's too-long hair, her scuffed flats and lack of make-up or earrings.

"I may need to consult with you, actually," Abony said, "since the assault happened to one of our employees on company property during company time."

Suzanne's face blanched and beads of sweat stood out on her upper lip. She slid the hangers on the nearest rack carefully apart and put back the blazer she'd been holding.

"Have you—or has this individual—reported the assault to the authorities?"

"No," Abony said, and waited.

Suzanne hitched her purse higher on her shoulder, tucked her hair behind her ear, then looked at Abony without meeting her eyes and asked, "Why not?"

But she'd waited a beat too long to ask, too long for the question to be genuine. And while she was visibly tense and unhappy about this conversation, she wasn't surprised.

"It *did* happen to you too," Abony said. "He assaulted you— and you—did you know about me?"

"No," Suzanne said. "I assumed I wasn't the only one, but I didn't know who else."

"You assumed—"

Abony opened her mouth to spit out names, then stopped.

"He's assaulted five women at the company including myself. You make six."

Whatever Suzanne might have been about to say in response was cut off by the loudspeaker announcement in a beautifully modulated female voice that the store was closing and customers should please bring all purchases to the register at this time.

Suzanne sighed. "The Cheesecake Factory is open until one. It'll be loud but that means no one will overhear us. If I'm going to have this conversation, I need a glass of wine."

"I'm sorry," Abony said, "is this *inconveniencing* you? You've been assaulted and cursed—and I'm standing here telling you he's done it to five other women at our company, one of them today—and you're acting like you can't even be bothered to talk about it?"

"Cursed?" Suzanne said, eyebrows raised. "Is that what you call it?"

She visibly shook herself. "Not here. I'll meet you at the restaurant. I need to call my husband and tell him I'll be home later than I thought."

She pulled out her phone and walked off, leaving Abony to follow, still so angry she was nearly panting with it, and even angrier because now she felt like her anger was inappropriate and unfair. Dammit, but she *disliked* that woman.

The Cheesecake Factory was, predictably, a madhouse, but the waits were for parties of six, eight and ten people. As a party of two, they were seated right away, and Suzanne was right; the ambient noise in the restaurant would clearly drown out their conversation. As soon as the server brought water and bread, Suzanne ordered a glass of Merlot and a slice of chocolate cheesecake, no whipped cream. Abony thought about getting a glass of wine herself, but she didn't want anything, and wasn't going to give Suzanne the satisfaction of having forced her to order something just for appearances.

"So," Abony said as soon as the server left, "he must have assaulted you not long after he started."

She'd remembered, walking over here, the unexplained spike, drop, and then second spike in the CEO's power on Maia and Simon's timeline, at three, four, and then five months into his tenure with the company. One of those must have been Suzanne.

"You left your compassionate HR persona at home this evening, I see," Suzanne said.

Her wine and cheesecake arrived. The server had forgotten her request for no whipped cream and so she spent a moment carefully removing the swirl of cream from the top of her piece of cake with the flat of her knife, depositing it on one of their unused bread plates, and then wiping the knife off. Something about the whole ridiculous process made Abony think of Ranjani and her constant pleating or tugging on things. This was the opposite of that—deliberate, focused—but it struck Abony that for someone as controlled and severe as Suzanne, surgically removing an unwanted ingredient from her plate was the equivalent of nervous fidgeting.

"I'm sorry," Abony said, sincerely this time. "When I approached you in the store, I was angry for a lot of reasons. I won't apologize for that—for being angry. But I do apologize for being a bitch to you."

"Would you like a bite?" Suzanne asked politely, gesturing to her cake with her fork.

"I'm good, thanks. Are you okay? Am I right that you've found a way to live with what he did to you?"

"I have," Suzanne said, "obviously." She took a drink of wine, then dug into the cheesecake. "You used the term *curse*," she said, "and you've referred to four other women at the company besides the two of us. I don't know anything about any of this. Can you give me a brief precis so I understand?"

She caught the look on Abony's face just as she was about to put a bite of cake in her mouth and paused with the fork at her lips.

"Please? I'll tell you what happened to me, but it sounds like it will make more sense to both of us if I have your context first."

So Abony narrated everything that Suzanne clearly didn't know, from Emily Sato's death as the likely reason the CEO had moved to their company to the things he'd done to each of them and the explanation from Chantal about curses, sorcerers, and where they drew their power. She didn't offer the other women's names and Suzanne didn't ask for them. She quietly, methodically, ate her entire piece of cheesecake while Abony talked, though at times—when Abony told her about Emily, and about what the CEO had done to Jo—it looked like Suzanne didn't particularly want to put food in her mouth.

"Wow," she said, when Abony had finished. She laid her fork on the side of her empty plate and slid it to the end of the table. "That explains everything. Thank you."

She wiped her mouth on her napkin.

"I assume you're going to tell the other women you're in contact with everything I tell you," she said. "That's fine. Just know that I have no wish to be involved in any of your activities and that if you tell anyone else—besides another impacted party, I mean—what I've told you, I will deny it."

"Impacted party? Really?"

Suzanne shrugged. "It's better than *victim*. Victims are helpless, and I don't think either of us would describe ourselves that way—or any of these other women, from the sound of it."

She reached for her wine, realized that her hand was shaking too badly to pick it up, and glared at Abony as if it was her fault.

"You're guessing that his assault on me explains *one* of the spikes in his power on the timelines you're working from. But if I understand how this all works, I suspect I explain all three of those points: the spike, then the drop, and then the second spike."

"How?" Abony asked. "Especially that drop. What did you do?"

Suzanne laughed, though there was no humor in it. "Don't you remember? I quit."

Suzanne had begun meeting with the CEO in his office weekly as soon as he started in July. There were dozens of company documents that needed to be re-executed with his signature on them, from attestations of financial and legal responsibility to innumerable federal regulatory forms. He waited nearly three months before raping her at the end of September—and waited until she'd gotten all the signatures she needed from him to do it. Afterwards, she zipped up her slacks with clumsy fingers and realized that he'd ripped the button off so they wouldn't close at the top.

I wouldn't try to tell anyone about this, Suzanne, he said, *unless of course you pass it off with a laugh. You've never struck me as having much of a sense of humor, but you'll learn.*

Suzanne went to the police station immediately, but when she opened her mouth to say what happened, she was overcome with hysterical laughter and couldn't speak. She left the building then went back in, but again when she tried to verbalize what the CEO had done to her, she burst into peals of wild, manic laughter that were met with shocked silence from everyone in the lobby. The young man at the desk stood up and leaned forward as if appealing to her, but Suzanne saw him use the movement as an excuse to press the panic button under the counter. She couldn't stop laughing, but she turned and walked out, and when she got to the sidewalk, the laughter drained away on its own.

She tried to report by phone with the same results, so she decided to regroup and find another way. Over those next few weeks, she continued to meet regularly with the CEO, though they were never alone together again. Suzanne brought one of her paralegals to each meeting—her *male* paralegal—whom the CEO acknowledged each time with a hearty handshake and a comment about what a powerhouse Suzanne was, how the company would be sunk without her, they were lucky she hadn't gone the partnership route in some big corporate outfit, blah blah blah.

Not knowing or understanding what the CEO had done to her, Suzanne nonetheless recognized that for the time being he had effectively prevented her from reporting him. That didn't mean she had to continue to work for him though. After a month of trying and failing to report and of meetings in his office at which no one acknowledged that she had been raped in that very room, she called up a law school classmate who had been trying for years to get her to join his firm. She had an offer in hand by the end of the week and submitted her resignation via email, effective immediately.

It was the end of October. Suzanne had enough accrued leave to cover her through the end of the year and she had arranged for a January 1 start date at the law firm. Meanwhile, she planned to spend the next two months with her family, doing such outlandish things as menu-planning for Thanksgiving more than two days in advance, making Christmas cookies with her kids, and going out to dinner with her husband and *not* talking about work. She had not tried to tell him about the rape; she'd assumed that she wouldn't be able to, so what was the point? Now that she was out of the job, she could put the assault in the past and move on.

Except she couldn't.

The CEO had accused Suzanne of not having a sense of humor, and within days of her resignation, she didn't, not anymore. Nothing was funny, or delightful, or silly or amusing or fun. When someone told her a joke, she just nodded. When her husband or a friend shared a can-you-even-believe-it story from work, she assured them that she did believe it. When her kids showed her the turkey-shaped place cards they'd made for the Thanksgiving table, she said they were beautiful and perfect—but she didn't smile as she said it, because she'd forgotten how to smile, and her daughter burst into tears and ran to hide under her bed.

She thinks you're mad at her, Suzanne's husband explained. *It kind of feels like you're mad at all of us—or maybe you're just really unhappy. Are you sure this job change was right for you?* He asked her to find a therapist, consider going on medication. She said she'd think about it, which she did, and rejected the idea. What was she going to do, walk into a therapist's office and laugh until she choked for fifty minutes?

On Thanksgiving night, as they were doing dishes together, her husband suggested that they might need to reconsider the trip to Disney World that they had planned for the week after

Christmas as the big present for the kids. *Or at least postpone it, Suze, until we figure out what's going on with you. Honestly, if we go while you're like this, no one's going to have a good time.*

And the next day, she got a Fed Ex envelope containing an offer, on company letterhead, to return to her job for 20% more than she'd been making, with all direct interactions with the CEO to be delegated to Zach, the paralegal she'd been bringing to meetings. Also enclosed was a note, unsigned and not on letterhead, that read, *Your family must miss your smile. And wouldn't you like to laugh again?* Clipped to it were four all-inclusive meal plan passes for Disney, which they hadn't bought when they'd booked the trip because they were so insanely expensive.

Abony wanted to sweep her arm across the table and dash Suzanne's empty plate to the floor just to hear the crash, even as she recognized the uselessness of her howling rage on the other woman's behalf. Suzanne knew that Abony didn't like her; she'd voiced it directly the last time they'd talked. And the emotionless recounting she'd given of what had happened seemed to dare Abony to respect her or sympathize with her— God forbid both.

"I had forgotten that you resigned last fall," Abony said, "because then I got the directive to rescind the resignation just a few weeks later. That took tremendous guts, Suzanne."

Suzanne's hand was still shaking slightly when she picked up her wine glass, but this time she lifted it and drank anyway.

"It was a stupid thing to do," she said. "I had no idea he could do what he did, but I should have known he'd never let me just walk away."

"He couldn't—it cost him when you left. That's what you're thinking about the pattern, isn't it? That he took a power hit when you quit?"

"Sure, I mean, the timing's right. And then so is the timing for the big power boost he got when I came back."

"Still," Abony pressed—this was going to blow Maia's mind— "there's something we can work with there, don't you see?"

Suzanne nodded at Abony's phone, which she'd silenced and put on the table. "You're buzzing."

The text was long enough that Abony had to scroll to read it all the way through.

"That was the most recent "impacted party's" sister," she said. "The woman he assaulted woke up an hour ago, had something to eat, then tried to go talk to their upstairs neighbor, who works for a rape crisis hotline."

Suzanne drew in a sharp breath. "Is she alright?"

"She's fine. She was on the first step. She's just asleep again." Abony put her phone back down. "At least she's waking up in between episodes."

"And she'll learn to stop trying," Suzanne said. "Then she'll be fine."

"For God's sake, Suzanne! Fine?"

Suzanne finished her wine and checked her own phone.

"I have to get home," she said. "My kids were in bed a while ago but if I'm not home soon, my husband will have turned in too."

"So that's it? He's assaulted seven women *that we know of*, cursed us all in the aftermath, and killed one woman with that curse! You actually got to him once, and now you know you're not alone, you wouldn't be alone the next time you tried."

Suzanne pulled her purse onto her lap, got out her wallet, and took $30 out. She smoothed the bills and tucked them under the base of her wine glass.

"I think that should cover it," she said, then smiled bitterly. "I can afford to overtip these days." She looked at Abony, then at the Neiman bag beside her. "Is that why you didn't order anything, because of the curse? I would have bought you a piece of cheesecake."

"I don't need you to buy me a piece of damn cheesecake," Abony snapped. "I need you to listen to me—"

"Nope, nope, nope." Suzanne's rather limp hair slapped against her cheeks with the force of her denial. "I'm out, Abony. I told you what happened to me and gave you permission to tell the other women—and I won't try to find out who any of them are, by the way, you can reassure them on that point. I don't want to know."

She shouldered her purse, met Abony's furious eyes for a long moment, and then slid out of the seat.

"He almost cost me my family," she said. "He almost cost me my ability to be happy. Keeping quiet about what he did to me is worth having those things back. Your inability to understand or accept that isn't my problem. Have a good weekend."

And she walked out.

On the Metro trip home, Abony wondered what fairy tale the CEO had used on Suzanne. She ran a web search on "fairy tales" and "couldn't laugh" and Google offered her several stories, along with the corrective that they were all about a princess who *wouldn't* laugh, not one who *couldn't*. She shut her eyes for the rest of the ride to her stop, one hand on the bag containing her new $950 shoes, because God knew what she'd do if someone tried to steal them.

Fairy Tales Forever Discord Channel

*We are an inclusive community; we celebrate all voices and identities. Expressions of hate, bias, or general assholery (yes, we know it's not a word) will not be tolerated. For full channel rules and guidelines click **here**.*

Discussion Boards: **Fairy Tale of the Day** | Question of the Day | Fairy Tales for Our Time

Fairy Tale of the Day: "The Princess Who Wouldn't Laugh"
submitted by kathys (member since 2017)

Once upon a time, there was a princess who had everything: beauty, wealth, grace, and her father's love. But she never laughed. The king consulted physicians and wise men, but though they examined her thoroughly, they could find no reason why she shouldn't laugh.

For her part, the princess did not understand why it was so important that she laugh. She was bored with her life at court and wanted to know how the ordinary people of the kingdom lived. One day, she disguised herself, snuck into the town, and stole a pair of sturdy peasant shoes (she herself had only dancing slippers). Unfortunately, she was caught by the city guard and brought back to the palace in disgrace. The king was horrified to learn what she had done but was forced by his own laws to sentence her as a thief to a day in the stocks in the town square.

While the princess endured her punishment, a young man named Jack happened by and asked everyone who the beautiful girl in the stocks was. "Why, it's the princess!" he was told. "The one who has never laughed a day in her life." Jack couldn't believe that a girl so beautiful could have never laughed. He plucked a branch of pussywillow from the side of the road, approached the princess, and used it to tickle the bottom of her foot. The princess screamed for him to stop, and tried to wriggle away from the strange sensation, but of course she was trapped and Jack did not stop. And after a while, though the princess continued to beg Jack to stop, she couldn't stop her own lips from curving up in a smile or her mouth opening wide, and she began to laugh. She laughed and laughed, while Jack tickled her all over, and when she was released from the stocks, they were married.

Throughout their lives together, Jack could always make the princess—later the queen—laugh by tickling her. Whether she *wanted* to laugh or not.

AUGUST 10: RANJANI

The kitchen smelled of onions and cumin and fresh ginger and there were dishes in the sink and spatters of grease around the stove. Ranjani left her purse and the bag of takeout food that clearly wasn't going to be eaten on a chair and went down the hall to what was supposed to be a first-floor master suite. They'd converted it into Shreshthi's rooms when her mother had come to live with them. The door was open and Amit was sitting on the bed, scrolling through his phone. He glanced up when Ranjani slipped into the room.

"She's brushing her teeth," he said. "We tried to wait for you to get home but she was getting tired."

"I'm sorry. I stopped to get you some food. Do you want me to take over?"

Amit shrugged and returned to his phone.

"We ate," he said. "She's been asking for you but she's okay. She got upset about the toothpaste for a minute."

One of the peculiarities of dementia, as Shreshthi's neurologist had explained it, was how the brain forgot things in pieces, so that one night, presented with a toothbrush and a tube of toothpaste, Shreshthi might simply stand and stare. Put the toothpaste on the brush and the brush in her hand and she performed the ablution automatically, brushing each quadrant of her mouth for thirty seconds as if she was on a timer, spitting after each, then rinsing the brush and replacing it in the holder. But hand her the brush again five minutes later and she would stare again, then grow increasingly agitated the longer she stood with it in her hand, knowing that she held something familiar, something she ought to know how to use, but unable to fathom the mystery of its damp bristles. It wasn't for surgery, or for cooking or cleaning, for writing or grooming: what was it for? *What was it for?*

Then the next morning she might wake up and brush her teeth on her own without any hesitation, or any recollection of the angry tears the toothbrush had elicited the night before.

"I'm sorry," Ranjani said again. "I'll get her to bed and then do the dishes."

"Everything okay at the office?" Amit asked, still not looking up from his screen.

Ranjani shrugged, carefully casual. "It's fine, yes. There's a lot of work to do and a new deadline, but it's fine."

"You must have been pretty absorbed," Amit said. He lifted his head finally and the look on his round face reminded Ranjani of a child who has just been scolded and doesn't understand why.

"I called your office," he said. "A couple of times. You didn't answer."

"Why didn't you call my cell?"

"Because you said you were going to the office."

He let that hang long enough for Ranjani to sort it out: that he had been suspicious when she left the house this evening, that he thought she had lied to him about where she'd been and why. *Well, you did,* returned a voice in her head—Maia's voice, all but trumpeting 'I told you so'—*you lied and he caught you and now he thinks the worst.*

"Amit—" Ranjani began, just as he said, trying to sound rough and angry but sounding still like a frightened little boy—

"Do you think I'm stupid?"

"Jaan, no!"

When Amit flinched at the endearment, Ranjani flung herself across the room to put her hands on his shoulders and turn him, rigid and resisting, to face her. "It's not like that; there's no one else, Amit, no one. That's not what's happening."

"Then what is happening?" he cried, and of course at that moment, the water stopped running in the bathroom.

"Ranjani? Is that you?" Her mother didn't wait for an answer but poked her head around the door, her gray-shot black curls disheveled and her robe slipping off one shoulder. "You're home!" Shreshthi's face splintered with joyful surprise, tears on her cheeks and her hands trembling as she reached for her daughter. "I missed you! This young man was taking good care of me—" She shot an almost coquettish look at Amit, a look that she herself would once have snorted at, the look an old woman gave to a powerful man, at once submissive and coercive. "But he kept saying he didn't know when you were coming home, and so I knew it was a secret."

Ranjani wrapped her hands around her mother's, tried to still the tremors in the cold fingers, felt the tensile strength in them even now, a surgeon's hands. But her mother couldn't remember how to brush her teeth.

"I'm home, Mami," she said. "Let's get you to bed, alright? Shall I stay and sing to you?"

When she turned to the bed, Amit was gone. Ranjani pulled back the covers to help Shreshthi lie down, knelt to take the slippers off her mother's feet. The nail on Shreshthi's left big toe was cracked and blackened and there was dried blood flaking under the edge of the nail. Ranjani touched it gently.

"Did you stub your toe, Mami?"

"I dented it," Shreshthi said, and when Ranjani glanced up at her, mystified, she explained impatiently.

"The coconut milk. I dropped the can and dented it. I could hardly get it open afterwards."

Another moment of disorienting contradictions: she must have dropped the can of coconut milk on her toe, but she wasn't connecting the two events, nor did she seem to feel the pain in her toe.

Ranjani swung her mother's feet up into the bed, tucked the covers around her, made sure that the nightlights Amit had plugged in to make a pathway from the bed to the bathroom were all working. She found a playlist of classical music on Shreshthi's phone on the nightstand, then sat down awkwardly on the edge of the bed as a Bach cello concerto began. Shreshthi would be asleep before it was over, had taught herself to fall asleep to this music almost instantaneously when she was a young surgeon and sleep was at a premium. But Ranjani never left the room until Shreshthi had curled up on her side, one hand under her cheek and the other tucked against her breast. Once she was deeply asleep, her face, in the dim bluish light from the phone screen, was the face Ranjani remembered, sharp-featured and hollowed out by intensity and impatience. Her mother's face.

She found Amit washing the dishes, his sleeves rolled up and his back to her. Ranjani stood a moment taking him in, his dress shirt blousing out from his khaki pants because he was so skinny and hated belts, so his pants were always just a little too loose. His thick black hair was too long all over; usually when it started to look like this Ranjani told him she hadn't known she'd married a member of the Beatles. But she couldn't joke with him tonight. Every line of Amit's body spoke of terrible tension, from the angle of his head over the sink and the way he'd planted his feet, to the jerky movements of his ridiculously long arms as he moved dishes from the sink to the drying rack.

"She's asleep," Ranjani said.

Amit nodded.

"I said I'd do that. You've been here all evening."

"I'm almost done," he said, and then, with an audible indrawn breath, "You going to tell me his name?"

Ranjani was across the kitchen before she registered moving, pressed up against him from behind with her arms tight around his waist and her forehead pressed to his spine. "Jaan, I told you, there is no one else! No one! Please—"

He went rigid at her touch, though he didn't shrug her off. He gripped the edge of the sink with soapy hands.

"Rani, you haven't wanted to go out in months, not just the two of us. When I suggest something, even just going out for fucking dinner, you make up some excuse, usually your mom, like I don't know what's going on with her, what we can and can't do. I live here too you know."

"It's not what you think!"

"You jump three feet in the air whenever I touch you, suddenly want the lights off whenever we—you know—and you, you…"

This time he trailed off, but Ranjani knew how that sentence ended, or some version of it: *You don't seem to want me anymore. You don't seem to want sex anymore. You haven't gone down on me in months and the one time I tried to nudge you there you freaked and jerked away.*

"I was with some women from work tonight," she said, and when she felt him draw in an angry breath she squeezed him tighter. "Wait, wait, please, Amit. I'm trying to tell you. I should have told you when it happened—"

"Told me *what* when *what* happened? Jesus, Rani!"

"It's a support group, sort of," she said. "I mean, I guess you could call it that. Of women from work. We were all… assaulted by the same man."

He shook his head like he was trying to dislodge her words from his ears.

"You were… someone did that to you and you didn't tell me?"

Ranjani couldn't get words out around the lump in her throat. She nodded her head against Amit's back.

"How could you not tell me?" he whispered. "What did you think? Did you think I wouldn't be able to handle it?"

"No! I just—every time I thought about telling you I pictured the look on your face and I couldn't. I didn't want to see you hurt like that."

"Rani—" Amit began, but she cut him off in a rush.

"I know, I hurt you anyway because you thought the wrong thing and I'm sorry, Amit, I don't know what to do to fix it!"

Amit released his death grip on the sink and carefully, so carefully, laid his hands over hers.

"Tell me," he said. "Tell me now."

Ranjani felt him adjust his stance so she could rest against him. Then she told him everything from the beginning.

Afterwards, after Amit had pulled away from her halfway through her story and begun to pace, after he'd sunk to the floor in the corner of the kitchen and hid his face behind a thicket of elbows and wrists, after she'd realized he was crying, uneven tearing sobs that he didn't want her to see, Ranjani wormed her way onto his lap and they sat there together, exquisitely uncomfortable but unwilling—both of them, she was sure—to move, because it would have meant untangling their bodies.

Amit wanted to kill the CEO. Ranjani didn't need to hear him whisper that against her hair to know that was why he was crying, nor did she need him to tell her that he was also crying in shock and horror at the strength of his rage. Amit hated being angry. He apologized to other cars on the Beltway when they cut him off, ignored slights at work or at family gatherings so he could avoid feeling angry about them. In five years of marriage, Ranjani remembered *one time* he'd gotten angry with her. As soon as she'd apologized, he'd left the room, only to come back a few minutes later as if nothing had happened. If she'd been able to tease him about this aspect of his temperament she would have asked if he'd rebooted their conversation in those few minutes, the way he rebooted a computer that was giving him an error message.

But she loved that her husband was almost allergic to anger. It was part of his sweetness, part of his calm. Ranjani hugged him tight while he clenched and unclenched his hands against her back, trying not to let her feel his need to hit something, tear something, *hurt* something because of what had been done to her.

"You can't hurt him," she said. "You can't. And it's not that he's so powerful—he is, he is, I'm not denying that," she hurried on, when Amit made a disbelieving sound. "But he's evil, Amit. That's how he can do these things, not just why. *How.* No one would even think of doing the things he does to people—the assaults or the curses afterwards—if they weren't evil."

"I should be able to protect you," Amit said, his voice clogged. "From monsters, from evil, whatever. You and your mother.

I should at least be able to help you *now*." He closed his arms around her. Ranjani nestled closer.

"You can help me with the thing we're going to try, to get free," she said.

"Helping you come up with some power of your own?"

Ranjani made a face. "Yes, but remember, it's about power *within the stories he's trapped us in*—that's how the witch put it—so some kind of fairy-tale symbol, I guess. And that just feels silly, if you think about the Disney versions, which is mostly what I know."

"And it sounds like the stories that he knows are way different," Amit said. "Like, scary and bloody." He held her a long moment in silence, though Ranjani sensed he was thinking. Meanwhile, her arm was falling asleep, trapped between their bodies. She shifted to ease the tingling and her braid slipped over her shoulder to bang against Amit's chest.

"Sorry!"

"You had the extra arm, silly, you had to fix it." Amit gently tucked her braid forward again. "Though if you ever really want to hurt someone, you could probably swing your braid at them and do some damage."

She elbowed him.

"You were thinking about our problem," she said. "Any brilliant insights?"

"What if it's not a *thing*?" he asked. "I mean, maybe you have something to show for it, but what if you have to *do* something symbolically powerful?"

Ranjani sat up, nearly knocking Amit in the chin with her head.

"Jaan, you're a genius."

She clutched her braid a moment, thinking it through in her turn, then had to laugh.

222 | ANN CLAYCOMB

"When I tell the others this, they'll know right away it was you and not me saying we have to *do* something powerful," she said. "I've been resisting doing *anything* for so long."

"You were protecting your mother!" Amit protested.

"Sshh," Ranjani leaned up and kissed him. "Yes, I was. But what you said just now—it's right, I *know* it is. It's what we were missing about what Chantal told us. And it's given me an idea."

She pulled far enough away to see his face.

"It's something I can do, something powerful. And it even has some fairy-tale symbolism, I think. But it's… I don't know what you'll think, jaan."

He was quiet for a long while after she told him.

"I'll miss it," he said finally. "But you'll still be beautiful. Do you think your mother will care?"

"My mother might not even notice," Ranjani said, half-laughing again. "*Your* mother will be horrified."

"My mother will be horrified," Amit confirmed. "She and my grandmother and all my aunties will roll their eyes and sigh over how you were so pretty until you went and did that to yourself. But they'll all be wrong."

"Well, it's not like we're going to India anytime soon," Ranjani said. "I can't even think about how we'd manage that. There are like a hundred new doors between here and there."

"I see where this is going," Amit said. "You're setting yourself up with an excuse not to go visit my relatives."

He poked her in the ribs and Ranjani giggled, a moment that was a small miracle in itself.

"Still," Amit said thoughtfully, "it wouldn't hurt to treat this like a sacrifice. That's what it is for you, for us. Maybe it will make it more powerful."

Ranjani didn't say anything to that, but when they were ready she lit red candles (for protection from evil) on the dressing table in their bedroom and put a red towel around her shoulders before she sat down. She wrapped a hair tie around the top of her braid so that the hair would stay tightly woven even after it was removed, bound on both ends. Then Amit lifted the braid off her neck and began to cut.

Ranjani kept her eyes on the mirror. Her skin was flushed and rosy in the red-tinged candlelight, twin flames glowing in her dark eyes. She looked like she knew what she was doing. Amit wore an expression of meditative intensity, his big hands steady. As the scissors bit through her hair, Ranjani murmured a prayer to Ganesha under her breath. It was one that her mother had taught her when she was little, and which Shreshthi herself used to recite as she washed her hands before every surgery.

Fairy Tales Forever Discord Channel

*We are an inclusive community; we celebrate all voices and identities. Expressions of hate, bias, or general assholery (yes, we know it's not a word) will not be tolerated. For full channel rules and guidelines click **here**.*

Discussion Boards: Fairy Tale of the Day | Question of the Day | **Fairy Tales for Our Time**

Fairy Tales for Our Time: "The Princess Who Cut Her Hair"
submitted by steph (member since 2016)

Once upon a time, my sister got cancer and all her hair started to fall out. What you have to understand about this is that she had the most amazing hair you've ever seen, that thick, shiny brown hair that she could just stick a pencil in without even realizing she was doing it, just wrap, stick, boom, and it would stay in a twist for hours. She had grown it down to her waist in high school and everyone called her Rapunzel, which she did not love, but then she convinced people to shorten it to Rap and that's what her friends called her for the next 20 years.

Then when she was 37 and had two kids, she got breast cancer and chemo made her hair fall out. A bunch of her friends and I talked about all shaving our heads in solidarity, but she didn't want us to and we wanted to respect that. The thing that she didn't say was that it wouldn't have been nearly as meaningful for any of us to shave our heads because we all had varying degrees of perfectly ordinary or even lackluster hair. We couldn't understand what she was losing when her hair fell out, because none of us had ever had that amazing hair. And even though I was her sister, I didn't know what to say to make her feel better.

One day I came over to her house and she was totally bald. Totally. And her scalp was all white and soft-looking. She showed me, then put her baseball cap back. "My skin looks like maggots," she said.

And without even thinking about it, I said back, "You know, Rapunzel's hair never helped her. All it was good for was for her actual jailer, *the person who was keeping her a prisoner*, to get in to see her. I bet she was never happier than when it was all gone." And she just stared at me.

But it was true, really. And even the prince who climbed up—I mean, how consensual was Rapunzel's relationship with him, really? He was literally the only other person she'd ever seen besides the person keeping her prisoner. All I know is that after my sister beat the cancer, she never grew her hair long again. And I'm so proud of her for that.

<click to see comments>

AUGUST 12: JO

"I can't believe you!" Jo sputtered. She negotiated the merge onto the DC Beltway and then shot a furious glance at her passenger. "You slept in my car all night, for God's sake! And what the hell did you tell Dad?"

Her stepmother Jane, who was busy folding up an afghan, looked mildly indignant.

"I did not sleep in your car *all night*," she said. "I slept in my bed until four a.m., which is when I usually wake up to your father's snoring anyway. *Then* I slept in your car."

"You stole my keys!"

Jane snorted. "They were lying on the kitchen counter."

Having tucked the afghan under her feet, she straightened up in her seat, smoothing the wrinkles out of her oversized linen shirt and absently ruffling her short, graying blonde hair. "I picked them up to unlock your car, then put them right back down where I'd found them. That's hardly 'stealing,' Jo. And as for your father, you know perfectly well he's still happily asleep. I told him last night I was going back to DC with you for a couple of days. He'll drive over and pick me up when I'm ready to come home."

"We don't even know what we're doing," Jo said. "I told you that. We're all supposed to spend the weekend brainstorming—"

"Fairy-tale symbols with power," Jane finished. "And as *I've* already told *you*, a wicked stepmother is a very powerful fairy-tale symbol."

"The fact that I used to call you my wicked stepmother just to try to make you mad does not actually make you one."

"Why not?" Jane asked. "You had a long list of the wicked things I did to you. Lima beans, as I recall, featured prominently. And broccoli."

"I was *ten*!"

"I don't know about you, but I could definitely use a Bloody Mary," Jane said. "Isn't there a nice brunch spot not far from your apartment? What's it called? And do they take reservations?"

Jo shook her head. She wondered if Jane understood that snapping and snarling was the only way Jo could keep from bursting into tears of weakness and relief because Jane now knew Jo's whole story and believed her. But that was stupid. Of course Jane understood.

"Pearl Dive Oysters," she said. "That's the place where Dad tried to sprinkle powdered sugar on his beignets and the lid to the shaker fell off."

"That's the one!" Jane crowed. "His plate looked like the Alps. I'll see if they're on Open Table."

Jo's father and Jane lived near Annapolis, just an hour outside the city. Usually they saw each other once a month, but this weekend was the first time Jo had visited since May. That time, she had neglected to mention that while she was with them, Eileen was moving out of the apartment. Unfortunately, Eileen had called Jane on Sunday afternoon to ask her tearfully to please take care of Jo, and Jane had then ruined a perfectly good cribbage game between Jo and her father by coming into the den, saying casually that she'd just gotten off the phone with Eileen, and picking up her book without another word. She didn't say—didn't need to say—that she was immeasurably sad that they'd broken up, that she knew Jo was wrecked but didn't want to talk about it, or that she was there if Jo changed her mind. Jo left an hour later. The problem was that the two of them insisted on knowing her far too well and accepting her exactly as she was—emotionally stifled and everything. Jo felt so goddamned *loved* when she was around them that she hadn't been able to deal. Not when the person she was hadn't been enough for Eileen.

This time she made it through all of Saturday at the house, and even thought she'd gotten away with just picking at Jane's famous chicken with olives, only to be ambushed while she was doing the dishes afterwards. Picking up a towel and plucking a wet pot from Jo's hands, Jane said firmly that she'd sent Jo's father off to bed with a promise to find out what was wrong. Because of course something *was* wrong. Jo was jumpy, exhausted, and far too skinny, which was no wonder, if her appetite at dinner was any indication of how she was eating generally.

"Your dad thinks it's the break-up, which is perfectly understandable," she said. "But—and I don't say this to minimize your heartbreak—I think something really dreadful has happened, and I think you'd better tell me what it is."

"You wouldn't believe me."

"Try me," Jane said.

Jo sighed, grabbed Jane's dishtowel to dry her hands, then went and got her laptop. She let Jane read the account she'd written of what happened to her while she started the dishwasher, then leaned one hip against the sink and waited.

"You want to come over here and sit down?" Jane asked.

"I will," Jo said. "But first you need to understand that I can't talk about it."

"I know—"

"No," Jo said. "You don't. I mean that I literally cannot talk about it." She folded her arms. "You're not going to freak out on me, right?"

Jane looked offended. "When in your life have you ever known me to *freak out*?"

So Jo formed the words to say what the CEO had done to her, gagging several fat cream-colored spiders and a slug into the sink. Jane let out a strangled shriek when the first spider emerged and looked ready to gag herself by the end.

Jo wiped her mouth, ran the faucet then the disposal, and came over to sit across from Jane at the kitchen table.

"So that's what happens when you try to talk about it?" Jane asked faintly. "That's—" she turned back to Jo's screen and murmured aloud what the CEO had said to Jo after he'd raped her: *You won't want to talk about this, Jo. You think you do now, but trust me, you won't.* Then she glared at Jo.

"That's impossible."

"Do you want to hear the rest or not?" Jo asked. "I think that if I just write down the parts I can't say aloud I should be able to tell you everything. I can't promise no more bugs or snakes but I can try."

"There are *snakes*?" Jane caught Jo's raised eyebrows and glared harder. "I am *not* freaking out. Here—and move over." She pushed Jo's computer over to her, then scooted her chair around so she could read anything Jo typed.

Once she knew everything, through a piecemeal combination of verbal and written narrative, Jane announced that she was accompanying Jo back to DC the next day. She didn't bother to vary her argument, just kept restating it while Jo made tea and drank it too hot and at one point even set down her mug and put her hands over her ears like a child.

"Stop it, stop it, I'm not listening to you!"

But, (said Jane—reasonably, calmly, patiently) a real-life, in-the-flesh wicked stepmother was a powerful fairy-tale symbol. No, of course she didn't have a specific idea for how Jo might use her in whatever plan she and her friends formulated. But she was sure they would think of something, and she certainly wasn't going to stay home while Jo confronted her rapist and possibly put herself in immeasurable danger, not if there was any chance that her very presence could be useful.

In the end Jo declared herself too tired to keep arguing and went to bed in her old room. She *was* tired, but she lay half-awake for a long time. They had to figure out what to do next, and soon. Otherwise, Jo knew with absolute certainty that Jane would march into the CEO's office in her favorite walking shoes and order him to remove the curses immediately. When she did fall asleep, she dreamt this very scene, at the end of which the CEO turned into a dragon and blew a gout of flame at Jane, who withstood it without faltering or crying out, but was nonetheless burnt to ash.

After she woke from her nightmare, Jo didn't fall back asleep until dawn, then overslept, foiling her own plan to slip out of the house early Sunday morning. It was nearly nine by the time she ventured downstairs, braced to find Jane waiting for her, and she was briefly relieved to find the kitchen empty. She scribbled a note about needing to catch up on some work in the office that afternoon, snatched up her purse and keys, and went out to her car—only to find her stepmother snuggled down in the passenger seat under an afghan, fast asleep. Looking down at Jane through the car window, cracked open to let in some fresh air, Jo felt a fresh surge of terror. Jane didn't look older or more fragile in her sleep. She looked exactly as capable and unflappable as ever, with a pink line of sunburn across her cheeks and her hair rumpled against the headrest. But she was just a smallish middle-aged woman with a will of iron and what struck Jo now as a dangerous overreliance on the practical, the sensible, the real.

Jane woke up and rolled the window the rest of the way down.

"Well," she said, "shall we get on the road?"

Jo scowled ferociously at her and stalked around the car to slide behind the wheel.

Two hours later, they were sitting on the patio at the Pearl Dive Oyster Palace and Jo was on her second mimosa at Jane's insistence. She'd also polished off a chocolate Belgian waffle and felt deliciously full and sleepy. How long had it been since she'd had this uniquely Sunday-afternoon-after-brunch feeling? Months, certainly, and not just because of the goddamned CEO. She'd stopped going to brunch when Eileen left.

Jane mopped up the last of her eggs Benedict with a crust of bread and took a sip of her coffee.

"So from the looks of her Facebook page, Eileen is having a good time in China," she said. "The furthest I ever took students was to the Smithsonian."

"You know what she's like," Jo said. "She can't get enough of those kids."

"I would also have said she couldn't get enough of you, though," Jane said. "Have you talked to her, Jo?"

"We've texted."

"But she doesn't know what's happened."

"She's been in China."

"She's back this weekend," Jane said.

Jo drained her glass and put it down, nearly tipping it when the base of the flute caught on the rim of her plate.

"I should warn you," she said, "that if you're steering this conversation where I think you're steering it, you're treading over old ground, at least in our little group of four."

"What do you mean?"

"Well, there's some significant disagreement about telling people what's happened to us, and not just because they won't believe us. On the one side is Maia, who told her husband, but I mean, as even she'll admit, she didn't really have a choice. And on the other side is Ranjani, who hasn't told her husband or her mother and turns into a puddle at the very thought."

"You never did have much patience for criers," Jane observed.

"I'm on her side!" Jo snapped. "Why tell someone you love something that will hurt them, that they can't do anything about, and that makes you even harder to be around?"

"So you do still love Eileen."

Check and mate, Jo thought, as her eyes abruptly filled with tears.

"But I could never *tell* her that I loved her, not enough or the way she needed me to, and now look at me. You think spitting out bugs and snakes instead of talking makes me more appealing? I miss her every day, okay? I miss her rubbing my legs—I'm so *sore* all the time—and I miss her cooking and her music. I even miss her talking about her students all the—"

She broke off and clapped her hand to her mouth, gagging convulsively, then turned a face of wild-eyed horror to Jane.

Jane put a hand on the back of Jo's neck. "Let it come, Jo," Jane said. "Let it come out. You have to, or you'll choke."

Jo gave in and spit into her cupped hand.

"And now look! Look! He's poisoned even that. I can't even talk about Eileen without vomiting up something vile!"

Jane leaned in, unfurled Jo's clenched fingers, and smiled slowly.

"Tell me something else you love about Eileen," she said.

Jo looked down at what was in her palm.

"I love her freckles," she said, and felt the slide of something smooth from between her lips, a shining white ball that dropped on her plate with a melodious clink. "Especially the ones that no one knows about but me." Two flower petals drifted down. "I love how she grades papers standing up because she gets so antsy, and how she grades in pink because she thinks red is too mean." She put her hand under her chin and spat a deep blue gemstone into it, teardrop-shaped and as long as her fingernail.

"I'm still able to get the words out," Jo said shakily. "That's different. I can say what I want but these things come out too."

The handful of jewels and flowers in her palm were slick with her saliva, but that only made them sparkle more.

"Do you think they're real?"

"The bugs and snakes are real," Jane said. "Why shouldn't the roses be? Or the sapphire?" She picked up the white sphere and added it to the pile. "Or the pearl?"

"Jesus," Jo said. "I can't imagine he meant for *this* to happen."

"No," Jane agreed. "But didn't you say that this also happens in the story he cursed you with? I wonder if he forgot about that part."

"Maybe." Jo shook her hand so that the jewels tumbled against each other. "I hope so. But then what does it mean that this happened when I started talking about Eileen?"

Jane laughed softly.

"It means something splendidly symbolic and dreadfully cliché," she said. "It means that telling someone all the reasons you love them is a gift, one you've been withholding. My question is, if this—" she nodded her head at the gems Jo was holding— "is how you feel about her, why won't you tell her?"

It had been uncomfortable to choke on jewels and flowers, almost as much as choking on bugs and toads. But now that Jo held these things in her hand she knew that discomfort had never been what stopped her from being more (sigh) *vulnerable* with Eileen. It was the fear that her love—now coalesced into something tangible—might not be valuable enough, might even turn out to be a cheap imitation of the real thing Eileen deserved.

"Can I just not answer right now?" she begged. "Please? I've had two glasses of champagne and more sugar than I usually eat in a week."

"Oh, you don't have to answer *me* at all," Jane said. "I just wanted you to think about it." Then her face clouded. "There is one other thing to consider."

"Which is?"

"What if this sorcerer didn't worry about the possible upside to the way he cursed you—the fact that you might spit out beautiful things when you talked about the woman you love—because he assumed you'd never do it?"

Jane spoke gently—for Jane—but the words still struck like stones. Jo dropped her eyes to her fist.

"The scariest part of that idea is that he could have known that much about me," she said.

She unfurled her fingers, plucked the bruised flowers out, and dropped them into her water glass. Then she put the stones on her napkin and wiped her hand on her skirt.

"Jane," she said slowly, "you are a total pain in the ass. You're bossy and good at everything and totally without vanity and always right. It's really annoying."

"And?" Jane prompted. Her smile threatened to turn into a grin.

"And I love you," Jo said grumpily. "I don't know how I got so damned lucky to have you for a stepmother. You're like my second-favorite person in the whole world, and—" she retched slightly but managed to finish— "I don't know what I would do without you, I really don't—" before she had to cup her hand under her chin.

"Oh, for God's sake," she said when she was finished. "Here."

And she dumped a fragrant petal, as thick and matte as a piece of linen, onto Jane's empty bread plate, along with two black pearls.

"Oh!" Jane exclaimed, visibly startled. Jo felt her heart clench. Did Jane truly not know Jo adored her?

"What?" she said. "No gloating? No 'I knew you were a softie at heart, Jo'?"

Jane shook her head. She was still smiling, but her eyes were brimming.

"Thank you, darling," she said. "I love you too. And I'm going to have these—" she rolled the pearls across the plate with a fingertip— "made into earrings, I think."

She brushed a hand across her eyes. "I'm so proud of you— no, don't make that face at me." She put her hand on Jo's wrist and shook lightly. "He tried to take away your voice, Jo," she said, "and he assumed you'd cooperate. Look what happens when you don't."

Fairy Tales Forever Discord Channel

*We are an inclusive community; we celebrate all voices and identities. Expressions of hate, bias, or general assholery (yes, we know it's not a word) will not be tolerated. For full channel rules and guidelines click **here**.*

Discussion Boards: Fairy Tale of the Day |
Question of the Day | Fairy Tales for Our Time

Question of the Day: Why are stepmothers in fairy tales always monsters?
submitted by Eden (member since 2017)

Eden: So I raised this in the conversation about why witches in fairy tales are always evil (see that one here) and @Angelofthehouse suggested that this would make a good separate thread. I hope people don't feel like it's repetitive. I get that a lot of stepmothers in these stories are ALSO wicked witches, but even the ones who aren't witches are still awful. Like Hansel and Gretel where the stepmother convinces her husband to take the kids out to the woods to starve. I mean—come on! I pack my stepkids lunch every damn day (and they still sometimes treat me like crap, tbh. Ask me if I've ever heard, "you're not even my real mom.")

Angelofthehouse: @Eden I am so glad you raised this one separately. It is a different question. Like I think I said, the reality that's left out is that sometimes widowers who had kids already married again (because they needed someone to take care of said kids!), then the second wives had their own babies. And we can imagine realistic tensions during famine or drought when they might have felt like they had to choose between their stepkids and their own babies. That doesn't make them monsters, though.

Jess: No, it doesn't. What it actually reveals is the point of view in a lot of fairy tales. I mean, they're told in third-person but they're implicitly from the point of view of the young person, the princess or the clever youngest son or whatever. We're not getting the stepmothers' stories. So the message that your stepmother may not have your best interests at heart is all that comes through. That make sense?

Eden: I guess so. And I started to ask why there aren't any stepfathers but then, duh, men didn't die in childbirth back then and of course so many women did. I really can't imagine having to choose between my own (biological) child and my stepkids. It's awful.

JennyK: Hey @Eden, I'm a stepmom too. What's so frustrating is that the "evil stepmother" trope has totally escaped the fairy-tale context. When my husband and I got married, my sister got me a t-shirt that said "I'm the Wicked Stepmother" and expected me to think it was hilarious!

steph: Wow, that's crazy. FWIW, my stepmom totally raised me. My mom died when I was little and then my dad died when I was 12. So literally she wasn't even my blood relation, but she was the absolute best. I don't call her my stepmother either. She's just my mom.

Eden: Thanks for that, @steph! I hope my (step)kids feel that way someday.

Angelofthehouse: Well, and sorry to get Freudian here, but the other way to read the "wicked stepmother" figure is that she's the mom you start to be angry at all the time when you're a teenager, and the "real mother" is the mom you remember loving when you were a little kid. I guess when you're an angsty teenager mad at your mom, you feel validated by stories in which (step)mothers treat their daughters like slaves or want to eat their hearts out. Literally.

<click for more comments>

AUGUST 12: MAIA

Maia and Simon spent the weekend puzzling over ways to show the CEO that Maia had power over the Thumbelina story—or was it *in* the Thumbelina story? Or *as* Thumbelina?

The semantics didn't help.

By Sunday afternoon, they were both punchy and irritable, and Maia had read way too many versions of the story, most of which seemed determined to turn "Thumbelina" into a children's cartoon that would have crossover episodes with *My Little Pony.*

"It doesn't matter how we interpret this. Thumbelina doesn't have anything like power," Maia said. "She puts a blanket on a fucking dead bird. That is the entire extent of her agency in the story."

"I'm not letting your witch off the hook, though," Simon said, "no matter how good her gingerbread is. Do you think all real-life magic users are as committed to unhelpful advice as the fictional ones are? Do they teach it as part of their training, like, *When you see someone under a horrible curse, be sure to only offer suggestions in vague, portentous language?*"

"One ring to rule them all, one ring to bind them..." Maia muttered, rubbing her eyes.

They had just scuttled their latest idea of making Maia wings on the 3-D printer, since Thumbelina gets wings at the end of the story. The design challenges involved revealed the fatal flaw in this one: since there was no way to make the wings functional, they'd just be a fairy-tale prop, which was exactly what Maia was trying to avoid.

"Forget it, Si," she said, leaning on his wrist and looking up at the image of lavender filigreed wings slowly spinning on his screen. "But, you know, save the file. If we don't figure this out, I can go as Thumbelina, Queen of the Fairies, for fucking Halloween."

"Maia—"

"I'm just hungry," she said. "I have a headache. I think everyone is expecting us to order food again. What about Lebanese this time?"

The other women were due to arrive soon. Maybe one of them had come up with something. Maia had Simon unlock the front door, then sent him up to take a shower while she ordered the food. When the doorbell rang, she texted all three women: *It's open come on in.*

Jo was the first to arrive again, but not sweaty and disheveled this time. In fact, Maia thought she looked better—less bony somehow, though it had only been a couple of days. Then Ranjani showed up as Simon was coming downstairs and stunned them all into silence with her haircut. She still looked beautiful, of course. Now that it was shorter, her thick, glossy black hair turned out to have a slight wave that made it ripple around her face. She too seemed better: lighter and less frightened, though she kept putting a hand up to the back of her neck as though shocked to feel it exposed to the air.

But there was no time to ask Ranjani about her hair because Abony came in looking blotchy and haggard.

"I ran into the delivery driver on your steps," she said, holding up two bags, then nearly dropped them when she caught sight of Ranjani. "Rani, holy shit. Wow."

Ranjani touched her neck again.

"Does it look okay?"

"It looks gorgeous," Abony said. "But—"

She pressed her lips together, strode into the dining room, and put the bags on the table.

"I've got stuff to tell you," she said, "before we ask why you cut your hair, Rani. Honestly, before we talk about anything else, I need to tell you what I found out on Friday night."

"At Renee's apartment?" Jo asked. "And should we eat while you tell us or wait?"

Abony looked like she was already exhausted by what she had to say.

"Let's eat," she said. "You may not want to when I'm done."

So Simon put several grains of seasoned rice, a scrap of grape leaf, and a shred of lamb on Maia's plate and Abony told them about her visit to Renee Peterson's apartment and her ongoing text conversation with Renee's sister. Based on Renee's own behavior when she was awake, it seemed almost certain that the CEO had assaulted Renee on Friday and then cursed her to fall asleep every time she tried to report him. The fact that they had already figured out the basic outline didn't make the story any less horrible. They hadn't known the details, like how suddenly sleep hit Renee or how often she'd tried to report anyway, with what sounded like the same combination of denial and determination that had driven Abony.

Then Abony told them about Suzanne.

Maia pushed her plate away. She knew a certain grim

satisfaction at having all the puzzle pieces fit into place; they now had a specific woman matched to every data point on the timeline they'd constructed around the CEO. But it was hardly a triumph. Mostly what she felt was a hopelessness that absolutely negated action, including chewing and swallowing.

"God," Jo said, putting down her own plate, "I don't know about you all but I'm so *tired* of being angry."

"I feel that," Abony said. "I've been sitting with this shit all weekend and I wish I could tell you I feel better now than I did Friday, but I don't. I thought about not telling you all."

"Fuck that," Maia said, but without heat. "You had to tell us. You couldn't sit with that alone."

Abony shrugged. "I could have," she said. "Suzanne did, all this time."

"Fuck," Maia said again, which seemed to sum everything up, because for a long time no one said anything.

Hugging her knees in the middle of the dining-room table, Maia shut her eyes to block out the other women's overwhelming physicality: their slumped shoulders, empty hands, even Ranjani's poor tender neck. Having them here with her had felt powerful just a few days ago, but now they had to acknowledge that in the coming days, Renee *might* call Abony's cell and *might* join them in trying to stop the CEO and break her curse. Or she might decide, as Suzanne had, that whatever her new reality was, she was better off facing it alone rather than trying to fight it with the rest of them.

And what did "fighting" their curses look like anyway? Maia's own last idea had been a goddamn fairy costume.

"We were on fire for a while there," she said without opening her eyes. "There's that."

"What are you talking about?" Abony asked.

"I got to the place where I was tired of being angry months ago," Maia said, "when it was just me and Simon trying to figure things out. Then we all connected and it was like—whoa—this is different. I mean, we didn't just sit around being angry. Abony went to The Gingerbread House. We ate witch cookies, for God's sake. But then we got super-cryptic advice that I don't understand. We've been trying to come up with something all weekend and my brain is mush. That's bad enough. Now finding out for sure about Renee—and about what he did to Suzanne, Jesus—it's like we've just totally flamed out."

"Ashes, ashes," Jo said in bitter singsong. "We all fall down."

"Is that from a fairy tale?" Ranjani asked in a small voice.

"Nah," Maia said. "We're just spouting nonsense now."

Abony's phone blared out what sounded like an emergency alert, and they all jumped.

"Sorry," she said. "It's just an email, but that alarm means it's urgent."

She picked up her phone, jerked back from it as though whatever she saw on the screen might bite, and then looked up, frowning.

Maia clambered to her feet.

"What's wrong? Did he just email you?"

"No," Abony said. "It looks like it's from Chantal, and it bypassed my alert parameters. She wants to know if we're free to do a video call."

Ranjani huddled in her chair. "Right now?"

"How does she know you're together?" Simon rose from his seat and frowned at Maia. "Could she be tracking you all?"

"I don't know how," Maia said. "Abony, what's the exact wording on the message?"

"For what it's worth," Abony said, "this does sound like her.

Gets right to the point: *This is Chantal. I need to talk to you and your friends. Video call?*"

"How do we know it's really her?" Jo asked.

"I don't." Abony put her phone down on the table at Maia's gesture and Maia went and stood over it.

"The email address is the one The Gingerbread House has on their website for special orders," she said. "Obviously that could be hacked, but—I mean if we're thinking the CEO, why would he bother impersonating Chantal? He knows how to get to all of us."

"Using normal work channels or his damn magic," Abony agreed.

"You want to take that chance?" Simon demanded.

"Si, we've got firewalls on top of firewalls," Maia said. "If this is a magical attack, it's a really stupid and inefficient one. And besides, what if it *is* her and she has something else to tell us, something actually useful?"

Simon pushed both hands through his hair and turned his back to her.

"Fine," he said. "It's not my call."

Maia looked up at the other women, resisting the urge to clasp her hands pleadingly. "Let's take the call. If it goes south, we shut everything down and block the bastard."

Abony waited for both Jo and Ranjani to nod assent before replying to the email. Maia went to wake up both of her monitors.

"Abony," she said over her shoulder, "can you forward me the link when Chantal sends it? I'll pull it up here so we can all see."

Ranjani shrieked, Simon cursed and lunged for his own monitor array, and Maia turned back to see that all of the monitors in the room—they had six set up between the two of them—had been taken over by a woman with light brown skin, hazel eyes, and a disgusted expression on her face.

"For God's sake, Abony," the woman said, "when someone gives you a goddamn gift, you're supposed to goddamn accept it."

"What the hell?" Simon tapped rapid-fire at his own keyboard, then lunged to lean over Maia to try hers, nearly knocking her down.

"Sorry!" he said as she braced herself on his knuckles.

He curled one hand around her to protect her from the furious typing and scrolling he was doing with his other hand. "I don't get it. We're not on Zoom. The camera's not even on. I can't figure out what app she's using or how she got in."

The woman on the screens rolled her eyes.

"I'm a witch," she said. "I don't need an app to 'get in.' I asked if you were free for a video call to make sure I had permission to contact you. I'm not in the habit of taking over people's computers without asking. But now that I have—" she sat back from the screen and surveyed them— "it would be helpful if you all scooted in a bit."

She waited, clearly expecting them to oblige her, which they did. Abony and Jo slid their chairs over to flank Ranjani's, while Simon flung up his hands in defeat and rolled his stool over.

"Much better," Chantal said.

"Before you scold me anymore," Abony said coldly, "you should know what's happened, and what we've learned, since I was at your shop on Friday."

She explained briefly about Renee and Suzanne.

The witch listened with her head down, muttering an occasional expletive under her breath. When Abony was done, Chantal looked up and fixed them all with her enormous, green-flecked eyes.

246 | ANN CLAYCOMB

"This man scares me," she said. "He's threatened me once for helping you, Abony probably told you that. And I'm not ashamed of being scared, for myself or for my daughter."

She drew in a breath deep enough to lift her arms where she'd crossed them over her chest.

"Ebonie ran a finding spell on Abony's curse after we closed up on Friday night and found the rest of you—and these two other women as well. It's a level of magic she should *not* have been doing on her own, you understand, but the upshot is that she asked me Saturday morning why I hadn't offered you more help."

Chantal's expression reflected mingled pride and frustration.

"My daughter thinks she's a woman," she said, "while I know she's still a child. But in either case she's witch enough to know something of what this man is doing to women. I won't be complicit to that evil, not if I can help you without putting Ebonie in danger. So here I am."

Maia felt a flicker of what might have been energy. Or hope.

"Thank you," she said carefully. "We'll take anything you have to give."

"Wonderful," Chantal said crisply. "I've got good news, bad news, and—" she shot a look at Abony— "I'll save the rest of my *scolding* for last. The good news is that you've already done something powerful, or at least two of you have."

Maia glanced over her shoulder at the others. Abony looked puzzled, Jo thoughtful. Ranjani was pleating her skirt in her lap.

"I told someone else what happened to me," Jo said.

"So did I," Ranjani said. She met Maia's eyes with a tiny smile. "I told Amit. So you can stop nagging me."

"You also cut your hair," Maia said. She swung back to face the screen. "That's it, isn't it? Rani cutting her hair?"

Chantal inclined her head.

"But why? That story—'Rapunzel'—isn't the one he cursed her with. And it's so obvious. If that was the sort of thing we needed to do, then Abony could—what was it we talked about?"

"Buy a pair of glass slippers and confront him in them," Abony said.

"He'd turn them red-hot and laugh while you tried to get out of them," Chantal said. "He gets to do that sort of thing. He's just dripping with the power he's pulling from people's belief in the awful things at the heart of these stories. But you need to do something more."

She looked at Ranjani. "You didn't do anything to free you from that key I assume you're wearing around your neck right now. But you *did* something all the same."

"Oh!" Ranjani, who had clutched her necklace instinctively, jumped at this. "That's what Amit said we should do—focus on actions not things. Then I had the idea about my hair. Amit loves—loved my hair," she added, "but he still cut it for me."

"So it was hard for both of you," Jo said. "So is that where the power came from? From doing something so painful?"

Chantal looked inscrutable and encouraging again.

Ranjani's chin wobbled. "When my mother saw me the next morning she cried," she said, "because this is the haircut I had when I was little. She never used to be sentimental but now she is. All day she kept asking me if I remembered things, like my stuffed tiger and my favorite purple dress and how much I hated eggplant."

"That made cutting it off even more powerful," Chantal said, her voice gentling for the first time. "That you summoned all those memories for her."

"What about the actual fairy-tale symbolism though?" Maia asked. "Was there power in that, even though it's not the story he cursed Rani with?"

"Oh, yes," Chantal said. "In the story, the witch uses Rapunzel's hair to keep her prisoner. People can climb the hair into the tower but Rapunzel herself can't climb down to escape. But what if she did? What if she cut off her hair herself and then climbed down the severed braid?"

"Different story, for sure," Maia said thoughtfully. "And much better too without the prince who climbs up her hair and gets her pregnant. Hard to know just how consensual that was, given that he would have been the only other person she'd ever seen besides her jailor."

"Ugh," Ranjani said. "Is that really what happens?"

"Yes, unfortunately. But not the way you retold it, Rani," Jo said. "In your version, Rapunzel would decide she wanted to cut her hair and she would find someone she trusted completely to help her."

"You have to show him that these stories can be reread," Chantal said. "Even better—re*written*. Do something to show him that the so-called truths at the core of them aren't truths at all. That's how you shake his belief, in the stories and by extension in his own power."

"Like, say for example in my story," Jo said, "the one—" she stopped and swallowed hard. "Sorry. You remember the other sister?"

"The one who spits out flowers and jewels?" Abony asked.

Jo nodded. "As it turns out," she said, "I do that too, but only when I tell people I love them." She looked sheepish. "Like, out loud and everything."

"Oooh!" Maia clasped her hands. "Can you show us, Jo? Right now?"

"No," Jo said grumpily. "And don't tell me that I need to get better at doing it because I know I do. But it's hard for me. It feels scary." Her face lightened as she made the connection. "Like cutting your hair, Rani. Clearly you're braver than I am."

"I only had to do it once," Ranjani pointed out. "And I didn't even hold the scissors myself. I just sat really still."

"I just talked," Jo said, "and said the things I'm scared to say because I'm worried they sound stupid or fake or incoherent or—Christ, I don't even know. And I came up with this."

She wiggled two fingers into the pocket of her jeans and tossed a bright, glinting object onto the table. It clattered unevenly toward Maia, reminding her of a gaming die. She half-expected to see numbers on the sides when it stopped moving.

But it was not a gaming die. It was a dark red gemstone *the size* of a gaming die.

"Good lord," Maia said. "You spat that out?"

"Along with some flowers and pearls and maybe a sapphire? It was blue."

Ranjani touched the gem on the table with a reverent fingertip. "This looks like a ruby."

Abony held the stone up to the screen.

"I can see it just fine," Chantal said. "It's blazing with magic, though that'll wear off. But Ranjani's right. It's a ruby."

Abony held it out to Jo, who reached for it automatically, then pulled her hand back.

"Keep it," she said.

"What? No. Come on, Jo, just put it back in your pocket."

Jo's expression turned fierce.

"I'm serious, Abony. Keep it. Sell it and pay for some of your shoes."

Abony shook her head and placed the jewel carefully back on the table.

"What's the bad news, Chantal?" she asked.

Chantal had been watching the exchange between Abony and Jo with narrowed eyes. Now she waved a dismissive hand.

"That's not exactly the right phrase. It's just a caution. We keep talking about how you have to 'show' him—" she used the air quotes— "ways you can take these stories back. You need to do that literally, no way around it."

"You mean confront him in person," Maia said.

"Yep, live and in person, I'm afraid."

Maia cast an anxious glance at Simon. They had their protocol in place for leaving the house, but they hadn't tried it yet. This would make a heck of a dry run.

Simon rocked forward on his stool. "Does it matter where? I mean, sounds like the most obvious place to go would be his office, but that's—" he looked around at the women flanking him— "well, I can't imagine any of you want to go back there."

Ranjani grabbed for her non-existent braid and then let her hand slide to her lap. She looked sick.

"I can't decide if it's smart because he won't expect us to dare go there or stupid because he'll see us coming," Jo said.

"Can you tell us if he's got magical protections around his office?" Abony asked Chantal. "Anything that would stop us from just knocking on the door?"

"No. He's clearly storing all his power in the building," Chantal said. "I told you, Abony, the whole place is lit up."

"But I think we *have* to go to his office," Maia said slowly. "Doesn't matter whether it's smart or stupid. Either way, it's where *he* feels most powerful because it's where he assaulted all of us. And it's where he assumes *we'll* all feel weakest."

"So if we show him we don't feel weak there—" Abony began.

"Don't we?" Ranjani murmured.

Unexpectedly, Jo reached over and curled her hand over Ranjani's, capturing the other woman's fidgety fingers.

"You won't be there alone this time," she said.

"Aha!" Chantal said, sitting up straight. "I like to hear that. But you've got to mean it."

Jo lifted an eyebrow. "Excuse me?"

"Remember Abony thought I called to 'scold' you?" Chantal asked, making the air quotes with her fingers. "You haven't tried my apple. And don't lie and say you did because I checked the spell. You haven't activated it."

Maia had forgotten all about the candy apple. It had been on the dining-room table Friday night, but she hadn't seen it since, and she couldn't very well spin around now to look for it without pissing Chantal off even more.

"I put it in the kitchen," Simon said under his breath.

Maia sighed in relief. "Maybe go get it," she murmured.

"It's my fault," Jo said. "When we realized what had probably happened to Renee on Friday, I got really upset, tried to say some stuff about it, and puked out a snake. After that I just couldn't stomach any more food, so I asked if we could wait and try the apple another time."

"Fair enough," Chantal said. "You understand what the apple can do for you?"

"According to Abony, bring us back to ourselves," Maia said.

"That's right. But it's a magic spell, not a miracle. You've still got to do the hard work yourselves." She jerked her chin at Ranjani and Jo in turn. "Cutting your beautiful hair off or getting over your WASP-y self enough to tell people you love them."

Jo snorted with reluctant laughter. "So it's no miracle," she said. "But didn't you also tell Abony that if we eat it together we'll trust each other more?"

Chantal smacked her hand on whatever hard surface was in front of her, making Ranjani jump.

"And *that's* what's got me worried. Because no, that's not what I said. What I said was that when you eat one of my candy apples with other people, you belong to each other. So you should only eat it with people you trust, because it will strengthen the bonds between you."

"And you don't think we trust each other?" Jo asked.

Chantal leaned back and ticked off her fingers.

"You don't know how to tell anyone you care about them. Maia's pretty sure she's the smartest person in the room and wishes you all would just do as she says. Rani feels a little—or a lot—bullied by the rest of you. And *you*—" she stabbed a finger at Abony— "just turned down a two-thousand-dollar jewel that someone offered you because you're too proud to admit this curse is going to bankrupt you."

She sat back, folded her arms, and looked ready to watch them all try to deny anything she'd just said, but just then the wall behind her resolved itself into a door as it opened and a teenage girl stuck her head in.

"Mom," she stage-whispered. "It's been like a half-hour and you said you'd help me. My paper is due tomorrow!"

The girl caught sight of Abony on the screen, recognized her, and offered a dimpled smile and wave.

"Eat the apple, don't eat the apple," Chantal said. "Trust each other or don't. It's what sorcerers and men who assault women have counted on for centuries. I've got to go."

She made a pass across the screen with her hand, an elegant

gesture that was more than a farewell wave. It might have been a benediction.

"Good luck."

And the monitors all went dark.

Fairy Tales Forever Discord Channel

*We are an inclusive community; we celebrate all voices and identities. Expressions of hate, bias, or general assholery (yes, we know it's not a word) will not be tolerated. For full channel rules and guidelines click **here**.*

Discussion Boards: Fairy Tale of the Day |
Question of the Day | **Fairy Tales for Our Time**

Fairy Tales for Our Time: "The Princesses Who Wore Out Their Dancing Shoes"
submitted by JennyK (member since 2017)

Once upon a time, princesses wore only thin-soled dancing slippers, because they did (or were expected to do) nothing strenuous besides dancing. This became a problem for princesses all around the world when they heard about terrible things happening in all of their provinces and kingdoms: princesses being put to sleep, kissed without consent, cheated out of coin they had earned, and forbidden by some kings and courts from deciding what to do with their own bodies.

Realizing that they all had the same problems, the princesses arranged to meet, and they came from all over—in carriages that had once been pumpkins, on white horses that talked, and wearing seven-league boots they'd borrowed or stolen from their brothers. They agreed that they couldn't all return to their own courts and kingdoms without a plan for how to stop or change the terrible things they were all witnessing or experiencing. But what could they do? They were princesses, after all. When they slept on peas, they got bruised. When they were kissed, they fell in love. When they danced too long, they wore out the soles of their pretty shoes and got blisters.

"That's it!" said one princess at last. "We're thinking that we can't do anything but dance because we'll wear through our shoes. But what if we just stopped wearing dancing shoes and wore instead— I don't know—"

"How about boots?" another princess suggested. "Good sturdy boots with lots of arch support." (She was one of those who had stolen a pair of seven-league boots to come to the meeting.)

"What on earth will we do in boots?" asked another.

"Same thing men do," said a princess from a particularly martial province. "We'll march."

"By ourselves?" Several princesses looked alarmed at this idea.

"No," others said decisively. "Not by ourselves. Together."

And so they did.

<click for comments>

AUGUST 12: MAIA

"Damn," Maia said. "I thought *I* was good at getting the last word."

Ranjani started gathering their plates. Abony and Jo stood up and joined her. Maia looked around for Simon, then remembered that she'd sent him to the kitchen. The way the end of that call had gone, she didn't blame him for just deciding to stay out of sight.

She watched the other women cleaning up, feeling helpless as usual. They moved in easy rhythm, scraping food scraps onto a single plate, resealing the containers of leftovers and stacking them, collecting napkins and other trash into the bag the food had come in.

Abony picked up the last crumpled napkin, revealed the ruby underneath, and stopped with her hand in mid-air. Then she, Maia, and Ranjani all looked at Jo.

"Come on, Abony," Jo said. "Don't make me beg."

Abony's mouth twitched. She picked up the ruby and tucked it into her own pocket.

"Thank you."

Maia felt something ease inside her. She thought she might smile too.

The other three women went into the kitchen and came back with fresh glasses of water and trailing Simon. Who had The Gingerbread House bag in one hand. He put it down next to his computer, out of the way, and joined the group at the table.

"Okay, Maia," Abony said. "What's the plan?"

"What?"

"Well," Abony flicked an amused glance at everyone else, then back to Maia, "I mean, you do have a plan, right? And you do just want to tell it to us and have us all agree?"

"Goddamnit," Maia said, trying not to laugh. "I do not."

But she did—sort of.

"The thing is," she said, "we're much better off than we were before Chantal called. I mean, forget about the apple, at least for now. When she called Abony, we were all sitting here feeling— correct me if I'm wrong—completely hopeless."

"No correction here," Jo said.

"But now we've got stuff to work with. First off, we know we need to confront him, in person, together."

"In his office," Ranjani said. "Maia, won't it be dangerous for you to even get there?"

Maia lifted an eyebrow at her husband.

"We've discussed how to safely get Maia out of the house," he said reluctantly.

"It'll be fine, Rani," Maia said. "Simon's not thrilled about it, but what he's not saying is that he came up with all the safety measures himself and it's really smart."

Simon flushed, though he still looked unhappy.

"Anyway, we know we've got to go to his office. And we know we've got to do it soon, because what he did to Renee—and when he did it—proves that he doesn't have a timeline we can count on. Any little bullshit thing that he thinks he might need power for could prompt him to assault someone."

"One hundred percent agree on that," Abony said. "I think we should take this week to plan, then move on Friday."

"That's what I was thinking too," Maia said, and pressed on. "The open question is still what we mean when we talk about 'planning,' because I for one don't suddenly have a brilliant idea for how to take back or find some power for myself in the Thumbelina story. But I think that's what we each do between now and then. We think of things, along the lines of what Rani and Jo have already done, and we—I don't know—test them out, I guess?"

"And keep each other in the loop," Abony said, "even just over text."

Maia nodded. "Totally. The point being that we're in this together and we're not going to just spring our ideas on each other at the last minute, like on Friday morning."

"And people need to keep in mind how what they're going to do affects the others," Simon put in. "Because if Maia's there—I mean, she'll be protected as much as possible but—"

"But no creepy-crawlies launched without warning," Jo agreed. "That's a non-starter."

She didn't sound offended, just matter-of-fact. Maia drew in a deep breath and dared to voice the last piece of her—it really wasn't a plan—general sense of what they ought to do.

"And I do think we should try the apple before you all leave," she said. "Whether the spell in there is going to help or not."

"To prove that we trust each other?" Abony asked.

"Nah." Maia lifted one shoulder in a deliberately casual shrug. "I think we do. But Chantal meant us to eat the apple together. I think it's important to do what she thinks we need to do in case we need her help again."

"That's a good point," Abony said. "And I think there's value in a symbolic gesture, even for all of us. Don't forget—" she grinned— "I *am* in HR. You want to build a stronger team, you send them all out on an obstacle course, that kind of shit."

Ranjani shuddered. "I've had to do those," she said. "I'd much rather eat a piece of candy apple. But Chantal wasn't right in everything she said at the end. I don't think you guys bully me."

"Really?" Jo asked, smiling slightly. "Not even a little?"

"Not even a little," Ranjani said firmly. "You're all very decisive and brave, and maybe I'm not, but I'm used to women who are. I was raised by one. I don't feel bullied by you."

She tugged on the chain around her neck and let the key fall onto the front of her t-shirt.

"I feel bullied by this," she said, then winced at the expressions on their faces.

"Sorry. I guess I made everything serious again, huh?"

"Damn right, you did," Maia said. "Thank you." She stood up. "You want to get plates and stuff, Si? Please?"

Simon went back into the kitchen and reappeared with plates and a carving knife that Maia could have used as a slide. Abony, meanwhile, lifted the apple out of the bag and tugged the knot out of the ribbons at the top. When she pulled the red cellophane away from the apple, Maia smelled sugar and apple juice so strongly that she felt sticky with it.

Abony leaned her weight on the knife to cut into the apple, scattering bright shards of candy shell across the table.

"Simon," she said, handing him a plate. "I don't think it can hurt for you to have some too. And I'll let you and Maia figure out how to share."

Simon pinched off a sliver of the white flesh and held it out for Maia. She had to hold it in two hands and bite into it as if it was a wedge of watermelon.

It tasted like any other apple. She set the uneaten part down and carefully took a shard of the candy coating off the plate. Might as well have some of that too in case the magic was in the shell or in the combination of the two. It was hard to eat, though; the edges were razor sharp against her fingers and she was afraid she'd cut her tongue. She gave the flat side a careful lick.

The horror of her smallness broke over her like a wave. Maia dropped to her knees and rode it out, feeling how little space she took up, how little weight she had to push against anything. She was just a speck, a tiny speck, and she couldn't open her eyes because then she'd see the nothing that was everything else being so terribly big, so big that it no longer made any sense, nothing made any sense except that Chantal had lied, had tricked them into eating her poisoned apple—shouldn't they have seen right through her from the beginning? Goddamnit, the gingerbread had been a dead giveaway, a gingerbread house to nibble until the witch lured them in, stuffed the boy in a cage for fattening up, and put the girl to work. And as for the apple itself, in "Snow White," the apple was a shining, beautiful thing that the stupid girl should have known better than to take a bite of because real fruit doesn't look like that, it's not that perfect, it has worm holes and bruises and—

"Good, Maia. You've cut right to the chase, as usual. Does anyone else see the problem with the program?"

She wasn't a speck anymore. She was in the computer lab where she'd taken most of her advanced Comp Sci classes in undergrad, the only girl in the lab as usual, and the professor was grinning. "Maia, why don't you explain to everyone else—and slow down this time, okay? Use small words so we can keep up."

He winked at her.

The feel of computer keys worn silky from use and shiny from the oils in her fingertips. The taste of stale coffee. The unfurling of lines of code on a screen, clean and beautiful as ink on snow, concentric ripples in a clear pond. The burning behind her eyes that reminded her she'd been at the computer too long, the ache in her lower back from sitting, the sense of unreality when she stood up to stretch and saw the same chair and table and window and wall. Amazing, how static the analog world was compared to the worlds she could manipulate online.

"Ah," said another voice, her own this time, sounding relieved. "There you are."

Maia unfurled herself and opened her eyes. She was still too small, but now she felt the wrong size like an uncomfortable pair of pants, something she *wore*, not what she *was*.

"I think I owe Chantal an apology," she said. "I knew there was a spell in there that she was really proud of, but I couldn't imagine how it would *work*."

"It was definitely not what I expected," Jo said. "It wasn't bad, though. Not at all."

Maia tugged on Simon's sleeve until he looked down.

"You okay?" she asked.

He smiled reassuringly at her. "I'm fine. I didn't try any. It was for you guys, not me."

He hadn't even tried it. She should have known he wouldn't. Maia took her hand off his sleeve and turned back to the other women.

"What about you, Rani?" she asked.

But Ranjani had snatched up her phone. She read the screen, then fumbled frantically for the key that lay between her breasts. They could all see that it was still pure white.

"What's happened, Rani?" Abony asked. "What's wrong?"

Ranjani closed one hand around the key and typed a reply text with the other.

"I've got to go home, I'm sorry," she said. "My mother knocked over the water glass on her nightstand and then stepped in the broken glass. Her feet are all cut up and she won't let Deb near them to get the glass out."

"But—" Jo began, gesturing towards Ranjani's clenched hand.

"It wasn't that, no," Ranjani said. She finished her text and drew in a deep breath; Maia saw her nostrils flare with it. "It was just an accident. It's the sort of thing that's been happening more often now even without my curse, because of my mom's illness."

She got ready to leave as she talked: tucking the key back under her shirt, swinging her purse onto her shoulder, spinning to push in the chair she'd been using. Watching the flow of graceful, purposeful movements, Maia remembered that Ranjani made her living as an artist and also taught Indian classical dance at a studio near her house. *It will bring you back to yourself,* she thought. *Yeah, good spell, Chantal.*

"I still have to go home though," Ranjani was saying. "This happened half an hour ago, apparently, and Deb tried to just take care of it herself, but my mother's being stubborn."

"Text us how she's doing," Abony said, "and also if we can help."

"I will." Ranjani paused in the doorway. "And I'm good with the plan. I'll try to think of a way to get power over this—" she touched the chain— "by the end of the week."

"You'll think of something, Rani," Maia assured her. "We trust you."

Ranjani smiled briefly, dazzlingly, and then darted out the door.

Abony and Jo left too, after Abony had wrapped the remains of the apple back up and Jo had produced the dress she'd borrowed on Friday out of her tote bag.

"Your bathrobe belt is in there too," she told Simon as she handed him the clothes. "I'm glad I remembered to give this to you before I left."

While Simon locked the front door and turned off lights, Maia looked at the dress on the table, trying to remember being the right size to wear it on her body. She had believed that it was a solid object, this dress, because it was made of fabric, but now she could see that the fabric wasn't solid at all. It was a woven network of threads, and the weave was full of flaws and snags, pinpoint holes and uneven wavering sections. She stared at it until it reminded her of lines of code, and then closed her eyes and stared at the lines of code in her head until Simon came back in the room and startled her by clearing his throat.

"You want to work on the wings again?" he asked.

"No," Maia said. "I've had another idea. The story that asshole trapped me in, the original title isn't 'Thumbelina,' it's 'Little Tiny,' remember?"

"So?" Simon asked. He sat down facing her, resting his chin on his folded arms.

"So the character he cursed me with doesn't have any power, but plenty of tiny things do. If I pulled in the right place on that—" she waved her hand at her dress— "it would come completely apart. All from one little pull on one little string, which I can see clearly because I'm so small myself."

"You're talking about little things having the power to take down big things," Simon said. "I get that. Like bacteria, too, right? Or viruses?"

He jerked upright at his own words, his eyes wide.

Maia smiled.

"Like viruses, Si. Exactly."

AUGUST 12: RANJANI

Whatever Ranjani had expected when she burst into her mother's bedroom, it wasn't the scene that greeted her, or the voice that brought her up short in the doorway.

"Light, please," the surgeon said crisply. "Higher and turn to the right. If you can get the light to catch the glass I can see it better—ah, yes. Hold it there."

Deb obliged, holding her phone steady above Shreshthi's foot as Shreshthi herself plucked a splinter of glass out of the sole and dropped it with a clink onto a bloodied paper towel that bore a heap of jagged pieces already. She had her right foot propped up on a towel draped over her left thigh and had already sutured three other gashes in her skin: one across her heel, one in her instep and one right along the ball of her foot. The cut she was working on now ran along the outside edge of her sole and was the smallest of the lot. Shreshthi put down the tweezers, picked up her threaded suture needle and scissors, and waited while Deb wiped the blood away from the wound before executing three rapid, close stitches that foreclosed any further bleeding. She whipped the needle around to make a tiny knot at the end of the last stitch, snipped, and then took her foot down and flexed it several times. Deb swiped a cloth over the whole surface of the surgical field. It left streaks of brown behind—

iodine—which must have stung. But Shreshthi only nodded in satisfaction.

"Thank you, Deb. Do we have a clean sock to put over the whole foot—white, ideally, so I can easily check for excessive bleeding?"

"Shall I wrap some gauze first?" Deb suggested. Suggested, Ranjani noted, not insisted, deferring to the doctor in charge.

Shreshthi shrugged. "Gauze is fine, just not too tight. And I imagine the heel is going to give you some trouble just because of where the cut is. A thick white sock would be fine too, and certainly after the gauze."

"How about I get you a pair of mine?" Amit offered, emerging from Shreshthi's bathroom. He had the mop in one hand and the handheld vacuum in the other.

Shreshthi laughed. "From your big feet? They'll be perfect. I can fold them over to double thickness."

Amit stopped beside Ranjani to lean the appliances against the wall.

"She's fine," he said. "I got home right after Deb texted us both. She was going to run back to her house for her first aid kit, but I pulled out your mother's, the one she keeps in the bathroom. I didn't realize there was a full suture kit in there. I feel like I just got a glimpse of her operating room."

"Are you sure you got all the glass? It must have gone everywhere."

"I've gone over the floor three times," Amit said, "and I scooted under the bed with a light and the dust-buster and grabbed a couple of pieces there too."

"Thank you, jaan. You saw my other text too, right?"

"That this didn't happen because of—you didn't have to go through a new door? Yeah, I saw that. I'm glad."

Ranjani put both hands on Amit's chest to feel his heartbeat under her palms, slid her fingers up to tap the smooth skin of his throat. The apple that the witch had made had tasted one minute of fruit, the next of Baskin-Robbins ice cream, then of the puri that Shreshthi only made once a year—hot and flaky and sharp with pepper, then of Amit's mouth the first time he ever kissed her. Each flavor had run like a current inside her, to the soles of her feet, to her hands, to her eyes.

"I won't let him have us," she murmured. And she savored, briefly, the flavor of those words in her mouth too, words that claimed both action and power for herself.

Amit's arms closed around her as she leaned against him and turned her head to watch Shreshthi supervise the surgery clean-up.

"Look at her," Ranjani said wonderingly. "She just put stitches in her own foot without any anesthesia."

"Actually," Amit said, "she put stitches in *both* feet without anesthesia. "The left foot was even worse."

There was blood on the bottom sheet, long messy smears of it. Ranjani and Amit stripped the bed after Deb left, while Shreshthi sat in a chair with a cup of tea. Then Ranjani helped her mother back into bed.

"You need to rest, now, Mami. Do you want something for the pain?"

Shreshthi made a dismissive gesture. "The cuts were clean and I got all the glass out, so there shouldn't be any risk of infection. I'll take the stitches out in a week or so."

She took a sip of her tea and assessed Ranjani over the rim of the cup.

"You've cut your hair. I like it. It's very elegant."

Ranjani touched her hair self-consciously, thinking of Shreshthi's weepy response the day before. The woman sitting very upright in bed now was a surgeon again, quick and direct as a blade.

"We need to get a new neurological consult, Rani, and I want some more bloodwork done. This… the progression is happening rapidly and I'm not…" She masked this faltering with another sip of tea. "I'm not ready. Can we get in with someone else soon?"

Of all the things for her mother to ask of her, this is what Ranjani should have absolutely expected, that Shreshthi, restored however briefly to her incisive, rational self, would recognize how much she'd deteriorated and map out a new course of action.

"I'll call the doctor's office tomorrow," Ranjani said. And she'd figure out how to actually get Shreshthi to the doctor's office when the time came.

"Good." Shreshthi set her tea down on the nightstand and reached for the black leather bag that Deb had left there. She pulled out a scalpel, still sheathed, and handed it to Ranjani.

"Show me," she said.

"Just how much surgical equipment did you pack into this kit?" Ranjani asked.

"Enough to handle small incidents at home," Shreshthi said. "Show me you remember how to make a first cut."

"I remember."

Ranjani held the scalpel poised over the bedclothes the way her mother had taught her and put a forefinger on the top of the blade to guide it. "You have to press down and pull towards you, no hesitation."

"Good," Shreshthi said again. "You have the hands for surgery, you know, just not the temperament."

"I'm not strong enough."

"No!" Shreshthi said sharply. "There is plenty of strength in you, but you are supple, like a dancer, and you bend into your strength. *I* couldn't bend. I worry that what I had to teach you…" she nodded at Ranjani's hand, still gripping the scalpel, "wasn't what you needed from me."

"You taught me everything," Ranjani said, as horrified by this admission as she'd been by the sight of her mother's blood.

Shreshthi smiled slightly. "Don't look so alarmed, Rani. Most of my life I've been quite sure of myself. But I want you to know that I'm proud of who you are, even if you never use a scalpel in your life."

"But if I ever need to," Ranjani said, smiling back, "I know how to make the first cut."

Shreshthi put her hand on top of her daughter's. "Hold it steady and press hard," she said. "Harder than you think you'll need to. Cut until the blood wells out."

And Ranjani, looking down at their stacked hands and at the wickedly sharp blade she held, felt her smile widen with the surety of what she could do when the time came.

AUGUST 12: ABONY

Abony drove home, parked, rode the elevator up to her own apartment, let herself in, and poured herself a glass of wine. Then she walked around her space, sipping wine and still tasting the sugary residue of the apple on her lips.

She was deeply glad that they hadn't all felt the need to share their experience of being brought back to themselves. She didn't want to share hers, not because it had been traumatic, as Maia's seemed to have been, or even surprising, but because it was in some ways a refutation of everything the others believed about her.

Talented. Gifted. Good at—fill in the blank. For most of her life, Abony had heard that she was all these things, singly and together, sometimes "despite" being a girl or a woman, being Black, or being a Black woman. She knew that she *was* talented, gifted, and good at many things that mattered: managing challenging employees, running a difficult meeting, putting together a strategic budget, making chicken cacciatore and a chocolate cake no one could stop eating, taking the lead in a crisis, designing a room or an outfit with elegance and style.

But before she'd known that she was good at things, she had just *felt* good at things—not necessarily things that mattered or could be measured, and not even the same thing every day.

She had always had the capacity to do something in a way that pleased *her*, felt right to *her*, and not in a way that meant "to hell with what other people thought" but in a deep, settled, sure way that made what the world thought truly irrelevant.

She had known that she was enough for herself. And now she remembered.

In her bedroom, Abony put down her wine and assessed the stacked shoeboxes that took up most of one wall. Abony took every single pair of Louboutins out of their boxes and lined them up in rows on the floor to the right of her closet, where she wouldn't step on them going to and from her room or into the adjoining bathroom.

In the fairy tale, the pair of red shoes had a mind of their own. They forced that poor girl to dance until she nearly died. By contrast, Abony's shoes were just sitting there waiting to be worn. What she wanted to do was convince them that they were enough in themselves, that they didn't need feet in them to move, or someone else's will to carry them forward.

She got her wine off the dresser, went to the kitchen to refill the glass. Then she came back in and began to tell her suede and patent and lucite and leather audience about all the ways that men tortured or mistreated women by means of their feet. She went through "The Red Shoes," "Cinderella," "Snow White," and "The Twelve Dancing Princesses," on to "The Little Mermaid." She told them real stories about the indignities of women's footwear over centuries. She showed them pictures of foot-binding. She told them her own story, then about Emily Sato, about Maia and Ranjani and Jo, about Suzanne and Renee.

Her audience didn't disagree with her or refuse to cooperate. But they were unmoved, because they were just empty shoes and determined, apparently, to stay that way.

Abony took her wine glass into the kitchen and rinsed it out. She told herself it had been worth a try, and also gave herself permission to wait until tomorrow to put all those damn shoes away again, each pair nestled first into their flannel bag and then into their tissue-lined box.

But when she came back into her bedroom, she detected a peculiar smell in the air, like someone had left an iron on too long and scorched a shirt. A shoe box that should have still been in her closet had tumbled to the floor, right in the middle of her path across the room where she couldn't miss it. Abony realized that she hadn't laid *all* of her Louboutins out as part of her audience. She'd left behind the pair she'd bought herself when she got promoted, the pair she'd been wearing the day the CEO raped her. She hadn't worn those shoes since; she didn't even want to look at them now. She'd been so in love with those shoes.

Abony eyed the box balefully; the burning smell was clearly coming from inside. She lifted the lid off, releasing a cloud of smoke, and saw that the soles of the shoes had burned a hole right through their protective flannel bag. She took one out, careful to touch only the inside of the shoe, and put her hand close to the sole. She could feel the heat coming off it from an inch away, though the glossy red leather was undamaged. In "Snow White," she had told the others, the wicked stepmother is killed by being forced to put on red-hot iron shoes and dance in them until she falls down dead.

"So," she said aloud, "someone was listening after all."

The shoe shivered in her hand, and Abony had the impression it was conveying incredulity. *Of course I was listening! I was there with you, remember.*

"Fair enough," she said.

The other shoe, still trapped inside the bag, tapped its heel against the side of the box and nudged its toe at the drawstring, clearly wanting out. So she didn't have a whole army, she had two... well, the term "foot soldiers" was almost irresistible. She could work with that.

Jo walked into her apartment to find Jane curled up on the sofa with her reading glasses on. She pushed them to the top of her head, catching a feathery piece of her hair over one ear, and put her Kindle on the coffee table.

"I've got the kettle full in case you want tea, and I found your good tequila," she said. "I'm prepared for you to have had a wonderful evening, or for everything to have gone to hell. If you need something sort of in between—like, I don't know, Pinot Grigio?— you're out of luck."

"Tea sounds wonderful," Jo said. "And I will pretend you didn't mention Pinot Grigio."

She sat down on the other end of the sofa and tugged out her ponytail holder.

"You didn't have to wait up."

"I didn't," Jane said. "I was reading. I'm going to put the tea on and then you can tell me what you all talked about and how I can help."

She padded into the kitchen.

Jo put her head back, wondering what Jane would experience if she ate a piece of Chantal's magic apple, just how far Jane had to go to get back to herself. Not far, Jo thought.

She had expected to feel something visceral, a thrumming

echo in her muscles and bones and lungs and heart of how she felt after a long run. But the apple hadn't taken her on a long, punishing run. It had taken her to the playground, to the mingled smell of dirt and kid-sweat and the soft solid feel of some kid's belly against her head as she ploughed into him to stop him from bullying a smaller boy. Then she was a new driver, white-knuckling her way through a sudden blinding rainstorm with her dad in the passenger seat calmly assuring her she could do this. The car in front had hit the brakes and so had Jo—while at the same moment, she flung her arm out to keep her dad from flying forward. Then Eileen was clutching her arm on a DC sidewalk, a slurring, ugly voice behind them speculating about what two women might do together in bed and whether he could watch. Jo's hair slapped at her face as she spun on her heel, tucking Eileen behind her and startling the guy so much that he stumbled into the gutter and rolled his ankle.

When her cell phone rang, she knew it was Eileen before she even picked it up.

"You're back," Jo said by way of greeting. "How was your trip? How's the jet-lag?"

Eileen's laugh was relieved and delighted and exasperated all at once. God, she had the best laugh.

"It was amazing and I'm not so much tired as just all mixed-up," Eileen said. "Since school doesn't start for a couple weeks, I'm pretending it's fine that I wake up at three a.m. and then want to go to bed at dinner time. I know I have to get back on the right time eventually, but for now…" She hesitated. "I mean, it's weird, honestly, because if I wasn't living alone I would have forced myself to get over it much sooner."

"So you've discovered a benefit to moving out besides getting away from me," Jo said.

Eileen was silent.

"Sorry. That was supposed to be a joke."

"It was extremely unfunny," Eileen said. "I missed you. You know people run on the Great Wall of China—like, recreational running, it's sort of surreal. Every time I saw a girl with long black hair in a ponytail streaming out behind her, I'd think, *Oh, it's Jo! She's here!* How's that for stupid?"

Jane set a steaming mug down on the coaster in front of Jo, then mimed going to sleep and disappeared into the guest room with her own tea, shutting the door firmly behind her.

"It's not stupid," Jo said. "I missed you too. I miss you every day. I—I know I'm not good at talking the way you want me to, and I know it's too late, but I've been trying to get better at it. It's just that it feels so awkward and hard, like—"

"Like the time I tried to take up running?" Eileen asked, and this time her voice was so tender and humorous that Jo started to cry. She swallowed hard, but it was no good. Whatever was in her throat was determined to choke its way out along with a sob that she couldn't keep Eileen from hearing.

"Oh, baby, don't!" And then of course Eileen was crying too because Eileen cried at everything: at commercials with puppies or babies in them; at thank-you cards from her students; after sex, and whenever she talked to her grandmother on the phone.

"I love you," Jo said, and spat a smattering of tiny gemstones like sprinkles into her hand, pink and blue and green and yellow.

"I love you too. Are you okay? I haven't even asked how you've been. You sound hoarse. Are you sick?"

"I'm fine." Jo leaned forward and trickled the jewels onto the coffee table. "Tell me more about the trip." She let herself sink down into the cushions as Eileen talked.

"Hey," Eileen said softly, then a little louder. "Jo-Jo. Are you awake?"

"What? Yes. You went to see the Terracotta Warriors and one of your kids, Shawn—"

"Shane."

"Shane slipped away from the group to try to get down into the statues."

"And what did I do when I caught him?" Eileen asked.

"Umm... you beat him?"

"Uh-huh. You were totally asleep."

Jo surveyed the jewels on her coffee table, which from this angle looked like a pile of sequins or brightly colored seeds.

"I was maybe a little bit asleep," she said, "but because I'm tired, not because your stories were boring."

"Fine, but I should still let you get to bed."

"No, wait." Jo sat up. "Can I ask you a question?"

"Should I be nervous?"

"No, silly, it's just... what's your favorite gemstone? I realized the other day that I know so many of your favorite things but not that."

Eileen started to cry again. "I had your ring all picked out, you know. It was going to have a sliced diamond in it. That's where they cut across the facets instead of with them so that it looks kind of rough, almost gray, but it has this gleam to it."

Jo could picture the ring. It was perfect.

"It sounds perfect," she said. "And I'm an idiot. I didn't mean to make you cry."

"Amethysts," Eileen said.

"Are those the purple ones?"

"Yes, those are the purple ones. I've got to go, Jo. We're both tired."

Jo picked up her tea, set it down again. "Can I see you?"

"I don't know," Eileen said. "Maybe. I'll text you, okay?" And she hung up.

Jo drank her tea while she looked at pictures of amethysts on her phone and read about their supposed protective and healing properties. Then she scrolled through her photos until she found her earliest shots of Eileen, from the summer they'd started dating.

"You want amethysts?" she asked the smiling woman on her screen. "Let's see if I can give you amethysts."

She woke to the smell of coffee quite close by and opened her eyes to see Jane sitting beside her again and a new steaming mug on the table.

"It was hard to find a place to put your cup," Jane said. "I hope I didn't disturb anything."

Jo sat up and pressed the heels of her hands against her eyes.

"No, it's fine. It's not really organized."

"Did you sleep at all?"

"I mean, I must have," Jo said mildly, hearing the sharpness in Jane's voice that meant she was worried, "since the coffee smell woke me up."

"You know what I mean," Jane said. "And your lip is bleeding. What the hell were you *doing*, Jo?"

Jo picked up her coffee, careful not to disturb the dazzling piles all over the table. "I was… trying something. Eileen's favorite jewels are amethysts."

"Ah," said Jane. "So these are the ones that matter?"

She pointed to the smallest pile, of gemstones in varying shades of purple, from almost clear with a faint lavender tint to a gleaming stone the size and shape of a blackberry.

"Those are the ones that matter."

"They're lovely," Jane said.

"Thanks," Jo said. "I think. I stayed up half the night finding a way to win my girlfriend back when I'm supposed to be figuring out how to fight that—goddamnit!" She gagged a fat slug into her coffee cup and jerked away from the splash.

"Ugh." She shuddered. "Sorry. I'm not quite awake. And I'm seriously never going to be able to eat anything mushy and salty ever again."

"Slugs are salty?"

Jo glared, then got up and took her cup into the kitchen to dump it. Jane followed her.

"I know you've got to get to work," she said, "and your dad wants to come all the way into the city so we can take you to dinner before he and I head home. But do you have time to fill me in on what happened yesterday at Maia's? What is it you're supposed to be doing? And does this mean you all have a plan?"

Jo got a clean cup and poured herself more coffee.

"We have pieces of a plan," she said. "And I definitely have time to fill you in. I think I could use your strategic brain, for one thing, and for another thing, I can't deprive you of hearing about our conversation with Chantal."

Jane's eyes lit up. "You talked to the witch directly? From The Gingerbread House? In the flesh?"

"No, actually," Jo said, "it was a magical video call."

She laughed so hard at the expression on Jane's face that she almost snorted her coffee and had to sit down at the kitchen table. Then Jane insisted on making French toast with the stale bread on the counter, while Jo told her everything they'd learned, discussed and decided the night before. When Jo was done talking, Jane brought their plates to the table, topped up both coffee cups, and sat down.

"So you've already gotten some power over your story—or maybe you had it all along but neither you nor the CEO knew it—in that you're able to cough out both the desirable and undesirable things, depending on what you're saying."

"Or trying to say," Jo corrected her.

"Or trying to say."

"And you've figured out how to spit out exactly what you want when it comes to the gems and flowers. Did you try specific flowers?"

Jo shook her head. "No, but I think I could. It's just that since they come out kind of, you know, covered in my saliva and usually not intact, that doesn't feel quite as desirable."

"Fair," Jane said. She took a thoughtful bite of French toast. "What if you could control the icky things too?"

"You mean control what I spit out when I want to talk about— what happened?"

"Well, it feels like controlling specific *things*—" Jane grimaced— "would be more effective if you knew this man had a snake phobia or something. But barring that, could you control what the things you spit out *do*?"

Jo thought about the story itself, and the helplessness of both sisters, just spilling things from their lips every time they spoke.

"What if I tried to *train* them, is that what you mean? That's—" she grinned, splitting her lip open again— "that's insane. I like it," she added, "but I don't understand how I'd go about doing it."

"How did you work your way through to amethysts last night?" Jane asked.

"Chantal said we had to do something hard, so I tried saying not just the reasons I love Eileen that I could—I don't know—put in a card or something, but the things I should have apologized for when we were together but never did, ways I've always held back, and things I want—wanted—for the future. The future stuff—" she squirmed a little— "like that I wanted to marry her after our first date, but that I'm not sure she can still love me long enough to buy a house, have a kid. That's been what I was always the most scared to say out loud."

"I think it's okay to say that you *want* a future with Eileen, using the present tense," Jane said. "And that's what produced the amethysts, huh?"

Jo nodded. "But what's the equivalent with the other stuff?"

She got up and took their dishes to the sink, then looked down into it, remembering that first long weekend of trying to figure out how to *not* produce centipedes.

"The actual physical act of bringing these things up is incredibly awful," she said. "I mean, in order to train these things I'd have to do a *lot* of trial and error."

"And what do you think you'd have to say—or try to say?"

Jo sat back down. "That's the key," she said slowly. "I have to think about these things as my *words*, my words that I'm directing at him, forcing him to listen to—"

She stopped abruptly. "*Forcing* him to listen to me," she said again.

"What?" Jane demanded.

Jo spoke so low she feared Jane would have to ask her to repeat herself. "It makes me worried that what I'm talking about is revenge."

"And you're not interested in revenge?" Jane asked in a neutral voice.

Jo shook her head violently.

"We've never even talked about it, but no. No. Revenge is how *his* mind works, not mine. Not any of ours. Revenge just spews out more violence and rage, and we're all so sick of being angry. We want to be *done*. Making him small, trapping him somewhere spitting disgusting things out—it doesn't get us our lives back."

"No," Jane said. "It doesn't. And I have never been more proud of you than I am hearing you articulate that. You are *right*, Jo. All of you. I hope I get to meet these friends of yours someday so I can tell them how much I admire them."

She caught Jo's hands and shook them lightly.

"But what you want to do *isn't* revenge. Forcing the man who sexually assaulted you to stand there and hear the impact his actions have had on you, how much they've hurt you—that's part of the criminal justice system, for God's sake. If you all succeed in breaking these curses, I hope you take this man to court and put him in jail.

"I know," she said, when Jo's hands twitched in hers. "You're not even thinking about that yet. But listen to me. You want him to bear the weight of what he's done. Do it. *Make* him carry it. And if he buckles under that weight well, then—" she let go of Jo's hands and sat back— "then he's not nearly as strong as you are, my darling. So *fuck him*."

They were both quiet, Jane sipping her coffee and Jo staring at her hands.

"You know," Jo said finally, "you were right. Having a wicked stepmother in my corner is turning out to be incredibly helpful."

Jane laughed and shooed Jo off to get ready for work.

In the bathroom, Jo faced the mirror and shaped words in her head. *You made me feel weak, actually physically weak, not just in my muscles but in my tendons and bones, like I wasn't even a person but this breakable* thing.

She opened her mouth, feeling things pushing and shoving against each other to emerge in a welter of wings and teeth and mandibles and furry legs. She spit them into the sink and watched them scuttle about. They really did look like they were waiting for her direction, so she tried it. The beetles and spiders kept trying to climb up the slick sides of the sink and falling back down, but the trio of ants marched obediently down the drain. And after waving its legs and antennae about defiantly, the fucking centipede went down after them.

Jo washed the spiders and beetles down the drain with hot water and plugged the sink so nothing could come back up. Not bad for a first trial run.

Fairy Tales Forever Discord Channel

*We are an inclusive community; we celebrate all voices and identities. Expressions of hate, bias, or general assholery (yes, we know it's not a word) will not be tolerated. For full channel rules and guidelines click **here**.*

Discussion Boards: Fairy Tale of the Day |
Question of the Day | Fairy Tales for Our Time

Question of the Day: Are there any actual female friendships in fairy tales?
submitted by Natalie (member since 2018)

Natalie: So I think I know why there are so many toxic female relationships in fairy tales, partly from conversations on here! (Thanks, everyone!) Whether it's sisters or a stepmother and stepdaughter, women are so often in competition with each other for men and everything they offer: safety, financial security, and basically legitimizing you as conventionally attractive and valuable. So I'm not really asking why there are so many of these bad relationships between women in fairy tales. What I want to know is are there any good ones? I'm drawing a blank!

Rebekah: Good question, I had to think about it. I don't know if this counts, but there are a bunch of positive sister relationships: Snow White and Rose Red for sure, and the Twelve Dancing Princesses, who may not be best friends but probably at least have some trauma bonding from the whole being-forced-to-dance-with-demon-princes-every-night thing.

Cleotheprettyrat: Adding to your list @Rebekah: the Little Mermaid's sisters. She chooses to totally torture and transform her body for a man she's never met and they don't give up on her. Instead, they let the sea witch shave their hair to get her back. In illustrated versions, there is always a picture of the sisters with their little bald heads pleading with the Little Mermaid to come home and for some reason I always find it really heart-breaking, because she still chooses the guy over them in the end.

Jess: So I wanted to jump in and suggest the little robber girl and Gerda in "The Snow Queen," but then I went and reread it and I'm going to save that for when someone asks about lesbian relationships in fairy tales. ☺ Because wow. I did not remember that little robber girl wanting Gerda to sleep in the bed with her and kissing her on the mouth...

badassvp: Natalie, per all the context you offered along with your question, I think that the sister relationships people have suggested are probably standing in for friendships more generally, just because there weren't social structures for women to interact unless they were related. So if you were lucky, your sisters were your friends and if you weren't, you know, they tried to push you into wells or abandon you in the forest. It's kind of funny that now we've turned things around and a lot of us call our friends our "sisters" when we're trying to make the point that we'll be there for each other no matter what.

<click for more comments>

Abony and Ranjani had been ready to go since Monday. Jo was relieved not to be the only one holding things up; Maia had sent a terse-bordering-on-snippy text explaining what she was trying to do and that it would take a couple more days. Jo had followed up with her own explanation, and the other women vehemently agreed that she and Maia needed the time, that what they were trying to do was worth doing.

By Thursday night, they were all ready. Jo sent a message to their text chain wishing everyone a good night's sleep, to which Ranjani said, *Thank you, you too,* Abony sent wine glass and bed emojis, and Maia replied, *Sleep is for the weak.*

Jo went to bed and stared at the ceiling. Her throat burned from all the work this week, her stomach was extremely unhappy with her, and her lips were chapped. She should get up and do something about all of these things, but she was too tired to move.

Near morning, of course, she finally fell into a deep sleep and dreamed she was sitting at a table in an unfamiliar, windowless conference room. Sitting directly across from her was a woman with shoulder-length brown hair parted to one side. She wore a navy blazer over a pale blue silk top, and she was reading from a thick sheaf of papers, turning each page over as she finished with it.

"…and in terms of stipulations, there is really nothing out of the ordinary. There's a standard non-disclosure agreement and you void the contract if you violate that. The only unusual thing is the language that we're using here, but while it's unusual, it's not unheard of, which is to say that you void the contract the *moment* you violate or attempt to violate the non-disclosure agreement." She paused and looked up. "Good so far?"

"What?"

Jo looked at the stack of pages already face-down. It was significantly higher than the stack the woman was still holding.

"What are you talking about? Have you already read all of that out loud?"

The woman frowned. "It's standard procedure."

"But I don't remember any of it," Jo said. "I don't know what we're talking about. I haven't signed anything…" she trailed off because there was a pen in her hand. Had it been there before?

The woman sighed, put down the papers, and leaned across the table to touch Jo's wrist.

"Jo, listen to me. We've been over this. What he's offering is really an extraordinary deal. He's offering to lift the curse entirely."

"Where is everyone?" Jo asked. She looked around the conference room. There should be more people here, shouldn't there? Other women.

"Where is everyone else?" she asked.

"This is about *you*," the woman said. "About taking care of yourself."

She sat back and tapped the stack of face-down paper to her left. "I've gone over the caveats," she said, "the non-disclosure, and of course the clause confirming that if you do break the contract the curse comes back redoubled. You understand all that, right?"

"Redoubled?" Jo could barely get the word out. What the hell would *that* look like. Jesus. She squeezed the pen she was holding until it wobbled.

"*Have* I signed anything?"

The woman shook her head. "This is the mandatory fine print that I have to go over, that's all. So long as you keep to the agreement, you don't even need to remember this stuff. Now, just sign there—" she plucked a piece of paper from the pile and slid it across the table— "and then we'll lift the curse. You'll be free!"

The paper was covered in gibberish, but there was a thick black line across the bottom where Jo was supposed to sign her name.

"*We'll* lift the curse?"

"*He* will lift the curse, of course, but I will do everything I can to make sure—and he has assured me that—the point is, it will be gone."

The pen was a fountain-tip. When Jo put it to the paper a drop of ink appeared instantly on the page. She pulled the pen up.

"What's the catch?"

"The catch?"

"To remove the curse from me, you must be making me sign something else away. What is it? I can't read these words."

This woman was clearly a lawyer, and a pro. She managed to keep all but the faintest whiff of impatience out of her voice.

"There's no catch. You're not going to sign away anything that affects you at all. You're just signing to confirm that you won't give any power, support, or aid to any of the women named here. To be clear, once you sign you won't be *able* to help them in any way. That's it."

"But I can't read this!"

Jo leaned over the paper, but the words refused to come into focus. Another drop of ink fell and spread. The woman clicked her tongue in irritation.

Jo remembered their names.

"Are they listed here?" she demanded. "Abony and Ranjani and Maia and Renee. Are their names here? And what about yours?" But she couldn't remember the woman's name.

The woman flinched.

"My name is definitely not in there," she snapped. "For God's sakes, Jo, this is only a dream. If you'll just *sign* it—"

Jo squeezed the pen as hard as she could, squeezed it until, by whatever logic possessed this dream, she did what she wanted to do and turned it into a black snake that reared up over her fingers and launched itself, hissing, across the table. The woman made no sound at all but flung up her arms and threw herself backwards so hard that her chair hit the wall and then seemed to sink into it, until the woman—and her chair—vanished and Jo sat facing a blank white surface.

"Go fuck yourself," Jo said.

She woke mumbling the same phrase and caught a glimpse of a black snake dropping off the edge of her bed before she heard it hit the floor with a soft thump.

"Jesus."

Ugh. She'd never coughed anything up in her sleep before.

Jo rolled onto her back and tried to make sense of the dream. After a minute, she grabbed her phone and checked the company website. The woman who had been trying to get her to sign that indecipherable contract was indeed Suzanne, the company's lawyer.

Jo texted the group chain—*anyone else have a really weird dream about Suzanne last night?*—then leaned over the edge of the bed and directed the snake to come out from under it and slither over to the wheeled suitcase waiting near her front door. She deposited the snake inside, which no one was happy about, checked the lock, then went to get dressed for work.

They had agreed to meet in the parking garage first thing in the morning, since Jo and Simon were both driving in with tricky cargo of sorts. Jo had double-checked the lock on her suitcase before she left the house, but that didn't mean she wanted to put it to the test on the Metro during rush hour. As for Simon, he planned to leave the house well before dawn to avoid as much traffic as possible.

There were plenty of cars in the lot when Jo pulled in, but she guessed that the car right in front of the ramp that led to the elevator lobby was Simon's. She parked beside it and cut her engine, then went around and looked in the driver's side window. Simon was asleep with the seat fully reclined. Jo tapped lightly on the window and he jerked awake and upright all at once, looking so alarmed that she took a step back and held her hands up.

"Sorry!"

Simon rubbed his eyes, levered the seat up, and rolled down the window.

"No, it's fine. I've got an alarm set to go off in a few minutes anyway."

He was wearing jeans, a rumpled t-shirt, and a long cord around his neck with some piece of tech at the end of it which now crackled into life and emitted Maia's amplified voice.

"Si? You awake? Who's there? Can I come out yet?"

"Not yet," Simon said. "It's Jo. Hang on."

"Hey, Maia," Jo said. "Did you get my text?"

Maia's answer would have to wait. Simon was moving: opening the car door, shutting it behind him, then going around to the back passenger seat to open that door. Jo backed up and let him do his thing. When he came around the car again, though, she burst into incredulous laughter.

"Is that where Maia is? Seriously?" She glanced toward the trunk of her own car. "We kind of match."

Simon was wheeling a sleek, hard-sided suitcase with more than a dozen holes drilled into the top of it, presumably for both air and light. It was plastered all over with dire warning labels: *Live Animals; Venomous Animals; Hazardous Materials; Do Not Approach.*

"You admiring my ride, Jo?" Maia asked.

"You better believe it."

"It seemed like the best way to keep people from getting too close or jostling her," Simon said. "She's seat-belted inside and there's a cellphone in there with her. That's what this speaker—" he pulled up the cord around his neck— "is connected to."

"It's genius," Jo said. "When do you feel like it'll be safe for her to get out? Won't she need to use her keyboard soon?"

"I think in the elevator will be okay," Simon said, "which reminds me. I've got to get our bag out of the trunk."

"I can hold onto Maia," Jo offered, then seeing the look of horror on Simon's face suggested that instead he give her the car keys and let *her* get the backpack.

Another car pulled up as Jo handed Simon his keys and Ranjani emerged wearing a deep blue washed silk dress, her canvas tote bag over one shoulder.

"Hi." She registered Simon's suitcase and her eyes widened. "Wow."

"Wow, yourself," Jo said, trying to telegraph with a tiny shake of her head just how tightly wound Simon was, understandably, right now. "Your dress is stunning."

Ranjani smiled wryly. "I had no idea what to wear for this—whatever it is we're doing, you know? And then I thought about Bluebeard. So I wore blue."

They heard the ringing sound of heels on concrete coming from around the corner, then Abony appeared. She had clearly dressed just as carefully for the occasion as Ranjani had, in a red silk blouse, black leather pencil skirt, and black patent leather slingbacks.

"Damn," Jo said. "I just wore this dress because it's stretchy and I can move in it."

"Good plan," Abony said as she reached the group. "You might need to."

She too noticed Simon's suitcase, raised her eyebrows, but didn't comment.

"Maia," Simon said, "everyone's here."

"Oh great," she said, "because I can't hear shit through this whole cellphone-speaker set-up. As far as I can tell, everybody thinks everybody looks fabulous. Can we go inside now so I can get out of here and get to work?"

"Hang on," Jo said. "Maia, we'll try to talk really clearly and only one at a time, okay? But did everyone get my text? No one responded."

Abony looked grim.

"I got it," she said. "And yes, I dreamed about Suzanne too. I didn't respond because I figured we were better off having this conversation in person."

"She was trying to make me sign something," Ranjani said softly, then glanced at Simon and said it louder. "Like a non-disclosure or something. I don't know what it was."

"Did you sign?" Abony asked.

Ranjani shook her head, her short hair swinging.

"Me either," Jo said. "I turned the pen she gave me into a snake instead."

Abony let out a bark of laughter. "I broke the pen in half and what looked like blood poured out of it, but it hardened into a shiny surface all over the table, like this." She tipped one foot inwards to show them the red sole of her shoe.

"Maia?" Jo asked. "You hearing this?"

"Enough," Maia said. "We all dreamed that Suzanne showed up and tried to make us betray each other." A whine of feedback drowned out her next words, but they clearly heard the end of her question— "affect what we're going to do?"

"You think we should change our plan?" Ranjani asked. "Not go through with it?"

She didn't look relieved at this prospect. There was a crease between her eyes as if the idea of not confronting the CEO made her head hurt. *We've come a very, very long way if* Rani's *prepared to do this,* Jo thought. *Too late to turn back now.*

She said as much.

"Agree," Maia said.

Abony frowned. "The dreams were clearly threats," she said, "but that may not be a bad thing. It could mean we've made him nervous. I mean, in our dreams, he was essentially trying to negotiate with us."

"And pit us against each other," Jo added. "But it didn't work. I think we should do this before he tries another way."

"What about Suzanne?" Ranjani asked. "What does it mean that she was there? Was she dreaming too, or did she agree to come into our dreams and offer us each a deal?"

"Whatever she did, he made her do it, no question," Abony said. "That said, he's already made her choose once, between losing a lot—including her integrity—and losing *everything*. I think she'd make the same choice again. And what she was asking us to do in the dreams wasn't all that much different than what she did in real life."

Simon shifted restlessly, clenching and unclenching his fingers around the handle of the suitcase.

"Listen," he said, "I didn't have a dream and I can't make this decision for you all. But the longer Maia's exposed like this, out of the apartment and in this makeshift set-up out in the open, the less comfortable I am with the situation."

"Goddamnit, Si, you don't get to—" Maia's voice was overwhelmed by a series of beeps, as though she'd accidentally hit a button on the cellphone she was using and initiated a call, which was probably exactly what had happened.

It didn't matter. They all knew what she'd been trying to say. Jo wondered if Simon realized that by insinuating that he had control of Maia, he had galvanized them all into action. None of the women said anything else, just turned together towards the building.

"Shit, hold on," Jo said, "I've got to get my stuff."

She lifted her suitcase carefully from the trunk and wheeled it up the ramp and into the elevator lobby. Ranjani pressed the call button, and when a car arrived, hit the "P" for the penthouse.

The only problem was, the elevator didn't move. The doors slid shut, the "P" lit up, and absolutely nothing happened.

Jo hit the button to open the doors, but they stayed shut.

"Fuck," she muttered.

Abony pressed first "P" and then "Doors Open" with the gleaming red nail of her index finger. Nothing.

"What the hell is going on?" Maia asked.

"We're in the elevator, Maia," Simon said. "We've pressed the button for the penthouse but it's not responding, and now the doors won't open at all."

"Are you fucking kidding me?" Maia spat into the mike. "Si, come on. Open up."

Simon shook his head and opened his mouth to speak, but Jo cut him off.

"Get her out or I will," she practically snarled at him. "I get that this is scary and unsafe and you're trying to protect her, but you need to Do. What. She. Says."

Simon looked like he wanted to argue with her but was also afraid she might spit a snake at him. He knelt on the floor of the elevator and carefully opened the suitcase.

The inside had been lined with heavy-duty foam cushioning ventilated by the holes Simon had drilled and cut out to accommodate different sections: Maia's seat, which she was indeed belted into with a safety harness, the cellphone that was affixed within her reach on the opposite side of the suitcase, and a whole network of wires connecting various small black boxes and ports.

Maia pushed sweaty hair out of her face and tipped her head back to survey the situation.

"We can't get out of the elevator now?" she asked.

"Looks that way," Jo said. She supposed they should be panicking—what if the CEO's plan was to literally trap them in this elevator indefinitely?—but she mostly just wanted the damn elevator to *work*, to do their bidding not his.

Maia strained forward in her harness to peer at the control panel.

"And we can't get to the top either?"

Ranjani drew in a sharp breath. She opened her tote bag and stared into the depths of it.

"What is it?" Abony asked her. "You okay?"

"We need to get to the top, right?" Ranjani asked. "I—this is probably really stupid but if it was a tower—well, actually it is, isn't it? An elevator tower?"

And she reached into her tote bag and pulled out a heavy braid of shining black hair, bound on both ends with red thread.

There was a moment of electric silence, but then Maia began to nod, her face set and white.

"Try it."

Jo realized that she was nodding too.

Abony stepped back from the panel to give Ranjani room. "If this works," she said, "we need to be sure to tell Chantal."

"*If* this works,'" Ranjani repeated. "I don't even know what to do!"

She held the braid like it was a living thing, a cat resting along her forearm and curling its tail down into the crease of her elbow.

"Make sure you use the cut end," Jo said suddenly. She glanced at Maia for confirmation. "That's the part you put power into, right? Where you cut it? So use that end."

"I am," Ranjani said. She touched the "P" button with the ragged, severed end of her braid.

There was a spark and a flare of fire from the button that ignited the braid like a torch, with the accompanying stench of burned hair. Ranjani jerked the braid away from the panel with a stifled scream and dropped it. Simon, who was wearing sneakers, stomped on the burning end until it went out.

The bottom dropped out of Jo's stomach. The elevator was ascending.

"It's too fast, we're going too fast." The amplification on Maia's voice turned her whisper into a something terribly urgent, but what could they do? They were flying upwards, the button for each floor lighting briefly as they passed—5, 6 . . . 12, 14 . . . and then the car stopped as suddenly as it had started, hard enough that Jo lost her balance and smacked her hip painfully against the side railing.

The doors slid open to reveal a tall figure in a black pantsuit. For a terrible moment Jo thought it was the CEO and realized that she wasn't ready to see him again, not now, not ever—what the hell had she been thinking?

But it wasn't the CEO. It was Suzanne.

She was doing an excellent impression of being completely at ease, with her arms folded over her breasts and her feet planted, but her face was washed of all color and the center of her lower lip was bleeding. Jo suspected that she'd bitten it when she realized that they'd figured out how to make the elevator work.

"Just move out of the way, Suzanne," Abony said quietly—gently even. "You've done what you had to do, but we're here now."

"Unfortunately," Suzanne said, "per the contract that was signed last night, none of you can come any further onto the premises."

"We can't?" Abony asked. "As in, *literally* can't? Because you're going to continue to bar the way?"

Suzanne took a step back, far enough that they could all leave the elevator without running into or having to go around her.

Jo tried. The air in front of the open doors was thick and gluey. It clung to her in a repellent, lingering way, like unwanted hands on her skin, until she retreated fully back into the elevator car.

"I didn't sign the damn thing," she said, "or don't you remember what happened to your pen?"

Suzanne twitched—she remembered alright—but stood her ground.

"Without a united intention, none of you can access this floor, Jo," she said. "Those who refused to sign the contract implicitly acknowledged in doing so your membership in the group identified in the contract—the same group that the undersigned party to the contract forfeited her ability to assist. I'm sorry for all the legal language but—"

"But none of us signed it!" Ranjani cried. "You're lying!"

Suzanne pressed her teeth into her lip again, making blood well up. She wiped it off with her fingers.

"I'm not lying, Ranjani. I assure you that the elevator will not give you any more trouble. It will now take you to any other floor of the building, including to your own offices should you wish to go to your desks and begin your workdays, or to the parking garage where you left your vehicles should you wish to go home."

"Suzanne, stop it," Abony said. Her voice had hardened. "You can't be serious. You're saying that one of us signed that fucking contract in a dream last night? Do you actually *believe* that?"

"I was there," Suzanne said. "I am in possession of the contract. I'm sorry. You could have saved yourselves the trip here and—" she nodded at Ranjani's scorched braid curled on the floor of the elevator— "not wasted all that beautiful hair. The fact is that the undersigned party promised not to aid or assist any of the others of your party and furthermore acknowledged per her signature that in signing she would in fact be rendering herself *unable* to help you."

Her eyes dropped again to focus on something near the bottom of the car.

"I'll let you explain it to them," she said quietly. And she turned and walked away.

Jo looked at Maia. Everyone looked at Maia.

She was fumbling with her harness. "Si, help me out!"

He crouched down and caught her when she got it open and literally fell into his waiting hands. He started to lift her so she could see the rest of them, but she flung her arm out, gesturing at something in the case. Jo realized that Maia was speaking, but even a few feet from the cellphone that had been capturing her voice, it was impossible to make out anything but a tinny squeaking sound. Simon snagged her lavalier mike from one of the snug foam compartments, turned it on, and laid it on his palm beside her. Then he picked her up and stood, angling his body so that Maia could talk to the other women over his fingers as though she were at a podium.

"I thought it was a dream," she said miserably. "It *was* a dream."

"But you said you didn't—" Jo broke off.

No, Maia hadn't actually said she hadn't signed Suzanne's contract. They'd just all assumed she hadn't because—Jesus—it was *Maia*.

Maia clung to two of Simon's fingertips. She looked awful, her hair frizzy and her face and neck flushed so deep with mortification that she seemed to be breaking out in a rash.

"I'm sorry," she said. "I'm so, so—God, it's pointless to say that. I've screwed all of you over. A fucking apology—"

She swayed slightly.

"Maia," Simon said stoutly. "Don't do this to yourself. You'd never betray anyone."

"But I did!" she cried. "I convinced myself it was a dream because the minute I woke up I was so freaked out, but I also wondered whether—oh, God."

She sat down abruptly inside Simon's hand and huddled into the curve of his fingers to escape their accusing eyes.

"Oh, Maia." Ranjani was crying. She picked up her braid and stuffed it back into her tote bag.

"I don't understand," Abony said. "If you signed away your ability to help us, why are you still tiny? Why hasn't he lifted your curse?"

"Because," Maia said, "what they offered wasn't to lift the curse. It was to leave it on."

Fairy Tales Forever Discord Channel

*We are an inclusive community; we celebrate all voices and identities. Expressions of hate, bias, or general assholery (yes, we know it's not a word) will not be tolerated. For full channel rules and guidelines click **here**.*

Discussion Boards: **Fairy Tale of the Day** |
Question of the Day | Fairy Tales for Our Time

Fairy Tale of the Day: "Thumbelina"
submitted by happilyneverafter (member since 2018)

...As they flew through the morning sunshine, Thumbelina assured the swallow that she was happy just to be out of the dark, damp tunnels where the field mouse lived, and away from the mole with his sharp claws and constantly snuffling nose. She told her friend to set her down anywhere he liked, so long as there were flowers, and she would make a life for herself.

But the swallow knew better. He flew on and on, all the way to the land of the Fairies, and then flew down into a meadow full of the most beautiful flowers Thumbelina had ever seen. Imagine her even greater astonishment when she slid off the swallow's back onto a flower and discovered inside it a fairy, hardly bigger than herself! There were fairies in every flower and soon they had all gathered around Thumbelina, exclaiming over her, because she, of course, was the smallest and the loveliest of all of them. "Look at how dainty she is!" they said to one another. "Why, she barely dents the petals when she walks!"

At last the King of the Flower Fairies heard the commotion and came to see the cause. The moment he beheld Thumbelina, he loved her, for she was the most exquisite, delicate creature he had ever seen. He asked her to marry him and become his queen, and for her wedding gift he gave her a pair of wings. He taught her to fly with them and took her all around the kingdom, showing off his beautiful, tiny bride.

<click for comments>

AUGUST 17: MAIA

Simon leaned down close enough that Maia could feel the damp warmth of his breath on her skin.

"Maia, why on *earth*?"

He hadn't brushed his teeth this morning and she wanted to tell him to please stop breathing on her, but of course she couldn't because the reason he hadn't brushed his teeth was that he'd set an alarm for 3:30 a.m. so he could pack her up in her suitcase and drive her to the office building through silent and empty streets. Safe streets.

As she braced herself on Simon's palm to stand up, Maia heard the other women talking far above her.

"Hang on, Rani," Jo was saying. "Try touching your braid to the spell or whatever it is that's keeping us from leaving the elevator. See if we can break the barrier that way."

"Be careful," Abony warned.

Simon was facing away from the doors, his body blocking Maia's view.

"Simon, let me see," she said.

He turned and held his hands up so she could see the doorway. There was something obviously wrong with the air there. It was *visible*, barely, as though there was a sheet of plastic wrap across the doors, or some thin film smeared with grease.

Ranjani wiped her eyes and touched the blackened end of her braid to the wavering space. Maia held her breath, but there were no sparks or flames. The braid seemed to encounter a rubbery sort of resistance and just wouldn't move past the doorway.

"Dammit," Jo said.

Abony stalked from one side of the elevator to the other as Ranjani put her braid away again. "You going to tell Simon why?" she asked Maia, her voice level. "I get that it's awkward that we're all here listening, but—"

"We could go back down now, couldn't we?" Ranjani ventured.

"I think we should," Simon said. "Maia, let's just go home and then we can—"

"No!" Maia said. "No, wait, please! We're so close!"

She glared at the open-but-not-really-open doorway just a few feet away.

"I thought it was a dream," she said. "I swear I did, the whole time it was happening, and even when I woke up. It wasn't until your text—" she nodded at Jo— "that I realized it might have been, well, still a dream, but a dream with consequences. But there was no way to know and so I just hoped—"

Abony frowned. "What do you mean, there was no way to know?"

Jo pushed herself off from the wall she'd been leaning on.

"She means that if it was just a dream, then of course she'd still be small, because nothing happened to change that. And if it was an actual binding negotiation session *conducted in a dream*—which as it turns out it was—then she'd also still be small, because that's what she agreed to. Right?"

She glanced at Maia for confirmation.

Maia clenched her hands together so she couldn't hide her face in them.

"Yeah."

"But *why*?" Simon asked again, his voice anguished this time. "Why would you want to stay like this?"

"I don't!" Maia cried. "Jesus. I don't! I just—" she knew she should look at Simon but she addressed his sheltering hand instead— "I just don't want to lose you."

"What are you talking about? I'd never leave you!"

"Not while I'm like this you won't," Maia said. Horribly, she started to cry, stupid, ugly tears that came with lots of snot. "Not now that I need you all the time."

"Oh, Maia, don't! Don't cry." Simon juggled her carefully into just one of his hands so he could touch one fingertip of the other to her cheek, the caress as gentle as if he were touching a butterfly.

"But I didn't mean it." Maia swiped angrily at her nose with her sleeve. "Jesus, I can't even blow my fucking nose like this. I don't want to be this small forever. And not at the expense of the rest of you."

She turned back towards the other women, staggering a little.

"Abony, there's got to be a way to break a standard contract— I mean, it's not so different from a non-disclosure agreement, is it?"

"In principle, no," Abony said. "The moment you break it, you're no longer entitled to whatever you got when you signed. Usually it's money, but in this case—I mean, I suppose as soon as you break it, he'll lift the curse."

"And I'll be my regular size again." Maia nodded. "So how do I break it?"

She rubbed her sleeve under her nose again, then used the other sleeve to wipe her eyes. "And will you all help?" The tears kept coming, dammit, but she talked through them. "I know I don't deserve your help but—"

"Oh, shut the fuck up," Jo said. "Of course we'll help. The problem is whether we can actually *do* anything, because what you agreed to doesn't sound like a contract. Abony?"

Abony was frowning. "I'm going back over the language in my head. Everything Suzanne said, in my dream and when she was talking to us earlier, was all standard legalese, except that you didn't sign *agreeing* not to help us, Maia. You apparently signed an understanding that you *can't*. I assume this means you physically can't help us confront him, which is why we can't get through those doors."

"Oh," Ranjani said. "Oh, I see. It was a spell."

"We could do what Simon suggested," Maia said dully. "Take the elevator down, drop us off, then come back up and try again."

"No," Ranjani said. "Maia, since when do you give up so fast? If it's a spell, there has to be a way to break it. My hair worked on the elevator and we definitely didn't plan or predict that."

"You're right, Rani," Abony said. "From the way Chantal talks about magic, there's always a way to break a spell. In this case, he was probably counting first on Maia not wanting to."

"And second on the rest of you being so mad at me that we'd all fall to pieces," Maia said. She pushed her hair off her sticky face. "But he fucking underestimated all of you. That's got to be something."

"Which leaves us united in wanting to break the spell," Jo said, "but not knowing how. Which I bet he's getting a terrific laugh out of because he's a—"

She clapped a hand over her mouth, coughed, flung the contents of her hand at the floor, and stomped hard. "Sorry."

"That could be useful," Abony said, then laughed shortly. "Not what you just spit out, Jo. Your point about him having *fun* with all this. Chantal said that too, that he's getting off on injecting his sick sense of humor into all these fairy-tale curses. So how do you usually break a spell in a fairy tale?"

"Oh for fuck's sake," Maia said. She spun around again. "Simon, pick me up higher."

Simon lifted her up to the level of his chin. From farther away she'd been able to see that he was both bewildered and deeply hurt. But from this close, all she could comprehend was a thicket of unshaven whiskers, each one nearly as long as her hands, and the clearly defined line between the pale pink skin of his face and the deeper pink of his mouth, roughened with cracks of chapping.

"Higher, please."

Simon raised her a little more.

"I'm so sorry," she whispered. "I love you."

And she leaned in and pressed her lips to her husband's, kissing him for the first time since the CEO had cursed her now nearly seven months before.

There was a horrible grinding sound over their heads, the door panel flashed wildly on and off, and the whole elevator began to shake so violently that Maia wasn't the least bit surprised when the lights went out, plunging them all into blackness.

In the first moment of the kiss, Maia did all the work, pressing her lips to the seam of Simon's mouth and keeping her hands on the pillow of his lower lip to hold herself steady. But that was alright, because Simon didn't know what was going to happen yet—and besides, if he'd opened his mouth he could have swallowed her whole.

As the car continued to convulse, the other women screamed and cursed. Someone fell and made a stifled sound of pain. Simon's hands tightened convulsively, and Maia reeled from a surge of nauseating dizziness. She squeezed her eyes shut and rode it out, like an entire course of the flu on fast-forward—she was shivering, she was sweating, she was boneless with fever, she was going to throw up.

The vertigo passed when her feet hit the floor and her hands were in the way of their mouths, big enough that Maia slid them around to scrape across the stubble on Simon's jawline and then tangle in his hair. Simon opened his mouth against hers and the taste of him was so sweetly familiar despite the morning breath that Maia kissed him harder. When he jerked his head back, breaking contact, she could have cried again—except that Simon was staring at the opening to the elevator, which was smoking as the magical barrier dissolved.

Maia tore herself out of Simon's arms, registered that she was naked, and pushed the awareness away with ferocious intent. She looked around wildly for their backpack. God, everything was so *close*—just a few steps and she was across the elevator.

"Come on!" she urged over her shoulder. "We may not get another chance."

She caught her toe against the metal rim of the doorframe and stumbled so hard she went down on her knees, unable to catch herself sooner because of the bag in her hands. She crawled across the plush carpet of the hallway and then scrambled to put her back to the wall because Jesus, everyone had just seen everything there was to see of her, hadn't they? Cellulite on her ass and her boobs hanging down, not to mention that the CEO must know she'd broken her contract. Maia checked the hall in both directions, but there was no one coming. She turned back in time to see the elevator doors start to close behind Ranjani, the last one out.

They'd all made it. They were out. And she was naked and everyone was staring at her.

Maia fished in the backpack for the clothes she'd made Simon stash in there in one of her optimistic moments. She didn't even know where the dress she'd been wearing had gone. She shimmied into her underwear, which was snug, dammit. *Six months without spin class*—she forced her brain away, found her bra and put it on, then her t-shirt, then stood up to step into her skirt. She knew she was being ridiculous not making eye contact while she did all this, as if that would make her invisible while she got dressed, but she felt like she was putting armor on and she wouldn't be able to face anyone until she was done.

But as soon as she was fully clothed, she felt a warm hand on her arm.

"Maia?" Ranjani made her name a question, but she was smiling. "You did it! Welcome back."

She hugged Maia hard. Maia's vision blurred.

"I probably stink."

"I don't care."

But there was no time. Maia set Ranjani away and sat down cross-legged, pulling their laptops out of the backpack.

"Simon," she said. "We've got to get logged in and get the programs running. Do you want to take one and I'll take the other?"

She held out a computer to her husband, who took it automatically, but didn't take his eyes off her. He didn't even seem to realize he was holding the laptop until she said his name again, sharply this time.

"Si!"

"Maia, you're…"

He registered the urgency in her voice and shook himself.

"You want me to just work on getting you in past the firewall, right?"

"Yeah. I'll be right behind you."

Their plan was distraction and destabilization: *Look over here at this very alarming thing, while the women you've assaulted launch a coordinated strike right in front of you and show you that you're not invincible after all.* Maia and Simon had written a cascading series of viral programs designed to first get the CEO's attention by making it look like the company's stock was plummeting, then to escalate his initial (hopefully panicky) response by thwarting every attempt he made to stop the plunge with yet another apparently disastrous development. It would look like there was a sell-off happening, then an FEC flag would go up on the company trading patterns, then a second one…

All week, they'd tested the parameters of what they could do given the company's excellent IT security, which Maia had designed herself. They couldn't wreak complete havoc without crashing payroll or risking the employee retirement funds. What they *could* do was target the CEO's obsession with the company's public-facing finances and try to throw him off-balance enough that he'd be vulnerable, literally and magically, to the other women's tactics.

"Remember what I told you all over text," Maia said as she logged in and started prepping her virus software to upload. "We're basically—hopefully—buying you time and dividing his attention. It's the best I can do."

"No, it's not," Abony said. "Maia, stop. Just wait a second. Jo, you want to, I don't know, keep watch?"

Jo nodded. "Who could we expect? Whose offices are on this floor?"

"Just the CEO's, the General Counsel's, their assistants', and a couple of big conference rooms," Abony said. "And it looks like we've made sure no one else is coming up for a while."

"Or going down," Jo added.

Maia peered past them and saw Ranjani's braid lying in between the elevator doors. The braid—or maybe the air around it—was smoking gently, and the doors were making weak thunking sounds as they tried to close on the thick rope of Ranjani's hair.

"Jesus," she said.

Ranjani, astonishingly, grinned.

"Aren't there other elevators?" Simon asked.

Abony shook her head. "There are four in the lobby, but only one with access to this floor. Listen, we've got a little time, but likely just a little. Maia, stop and think."

"There's not time!" Maia snapped. "You just said it yourself. If you all want to go catch him in his office, then we've got to get these viruses going so he's freaked out when you get there."

"Or you could put down the computer and go to the police."

"And the Board," Jo added. "Call the company grievance line."

"Call the *Post* and offer them an exclusive," Abony said. "Hell, Maia, get out of here and contact the damn FBI. But stop worrying about distracting him with a computer virus and *go report him*."

Maia felt sweat run down her sides under her t-shirt. Her hands were clammy on the computer as she closed the lid.

"I forgot shoes," she said.

"No, I've got them."

Simon passed her a pair of squashed ballet flats. She slipped them on and scrambled to her feet, clutching her laptop to her chest.

"I look like shit."

"You look like a woman who's been assaulted and then terrorized for six months by the man who assaulted her," Abony said.

"They'll want to know why I waited six months."

"It's well within the statute," Jo said. "And they'll consider it urgent if you tell them that three *other* women he assaulted are confronting him in his office right now and you're worried what's going to happen to them—or him."

"I am *not* worried about what's going to happen to him," Maia retorted, but she didn't move. Now that she was paying attention to her body, she realized that she felt physically awful, bloated and queasy and too big and too small all at once. It was as though the hallway they were standing in was one of those funhouse corridors with mirrors everywhere, floor and ceiling too, and as you walked the floor became the wall and the wall became first the ceiling and then the other wall and then the floor again. She clutched her laptop until the sides bit into her upper arms and tried to remember that this was who she was, this size, this shape.

So little and yet so fierce, he'd taunted her. She didn't feel fierce now.

But she had been. She *was*.

"You son of a bitch," she said, the words she'd said to him that day in his office. "There is no way you're getting away with this. No fucking way."

She stepped around Abony, pressed the "down" button on the elevator panel, and picked up Ranjani's braid when the doors opened.

"I'll keep this for you," she said to Ranjani. "Si, is there room in the backpack for it?"

Simon got into the elevator, took both her computer and the braid from her, and crouched to tuck everything back into their bag.

Maia looked across the threshold at the other women.

"Go, get out of here. Give him hell for me or something like that. I don't have any snappy lines right now. Just—" she faltered—"stay safe."

Abony nodded once, as though she was approving something, and Maia pressed the down button on the elevator again. Ranjani waved to Maia as the doors closed. Jo was already moving down the hall, pulling her suitcase behind her.

In the elevator, Maia pressed the button for the parking garage, then lunged for the backpack.

"Si, where's your phone? I want to see if I can call the grievance line from the car on the way to the station. I just want to pull the number up now—shit, no signal in here."

She rummaged further and turned up the toiletry bag she used to take to the gym.

"Oh, thank God! I forgot I asked you to pack this."

Maia did an inventory: wet wipes, deodorant, a hairbrush with several elastics wrapped around the handle. She could make herself something close to presentable, instead of showing up at the police station looking like a madwoman fresh from her attic.

Swiping a cleansing wipe under her arms, she turned to see what Simon was doing.

He was crawling on the floor retrieving the wires and connectors that had comprised Maia's elaborate communications system inside the suitcase. The case itself was open beside him, the beautifully constructed foam interior torn and squashed from the chaotic ride up.

"It doesn't matter," Simon said over his shoulder. "I mean, it's not like we'll need to use it again."

Nevertheless, he tucked all the tech carefully back into the case before closing it and standing up.

"You want me to drive you to the police station?"

Maia laughed, remembering Abony's suggestion of the FBI.

"Yes, please," she said, "unless you have a better idea."

"We could just leave," Simon said in a rush. "We could leave DC and never come back."

Maia froze in the midst of a stroke of deodorant and stared at her husband. She tried not to search his face for dismay at the reality of her, regular-sized and already bossing him around— and not to let her own dismay at his suggestion show on hers.

"Yeah," Simon said after a moment. "Never mind."

The elevator stopped at the garage and he got out, then held the door open while Maia gathered up the explosion of stuff she'd dumped from the backpack. Once they were in the car, he took his phone back, plugged in the address of the nearest police station, and carefully backed out of the spot.

Fairy Tales Forever Discord Channel

*We are an inclusive community; we celebrate all voices and identities. Expressions of hate, bias, or general assholery (yes, we know it's not a word) will not be tolerated. For full channel rules and guidelines click **here**.*

Discussion Boards: Fairy Tale of the Day |
Question of the Day | Fairy Tales for Our Time

Question of the Day: Are there any stories where the princess does the kissing instead of needing to be kissed?
submitted by ellerythegreat (member since 2018)

ellerythegreat: Hi, I am 12 and I am writing this question with my mom's permission for a school project. She's already a member of this group and said I could join to ask this question. Her name on here is @blackcatlover because of our amazing black cat who my mom named Mephistopheles. But nobody but her can pronounce that so we call him Meff. My question is the one I put in the question field: Are there any fairy tales where the princess kisses the prince first instead of him having to kiss her?

Angelofthehouse: Hi @ellerythegreat, welcome to the group! I hope your mom lets you join more conversations. The only one I can think of is "The Frog Prince," where the prince is trapped in the body of a frog until the princess kisses him to turn him back into a prince. Anyone else?

Jess: What's interesting is that there are a lot of other fairy tales where the prince is trapped in the body of an animal (or, you know, a Beast) and has to be freed by a princess, but none of those use a kiss as the way to free him. It's usually that the princess has to fall in love with him, but in many of them, she has to go through a lot of really hard challenges to PROVE that she loves him. "In East of the Sun, West of the Moon," for example, she has to cut off her little fingers! Don't worry, that's still a good story and I bet you'll like it. But I can't think of other fairy tales where a prince is just awakened or freed from a spell with a kiss.

JennyK: People are right. There's also "The Brown Bear of Norroway," "Hans My Hedgehog," and of course "Cupid and Psyche." Consistently, in stories where the prince has to win the princess, he literally just has to kiss her awake and bam, they fall in love and get married. But in stories where the princess has to win the prince, she has to endure or go through a lot of hardship. She doesn't get to pick a prince, kiss him, and then live happily ever after.

AUGUST 17: ABONY

Abony knew that asking Maia to go to the police had been the right call. But she also knew that it would leave the rest of them vulnerable from the moment they opened the door to the CEO's office. They'd counted on storming in while he was screaming and clutching his hair (Abony relished that particular visual) at the evidence that all his hard-earned fiscal gains for the company were melting away even as he watched. They'd counted on catching him off guard.

And now he wasn't.

Outside the office, Abony looked at the other women and silently raised her eyebrows: *Do it or not?*

Jo nodded immediately. After a fraction of a second, Ranjani did too.

Abony pushed the door open and stepped inside the CEO's office for the first time since he'd raped her there almost five months before.

He was at his desk. Without looking up, he thrust out his hand and froze them all where they stood. Abony instinctively backed up—except she couldn't. She was paralyzed, unable even to turn her head. Behind her she heard a metal thunk; he'd locked them in.

He lowered his hand and made a show—Abony was sure it was a show—of finishing whatever task he was doing, furrowing his brow as he read something on the screen, then typing with two-fingered concentration. At last he leaned back and surveyed them from behind his gleaming mahogany moat.

He was a big man, wide as well as tall, though there was no softness to him. He wore his hair slicked back from a point on his forehead and his suit was either navy blue or black—or perhaps it was actually shifting, as Abony looked at it, between the two colors. His shirt collar was very white and so were his cuffs when he shook out his arms and folded his hands at his waist. There were gemstones at his wrists, square sapphires as big as postage stamps.

"Ladies," he said, "this is unexpected. And I'd say it was a pleasure, but I don't like to lie unless it's absolutely necessary. You should have called first, really you should have."

He smiled.

"Where's Maia, by the way?"

Did he not know? Curious. Abony wondered how that was possible, and if Suzanne knew and hadn't told him yet. She wanted to believe it, that Suzanne had bought them time. But of course, time was no use to them when they were all frozen in place.

She remembered clearly that he'd done this to her right after he'd raped her, in the moment when she might otherwise have raked bloody furrows down his face with her nails.

"No one wants to talk about Maia?" The CEO pulled his mouth down into a parody of a sorrowful face. "Is she on her way to some police station even now, or did she have to go find some clothes that fit first?"

Oh. He knew. *Stupid!* Abony shouted at herself. *Stupid to think you could just walk in here and do anything to this man.*

They'd convinced themselves that the magic they'd discovered, not just Chantal's but their own, of a sort, would be a match for his. They'd believed that they could break his own perfect assurance of his power. Abony felt and heard herself panting and thought almost dispassionately that she seemed to be having a panic attack. Her mouth was dry, her heart pounding, her feet throbbing.

No, her feet weren't throbbing. They only felt that way because her shoes were growing hot. The shoes remembered the last time they'd been here too.

Abony tried to clench her feet inside her shoes to encourage them and discovered that she could. A few minutes ago she hadn't been able to turn her head. Had the spell loosened?

"Alright," the CEO said, "never mind Maia. Let's talk about you. As always, Abony, I love your shoes. You seem to have an endless collection. Is this pair new?"

"Actually," Abony said—so she could talk, for what it was worth; the paralysis didn't extend to her voice— "these are the shoes I was wearing the day you raped me right here in this office. I bought them because I *wanted* to buy them and not because you cursed me. They were my favorite shoes."

She'd played this interaction out in her head a hundred times. It would be the moment she'd make him hear just how much he'd taken from her, and the moment right before she took some of herself back. But locked in place in front of him, she heard her voice shake as she told him, *They were my favorite shoes.* She sounded shaken and sad instead of angry.

Her shoes were not fans of the way this was going. They were quivering on her feet now, like hunting animals being held back from springing at prey. The problem was that Abony couldn't take them off without him noticing.

But he was already tired of her. He strolled around the desk to stand in front of Jo.

Abony toed off one shoe.

"Jo," the CEO said, "I'm quite sure you would like to tell me just what you think of me. Shall I get a flyswatter ready? Or some Raid?"

Jo sneered.

Abony toed off her other shoe. Freed from her feet, they seemed to hesitate, to forget themselves. Abony tried to breathe slowly. She made herself remember more details and offered them to the shoes: how he'd pressed her cheek into his desk and held her hands tight in one of his, the bones in her wrists grinding together as he ground into her, how he'd talked about her shoes as if they were to blame for what he was doing to her.

The shoes twitched, shook themselves.

Just listen, Abony whispered to them. *Listen to him. He's got us all in a spell so we can't move, but he can't hold you.*

"And, Ranjani," he was saying, "what a shame about your hair. I really am sorry for that, you know, both that you cut it off—such beautiful hair—and that you did it for nothing. For an elevator ride."

"It was worth it," Ranjani said. "Maia got out."

"And your left eyebrow keeps twitching," Jo added. "Nervous tic?"

Smoke began to rise from under Abony's shoes.

"I'm disappointed about Maia," the CEO said, wheeling back to Jo, "but it was a calculated risk, offering each of you a way out at the expense of the others. When she signed a deal to stay small, I initially gained power rather than losing it. Now that she's changed her mind—" He shrugged, but Abony saw that Jo was right. His eyebrow was twitching, and his hands were tight-fisted at his sides.

"Again, it was a gamble," he went on. "And now she's sitting in an uncomfortable chair outside some detective's office trying to figure out how to tell a version of what happened to her that people can actually believe. Knowing Maia, she's wearing a t-shirt that reads *hashtag believe women*."

"People *will* believe her," Jo said. "If you weren't so scared that people would believe women, why have you tried so hard to silence us?"

"I *did* silence you!" he roared—and lunged at Jo.

"Go!" Abony cried aloud, and her shoes leapt forward, leaving scorch marks on the carpet in their wake. They moved in perfect synchrony, one on either side of him, slipping under his pant legs to sear the skin of his calves and ankles, then out and in again, stabbing at the tops of his dress shoes like scorpions stinging a bear. He screamed and swatted them, first instinctively with his hands, and then when he burned himself on the soles, with violent gestures that Abony guessed were thrusts of magic, and which the shoes ignored.

The spell holding the three women broke so suddenly that Abony stumbled forward.

"Hold him still!" she snapped. The shoes backed off the CEO's feet and took simultaneous running jumps to land halfway up his thighs and climb, forcing him back, cursing and flailing at them, until he hit the edge of his desk. He flung back his hands to brace himself and the shoes ran down his arms to his wrists, reared up, and then seemed to half-melt, smoking, into red and black manacles that bound him in place. He twisted and bucked up against them, the movement unintentionally obscene.

"Revenge, Abony?" he panted. "That's what you're here for? How long have you been dreaming up this little fantasy?"

"I didn't dream it up," Abony said. "You did. Don't you remember the story of the Red Shoes? They have minds of their own and they can't be controlled. Turns out that my red-soled shoes do too."

She cocked her head, considering him. He was sweating, enough that she could see patches of damp on his white shirt front and rivulets running down the sides of his face. "You know that already, don't you? You're trying spells and they're not working. Scary, isn't it, to feel helpless?"

"I am so far from helpless," he retorted. "When I'm done with you, all of you—"

"Oh, for God's sake," Jo cut in, "you sound like a James Bond villain. Do you even hear yourself?" She swung her suitcase flat on the floor so it opened toward him.

"Do you hear *yourself*?" the CEO snapped back. "Can anyone stand to hear you, or are they too busy running screaming every time you try to speak? And what could you possibly have in a *suitcase*—" he fairly spat the word— "that would change that?"

Jo stilled with her hand on the latch.

"Do you seriously not know what's in here?"

She looked incredulously around at the other women. "He really doesn't know."

Abony saw the moment he realized, his eyes going from Jo's face to the suitcase and back.

"Fine," he snarled. "I'll worry about these damn shoes later, Abony." He made a flicking motion in her direction with one constrained hand. "You worry about the ones you don't have yet. And you—" he made the same gesture at Jo— "stay still!"

Jo froze in place again, crouched over her suitcase with one hand on the lid and the other flung up as if to block the spell.

Ranjani was on her knees on Jo's other side, scrabbling in her tote bag for something. The CEO didn't even spare her a glance.

Then his words to Abony—*you worry about the ones you don't have yet*—did their work and her heightened curse crashed over her like a wave.

She had to have shoes, more shoes, who knew how many more, it didn't matter how many, or what size, whether she liked them or not, or whether or not they would fit. Abony had dropped her purse when she'd unfrozen. Now she fell to her knees so hard they hurt and fumbled in her purse for her phone. The Neiman Marcus site popped up without any prompting, which had to be part of his plan—no bargain shoes allowed. Abony's stomach roiled. She found the Louboutin listings and clicked *Add to Cart* over and over again: snakeskin wedges, rainbow-striped pumps, some hideous lucite and mesh things, even a pair of "nude" slingbacks that were only nude for a White woman.

Ten pairs, twelve. If she clicked *Complete Purchase,* she'd spend $10,000. But he didn't know everything about her curse, damn him, and he didn't know *anything* about her. Abony had about thirty seconds before she blacked out. If she could just resist buying the fucking shoes a little longer—she was shaking all over, her vision starting to swim—

"Hang on, Abony," Ranjani said breathlessly. "Hang on."

She was rushing to the desk, pulling her necklace over her head.

"Ranjani, Ranjani," the CEO said. "Think of your mother. What will happen to her if you're not careful?"

Ranjani put the exquisite white key down on the desk and uncapped the pen she had in her hand.

Abony blinked hard, trying to focus. Oh, not a pen. A scalpel.

"I know what happens to my mother when I'm not careful *now*," Ranjani said. "This key turns red as if it's stained with blood." She slanted a glance at the CEO. "I wonder how you made that work. Is there really blood inside the key?"

"You can't damage that," the CEO said, and Abony swallowed against the sudden wild hope that she'd heard fear in his voice. "Do you have any idea what will happen to your mother?"

Ranjani, incredibly, smiled. "Oh yes," she said. "She showed me exactly what to do. The trick is not to hesitate." And she lowered the scalpel with her index finger to guide it and sliced the key in half in one clean stroke.

Everything happened at once then. The CEO let out a roar of rage and denial. Blood fountained up out of the key, an impossible geyser that nearly caught Ranjani in the face before it subsided into the desktop and began to spread. Jo shook free of the binding and spat out a cloud of iridescent green flies that stung the CEO's face and ears and burrowed into his hair, while he screamed and twisted ineffectually away, unable to use his hands to slap at them. And Abony's curse broke.

She hadn't spent time wondering how she'd know, whether she'd know, when her curse broke, but she felt it break just as viscerally as she'd felt it intensify a few minutes before. It was the easing of a headache from behind her eyes, the first pang of real hunger after the stomach flu, a deep breath after taking off a too-tight skirt. It was—Abony laughed out loud—something like the relief of taking off a pair of high-heeled shoes after she'd been walking in them all day.

No one else in the room turned to see why she had laughed. They were all watching the bloodstain spread across the CEO's desk. Rather than moving out in all directions or dripping onto the floor, it was flowing towards the CEO's nearest manacled hand as though drawn there. When it touched his hand—he tore so frantically at his bindings that Abony was sure she could hear seams ripping in her poor shoes—the blood simply vanished, even as he thrashed and protested. In moments, it was all gone.

Ranjani poked at the remains of the key with the scalpel.

"I don't know exactly what happened," she said apologetically to Abony and Jo. "I meant to just cut the curse out of the key, like lancing a wound—"

The CEO cut her off, spitting with impotent rage: "When I get free, there will be nowhere for you to hide, none of you."

"There never has been," Ranjani said, without inflection. She capped the scalpel and dropped it back into her bag, then stepped back, frowning.

"I didn't expect all that blood," she said, "or for it to have returned to him like that."

"I wonder…" Abony said and narrowed her eyes at her shoes. "Make him show us his hands."

The shoes visibly loosened their grip on his wrists and then, as he moved to free himself, clamped down again so he was trapped palms-up. They all saw what Abony had thought they might: his palms were stained red as if with blood.

"I can make this go away," the CEO said. "I created the spell. I can take care of this. Your gloating is premature, I assure you."

"Gloating?" Jo asked. "There's blood on your hands and you think we're gloating? That's *our* blood." She broke off, choking, but nothing threatened to come from her mouth but words.

"I bled," she said, "and I *leaked. You* leaked out of me, which made me want to vomit. And I hurt all over—between my legs, my back, my hips, my arms from where you held me still. It was *disgusting.*"

Improbably, the CEO seemed to rear back and shout a denial of what was going to happen before it did, but as she said the word *disgusting* Jo kicked her suitcase so that the lid sprang open and the things inside of it boiled out—crawling, slithering, hopping, scuttling, flying, buzzing—and swarmed. Abony's shoes sprang free at the last moment, releasing his hands, which he flung up too late to do any good. Within seconds, he disappeared under the seething mass.

On the carpet, the shoes shook themselves like dogs and scampered back to Abony. Behind her, someone began pounding on the doors of the office.

"Security!" a man's voice shouted. "Security. Is everyone okay in there?"

Abony slipped her shoes on, grabbed Jo's empty suitcase and righted it, locked it, and tucked it back against the wall. Jo stood watching the thing at the desk, man-shaped under its living blanket. Together, Abony and Ranjani tried to tug her away.

Another round of determined knocking on the door.

"Sir! Sir, are you alright? We've had a call that there might be someone in distress in this office. Can you answer, please? Sir?"

"Wait." Jo shook off the other women's hands and turned back towards the CEO.

"That's enough," she said.

The squirming, glittering mass lifted off like a black curtain being plucked straight up in the air by a magician's hand. The creatures kept rising—even the ones that shouldn't have been able to fly seemed borne aloft by sheer numbers—up to the enormous air vent on the ceiling. They poured into it in a steady stream, until the only things left were a half-dozen fat black flies, which turned their attention to the windows instead, buzzing stubbornly against the glass as though they could escape through sheer indignation.

The knocks at the door ceased. Instead they heard muffled sounds of radio static, raised voices, and then a man's voice saying urgently, "Sir, we're coming in. Please stand clear of the door."

Abony braced herself for the door to explode inward, but someone on the other side simply used a key. A moment later, two building security guards stepped in cautiously with their batons and radios out. The moment they saw the man lurching up from where he'd apparently been leaning on his desk, they raced forward to support him and ease him on his back onto the carpet in front of his desk.

The CEO stank of fear sweat and burnt meat, and he was breathing in dreadful gulps, his color ghastly. Abony assessed him narrowly. She needed to know what kinds of questions they'd be facing. There were no creatures crawling across his skin, no stings or welts or bites, nor any sign of the blistering burns that Abony's shoes had made on his wrists or of the blood on his palms. He looked like a man having a heart attack.

"Call 911," one of the guards snapped at his colleague. He himself was busy loosening the victim's tie, checking him for responsiveness.

"Should we leave?" Ranjani murmured. "*Can* we leave?"

"I think we can start by going out into the hall," Abony said.

"Does this mean Maia got to the police already?" Ranjani wanted to know once they were out of the office. "It seemed to all happen so fast."

"But this wasn't the police," Abony said. "It's just building security, which means someone from the company called it in."

"I did," said a voice behind them. Abony swung around to see Suzanne with her cell phone in her hand.

"I'm hoping that you will all agree to remain on the premises a bit longer," she said. "I can't force you to stay, but it would be helpful if you would give statements to the police when they arrive."

"Even if Maia's gotten to talk to someone at the police station by now, we won't see them here for hours," Abony said.

"But I called them too," Suzanne said, "about five minutes ago." She made a choked sound that might have been a laugh. "Imagine my surprise when the call actually went through."

She looked from one of them to the other and then abruptly dissolved into laughter. She laughed and laughed until she started to choke and sputter and one of the guards stuck his head out the door curiously.

"Everything alright?"

Jo waved him away.

Suzanne kept laughing. She let her cell phone fall, put her hands over her face and backed up to the wall, then slid down it to land with a thump, at which point the laughter turned into sobs and she pressed her face into her knees and sobbed until she couldn't breathe.

Ranjani put a hand on her back.

"Take a breath, that's right, another. Just try to breathe, okay? In and out, nice and deep."

The elevator dinged and a paramedic crew stepped off with a stretcher. They paused by the women.

"You all okay? Somebody need emergency services?"

"Over here!" shouted one of the guards from inside the office. "Possible heart attack!"

The paramedics hurried into the office. Abony heard them asking the CEO questions in measured cadence, interrupted by his voice in ragged bursts. She couldn't make out any of the words.

Suzanne spoke without lifting her head.

"Is the other girl okay? Renee?"

"I hadn't even thought—I'll find out." Abony fumbled for her phone and sent a text to Penny.

"She's okay," Ranjani said. "I know it. We're going to find out that she's okay."

She had sat down beside Suzanne to rub her back.

"I felt the curse break," Ranjani said softly, "the moment I cut into that key. You felt yours break too, didn't you?"

Abony nodded. "I knew I would feel relieved, but it felt better than that."

"Like getting part of yourself back," Jo said. She wasn't smiling, but something had visibly eased in her thin face. "What I've got back is my ability to *tell* you that the CEO raped me three weeks ago in his office and I intend to see that he goes to jail for it."

"For a long, long time," Suzanne said hoarsely. She turned her head sideways on her knees to meet Abony's eyes. "Mine's broken too," she said. "I'd already called security on the pretext that there was someone in his office harassing him. I called the police the moment I felt it break. But I don't know—" She shrugged miserably. "I don't think I got part of myself back."

"Do you feel any better?" Abony asked.

"I feel like I could sleep for a week, but yes, I feel better." Suzanne turned her face back to her knees. "Thank you," she said.

They sat in silence, all of them—except maybe Suzanne—straining slightly to hear what was happening inside the office behind them. One of the paramedics emerged, talking to a dispatcher, and walked a few paces down the hall in the other direction.

"No, this is a non-emergency," he was saying. "Aside from elevated blood pressure, the guy's vitals are normal. He's claiming he was attacked—burned, covered in bugs and blood—but there's not a mark on him. He's demanding to talk to the cops, so we'll stay and do the handoff."

Abony's phone pinged with a text alert.

"Renee's curse is broken too," she said. "Penny says I must be psychic—ha!—because right before I texted, Renee sat up in her hospital bed and started pulling out tubes."

"They won't let her off that easy," Jo said, "but still. I'm glad."

"Yeah," Suzanne said. "Thanks for finding out."

The murmur of voices inside the CEO's office dropped off as the CEO himself began to shout at people, his voice rising to a crescendo accompanied by a crash and a flurry of cursing. The paramedic who'd come out to the hallway went back in, then a few minutes later one of the guards appeared in the doorway, looked up and down the hall, and visibly relaxed when he saw them all sitting on the floor.

"Looks like they're glad we're all still here," Jo muttered. "I wonder why?"

"I'm guessing that asshole just accused us of something," Abony said.

The security guard started towards them.

"Ladies," he said. "I'd be grateful if you just stayed here so the police can talk to you when they arrive."

As if on cue, the elevator opened again and disgorged two uniformed officers, a young White man and a Black woman in her forties.

The security guard cast an anxious look at their group.

"We're not going anywhere," Abony assured him. He walked down the hall to meet the cops, then ushered them into the CEO's office, talking quickly. The CEO roared something so loud that they could clearly understand it even from the hall: *So if they're still here why aren't you fucking arresting them right now? The fuck is wrong with you people?*

Someone inside the office shut the door and the women couldn't hear anything clearly for a while.

Ranjani, who had moved away from Suzanne to sit cross-legged against the wall beside her, announced that she was texting with Maia.

"I told her what happened," she said. "It's kind of hard to explain over text."

Jo snorted. "It's hard to explain in my head and I was there."

"But here's the thing," Ranjani said. "She says she knew. Even though her curse was already broken, she still knew the minute it happened. She felt better all of a sudden, less weird about being her normal size again."

The office door reopened. The paramedics came out wheeling their empty stretcher and strolled back down to the elevator.

"Have a good day, ladies," one of them said as they passed. "Stay safe; don't get into any trouble and make us come back here."

Once the elevator doors had shut behind them, Abony turned back to Ranjani.

"So did Maia make any progress on reporting him?"

"Well, let's see," Ranjani said, scrolling. "She's already sent an anonymous tip to the *Post* about assault allegations that are about to come out against him along with the documents from the suit Emily Sato's parents filed against him at his last company."

"Fuck," Suzanne said without lifting her head.

"And she's called the Board's grievance line and left a message there. Meanwhile, she's at Metro PD and she's asked to make a report with Sex Crimes. They've told her it's not—*timely*, I guess?" Ranjani's face clouded. "Like, you know, she can't exactly do a rape kit."

"Or prove she was four fucking inches tall for nearly seven months," Jo added.

"Right, or anything like that. But they're taking her seriously. They've given her a contact person who's a detective and told her they'll call her to set up an appointment to take her statement. Meanwhile—" she smiled—"she's apparently going home to shower and put on real clothes and then she's making Simon take her to Cactus Cantina for a chimichanga and a margarita because apparently, Mexican food was impossible to manage when she was so small."

The office door opened and the female cop and one of the guards stepped out, then stopped in the doorway to finish their conversation. Inside the office, the CEO seemed to have run down. There were still voices, but no more bursts of shouting.

Suzanne stirred again.

"You said Maia reported him to the Board?"

"Yep," Abony said. "And as soon as that police officer who I guarantee is headed this way gets done with us, you better believe that I will also be reporting him to the Board, and not anonymously either. I will be opening four Title IX complaints against him immediately and I will add one for Renee as soon as she gives me permission—"

"And for me," Suzanne said. She lifted her head and got to her feet. "You can add mine now if you like. Abony, I trust you to talk to the police. I'm going to go deal with the Board."

"Deal with?"

Suzanne brushed off her butt, shook out the crumpled, tear-splotched legs of her pantsuit.

"Deal with," she said. "As in, tell them that there are about to be six Title IX complaints registered against their golden boy CEO, all of which will lead to criminal complaints. I will also tell them that I believe, in my capacity as General Counsel and as one of the complainants, that all the charges are going to stick to this fucking monster. So in my legal opinion, the Board should direct me to pull his contract and see just how fast they can fire him."

She paused. "And while I am happy to help the Board navigate this mess until he's in jail, after that I'm done. I quit."

She stooped to pick up her cell phone and started back down the hall towards her office.

"Suzanne," Abony said sharply.

Suzanne turned back around.

"You trust me to talk to the police, I trust you to talk to the Board," Abony said. "You'll do great. You're a very good lawyer."

Suzanne almost smiled. "That much I am."

The female cop reached them just as Suzanne was closing the door to her office.

"Do I need to talk to that young lady too?" she asked. "She one of the group of women who, according to the gentleman in there, *burst into his office an hour ago and attacked him unprovoked.*"

Jo made a choked sound but said nothing.

"No, ma'am," Abony said. "She's just the company's lawyer."

"Oh, Lord," the officer eyed Suzanne's door like she was willing it to stay shut. "I don't need to talk to her then."

She returned her attention to the three of them. "You're the ones then?"

Abony folded her arms. "The ones who what?"

The cop sighed, pulled up the notes app on her phone, and read aloud.

"Well, in no particular order and frankly without a whole lot of sense to the whole business, directed your high-heeled shoes to burn and restrain him, attacked him with—and I do quote here—*an army of trained insects, spiders, and snakes*—and did something else that involved slicing him in half with a scalpel, even though there's not a mark on him."

She looked up and gave them a minute.

No one said a word.

"Yeah," she sighed. "I figured as much. But listen, this one's going down swinging. Wants to make this all about how you all are out for revenge—thus the slicing him open and attacking him with shoes and bugs—but when I ask him what reason you might have to take this revenge, he says no idea. *You* have any idea?"

Her face was carefully neutral, but Abony liked what she saw in the line of the woman's jaw.

"I have no idea why he would think we were interested in revenge," Abony said.

Jo nodded vigorously. "Revenge is—it's not what normal people do, is it? It's for, I don't know—"

"James Bond villains?" Ranjani suggested. Abony shot her a look, which she returned, wide-eyed.

"Okay, so you're not interested in revenge," the officer said, "as a matter of principle. But you must have wanted something from this guy, otherwise why'd you go in there, all three of you together, and scare the living shit out of him, pardon my language?"

She planted her feet and prepared to stare them all down. Abony stared back. Since she was nearly a foot taller than the other woman in her heels, she wasn't worried about who was going to break first. And besides, the officer's heart wasn't really in it.

"If what's happened is what I think—and I don't know, obviously—then I hope you pursue your concerns," she said. "This one's not going to be easy, that worries me, and I say that as someone who's been in law enforcement a long time. He's going to fight you every step of the way. He's going to drag you all through hell and try to make you wish you'd never come forward. You sure you're up for it?"

Abony offered a smile that was mostly teeth.

"Oh yes," she said. "We're up for it."

Fairy Tales Forever Discord Channel

*We are an inclusive community; we celebrate all voices and identities. Expressions of hate, bias, or general assholery (yes, we know it's not a word) will not be tolerated. For full channel rules and guidelines click **here**.*

Discussion Boards: Fairy Tale of the Day |
Question of the Day | **Fairy Tales for Our Time**

Fairy Tales for Our Time: "Beauty and the ~~Beast~~ Man Who Used to be a Beast"
submitted by bellerules (member since 2015)

AND so Beauty and the Prince were married. After the wedding **THEY** moved in with Beauty's father to save money. The Prince took what was supposed to be a short-term job as a landscaper, but he discovered that he loved to make things grow, especially roses. Soon he was consulting with local rose growers and botanical gardens and he and Beauty were able to get their own place. Beauty convinced the Prince to buy a foreclosure and they **LIVED** in it while Beauty renovated it top to bottom. As it turned out, she had an instinct for seeing the potential in even the scariest fixer-uppers, so she opened her own real estate flipping company.

They were both **HAPPILY** building their careers when Beauty got pregnant with twins, whom they named Rose and Belle. ("We might as well lean in, sweetie," Beauty told the Prince.) Rose, who was neurodiverse, avoided speaking to people but was downright loquacious with animals. By kindergarten, she was a passionate activist against dragon extinction. Belle, meanwhile, changed his name to Beau when he was eight. He intended to be a prince when he grew up, though he assured Rose that if he **EVER** encountered a dragon, he would just wave.

Beauty had very little free time, between her marriage and the kids and the business. Occasionally, though, she would wake up in the middle of the night and look over at her sleeping husband, who frequently smelled faintly of compost and who always had dirt under his nails. She would smile to think of how naïve she'd been when she lived in an enchanted castle with a mysterious beast. She'd imagined someday finding and marrying a handsome prince, but she'd never once thought about what would come **AFTER**.

AUGUST 24: JO

As she approached the restaurant, she saw that she was the last
to arrive. Her friends were already seated at a table on the patio,
laughing at something Ranjani was saying.

Her friends.

Jo stopped by the wrought iron gate that surrounded the
patio and observed them. It had been a week since they'd broken
their curses and started rolling the boulder of real-life sexual
assault reporting uphill. Abony looked chic as always in a green
and yellow watercolor-print dress, but even from this distance,
Jo thought she also looked tired. Abony and Suzanne were
bearing the brunt of much of the company's upheaval in their
respective roles, as well as coordinating the Title IX, criminal,
and civil complaints against the CEO.

Jo looked down at Abony's feet and smiled. Abony was
wearing a fabulous pair of green and white striped heels, but the
bottoms were beige.

Maia, meanwhile, had cut several inches off her unruly hair
and was pink with sunburn. She was wearing a t-shirt and spandex
bike shorts and there was a helmet hanging off the arm of her seat.

"Hey!" she called, waving an arm at Jo. "You gonna join us or
just stand there looking at us all day?"

Jo went over and sat down.

"Sorry," she said. "I saw you all as I walked up and you know what popped into my head? *Oh, my friends are here already.*"

She saw from their expressions that she didn't need to explain further, but she did it anyway.

"You know—not, *Oh, the others are here.*"

"We get it." Maia grinned. "And we like to hear it. Getting easier is it? The expressing your emotions?"

"I work hard every day," Jo said solemnly. "It's a journey."

Abony snorted into her iced tea. "You want to order now or wait for Chantal?" she asked. "I do have some updates to share."

"Good or bad?" Jo asked, just as Chantal appeared over her left shoulder and deposited an enormous gold gift bag on the table in front of her.

"I'm here," Chantal said. "Had to make the cab pull over on a side street so I could get all these things out without crushing them." She walked around the table placing gold bags at everyone's place setting, then sat down in the empty chair. The waitress came over just then and asked if they were celebrating something.

"Absolutely," Chantal said. "And I'll take the bill." She looked around the table. "Champagne, ladies?"

Ranjani shook her head, but the others all accepted. When the waitress was gone, Chantal waved her hand at the bags.

"You can put those down next to you or something, save them for later. You've got a candy apple, a box of gingerbread tiles, and a batch of candied walnut truffles. Ebonie insisted on those. It's her first spell that I've approved for us to sell in the shop."

Ranjani pushed swaths of rustling gold tissue aside to peer into her bag. "They sound amazing," she said, "and look how pretty!" She dug out the small round box with a clear cellophane lid and showed them the truffles, each topped with a walnut half dusted in gold leaf.

Chantal sniffed. "She's too impatient with her tempering, but the flavor is right."

"What do they do?" Jo asked.

"They make you see the best in people. Ebonie had the idea after the Christmas Eve madness in the shop two years ago. All those people getting gifts to show how much they loved the people in their lives and screaming and snapping at each other the whole time. This past Christmas Eve we passed her first trial batch out as free samples at the front door."

"And?" Ranjani looked in fresh wonder at the box in her hand. "What happened?"

"It was heavy-handed," Chantal said. "Strangers started hugging each other, trying to hug me, and an impromptu caroling group convened on the sidewalk and blocked the door. But promising. And, of course"—she nodded at the box Ranjani was holding— "we've refined it since."

Ranjani put her bag down beside her as the waitress returned with their champagne and topped up Ranjani's iced tea.

"Anyone want to propose a toast?" Chantal asked, picking up her glass.

"Oh hell, I do," Jo said. "I mean—it feels obvious." She lifted her glass. "To seeing the best in one another, even without a spell. If we hadn't been able to do that, we wouldn't be here."

Abony raised an appreciative eyebrow, Chantal nodded as though this was exactly what she expected Jo to say, and they clinked glasses.

"Since I invited you all," Chantal said, "let's get my agenda out of the way." She set her glass down. "You know you broke the curses, your own plus Renee's and Suzanne's. What you may not know is that you did more than that. You broke his power entirely."

"What do you mean?" Jo asked.

"I mean," Chantal said, "that he's not a sorcerer anymore. He's lost access to the power he was drawing on. All of it."

"So he's just a man now," Ranjani said softly.

"Oh, he was *always* just a man," Chantal said. "But you all made him realize it."

She turned to Abony. "Tell me what's happened to him—non-magically, I mean. And don't give me any bullshit about confidentiality, Abony. I need to know everything you know."

"He's in the hospital under psychiatric observation," Abony said, "and he may also have suffered a stroke, or even several. They're running tests, of course, but some of his symptoms—itching and burning on his skin, dry mouth, loss of taste—are consistent with stroke or another neurological event. He's also being charged with six counts of forcible sexual assault, with sexual harassment and intimidation likely being added on top of those for the silencing campaign he waged against the women he assaulted."

"How will those other charges hold up, though?" Maia asked. "I mean, there's no way to prove that he cursed us."

"Well, that's the thing." Abony hesitated.

"Is this where we come around to the updates?" Jo asked.

"Yes. See, when Suzanne got us access to his computer and his email, we actually found evidence of ongoing threats to all of us."

She turned to Maia. "The forensic IT experts found messages to you in the CEO's sent email folder, a message every single day since January 26, which is the day he assaulted you, right? They establish a clear pattern of intimidation."

Maia reared back in her seat. "What the hell? I never got any emails from him, not a single one. Except for legitimate professional correspondence with you, Abony, there's no mention of any of us anywhere in his files and believe me, I looked. Simon and I both did."

"I know."

"Well, what did the emails say?"

Abony grimaced. "They're just a sentence each, different every day, calling you stupid or fat, mocking your taste in clothes or how you wear your hair, your love of Comic-Con, your ability to do your job."

Maia scrunched her forehead. She was clearly more frustrated by the mystery of the emails' appearance than by their content.

"I don't get it," she said. "He'd already cursed me. Why bother to send petty little emails on top of that?"

Beside her, Chantal drew in a sharp breath.

"He didn't."

Her expression was so similar to Maia's—a determined puzzling out of a problem they *knew* they could solve—that Jo almost laughed.

"How extraordinary," Chantal went on, her eyes unfocused. "And how splendid. I'm sure he *never* anticipated that."

"Chantal," Abony said, drawing her name out warningly. "Don't start with the vague bullshit."

"Sorry," Chantal said. "I'm astonished, is all. Maia, the messages Abony described—what do they sound like to you? What are they intended to do?"

Maia shrugged. "Insult me, bully me, make me feel—" she broke off and her face cleared just as Chantal's had a moment before.

"*Belittle* me," she said. "Holy shit!"

She bounced out of her seat, back into it, then leaned toward the table, beckoning the rest of them in close.

"The emails weren't there when I looked," she said, "when I was still cursed. Now our curses are broken, his power's broken, and these messages appear in his email. The emails to me are all intended to make me feel small. Abony, what were Jo's? And when did hers start?"

"The day she was assaulted," Abony said, "same as yours. Same as all of ours. There are emails sent to every woman he attacked that start the day he assaulted her. Us. So there aren't as many to Jo, obviously, and they're not even in his own words. They're quotes from social media or right-wing news about women."

"Let me guess," Maia said. "Are they about women's voices, specifically?"

Abony thought about it. "I suppose so, yes. Some are about the literal sound of a woman's voice—*it's like fingernails on a chalkboard, she whines like a baby*—and the rest claim that women who try to be heard in a public space, when they've been wronged, you name it, are shrill, aggressive, hysterical. There are some pretty bad suggestions in the mix about ways to effectively silence *the bitches.*"

She cast Jo an apologetic glance.

"Abony," Jo said, "the fact that this asshole sent me—or wanted to send me—an incel take-of-the-day isn't surprising. And listen to me—I just called him an asshole."

"But the point is," Maia cut in impatiently, "that his emails to Jo were about her voice. And I'm guessing Ranjani's were actual threats against her mother's health. What were yours about, Abony?"

"Oh," Abony said disgustedly, "photos and videos almost exclusively. I had no idea there was that much interest in images and recordings of women's mutilated feet."

"Oh, for fuck's sake," Jo said. "Really?"

Ranjani squeezed Abony's hand.

But Maia beamed. "No, not really. The emails you found aren't real—or at least, they weren't emails that would ever have appeared in our inboxes—and they're not things he was doing

344 | ANN CLAYCOMB

in addition to the curses. They *are* the curses. They weren't in his sent mail folder before we confronted him because he was so powerful that he could cover his tracks. But we broke his power, including his ability to conceal what he was doing to women. Ergo—email trails suddenly appear that match the timelines when we were each cursed."

She looked at Chantal. "How'd I do?"

"Couldn't have put it better," Chantal said. "Just don't ask me how it happened because I've got no idea. I don't mess with sorcery and my computer knowledge is limited to whether the damn thing saves my files or not."

"I don't care how it happened," Abony said.

She looked shaken, but also like she was thinking hard, rearranging information in her head. Jo realized that Abony must have been at least partly dreading this dinner, dreading having to tell them all that there was more the CEO had done to them than they'd already known. But there wasn't. There was instead, incredibly, more that *they* had done—not to him, not even deliberately, but they'd done it all the same.

"To your point earlier, Maia," Abony said, "these emails are admissible evidence of, not the literal curses obviously, but certainly of the intent of the curses. Suzanne is confident that we'll prevail on all the charges we've brought against him."

Maia sat back, looking satisfied.

The waitress sidled up to take their food order and Chantal held out her credit card.

"Can you put their tab on here and then come back? I don't want to get in any arguments about who's paying."

To the women at the table she said, "I'm heading home. You all stay here and toast each other again, toast what you accomplished. Oh, I know I helped you," she said, when they opened their mouths to protest, "but that was because you came looking for me. That was still *you*."

The waitress came back with Chantal's card. She took it, then pushed her chair back and stood up.

"I don't tell Ebonie I'm proud of her very often," she said. "I need her to grow up strong enough to trust in her own sense of who she is and what she can do, as a witch, as a woman, as a Black woman. But if she ever accomplishes anything like what you four did, you can be sure I will tell her flat-out: I am proud of you. *You saved yourselves*."

No one spoke as Chantal wended her way between tables to the sidewalk. Then Maia muttered, "Dammit, she is the freaking master of having the last word."

The waitress took their laughter as a sign that it was finally time to take their order. When she'd gone, Abony said, "I do have something else to share. The Board is concerned about civil suits that we might all bring against the company, given that they hired the CEO despite knowing about Emily Sato's parents' accusations, *and* that he subsequently assaulted women on the premises and harassed them—apparently—from his company email account. They're going to offer us money."

"On the condition that we don't sue," Jo said flatly.

"Yes."

Blood money, wasn't that the term? Jo didn't say it out loud.

"Fine, I'll bite," Maia said. "How much?"

Abony named the figure. Ranjani gasped.

"Well, damn," Maia said. "That'll make quitting easier."

Abony raised an eyebrow. "You're quitting?"

"I am. And I'll get you a letter of resignation, don't worry. I figured you had enough to deal with right at this minute. I can wait a few weeks."

"What are you going to do?" Jo asked.

"No idea," Maia said. "Well, that's not true. I'm going to travel. Europe, probably? Maybe Central America? We went to Costa Rica on our honeymoon and I made Simon hike." She half-smiled. "He hated every minute of it."

"So—he's not coming with you?" Ranjani asked tentatively.

"No. We're not... over... but he's staying here." Maia shrugged unhappily. "We're just going to see what happens, how we feel in a couple of months."

She tipped back her champagne glass and emptied it. The waitress arrived with their meals and there was the usual brief chaos of sorting out silverware and drink orders and the need for ketchup.

Once that was over, Ranjani looked across at Maia, who was cutting her burger in half.

"Maia, will this settlement money really make it a lot easier to quit and travel the way you want to?"

"Oh, I don't know about that," Maia said. "I plan to travel light, for one thing, and for another, I've got a lot saved up." She smiled wryly. "Turns out that when you can't leave your house for six months, you don't spend much, not to mention how little I ate."

"That's good," Ranjani said. "I mean, obviously having extra money would help. It would help us too, getting my mom more care and—" she blushed— "well, we're talking about trying to plan for—"

"A baby!" Maia shrieked. "Yes, yes, do it, do it, you guys will be such cute parents." She froze with her burger halfway to her mouth. "If you were going to say *puppy*, I'm going to feel like an idiot."

Ranjani giggled. "Nope. Baby. We've been talking to my mom's doctor—because we've been able to *go* back to the doctor, which is so, so good. There's maybe a clinical trial she can get into, plus some new meds on the market. Anyway, she's lost ground, but she's still her, and if we can keep her that way or even get her some ground back—well, we'd like her to know her first grandchild. Plus, I mean, we've always wanted to have a baby."

She put her fork down on the side of her plate and swallowed hard.

"So yeah, more money would be helpful, but I don't want *that* money. I really, really don't."

"Yeah," Jo said, relieved. "Me either."

"It's different for you, Abony," Ranjani added hurriedly. "All the money he made you spend—you should just consider it reimbursement."

"But that's not what it is," Abony said. "And if I need money, I can sell the damn shoes."

Maia was frowning fiercely. "I'm on board with not taking a cent from the company to keep us all quiet. But if we don't take it, then they just get off easily—"

"I think we should take it," Ranjani said. "But what if we gave it to Emily's family instead?"

"Oh God," Maia said. "That's a good idea. They're not getting anything from our company."

"Money won't bring their daughter back," Abony said. "But it could help other women."

She wiped her hands on her napkin and reached into her purse.

"Here," she said, passing them each a folded sheet of paper. "Suzanne and I had this conversation already. This was actually her idea. See what you think."

It was a proposal to establish a fund in Emily Sato's name with a DC organization called the Network for Victim Recovery.

"I'm in," Ranjani said as soon as she'd scanned the proposal.

"Me too," Maia said. "Show me where to sign. And listen to their mission statement." She read it aloud. "*Empowering victims of all crimes to achieve survivor-defined justice through a collaborative continuum of advocacy, case management, and legal services.*"

"Survivor-defined justice," Jo repeated. "I don't think we even knew that's what we wanted, but it's what we got for ourselves. Let's help other people get it too."

AUGUST 24: RANJANI

Amit was on the phone with his grandmother in India when Ranjani got home. She could hear him talking through the closed door of his office, his voice raised to a level just short of a shout because his grandmother was hard of hearing and their connection was often bad.

She unpacked The Gingerbread House bag on the kitchen counter and went to find her mother. Shreshthi was not in her bedroom. Ranjani found her bent over a pad of paper on the back patio.

"Mami?" she said. "What are you doing out here? Did you get dinner?"

"I made dinner for me and Amit," her mother said. "We were going to watch a movie but his amma called him and—" she waved her pen impatiently— "you know how she is with time zones and knowing when he's free. It was easier for him just to talk to her."

Ranjani didn't know whether to laugh or cry at this, given Shreshthi's own inconsistent ability to navigate even a simple phone call these days. She sat down in the chair facing her mother's.

"So what are you doing?" she asked. "You look like you're working on something."

"I'm making a list of criteria," her mother said. "When I'm done I'll rank them, but for now I'm just listing everything we need to consider: food, cleanliness, distance from your house, hospital affiliation, staff retention, and—" she stumbled over the list so briefly that Ranjani could have missed the break if she hadn't known her mother so well— "whether they have a memory care unit onsite."

"Mami!" Ranjani snatched the list and scanned it. "What is this for? What are you doing?"

"I think it's time we talk about places for me to live," Shreshthi said calmly. She took the pad back and busied herself sliding the pen through the spiral binding at the top. "You can't take care of me forever, Rani, you and Amit. You have busy jobs already and you'll want to have a family soon."

"We *can* take care of you forever," Ranjani said fiercely. "We don't want you to leave, do you hear me? This is your home, our home." She felt tears coming and tried to stave them off.

"Who would cook if you weren't here? You know I'm no good at puri. Mine come out greasy every time."

But it was no good. Tears slid down Ranjani's cheeks and splashed on her hands. "And I would miss you, Mami. Please don't go."

Slowly, Shreshthi sat back in her seat. She looked so bewildered that Ranjani was afraid she'd sunsetted, forgotten her own arguments, lost track of why she even had a pad covered in her own spiky handwriting in her lap.

But it wasn't that at all.

"Rani," her mother said, "I'm sorry. I didn't know you felt this way. Of course I don't want to leave you and go live in some apartment where the hallways always smell of bleach." She wrinkled her nose. "But I've been worried about you.

You've been so unhappy these past few weeks, maybe months. I—don't know exactly how long. But you never seem to leave the house, not even to go to a movie with your husband, and he loves you so much, Rani, you must know how much he loves you."

"Oh, Mami!"

Shreshthi put out a hand to touch Ranjani's wet face. "You've been working so late, going back into the office at night. And then you cut your hair. It looks very nice, but you don't seem happy. Why did you cut it, Rani, if you didn't want to?"

Ranjani's nose was running. "Wait," she said. "Mami, hold on."

She slipped inside for the box of tissues and came back out blowing her nose.

"I had to cut my hair," she said. "I can't explain why. I just had to and I'm glad I did. But I am going to grow it out."

"Have you been doing oil treatments at night? You need to do those if you want to grow it out."

Ranjani laughed shakily as she got a fresh tissue out.

"I haven't been, but I will. I need to go to the store, though, and get some jasmine oil."

She drew in a deep breath. "Do you want to come with me to do that? Tomorrow? Maybe we could do some shopping if you feel like it."

Her mother frowned at her. "Don't humor me, Rani. No going out for months and now suddenly you want to?"

"Yes," Ranjani said. She balled up the tissues she'd used and tossed them on the ground. "Suddenly I want to because suddenly I *can*. You were right about what's been going on. Something has been wrong, but it's not you, never you."

"And now it's alright? Whatever was wrong that you can't tell me, it's okay now? You fixed it?"

Ranjani smiled and took her mother's hand.

"Not by myself, no. I had a lot of help. *You* helped. But yes, I fixed it."

AUGUST 24: ABONY

It was still light when Abony pulled into her parking space and she felt an unexpected reluctance to head up to her apartment. She had plenty to look forward to this weekend, including brunch with some girlfriends she'd been neglecting and a day at the zoo with her brother Darnell and his family. She had also been so busy cleaning up the mess of the CEO's downfall all week that she should be bone tired. But she felt instead a restlessness akin to the way she remembered feeling at the start of summer vacation from school, full of a pent-up readiness for something good to happen. She decided to walk to the row of shops down the block, maybe pick up something for her nephews at the toy store or a bottle of wine for later.

Rounding the corner of her building, Abony looked into the gym, which was packed as usual on Friday evenings. Their juice bar was doing a brisk business and the high-top tables they'd squeezed into the space in front of the windows were all occupied. One of the patrons was a man sitting alone, scrolling through his phone and sipping something unreasonably green. Abony went in before she had time to think about it.

"Tell me that tastes better than it looks," she said.

Jon Martin, forensic accountant, looked up and started to

smile, checked himself, held up his juice, and tilted the plastic cup so that the murky contents sloshed up the side.

"I could tell you that," he said, "but I'd be lying. I don't suppose you'd be impressed if I told you that I just worked out pretty hard and figured some spinach was in order?"

"You're drinking *spinach*," Abony said. "Do you hear how wrong that is?"

He gave up and let her have the grin. "So wrong."

"How about drinking something that's meant to be a liquid instead?"

Jon nodded thoughtfully. "I hear people do that."

"I mean like getting a glass of wine, you fool, at a restaurant."

"With you?"

"With me."

"When are you thinking, Abony?"

She shrugged. "How about now? Unless, that is, you have somewhere else to be." *Please God, don't let him have a date.*

Jon leaned forward, caught her wrist very, very gently, and tugged her toward him.

"I want to say yes," he said. "But I'm not interested in fooling around, Abony. A couple of weeks ago, you didn't want anything to do with me and now you do. If there's someone else you're trying to make jealous or break free from, I don't want any part of that."

"Jon," Abony said, savoring his name—the first time she'd used it unprompted, "I am a free woman, and I'm asking you to dinner. Please."

"I've got to shower," he said. "I can't go out with you like this."

"So shower," Abony said. "I'll wait here."

She slid into his seat at the table as he left, watched how he hurried to the locker room, hurried to get back to *her*, and settled in to wait. It turned out it wasn't so hard to wait for something when you knew it was going to happen, and that it was going to be good.

AUGUST 24: MAIA

God, she was out of shape.

Maia came off a slight rise on the trail through Rock Creek Park and tried to decide, as she coasted the first part of the straightaway, which parts of her legs hurt most. Her calves were burning, and her ass was definitely not used to the bike seat anymore, but her quads were still the winners.

Tough. If she was going to backpack across Europe, she needed to push past her screaming quadriceps.

Maia had pulled her hair into a ponytail before stuffing it under her helmet, but frizzy strands had snuck out and she kept having to blow them out of her mouth as she rode. She tried to focus on the things that still felt extraordinary after just a week of being 5'4" again.

In the case of a bike ride, it was the awareness that she was having an effect on an inanimate object with her physical body. She pushed on the pedals and the bike rolled forward. She gripped the handlebars and it turned in the direction she wanted it to turn.

And the world she rode through was just her size. The pavement was bumpy and pitted in places, but none of the cracks she jounced over was big enough to swallow her. The grass on either side would barely have brushed her ankles. There were plenty of other people in the park at this hour—bicyclists and runners and people out walking with strollers and dogs and dogs in strollers—and they all did this amazing paradoxical thing. On the one hand, they *saw* Maia as she rode by. They smiled or nodded or waved, got out of her way as she passed, or called "on your left" when they came up behind her and wanted her to get out of theirs. On the other hand, they didn't see her at all: not as freakish or weird, neither too small nor too large. Because she wasn't any of those things anymore. She was just another woman riding her bike somewhat inexpertly through Rock Creek and taking up exactly the space she needed to take up.

Maia came to the bottom of the toughest part of this loop: a long, gradual incline that was all the worse for looking like nothing at all from the bottom but going on and on and ever so slightly up for much longer than seemed possible. She'd had to walk her bike halfway up every night so far this week. Tonight she put her head down so she didn't have to see how much farther she had to climb and just kept pedaling.

She tried picturing the places she wanted to go, turning the cities and countries into a litany in her head. But she didn't *know* where she wanted to go yet, or what she wanted to do when she got there. She thought about Simon, who looked a little bereft every time he came downstairs in the morning and saw their living room restored to ordinary-human-sized order. But what was there to think about? He was at home right now, and not even waiting for her, just working or playing a video game until he got tired.

Halfway up, Maia thought about her friends, about the dreadful moment in the elevator when she'd realized that she'd betrayed them and the almost more dreadful realization that they were going to forgive her for it. She thought about what

Chantal had said as she left the table earlier that evening: *You saved yourselves.*

And she was at the top, facing an equally long, open stretch of downhill trail.

Maia was gasping for breath, but she didn't hesitate. She shifted into high gear and crested the hill, feeling the increasing wind blow her rebellious hair out of her face and plaster her sweat-soaked t-shirt to her body. She went faster and faster, gulping in air and shivering from the rush of speed, almost like flying.

No wings, of course, but she managed.

AUGUST 24: JO

There was a woman sitting on the low brick wall in front of Jo's apartment building, a perfectly ordinary-looking woman with curly light brown hair. She was wearing a t-shirt dress and flat sandals and her head was bent over her Kindle. As Jo got out of her Uber, the woman tapped to turn the page. She was visibly absorbed in her book, but just as obviously only sitting there because she was waiting for someone. When Jo shut the car door behind her, the woman looked up, shading her eyes, and lowered the Kindle to her lap.

Jo stood where she was a moment. In the drawer of her nightstand was the bag of amethysts. She could say "wait here a minute," run up and get them, then come back and pour the contents into Eileen's hands, where the stones would dazzle in the evening light. She could say "come upstairs and let me show you something," and upend the bag across the white comforter on her bed, where the myriad shades of purple would be just as dazzling in their sheer diversity. Either way, Eileen would initially gasp in disbelief and then, when Jo had told her everything—and Jo was going to tell her everything—she would cry, because of what the jewels had cost Jo and because they were for her. She would give them another chance on the strength of words Jo had spoken that had worked magic, but which Eileen hadn't even heard. She would treasure the gems themselves, wear one of them set into a ring, and try to convince them both that this trove that proved Jo loved her was enough for a lifetime.

Jo crossed the sidewalk and sat down on the wall herself, close enough to touch but not daring. She thought about the first night she'd figured out how to make an amethyst, the clean, sharp feel of it against her teeth and tongue that was nothing at all like spitting out bugs. It had been exhilarating, seeing that first violet stone in her palm, but frightening too, because even as Jo had held the amethyst up to the light and marveled at it, she had worried that it was occluded, imperfect, not beautiful enough—and it was the best she could do.

"In twenty years," she said to Eileen now, shaping her mouth around her words to get them right, "you're going to have some gray in your hair; not a lot, just enough to make it curl differently and make you crazy and you'll complain about it and want to cut it all off but you won't because you think you don't have the right face for short hair. And I'll still be running and probably too thin, only I *will* cut my hair short. You'll still be teaching because you love it, though if you're not careful they're going to make you the department chair, which will mean more paperwork and less time in the classroom, and you'll stress about whether you should keep doing it because of the extra money, which we'll need to put the kids through college."

"Kids?" Eileen said faintly.

"I'm scared to have kids," Jo said. "I'm so scared that I feel sick when I think about it, like I'm going to throw up. I know you must have thought I didn't want them because every time you brought it up I changed the subject, but it wasn't that. It was because I'm scared, scared I won't be a good parent…"

Dammit, her voice was shaking, the words just as hard to get out as they'd always been, and with no jewel to prove that at least she'd *tried* to get them right. "Scared that I'll let you do all the hard work making them feel loved, because clearly I have a hard time making even another adult feel loved. How can I do it with a baby or a little kid?"

Jo stopped. Swallowed.

Eileen was crying.

"I thought you didn't want to talk about the future because you weren't sure we had one," she said.

Jo shook her head.

Eileen wiped at her cheeks with both hands and seemed to steel herself, sitting up straighter on the wall and drawing in a shuddering breath.

Jo closed her eyes against what was coming.

"I really don't *ever* want to be department chair," Eileen said. "Do you promise you won't let me do it?"

But Jo didn't get a chance to promise, not out loud, because Eileen was in her arms and her mouth was on Eileen's hair and on her wet cheek and then on Eileen's mouth finally, and everything was, amazingly, going to be okay. Even without amethysts.

ACKNOWLEDGEMENTS

Cameron McClure is so much more than a terrific, brilliant agent. She's also a passionate reader, an amazing mom (hour of cookie!), and a tireless advocate for her writers. In the six years since we've seen my first novel appear in print, she's held my hand virtually through several different project ideas, the fits and starts of writing during a pandemic, the rather grueling process of finding a home for this book, and the edits that took the manuscript far from where it had begun... and she's done so without ever complaining about my (virtual) sweaty palms and heart palpitations, or ever losing faith in me. Thank you!

I'm grateful to everyone who works with Cameron at DMLA, especially Katie Shea Boutillier for helping with audio and translation rights. And thanks to Anne Perry for being part of this book's journey to publication.

Thanks to Joanna Harwood for taking a chance on the manuscript we submitted to Titan Books in summer 2021. And to Cath Trechman, who inherited the task of editing a book she hadn't even read. Cath, your questions were challenging, incisive, logical, precise... and in the end what you did was practically fairy tale magic in itself, pushing me to spin straw into gold one strand at a time. I'm deeply grateful to you and to everyone at

Titan who turned their extraordinary talents to bring this book to readers: Julia Lloyd for the stunning cover, Katharine Carroll for getting the word out, and Hayley Shepherd for what was far more than copy-editing.

Many of the writers who inspire me remain constant stars in my firmament, from Hans Christian Andersen (for making plain, in the dreadful punishments he inflicts on women, just how ugly fairy tales are at their core) to Andrew Lang, Angela Carter, Robin McKinley, Guy Gavriel Kay, Neil Gaiman, Pamela Dean, and Emma Bull. In recent years, I've had the privilege of reading Emily St. John Mandel, Amor Towles, Mona Awad, Carol Rifka Blunt, Stella Newman (Pear Shaped is perfect), Cherie Dimaline, Naomi Novik, Melissa Olson, Abi Daré, and Eileen Wilks—so yes, I've been inspired by tales of everything from itinerant Shakespeareans to Chinese women who can turn into... nope, I won't spoil it.

Many of the fairy tale discord contributors in Silenced are inspired by real-live amazing women, particularly Jess, JennyK, and Angelofthehouse. Thank you for being the bad-ass voices in my head!

YB, JB, and Lauren White... Abony LePrince is not any of you, but she owes much of her strength, her grace, and her indomitable sense of self to the way each of you moves through the world. Abony and Rani both owe their names to two incredible young women whom I once had the privilege of teaching. And all of my heroines owe a great debt to the many, many women who came forward to say "Me too" in these past few years.

The list of extraordinary teachers who have made me a better writer still includes Claire Messud, Reg McKnight, Gail Galloway Adams, Kevin Oderman, Mark Brazaitis, and Emily Mitchell. In the past few years, my first readers have been the ones who have pushed me to tell my stories as well as they can be told, most especially Paula, Erin, and yes, Lilah.

Finally, this book demanded a great deal of me, and I woudn't have had anything to bring to the project without the sustained and sustaining support of Tom, Rosemary, Hawley, Emily S, Valerie, Mark L, Cherie, Bruce, and Joyce. Thanks to Collin, for being proud enough to tell his friends I'm a writer; to Artemis, who defies gravity while not throwing away their shot; and to Lilah, for reminding me regularly that there are always things to be thankful for.

And thanks to Ryan, who never let me give up hope that things would get better, this book would see the light of day, and it would be worth that light. Who said it was okay that the story kept getting darker—and added more mezcal to the glass at my elbow. Who is neither Eileen nor Amit nor Jon but who is nonetheless the reason I believe in happily ever after.

Elisabeth's Lists

A LIFE BETWEEN THE LINES

LULAH ELLENDER

GRANTA

Granta Publications, 12 Addison Avenue, London W11 4QR

First published in Great Britain by Granta Books, 2018
This paperback edition published by Granta Books, 2019

Copyright © Lulah Ellender, 2018
Images © Lulah Ellender

An essay based on an early draft of this book appeared in *The Junket*

Lines from *The Waste Land* by T. S. Eliot are reprinted by
kind permission of Faber & Faber (UK)

'Separation' from *The Second Four Books of Poems* by W. S. Merwin
is reprinted by kind permission of Bloodaxe Books

Lines from William E. Stafford's 'A Message from the Wanderer'
are reprinted by kind permission of Graywolf Press

A CIP catalogue record for this book is available
from the British Library.

1 3 5 7 9 10 8 6 4 2

ISBN 978 1 78378 385 4
eISBN 978 1 78378 384 7

Typeset in Calluna by Lindsay Nash
Printed and bound by CPI Group (UK) Ltd, Croydon, CR0 4YY

MIX
Paper from
responsible sources
FSC® C020471